No One Like You

Heather McGovern

LYRICAL SHINE
Kensington Publishing Corp.
www.kensingtonbooks.com

LYRICAL SHINE BOOKS are published by

Kensington Publishing Corp.
119 West 40th Street
New York, NY 10018

All Kensington titles, imprints, and distributed lines are available at special quantity discounts for bulk purchases for sales promotion, premiums, fund-raising, educational, or institutional use.

Special book excerpts or customized printings can also be created to fit specific needs. For details, write or phone the office of the Kensington Sales Manager: Kensington Publishing Corp., 119 West 40th Street, New York, NY 10018. Attn. Sales Department. Phone: 1-800-221-2647.

Lyrical Shine and Lyrical Shine logo Reg. U.S. Pat. & TM Off.

First Electronic Edition: October 2018
eISBN-13: 978-1-5161-0761-2
eISBN-10: 1-5161-0761-6

First Print Edition: October 2018
ISBN-13: 978-1-5161-0764-3
ISBN-10: 1-5161-0764-0

Printed in the United States of America

NO ONE LIKE YOU

"You should talk up the garden aspect of the chateau in your advertising, if you don't already. That rose is already my favorite." Trevor pointed to a peach-colored bloom, barely open.

Brooke walked toward the rose, but didn't let go of his arm. "Makes sense. The full bloom is a beautiful creamy peach. A lot like Honeywilde's signature shade. I can check with Laurel, she'd probably let you have a clipping if you want. She loves to share. You could take some back to the inn with you."

"Brooke Sargent, are you giving me flowers? I didn't think we were that serious yet."

Her mouth fell open, followed immediately by a grin. "I don't know how you do it, but I think we might actually pull this thing off."

"Because I'm awesome?"

"And so humble." She smiled, bumping the back of her hand against his chest.

He took her hand, clasping it in place. "I wanted to kiss you yesterday," he confessed. "Right inside that ballroom, before the prom committee rolled in on us."

"I know."

He moved in even closer, and he wasn't letting go. "I still want to kiss you..."

Books by Heather McGovern

A Honeywilde Romance
A Moment of Bliss
A Date with Desire
A Taste of Temptation

A Chateau Jolie Romance
No One Like You

Published by Kensington Publishing Corporation

Chapter 1

Brooke clung to her menu like it was a full skirt on a windy day. "Coffee," she said to the Honeywilde waiter.

Her hands cramped, palms sweaty, and the pinching start of a headache worked its way up both temples.

Meeting with Roark Bradley shouldn't set her on edge like this. Roark was professional and pleasant. All of the Bradleys were nice people.

Trevor Bradley in particular.

Nice looking too, though that was beside the point.

Since Devlin's wedding in August, she'd seen Trevor only in passing. In town, she'd see him maybe shopping or walking down the sidewalk, but the glimpses were enough to confirm what she already knew—he was still as wickedly handsome as ever.

Her muscles tensed, ready to jump out of her skin, but her nerves couldn't be because of Trevor.

"I'm back. Sorry to keep you waiting." Roark took the seat across from her and motioned for coffee. "Anyway, as I was saying, the high school needs Chateau Jolie's help with their prom."

Ding, ding, ding.

The prom.

That would be the source of her anxiety.

Didn't matter that she and her sisters had been running Chateau Jolie for almost a year, the prospect of being the location for the school's emergency prom had her more wound up than a set of novelty chattering teeth.

Brooke unclenched her jaw. "I believe you were about to ask if we could *host* the prom at Jolie." Both a blessing and a curse that couldn't come at a more inopportune time.

"Yes. The venue they were going to use went out of business last week. With no notification to the school, their prom is just…gone."

"Gone?"

"No place to have it, no backup plans. Nothing."

"Those poor kids."

Taking this project on wasn't ideal, but how could she say no to a bunch of sad teenagers who would get all dressed up and have no place to go?

Roark sipped his coffee and shook his head. "They lost their money too. That event place in Newton went bankrupt. All of the juniors and seniors had bought tickets, so that's their hard-earned cash gone. Which means they've got no budget."

Her stomach dropped. "Well, that—" Sucks. "That's awful."

And she couldn't help them without a budget. Chateau Jolie certainly didn't have the spare cash to fork over.

"The assistant principal came to me yesterday asking—actually, pleading is more accurate—to use Honeywilde. But we're booked solid for the whole season."

Of course they were.

Honeywilde was always booked. This season, next season. Every season two years from now. Honeywilde's success was one of the reasons for Jolie's lackluster couple of years.

But she wasn't about to tell Roark Bradley that.

"Then Sophie thought of Chateau Jolie. Thank goodness your ballroom is available."

She pasted on a smile. "Yes. Thank goodness."

"That is, if you can host the event. It's in two and a half weeks."

Her eyes almost popped out of her skull.

"I know, I know. It's not much time, but we're still going to help," he rushed to add. "You wouldn't be doing this alone. I'm ready to offer up a donation for food, décor, and other expenses. And some added manpower for the event itself, since Jolie is…well, we have a larger staff here."

He was understating to be polite. Honeywilde had the money and people to spare. Chateau Jolie did not.

The throb in her skull got a little bit worse. "I think…"

She didn't have the luxury of thinking. Chateau Jolie needed to catch a break, especially now that she had to shell out thousands of dollars to keep from losing part of Jolie to an evil a-hole of a man.

Not only was hosting the school's prom the right thing to do, but a community event and charity might give the hotel the kind of promotion and PR it needed to spark off their slumping reservation rates and make some much needed money.

"We wouldn't throw all of this on you to deal with alone." Roark leaned forward, his coffee mug cradled between his hands. "We plan to help out as much as we can. But what the school needs most is a location."

Brooke flexed her fingers to get some blood into them. Chateau Jolie could easily be the location, but they didn't have Honeywilde's financial resources to fund a party.

She wasn't about to tell Roark Bradley that either.

"We'd love for the school to use our ballroom," she said instead.

"Great!"

But she couldn't only offer up a location.

If all she provided was a room, then yet again, Honeywilde would be the hero of the day. They'd swoop in, save the town, and hog all the glory. Again. Chateau Jolie would be the little stepsister who got dragged along to the dance.

Her family's business couldn't afford to be the stepsister anymore.

Brooke stiffened her spine. "We'd want to do more than provide a location though. We have resources of our own." Pitifully few, but po-tay-toe, po-tah-toe. "If the prom is at our hotel, I'd prefer to be the one in charge of coordinating with the prom's committee chair."

Roark nodded. "Absolutely. I agree."

Proms weren't in her wheelhouse, but she knew enough about parties to handle one for teenagers.

Roark took another sip of his coffee, looking proud as a peacock. "That works out perfectly for us too. With the Blueberry Festival coming up, and peak season, we don't need to commit to managing more than we can handle."

Peak season. Must be nice.

She shook off the resentment to concentrate on the possibilities. This prom could be the very thing Jolie needed, and if she could run the show with a Honeywilde income, even better.

She could make this the goodwill event of the year, get on every social media platform, and prove her family's hotel was every bit as charitable and wonderful as Honeywilde, and she might be able to redeem herself. No, she *would* redeem herself.

"Hey." A deep voice interrupted her pep talk.

Brooke looked up, into striking blue eyes and dimples that ought to be outlawed.

Trevor Bradley.

The best-looking man to ever ask her out, and the one she'd turned down the hardest.

Brooke stared, trying to recall the reasons why.

Roark cleared his throat. "Our breakfast started at nine thirty, Trev."

Trevor checked his wrist, where a watch might be if he wore one. "What is it now? Nine forty?"

"Nine forty-five."

"Then you're getting to the good stuff." He pulled out a chair and sat beside her. "Besides, the first ten minutes of breakfast should be spent enjoying coffee and these biscuits. You haven't had a biscuit yet?" He scowled at the untouched basket as though it were a sin, then held the basket toward her until she took one.

Roark took one as well. "Chateau Jolie has agreed to be the location for the prom and we were about to discuss your involvement."

Brooke's gaze jerked toward Roark. "We were?"

"Like you said, Jolie would head up this project, but we want to lend our management's support too. Trevor eagerly volunteered. This way, our hotels can partner up and give the school the best prom they've ever had."

No! Brooke bit back the desire to snap at the perfectly nice offer.

"That's…very generous, but you guys don't have time to deal with all the minutiae of planning."

"I love minutiae." Trevor popped a bit of biscuit into his mouth.

She bet he did.

Last summer, Trevor had wooed her at Dev's wedding, the likes of which she'd never seen or experienced. She'd darned near kissed him too, until her reality came crashing in.

Men like Trevor were dangerous.

Delicious, but dangerous.

They could not partner, and not just because of his dimples. A partnership meant shared credit, and in the case of sharing with Honeywilde, it meant they'd get all the credit.

Brooke sat up a little straighter. "I can plan the majority and simply call on you as needed. No reason to assign one of your managers to this full time."

Especially not Trevor Bradley. She couldn't have him all up in her space, every day for the next two weeks.

Roark pinched his lips together with a thoughtful sound.

Not a good sign. A man like Roark, with a place like Honeywilde, was never going to let her do all the work and refuse his help. He also wasn't about to throw a bunch of money at the competition and walk away, trusting her to spend it well and wisely.

He didn't get to be a success by being stupid.

She'd be the exact same way.

"I'm only half-manager," Trevor argued, a lock of chocolate brown hair brushing his sun-kissed forehead as he leaned back.

Trevor's casual attitude might work in her favor. Goodness knew she'd never be able to take the reins with the likes of Roark around, but she'd already learned Trevor was easygoing and fun loving.

And charming and insanely good looking…

But the point was, he probably wouldn't care if she wanted to head up the project while he played second fiddle.

Still, having Trevor around all the time? When it'd taken him only one night to have her swooning in his arms, after years of no swooning at all, not even a sway?

Nothing good could come of that.

His eyes and dimples remained on full blast, like he knew exactly what she was thinking.

"I couldn't ask you to give up Trevor permanently for more than two weeks. The occasional conferring ought to be enough."

Roark shook off her objection. "No, he wants to help. He asked me to give him this job."

"And I want to work full time on this, not as a consultant." Still leaning back, looking like some Folgers commercial in his blue jeans and soft henley, Trevor drank his coffee.

Meeting with Roark at Honeywilde meant the chances of running into Trevor were high. She'd made peace with that, but she wasn't physically or emotionally prepared to work with him full time. Particularly not when he insisted on being like *that*.

Roark sat forward again, his elbows on the table. "I'm with Trevor. Honeywilde needs to be involved beyond consultation. Believe it or not, Trev's handy, works best under pressure, and he's become our go-to guy for last-minute creativity. If there's a lot to accomplish in very little time, he's your guy."

Trevor angled himself toward her, hair as dark and tousled as it was last summer, with teeth so perfect they were blinding. "See? I'm handy and available. That's also his code for saying I'm the most dispensable member of management."

Roark stiffened. "I didn't say that."

"Relax, Roark. Brooke is a friend. She knows I'm kidding." A mischievous smile crept across Trevor's lips. "He's so easy to outrage."

Brooke grabbed her coffee, focusing on the breakfast beverage as though life depended on it.

Months had passed since Devlin's wedding. Autumn and winter came and went, but that playful smile of his still made her insides flutter more than a migration of monarchs.

He'd been utterly gorgeous the night of the wedding. So guileless and determined in his pursuit, she'd forgotten herself. They'd laughed and flirted, spent almost the entire evening talking and dancing and, near the end of the night, she thought he might kiss her.

She'd wanted him to, even though the idea of letting a man close to her again made her physically ill.

"Dispensable or not, I can't take away one of your managers," she tried. "He'll be needed here as your season ramps up."

"They don't need me here full time." Trevor sat close enough to make out his long, envy-worthy lashes, the complete lack of laugh lines or crow's feet. "This prom needs to knock socks off. Those Windamere High kids are good kids. They got the raw end of the deal and that's not okay in my book."

Heat rushed up the back of her neck. His offer was considerate and kind, and under any other circumstance she'd accept, but this prom needed to be her baby.

"I know. I feel the same way, but—" The words froze on her tongue. She couldn't tell them all of the reasons why she needed this success to be hers.

Not only for Jolie, but for her.

"I'd prefer to oversee things alone."

She needed a win. She needed to know she could do something without making a mess and then failing miserably.

Roark frowned, his hackles almost visibly rising. "Wait. Are you saying you don't want us involved at all?"

Chapter 2

Brooke's face went blank, except for the flash of panic in her eyes.

Beautiful, bottomless, and so dark they were almost black. He'd thought about those eyes dozens of times since last August.

Even after he'd asked her out and she shot him down with the force of a torpedo fired from ten feet away, he'd pictured how the darkness danced in them when she laughed.

Roark hunkered down. "If we're donating money, we have to be involved."

Now her eyes were full of fear.

Trevor's understanding of why would have to wait for later. First, he had to run Roark interference.

"Of course we do. Brooke isn't saying otherwise." Trevor stepped in with a breezy tone before his oldest brother botched things completely. "And of course she wants us involved, don't you?" He shot her a wide-eyed glance.

"Yes?"

"See?" He looked back at his brother. "But Jolie is Brooke's hotel. That's her baby the same way Honeywilde is yours. Plus, she's more than capable, and she wants to be lead on the event without me stepping all over her toes. Right?" Another darted glance her way.

"Right," she agreed.

"Good. See? Brooke will head things up and I'll help out. We're all on the same page." Trevor gave his brother a narrow-eyed glare.

"Are we?" Roark scowled.

Brooke met Roark's stare. "We are now."

God, she was something.

Since he was fifteen, he knew who Brooke Sargent was. She'd been a senior, and so far out of his league they weren't even playing the same sport, but even then, she'd fascinated him.

Studious, serious, pretty, and perfect.

Until a couple of years ago, she'd been MIA somewhere. Probably living the high life. Didn't matter. All that mattered was he'd made her laugh so hard at Dev's wedding, he'd felt like a king.

They'd laughed and talked and dined. Even danced.

But when the clock struck midnight, and he'd asked her out for coffee or lunch sometime, her answer had been a carriage-back-into-a-pumpkin, gut-punching *no*.

He still couldn't figure out where he'd gone wrong, or how the hell he'd screwed things up.

Roark's surly expression remained firmly in place until his phone trilled with an incoming call. "Excuse me, I have to take this." He left the table and walked toward the kitchen.

With a sigh of relief, Trevor scooted his chair back up to the table. "Good, he's gone. Look, I understand your concern, but you've got to work with me, not against me. You keep arguing with Roark, and he'll argue right back 'til the cows come home."

"I wasn't trying to be argumentative."

"Really? You might want to try harder."

"I know, but I—"

"Look, I'm not going to get in your way or try to call the shots at your hotel. I know how you manager types like to run the show. Have you met my boss, Roark? I've learned to help out without being a hindrance. Trust me, I'm not in this to take over the event or, like, I don't know, take your hotel."

Brooke fidgeted with her napkin before folding it neatly to lie next to her plate. "I should go." She pushed her chair out and grabbed her purse.

"You're leaving? You haven't eaten. You barely tried your biscuit."

Her gaze darted around the restaurant. "I'm not hungry."

She started for the door like someone had pulled the fire alarm.

Whatever was going on with her, this was about more than a prom.

"Hey." He hurried to catch up, following her into the great room. "Don't stress about it. I'll help you with the prom. Roark's not going to pull out our money or anything like that. As for the rest, you run a hotel and winery. This is a prom. No big deal."

She came to a full stop. "That's easy for you to say. Your family throws events bigger than this on a weekly basis."

"I meant that as a compliment."

The corner of her mouth pulled down and she walked away again.

"Hang on." He was right behind her. "Hold up for a second."

She finally stopped at the front doors.

"If you're worried about the event happening on such short notice, I'm here for that. Like Roark said, I'm good under pressure. Great, actually. We can work together."

Brooke didn't respond. She stared. And stared some more. The silence stretched out until it was painful. "I'm not worried. But why would *you* help *me*?"

Trevor grinned. "Because my brother told me to?"

"You know what I mean. After Dev's wedding, why would you ever want to help me?"

"Because I want to and it's my job."

She studied him, her eyes fathomless, revealing nothing.

But he could render a guess. "Yes, I asked you out before, and you said no. Yes, that kind of took the wind out of my sails, but I'm a big boy. And yes, I find you attractive, but that's not why I'm offering to help."

Her stare remained steady.

"Fine. That is not the *only* reason I'm offering. I admit, hearing your name and Chateau Jolie made me pay attention in Roark's meeting, but hearing about the canceled prom is what made me want to help."

One dark eyebrow of disbelief crept up.

Trust issues much?

"I meant what I said about those kids. They deserve a prom, and I happen to know more about that school and teenagers than probably you or anyone else around here. I've volunteered there before and—"

"You have?" She blinked.

"Don't look so shocked. I make good use of my free time."

Brooke shook her head, one hand still on the door. "After Dev's wedding and…I don't know…using you feels wrong."

Her saying things like "using you" felt pretty good to him.

She bit at her bottom lip, clearly debating with herself. She released it, redder and plumper than before, and a fire lit inside him.

"It wouldn't be some kind of conflict of interest?"

"No." He'd gone for months wishing he could talk to her again, hoping he'd get another chance. Now the perfect opportunity stood before him, and all because he'd paid attention in a morning meeting.

Somehow, some way, he was going to help her with this prom and help those kids to boot.

But clearly, Brooke wasn't a woman to be pressured. She needed time to process.

He stepped away, hands up in resignation. "Look, I'm not going to badger you. I told you this would be your show, and it is. The prom is coming up soon, and I'm here for you."

Again, she went still and quiet. The woman would make a ridiculously good ninja.

Then she straightened and spoke, her voice firmer than before. "Seems your brother won't have it any other way."

"Then I guess I'll be seeing you."

She was halfway out the door before he could catch it. Her long dark hair swung over her shoulders as she hurried through the portico. "I guess so," she called out.

Chapter 3

"It's a good thing you're here." The Tavern's bartender chuckled and shook his head. "She's not too far gone, but I'm cutting her off."

Brooke searched the bar for her sister Reagan. "Good call. And thanks for calling the chateau."

"No problem. Seeing as how she never sets foot in here and now *this*.

This being preppy, self-proclaimed high-class Reagan, in a trucker hat, ratty jean shorts, and a T-shirt, clearly intoxicated and scream-singing "You Never Even Called Me by My Name" along with the jukebox.

"Reagan," Brooke called across the Tavern's makeshift dance floor at a normal volume.

Nothing.

"Reagan!"

Her sister gave her a sloppy grin and waved, but didn't stop dancing. "What're you doing here?"

"I came to give you a ride home."

"Pfffft." Reagan flapped her hands and lolled to the side. "I'm not ready to go."

"Yes. You are."

With her chin jutted out, Reagan threw her shoulders back, radiating the kind of indignation that only a middle sister could muster.

"I am not ready to go." The words came out so perfect and razor sharp, she almost appeared sober.

Except for the leaning.

"Reagan Sargent, it's been a long day. I know you're upset, but do not start with me right now."

A familiar deep voice filled Brooke's ears. "Maybe more honey, less vinegar. That is, if you want her to go with you. If you're trying to start a bar fight then, by all means, continue."

Brooke spun around.

Trevor, and his dimples, right there. Again. Inescapable. "What are you doing here?"

He thumbed to the chalkboard on the bar. "Buy one, get one free wing night. Everyone comes here on Tuesdays."

She shook off his logical explanation. A universal conspiracy against her made more sense.

Trevor rocked back and crossed his arms, his skin golden brown against the white T-shirt. "You should try being nice if you want to get her home. You yell at her, and I guarantee she's going to stay right there to spite you."

"Why, because it's what you'd do?"

"No, I'd go home with you the first time you asked. But I ain't your sister."

She tried glaring at him, though it'd do no good. "I don't have time to be nice."

"Suit yourself." Trevor shrugged and moved to the side to lean against the bar. "This should be entertaining."

Brooke pulled herself away from his bright blue eyes and studied her sister, now attempting to cha-cha slide with a bunch of strangers.

Reagan could stay here, have fun with bar patrons, enjoy dancing and singing, *or* she could go home—where she'd continue to wallow over her breakup and be subjected to Brooke stressing over this stupid prom and her attorney's fees.

Mmmm. Tough call.

Trevor and his dimples might be right. Honey instead of vinegar.

"Reagan?" She softened her voice as much as she could. "How about we go home? I'll make tea."

Reagan's face strained with a look of disgust. "Nah, I'm good."

"You love tea."

"I don't want to go home. I told you to leave me alone."

"You can't drive like this. I have to take you home."

"Would you stop mothering me. I'll call a cab."

"A cab?" Brooke tried breathing through her nose and counting to five. "There are no cabs in Windamere, Reagan. Get your stuff and let's go. Now!"

Trevor pushed off from the bar. "Yeah, you suck at this."

She slapped her hands down at her sides and turned on him. "And what would you suggest?"

"Not tea. Hey, Reagan!" Trevor shouted over the music. "We're going to get pizza. You in?"

Brooke could see the suggestion take hold of her sister. The subliminal magic of melted cheese, pepperoni, sauce, and a crispy crust cut through the haze of her drowned sorrows.

Long Island Ice Teas and bar music lost their allure when competing with piping hot pizza.

Reagan wet her lips as she slowly moved toward them. "Zita's Pizzeria pizza?"

"Is there any other kind?" Trevor pulled out his wallet as Reagan joined them. He handed the bartender some folded-up twenties.

There was no way he'd had that many wings.

"You don't have to pay my sister's tab," Brooke told him.

He waved her off and headed to the door. "This is faster. We've got her attention and you have to reel in the intoxicated family member while they're on the line or you lose them."

"You sound like you've done this before."

"Something like that."

Reagan followed them to the exit without argument.

They made it outside and to the parking lot before he added, "Plus, you're paying for the pizza. And I'm starving."

He'd gotten her sister all the way outside without so much as a hint of an argument. That act alone could qualify him for knighthood. The least she could do was buy pizza.

"Deal. But I get final call on the toppings."

"Ugh, no," Reagan shouted. "You'll have us eating ham and pineapple. Gross."

Trevor slowed his pace to match Reagan's. "Agreed. No pineapple on pizza."

They walked the three blocks to Zita's, not one complaint from Reagan. Brooke would've fallen over from shock except she was too busy trying to figure out how, and why, Trevor did it.

"Are you a veggie-lover kind of pizza person? Or I bet you're a meat lover."

Brooke took the lead and had to stop every half block to let them catch up. She had absolutely no grounds to object, but surely Trevor wasn't flirting with her sister.

Reagan made a face. "Supreme or don't bother. Extra sauce."

"I like your thinking."

Not that Brooke could be jealous if he was. Still, it'd be in bad taste. You didn't hit on one sister and then the other, unless you were some hound dog looking to get lucky.

Trevor didn't strike her as the type.

Once they reached the pizzeria, he caught up with Brooke, opening the door as he whispered, "I actually love pineapple on pizza, but if you play along with what she wants, the rest of the night will go a lot smoother. Trust me on this."

Brooke stepped into an almost empty restaurant, the coin dropping.

Trevor was right.

If she didn't run opposition for Reagan, there'd be nothing to argue about.

Trevor was entertaining Reagan to keep the peace, which meant he wasn't flirting with her.

Not that Brooke cared.

Her sister picked a booth halfway down the wall, she and Brooke on one side and Trevor across from them.

"I feel like deep dish," Reagan announced.

Brooke's thin-crust-loving heart broke, but she didn't say a word.

"One large deep-dish supreme?" Trevor put down the menu he'd barely picked up.

"Yes!"

"I don't like green peppers," she reminded Reagan.

Beneath the table, something bumped Brooke's knee.

As soon as she met Trevor's pointed look, his eyes relayed a thousand different messages without saying a word.

That was his knee banging into hers. So she did what any mature woman would do. She bumped him back, with an equally pointed look.

Reagan propped her elbows on the table, and her voice kicked up a notch. "Heaven forbid you get a little heartburn from green peppers. Can't you pick them off?"

She wanted an argument, Brooke reminded herself. Over something stupid that had nothing to do with why she was really upset.

"Or"—Trevor nudged Brooke's knee again, gently this time—"we could do half the pizza with peppers, half without."

She and her sister stared at one another.

"Good idea," Brooke agreed.

That, neither she nor her sister was reasonable enough to consider.

When the waiter came over, Trevor placed the order, along with three large waters all around. Once the waiter left, Reagan turned, waggling her finger back and forth between Brooke and Trevor. "So, how do you two know each other?"

Brooke pulled a napkin from the dispenser to have something to do. "I was at his brother's wedding. Do you want to talk about why you were drinking alone in a bar?"

"Oh, my God." Her sister's face flushed. "I don't want to talk about that in front of him."

"Really?" Brooke glared. "I can't imagine what that feels like."

Trevor leaned back in his booth. "I don't mind if y'all talk. Go ahead."

Reagan squinted back. "Were you his date?"

"No."

"Not for lack of me trying," Trevor interjected.

Reagan's grin was slow and wide, not unlike the Grinch's. "I knew it!"

"I wasn't his date." Brooke kept her voice even. "And I want to know what made you go drink too much in a bar, alone, on a Tuesday night. Was it this thing with Rex? Because so help me God, if that guy—"

"I told you. There is no Rex." Regan scooped up her water glass, sloshing it before she took a sip. "Not anymore. He dumped me. *He* dumped *me*."

Brooke tried to measure her reaction, because she'd been as shocked as her sister.

She meant to say something reassuring. Something sympathetic and inspirational to remind Reagan she was the kind of person anyone would be lucky to have.

What came out was "You should've dumped his ass months ago."

Beneath the table, she got another bump from Trevor's knee.

Her sister slumped back, rough enough to shake the booth. "That's all you have to say? I told you so?"

Trevor grimaced. "I think what your sister is trying to say is that she knew you could do better, and now you *can*, because Rex isn't holding you back anymore."

"That." Brooke pointed to Trevor. "*That* is what I'm trying to say."

Reagan shook her head. "Whatever."

They sipped their water and Brooke's glass was empty before anyone spoke again.

Reagan's voice was soft and more than a little sad. "But what if I can't do better? What if Rex is as good as it gets for me?"

Brooke glanced up, her gaze locking with Trevor's. If she had a desperate look in her eyes, then there was good reason.

She had an idea what to say, but more often than not, when it came to consoling her sisters or being sweet, she lacked the finesse. Even if she meant well, her most firmly held opinions had edge.

The only reason she'd been able to help Trevor's sister, Sophie, was because Sophie needed the direct approach.

Reagan was a softer touch, and the defeat in her voice was too much. Brooke couldn't say the wrong thing, and lately, everything she did was wrong. The possibility of flubbing had her lips frozen shut.

"You can do better," Trevor spoke up. "Without a doubt. I happen to know who Rex is. The guy's an ass, like your sister said. He doesn't deserve you. Not even when you have on *the* ugliest trucker hat I've ever seen."

Reagan laughed, sniffing back the tears threatening to fall as she took the hat off.

Trevor picked it up, turning it around for inspection. "To think, you actually went through the trouble of taking this thing away from someone else."

Reagan laughed again, her smile genuine.

Brooke finally took a breath, letting her shoulders slump. *Thank you*, she mouthed to Trevor.

You're welcome, he mouthed back, his sky-blue eyes twinkling.

He was quickly becoming the night's hero.

Crap.

Chapter 4

The chance he was wearing a dopey grin on his face right now?

One hundred percent.

Brooke's thank-you, that smile, the fact that she was loosening up and teasing him back again all sent waves of warmth through his body.

This was the Brooke he'd spent time with at Dev's wedding. Guarded, but good natured.

She didn't give away her smiles or gratitude lightly, which made them all the sweeter when she did.

Their pizza finally arrived and they ate in the kind of silence that descends upon the hungry.

He was on slice number three when Reagan pepped up. "Seriously, though, how do you two know each other?"

Brooke opened her mouth, but her sister cut her off. "Don't you dare deflect. I got dumped today. I deserve a good story."

Brooke glanced at him and her sister, probably wondering how to share the tale of their amazing time at Dev's wedding, only for things to end in her turning him down flat and taking off like Cinderella from the ball.

There had to be more to the story—parts he didn't know—but right now, he was more interested in the present.

And Reagan's request gave him the perfect opportunity to get in Brooke's way.

"I'm supposed to be helping your sister with the prom at Chateau Jolie, but she doesn't want me to."

"That's not what I said."

"What?" Reagan interrupted, putting both hands out and turning to Brooke. *"Why?* We need help."

He grinned. Somehow he knew Reagan would have his back.

"I didn't—" Brooke gave him the evil eye. "Thanks a lot."

"Seriously, if he's offering to give us a hand, say yes. They do this crap all the time at Honeywilde."

"It's not crap. It's a prom."

"Which is exactly why we need him."

Brooke shot him another scolding glance.

"You know I'd be happy to oblige."

Reagan's eyes widened before she began elbowing Brooke incessantly. "See? Say yes."

When Brooke didn't respond, still sitting there, steely eyed, Reagan picked up her pizza slice and gave Trevor a wink. "Don't worry. That look means she'll eventually say yes. You just have to survive the period of purgatory that comes before she finally does."

If looks could kill, Reagan would've choked to death on a pepperoni at that very moment.

Instead, she dropped her mangled crust and stood. "Be right back. I've got to go to the ladies' room."

Brooke turned her glare on him. "You dragged her into this on purpose."

"Yep."

"I'll have to accept your help or hear about it from her, all day, every day."

"Eh. You're stuck with me anyway. Roark and I discussed it yesterday and he's insistent. If we're throwing in money, we help throw this shindig."

With lips pursed into a funny little shape, she pushed her plate away.

That did it. His jimmies were officially rustled. "Is being stuck with me that damn bad? I thought you and I got along pretty well. You're acting like I'm Typhoid Mary."

She flinched, her eyes wide. "What? No! It's not—I don't think you're Typhoid Mary. I just don't want to take—"

"Advantage of me. You said that already. But that's not the situation here, okay? Even if it was, please, take advantage of me. You won't hear me complain."

His comment got the faintest whiff of a smile before she began twisting her napkin up into some god-awful origami.

"I know you need help with this prom, mainly because your sister is drunk and blurted out the truth."

Why wouldn't she want free help? Her resistance made no sense.

"If you're worried about reliability, you can count on me."

Her gaze met his and, for a moment, he thought he had her. Then she lifted her water glass to her lips, muttering as she sipped.

"Yeah, I've heard that before."

"What?"

"Nothing."

He might not have been the most involved in his family's business in years past, but by God, he did his share now. He'd never been afraid of a hard day's work. The family dynamic was what ran him off for a while, but Brooke wouldn't know that.

Maybe she'd heard things about the devil-may-care youngest Bradley, caught a few rumors about him running off to faraway lands—or nearby beaches and mountains—without a penny to his name just to see if he could survive day to day.

That was all true of course, but nowadays he pulled his weight. The wanderlust never went away, but work hard, play hard. That was his new motto.

"I am so done with this day." Reagan reappeared at their table like she'd been conjured up from thin air. "Can we go home now?"

"What a novel idea, sis." Brooke hopped up.

She paid the tab and they made their way back to the Tavern's parking lot, the conversation going nowhere near the topic of the upcoming prom.

"Are you planning to come back and get your sister's car tomorrow or..." Trevor let the question hang.

Brooke stopped in her tracks, her head falling back. "Dang it."

He grinned. She struck him as too polished for dang-its, but he loved surprises.

"So that's a no?"

"I can't come back here tomorrow. I don't have time to run up and down the mountain. I've got a morning meeting, we're still spring cleaning at the winery for tours, and—"

"I can follow you in your sister's car. But I'll need you to bring me back here tonight to get mine."

Brooke shifted on her feet while her sister went right ahead and crawled into the passenger seat of her car.

They could stand there all night waiting for Brooke to concede.

Rather than grow old waiting, he popped his head in the open passenger door of the Camry. "You have your keys?" he asked Reagan.

She dug into her purse and tossed them over.

He held them up to show Brooke and walked to her sister's car. "It's settled then. I'll follow you and you can bring me back to my car after we drop off your sister."

Brooke tracked him with her gaze, but remained motionless. "Okay?"

Chapter 5

Trevor slid behind the wheel of Reagan's car while Brooke stood there trying to come up with a good reason and good way to refuse him.

There wasn't one.

"Fine." She grumbled and got in her car.

She drove home with Reagan burning a hole in the side of her skull.

"What?" she finally asked with only a couple of miles to spare

"How do you know Trevor, really?"

"I told you, we were at the same wedding and he's supposed to help with this prom."

"And?"

Brooke kept driving.

"You might be able to stonewall everyone else in this town, but you aren't shutting me out. I know there's more going on than you two being casually acquainted. Spill."

"There is nothing to spill."

"Have you kissed him?"

"No."

"Did you make out?"

"Stop."

"Did you dance with him?"

Brooke stared straight ahead, silent.

"You danced with him at the wedding? You danced!" Reagan wiggled her fingers. "More than once, I bet."

"That's enough. I'm not a sixteen-year-old girl who met some boy at a party. We danced. So what? We had polite conversation, discussed business in Windamere, and—"

"Yeah, yeah, yeah. Everything was all very grown up and boring, I'm sure, except the part where Trevor Bradley is a smoking-hot hottie who doesn't seem boring at all."

The annoyed groan came from all the way down at her toes.

But she was more annoyed with herself than with her sister.

Reagan was right. Trevor was anything but boring. He might be an adult, but he had a kind of relaxed exuberance, an ease with life, that she'd never attained.

Their time together at Devlin's wedding was the happiest she'd been in years.

She'd giggled like a schoolgirl, talked, and eaten way too much cake. And when they danced, he'd held her too close, but she didn't object. In fact, she'd moved against him, considering things she hadn't wanted in ages.

She'd even gone so far as to take his arm as he walked her out, then skittered away like a frightened rabbit when he asked to see her again.

"I mean really, Brooke. At least you've got a guy interested in you. A *decent* guy. He's cute and nice and funny and wants to help. He's the exact opposite of that jerk I dated, and you can't even have coffee with him?"

"Coffee leads to dating."

"So?"

"I've done all of that already. The dating, the relationship, the engagement. The marriage, the divorce. You know what I've been through. It's pointless. Real-life relationships aren't the fairy tale we were brought up to believe. Finding a cute guy doesn't mean you end up with someone like Dad. Fun dates don't mean you get the kind of relationship our parents have."

"Ugh." Reagan made a show of slumping against the passenger door as they pulled into the chateau's parking lot. "No couple is like Mom and Dad. I've already learned. And I know you and Nick didn't work out, but that doesn't mean you give up on men. Or happiness."

Didn't work out.

That had to be the best euphemism yet for the hell that was the last year of her marriage.

"I am happy, Reags. And I don't need a man to remain so."

"Okay, sure." Her sister rolled her eyes.

This from a woman who'd been dumped by the town's biggest player and yet she still thought dating another guy was the answer.

"Your marriage went to shit and you're using that to avoid any connections to anyone from now until eternity, but whatever. You can sit around and grow old and die alone if you like. I won't stop you."

Heaven help her deal with Reagan's dramatics. "Die alone? That escalated quickly."

"Brooke." Her sister, several years her junior and often a decade more immature, suddenly grew serious. Her eyes clear, her voice unwavering. "I mean it. Don't say whatever it is you think will make me shut up and then ignore my advice like you do everything else. Trevor is nice. He's cute. He obviously likes you. He bought us pizza."

"I bought the pizza."

"I don't care. Promise me you'll try. You don't have to marry the guy, just let him help us with the prom and don't get all defensive when he's friendly."

"I'm not defensive."

Her sister cocked her head to the side with more attitude than Brooke could ever muster.

Reagan might have a point.

Over a year had passed since she'd let anyone close, other than her two sisters. Month after month of an odd sort of solitary. Every day she was around people, but she'd never been so alone.

At first, she'd needed the solitude to lick her wounds and find some kind of emotional solid ground. When she'd first come back home to Jolie, she'd burst into tears at the weirdest provocation, and without warning.

Better to be alone when you found yourself weeping over the inability to find your favorite fleecy pajama pants.

Even though solitude was growing old, the notion of dating made her stomach sway.

She'd been through hell and back with her ex, and Trevor couldn't be a dating option.

For crying out loud, he was a Bradley.

Too much was at stake with this prom. Where one Bradley appeared, three others followed. If she let Trevor truly be a partner on the prom project, before she knew it, they'd all be involved.

One date with him and she'd probably be neck deep in bossy Bradleys.

Right now, she needed to be the one in charge.

But...Trevor did have the connections with the high school and the Bradley name to smooth out the whole process. His family was footing the lion's share of the prom budget too, even if they hadn't discussed those details yet.

Trevor was the reason she got Reagan home safely tonight too, and spending time with him wasn't horrible.

She met her sister's gaze. "Okay. I promise to try. And I won't get defensive just because a cute guy is being nice to me."

"Thank you." Reagan's Grinch grin came back. "And I knew you thought he was cute."

* * * *

At night, with the entryway lit and the downstairs indoor lights glowing, Chateau Jolie looked like a dream.

Trevor crawled out of Reagan's Prius while Brooke and her sister stayed in the other car, chatting away.

He took a deep breath, appreciating the crisp, clean air. Spring in the mountains brought cool night air. And sometimes it could get downright cold.

Like now.

Trevor crossed his arms against the chill. They needed to hurry things up.

Reagan finally emerged, big Cheshire cat grin on her face. "Thanks for getting my car back. Y'all be safe on the way down. But not too safe."

He joined Brooke in her car. "Is she still tipsy or did I miss something?"

"With her, we're all missing something." She pulled out of the parking lot.

"Yeah, I kind of gathered she's a handful. And dated Rex Richards? Yeesh."

"Tell me about it. Only for a few months, but that's still a few too many. I told her he was trouble. She told me just because I was back didn't mean I could butt in."

Trevor grabbed onto the most telling word.

"Back? From where?"

When she didn't answer, he kept digging. "I'd noticed you moved away after school, but I didn't want to be nosey at Dev's wedding."

The corner of Brooke's lip turned down.

"Where'd you run off to?"

"Trevor."

He gaped dramatically. "You went to a place called Trevor?"

She lost her fight against smiling. "I thought you didn't want to be nosey."

"That was at Dev's wedding. Now I don't have a problem nosing."

"I moved back over a year ago. I thought we already talked about this."

"Um, no. I spent half an hour that night trying to find out if you preferred white wine over red. We talked about everything from TV shows to work to weddings we'd crashed—"

"*You* talked about weddings you've crashed. I don't do that."

"We talked a lot, but nothing too personal. I still don't know if you prefer white or red."

"I wasn't that bad."

He gave her a dead-eyed stare.

"Wow. Okay, guess I was."

"We still had a great time."

"Yes, we did." Her gaze met his briefly and a smile lit her dark features. "And I know I told you I prefer red."

They reached the valley and she pulled onto Main Street. The Tavern was on the edge of downtown and the only cars left in the parking lot were his and a few Tavern employees.

"Thank you," Brooke said as she parked.

"For?"

"For being here tonight. Otherwise my sister and I might still be inside the Tavern arguing. Probably causing a scene."

Trevor climbed out of her car but leaned back down. "From what I hear, it wouldn't be the first time y'all caused a scene in town."

Brooke popped up on the other side of the car with a gasp, her eyes wide and mouth open.

"Oh yeah, I heard about the two of you this past winter. Reagan, reading the riot act to some waitress who'd slept with her boyfriend, and you, cool as a cucumber, threatening to turn the whole matter over to the police."

"Small towns, I swear."

"Then it's true."

"No. Total exaggeration. I had a brief word with a waitress who was sending threatening text messages to my sister. I made it clear she would desist, by choice, or I'd make her, by force. I can't help it. I'm protective when it comes to my family."

He went around her car. "I bet you're a sight when you get fired up."

"I doubt it."

"I don't."

A frown pulled at her lips and she glanced away. "You'll have to take my word."

"I'd rather take you to lunch sometime."

"Trevor."

"I'm not asking you for an answer right now. Just stating my interest. Besides, it's one meal. Technically, we've already had dinner together. The only difference is it'd be a meal without your sister chaperoning."

"Ha. Reagan chaperoning? That'll be the day." Brooke studied him, not responding, but no longer objecting. Any time they were together, his skin hummed at the challenge she presented, his senses buzzing any time he could make her smile.

"We're already going to see a lot of each other while planning this prom. What's the big deal about throwing a meal into the mix?" he asked. "Even snacks. We could just do snacks."

She lost another battle with a smile and had to glance away.

There was no way this attraction was one-sided. Part of him wanted to push the issue, lean on the reckless ways of old Trevor and leap. But a more sensible side made him pump the brakes.

"Here. Reagan might be looking for these tomorrow." He held out Reagan's keys and Brooke's fingers brushed his palm as she took them.

Risking the tiniest leap—more like big step—he closed his hand gently around hers.

Brooke didn't pull away.

"Remember how much we danced at Dev's wedding?"

She studied her hand within his, her voice dropping to just above a whisper. "Yes. How could I forget? My legs were sore the next day."

"I wanted to kiss you that night."

"I know."

"But you took off."

A sigh lifted her shoulders. "I know. I…I wished I'd handled that better."

They stood in the dim stillness of the parking lot, the music of tree frogs filling the air. The scent of her shampoo or lotion or something reached him. Fresh strawberries picked on a sunny day. It was all he could do not to lean in closer, touch his lips to her temple, and breathe in deep.

After what seemed an eternity, Brooke looked up, her gaze unreadable. Regret or hope? Longing or guilt? She could feel all of the above, and he would never be sure unless she told him.

The sound of her voice startled the silence. "It's been a really long time since I've dated."

"I'm happy to mentor. You don't forget how."

"Like riding a bike?"

"Even better."

With another breath, her shoulders relaxed. "I'll think about it."

"I can't wait."

A glint of amusement touched her voice. "I didn't say yes."

"I know." He opened his hand, letting her go.

But she hadn't said no, either.

Chapter 6

"What about streamers?" Her youngest sister, Laurel, sat curled up in the window seat of Brooke's office, chin planted in the palm of her hand, a faraway look in her eyes.

From her spot in one of the straight-backed office chairs, Reagan groaned.

Laurel's pout was immediate. "I haven't had coffee yet and I'm supposed to come up with brilliant party ideas. Streamers are all I've got."

"Why do we need brilliant ideas right this second anyway?" Reagan crossed her legs with all the composure of royalty. A far cry from her night at the Tavern. But that was Reagan. A hot mess one second, queen of all she surveyed the next.

"Because right now is all we have. This prom is around the corner. We've got to get cracking."

Brooke's phone vibrated on her desk. She glanced at the screen, and her blood ran cold.

Her attorney's name stood out, stark and ominous.

The woman was great at her job, but Brooke should've wrapped up business with her months ago. Done with the divorce, done with her ex, done with phone calls that made her heart punch against her ribs.

Except Nick wouldn't let her go. Not as long as he could make her suffer more.

Eventually, she'd have to talk to her attorney, face the reality of what her ex-husband was trying to do, and figure out how to fight him.

Right after she came up with a plan for the prom battle.

"You're in the middle of booking a big tasting party." Reagan's voice pulled her back. "I'm trying to sell them all a weekend room package, and

Laurel is busy doing Laurel things. We don't have time to get cracking on a prom right now."

They were all up to their eyeballs with work for the winery and trying to prop up sagging room sales. They needed the exposure of this prom to do exactly that, and then maybe she could afford to pay her attorney for yet another war, but that was her problem to solve. Not theirs.

Brooke used her firmest manager tone. "We have to make time for this prom."

In the next second, a scratching sound came from the door. They were immediately joined by their newest and least helpful staff member, a round, six-month-old little pudge of a pug.

"Beans!" Laurel cooed with delight and scooped up the professed love of her life. "Hey, Beans. Hey, Beans. Hey, Beans."

Her repetitive greeting was met with much wiggling and licking.

"Unless the pug has an opinion on proms, we need to focus," Brooke said.

Reagan reached over to shower more affection on the puppy. "I have an idea. You could let me handle the winery bookings for a while. And Laurel could take over room reservations. Instead of being a control freak, you could let go of some responsibility. Then you'd be free to get cracking on this prom all you like."

"I don't know if that's the most—"

"You need to give Laurel and me more to do. You keep saying you will, but then you never do."

"I'm more experienced in business than either of you. Believe me, I don't want to hog all the work."

"Then don't. You don't have to prove anything to us. We already know you're the smart one."

Her sisters might think her smart and successful, but the smarts never came easy and the success was a sham.

Brooke worked her tail off for every success she'd ever had. Her determination was only surpassed by her ability to function on four hours of sleep for multiple days in a row. She had no choice.

Her grandfather was a professor at Brown. Her parents were hedge fund managers who "retired" at forty to buy a chateau, and then they took a fledgling winery and made it a triumph. Hired all the right people and raised three girls, only to retire again at sixty.

As the oldest, Brooke wasn't only expected to do well, but to do it as seemingly effortlessly as her parents.

Reagan harrumphed and shifted in her chair. "You're doing too much though and, if I'm blunt, kind of sucking at it."

Laurel finally focused on the two of them. "*If* you're blunt."

As tough as it was to admit, Reagan was right.

Brooke had taken over the management of Chateau Jolie's Boutique Winery and Hotel like a warlord with something to prove.

The responsibility shouldn't have been surprising—she'd watched her parents do this for years—but the daily workloads of a winery and hotel were proving to be more than any of the Sargent sisters had expected.

But they each wanted this. They'd agreed. Their parents said they wanted to retire and the three of them said they'd take over the family business. Reagan had given up her career in retail and Laurel ceased her endless pursuit of veterinary science.

Brooke moved home because she'd had little choice but to come back to Jolie, pouring what was left of her heart and soul into this business.

But it was time to delegate.

"You know what, you're right," Brooke said.

A few seconds passed before Reagan formed a response. "I am?"

"Yes. It's time you two did more. Until this prom is over, you can take over managing the tastings and act as primary contact for our viniculturist. And Laurel, you can take Reagan's place in managing hotel bookings and reception."

"Wait. I wasn't the one complaining about my responsibilities. I'm happy with—"

"No. As long as this prom is on our plate, I need to give it as much attention as possible. The school and the town need this."

Her sisters didn't have the full picture on how badly *she* needed this. All three of them being in a panic would equal disaster, but at some point she had to tell them.

"And it'll be good PR for us too. You guys can pick up the slack."

"Of course we can." Reagan practically glowed, delighted with being given a bigger role at Jolie.

Laurel couldn't be more opposite. Hotel duty meant more time inside. Laurel withered when cooped up indoors.

"You can still lead hikes and recreation for guests, Laurel. No one is taking that away from you. It'll be fine." Satisfied, Brooke closed her laptop. "Now that that's settled, we need to discuss decorations for the dance."

"What about those prom theme packages of decorations you can buy online? Are those still a thing?" Laurel asked.

Reagan smirked, that damnable gleam in her eyes. "Wait. Isn't Trevor supposed to be helping you with the prom details? Where is he anyway? He was really helpful when he brought us home."

"What?" Laurel perked up. "Who? What'd I miss? Who is Trevor?"

"The youngest Bradley brother. With the big blue eyes to prove it."

"Stop." Her phone buzzed with another call from her attorney.

"And he's got a thing for Brooke."

"He does not have a thing for me. We don't have time for nonsense, Reags."

"You should be roping Baby Blues into decoration discussions, not us. Invite him over, make tea. You guys can *plan* things together."

Her phone buzzed again.

"Who's calling you?" Reagan reached for Brooke's phone, but she grabbed it from her desk before her sister could.

"No one."

"Nice try. Who is it?"

Reagan always was the skilled liar in the family, not Brooke.

"It's my attorney."

Laurel's delicate features scrunched into a scowl. "Why is your attorney calling you? I thought you were done with her?"

"I was."

"But…" Reagan cocked an eyebrow.

Trying to hide anything from the Sargent Inquisition was futile.

"Nick is claiming he has rights to my half of Jolie."

"*What?*" Reagan jerked forward.

"No!" Laurel exclaimed simultaneously. "He can't do that."

"I know, I know." She tried settling her sisters with a level tone and a few calming hand gestures. Fat lot of good it'd do. This was precisely why she didn't want them to know. Full-blown Sargent panic didn't help their business. "He has no legal right to anything else, but he can try, and he is. That's why my attorney is blowing up my phone."

"Then talk to her." Reagan reached for her phone again. "You're a-hole ex-husband cannot have any part of Jolie. Sic the Barracuda on him."

"I am. I'll call her in a while. In private."

"I can't believe you haven't said anything until now."

"I found out last week."

Even Laurel didn't look convinced. "But you guys are divorced. You already settled."

"And got screwed," Reagan added.

"I thought it was over."

"He's saying I intentionally hid the hotel and my rights to it, so he wouldn't know about the property or try to get a portion."

"We didn't inherit the hotel and winery until after you were separated."

"I know all of this, Reags. But something else you learn while going through a divorce, it doesn't matter what you know. It only matters what you can prove."

Laurel nibbled at her bottom lip as she held Beans closer. "This means more money spent on attorneys and courts."

People who called her sister flighty or an airhead were idiots. Nothing that mattered got past Laurel.

"Can we afford the Barracuda again?"

A lump grew in Brooke's throat. *We*. There shouldn't be a *we* here. This was her past, her mistakes, coming back to haunt her. Her problems refused to let her move on and yet her sisters, when she needed them most, were still there for her.

Her sisters weren't bookkeepers or accountants. For as involved as they were with running the chateau, they trusted her with the financial side of the business.

The deserved nothing but the truth. "Barely? Maybe. But I will figure something out. This is my problem."

"You're our sister. We can help. What about money from the winery?" Reagan asked.

Brooke shook her head. "Times are tighter now. Borrowing more from the winery means a significant dent in the operational budget. We've got a lot of overhead with the vineyard."

"But having your attorney is more important," Laurel said.

"And we've already agreed to the prom. Backing out will hurt us more than help us. I can put off paying my attorney for a few months. I've paid her plenty already. We don't exactly have the money to spend on this prom, but we need the exposure. This prom is our best bet."

Reagan scooted forward in her chair. "Then you need to go talk to Trevor. Honeywilde has the money. They can handle the lion's share of the budget."

Finally, she and Reagan were on the same page.

"You need to focus on this prom. Laurel and I can take on more around the chateau while you do. Trevor should be your partner on this. Right, Laurel?"

Laurel paused, and then nodded fast enough to give herself a crick. "What she said. And when did he bring you home? I want to meet him. Do you like him?"

Even with the weight of the world bearing down on them, her sister defaulted to the romantic. Her world was on its way to being a certifiable wreck, yet here was Laurel, with notions of match making.

"I like him as a person, yes. But that's it."

"Boo."

Didn't matter that Brooke wasn't ready for a match, in her sisters' eyes, she'd only heal the hole in her heart with another man.

But she knew better.

She'd moved on, put one foot in front of the other, and did her best in life. She'd found a way to keep going, and lately she'd enjoyed a level of contentment found in routine.

The deterioration of her marriage destroyed that mythical happily-ever-after, but she was happy enough right now. She'd never be the optimistic, go-getting Pollyanna she once was, but she was doing okay.

Reagan and Laurel couldn't understand this. They'd never experienced her reality.

She hoped they'd never have to.

"Well, I still want to meet him. When is he coming to Jolie?" Laurel used her singsong voice and held Beans in front of her face, bobbing him up and down. "He will love us. He should come over. We like new people."

"Stop being weird. You're scaring the dog." Reagan reached for Beans, but got the side eye from both of them.

"Reagan does have a point though," Laurel said from behind the pug. "You need to get Trevor's involvement *now*. If we're counting on Honeywilde to fund this party, he should be the one discussing the streamers and stuff with you, not us."

With a calculating glint in her eyes, Reagan agreed. "Exactly. And, like I said, they do this stuff all the time at Honeywilde. We could use his help. If you're meeting with the prom committee tomorrow, you need to loop him in before then."

Brooke bristled, her defenses marching forward to fall in line. "I don't want this to be Honeywilde's project though. It needs to be ours."

With a wave of her hand, Laurel dismissed her concern. "And poor Trevor has to compete with you for credit. I trust you'll figure out a way to win. Don't you, Laurel?"

"Totally."

"I am not that bad."

Her sisters shared a glance that argued otherwise.

"Remember the time she wanted to compete to see who could decorate the prettiest Christmas tree?" Reagan asked.

"So instead of one big tree, we had to get three smaller ones." Laurel nodded.

"In my defense, I was eight."

Laurel leveled her with a look. "But you won, with flying colors. I had Mom's help and you still beat us!"

Reagan's rarely heard laugh filled the room. "Remember, Mom demanded a recount because she said Dad and Gigi and Papa were biased?"

Her sisters' laughter, each uniquely their own, shined some light into the shadows of Brooke's heart. They weren't sure what the future held. Jolie was in trouble, but the three of them had each other, and that was a lot more than most people had.

Surely, Brooke could figure out the rest.

"Come on, Laurel. The two of us have got to get cracking on our new jobs." Reagan snatched the calendar from Brooke's desk before she could argue. "You better call Baby Blue Eyes."

Without another word, her sisters popped up from their seats and left. Not even Beans stayed behind for moral support.

Brooke slumped back in her chair, the realization sinking in fully.

Her sisters were right; she needed Trevor Bradley's help. But even more than that, before she could do anything else, she needed Trevor Bradley's money.

She had to go back to Honeywilde.

Chapter 7

The sun-dappled western shore of Lake Anikawa was Trevor's favorite patch of earth. Dotted in mountain laurel and rocks, hiding narrow paths and small clearings, the lakeside made the perfect mini getaway.

Beau barked in agreement as they neared their preferred clearing.

Trevor set his blanket down to give his dog a two-handed scratch, making one of his back legs peddle. "I know, buddy. Best idea ever."

They could have a little peace and quiet, enjoy the out of doors. He'd even brought snacks.

If they needed to get away from the constant flurry of activity at the inn or wanted a break from his family, this place, just to the right of the cove, was the ideal hiding spot.

Except for today.

"I know you're trying to do your stretches or whatever," Devlin said, intruding their space with way too much pep in his step. "But I need a minute."

"It's yoga, not stretches. I'll give you a minute, if you swear you'll never call it stretching again."

"Fine. Yoga." Dev bent to pet Beau.

"What's up?"

Dev caught the edge of Trevor's blanket as he rolled it out and straightened the corners. "You know we've got the Blueberry Festival coming up next month."

His brother's tone made him look up. "Yeah."

"My schedule is basically nothing but this festival until the day of. Sophie and Roark are slammed with gearing up for the season. Our staff is scheduled out for the next eight weeks and—"

"Cut to the chase, Dev."

"We really need you to come through on this prom thing."

The two of them stared at one another a moment.

"I'll do my best not to screw things up," Trevor snapped.

"That is not what I meant."

He wanted to toss a "whatever" over his shoulder, make a smart remark or smother the moment in humor. Instead, he sat down and remained silent for a second, tamping down his frustration.

Devlin wasn't Roark. He wasn't Trevor's boss and he'd screwed up as much as Trevor ever had. Even more. His concern came from a good place.

A place of understanding.

"Look." Dev joined him on the blanket, Beau wedging himself between them for double the scratches. "Roark is....being Roark, and he's micromanaging me because he's concerned about you. The prom is your first project without one of us and I said I'd talk to you."

"Because he'd muck it up."

"Exactly."

Beau wriggled around, offering his belly and snuffing until someone complied.

"I'm not trying to micromanage you," Dev said. "Or hover or whatever it is you probably think I'm doing. I hate that shit. I know how it feels. I'm just trying to help."

"I know. For a second you reminded me of Roark—kind of freaked me out—but I get it."

With a good-natured smirk, Dev punched Trevor in the arm.

"Ow!"

"Call me Roark again."

"Damn." He rubbed his arm and laughed. "Have you always been that strong?"

"Yeah, but it's been a long time since you made me prove it."

Until the last year or so, he and Dev hadn't hung out at all. In their years as teens, hanging out with Devlin wasn't something he did. Laughing with him was a rarity.

But a lot had changed in the last couple of years. Namely, Trevor was no longer in Peru, hiding from his family and their problems, and Dev wasn't on self-destruct mode all the time.

Dev was the one who'd reached out over a year ago and asked him to come home.

For that, Trevor would be forever thankful.

Dev peered over the top of his sunglasses. "You're doing a good job around here. I don't know if anyone has said so, but you are. Roark gave you the high school's prom to pull off with a pretty tight budget, and you haven't really..."

"Ever done this on my own?"

"Basically, yeah."

Maybe not for Honeywilde, and certainly not when he had the three super Bradleys running everything in the family business, but while volunteering in Peru, he was no slouch. He had plenty of projects and he'd excelled.

His brothers and sister didn't know or understand what he did down there. But they should know how dedicated he'd been at Honeywilde since his return. Sure, he'd still had his own agenda when he reached out to their mom behind everyone's back, but that was for the good of the family.

He hadn't meant to ditch work here and there, but some things took priority over others.

"If this project gets to be too much, don't be afraid to say something," Dev said.

"It won't be too much."

"Being tied down to a bunch of work isn't your thing and that's fine."

His family had little comprehension about what *was* his thing, and that was okay. They didn't know, because he didn't tell them. He didn't tell them lots of things.

"Sophie told me about your wanting to go to South America again, so if you think you won't have time—"

Except for that.

"Let me stop you right there." Trevor turned toward his brother, and Beau's head popped up at his tone. "My summer plans aren't Sophie's to share. She knows only because she's nosey. I talked to Roark about it, in theory. But yeah, I want to take a few weeks off at the end of the summer to travel. End of the summer, as in months from now. As in long after this prom is over."

"Okay, okay." Dev's hands went up. "I'm only checking."

"Do you remember how much you loved people checking on you a year ago?"

His brother had the good sense to look contrite. "Fair enough. If you say you've got the prom thing covered, I'm done asking."

"I've got the prom thing covered. And if you make me reassure you again, I'm going to punch you back."

With a cocky smile, Dev leaned back. "You can try."

Trevor shoved him off balance and laughed.

"I might actually miss you if you leave for a month," Dev said.

"Sure you will."

"I will. You've earned the vacation time, but a few weeks is a long time."

"The three of you have this place clicking along like a fine-tuned car. And Marco is killing it in the kitchen. I think you'll do just fine without me for a few weeks."

"Your help is not what I meant. I'll miss that too, but more than that, I'll miss having you around."

Trevor studied his hands rather than pay too much attention to what could possibly pass as a compliment. "Oh."

"I'll have to deal with Roark and Sophie all by myself. Like two caffeinated bees buzzing around here. You should be worried about me, not the other way around."

Dev tried to keep his tone light, but there was obvious concern in his comment.

Older-brother habits died hard, and he was the only one who might understand why Trevor had to leave Honeywilde years ago.

"You don't need to worry. I'm not going to disappear on y'all again. I've saved up more than enough money because I haven't gone anywhere or done anything in almost two years. And I'll be back home afterward, business as usual."

Lips pinched, Dev nodded.

He didn't seem convinced. Understandable, considering that the last time Trevor went on vacation, he'd gone to Peru for a couple of weeks and ended up staying for over a year. He'd joined a nonprofit, traveled around a few countries, built houses, a school, hiked, met people. Lived a life outside of Windamere. Found some happiness and escaped the turmoil that used to be Honeywilde's default setting.

Things were different now.

Honeywilde was calm. More like home. He had no reason to run away.

Dev cleared his throat, shifting on the blanket. "Have you, uh, talked to Mom recently?"

Trevor fought not to let the surprise show.

Their mother was a tremulous topic. He and Sophie were the only Bradleys who kept the lines of communication open. Dev actively fought against it.

At least, at first.

"Not in a few weeks. I was thinking sometime before Mother's Day. Maybe."

His brother nodded.

"Just a phone call though, you know?"

"No more unannounced visits?" Dev asked.

"No, not again."

With a grunt, he nodded again. "But a phone call might be nice. You know, if you wanted to."

Trevor grinned. That was Devlin-ese for giving his approval on a phone call.

"I'll let you know when I call. And, Dev?" He waited until his brother looked his way. "I'm not going to take off again. I promise. I'm not that guy anymore."

A breeze from the lake rustled through the trees.

Dev straightened his legs and leaned back, tilting his chin up toward the sun. "Good. Nothing wrong with the guy you were, but I like having you around. Believe it or not, we all like having you around."

Again, his brother's tone was light, but meaning weighted his words.

Believing his family actually missed him remained a challenge. They'd always let him be himself, even if they never understood him, but his entire life he'd been the odd man out. Sure, Dev had his drama over the years, but a lot of Bradley energy was spent on worrying or rescuing him.

Trevor was the quiet one. No one tried to rescue him when he withdrew completely at fourteen, because no one really noticed. They were all too busy.

When he graduated high school and decided to road trip cross-country, he didn't bother telling anyone and no one asked. He just went.

And when he moved out of the inn the last two winters to stay in one of the empty yurts, his brothers and sister raised their collective eyebrows, but they didn't say a word.

Having them slowly involved, more and more, in his life, was weird. He'd gone it alone for so long, letting them in was unnatural, even if welcome.

"Trevor?"

He sat up straighter at the sound of his name, and he knew the voice before he laid eyes on her.

In a split second, he was on his feet. "Brooke. Hey. What are you doing here?"

Devlin's gaze followed his, and Beau popped up, tail wagging a million miles an hour. Then Beau charged toward Brooke, at full speed.

Rather than shrink back at the seventy pounds of brown, floppy fur barreling toward her, Brooke reached out to pet him. "My goodness, who are you? You weren't at the wedding."

"That's Beau." Trevor tried to grab his collar, but the boy wasn't having it. He circled Brooke, tongue lolling, eyes full of wonder.

Trevor could sympathize.

"Beau," he tried to scold.

"It's okay, he probably smells Beans."

"Beans? As in baked?"

Her nose wrinkled comically. "Huh? Oh! No, no, Beans is our pug's name. And this must be the dog you told me about at the wedding."

"The one and only. He's too rowdy to attend in person."

Brooke straightened and shielded her eyes from the sun with a hand on her forehead.

"You must be the Brooke from Chateau Jolie." Devlin rose from the blanket.

Trevor had lost track of his brother's presence. "Brooke was at your wedding."

"That's right. Sophie told me." Devlin offered his hand. "Sorry, I had tunnel vision that day. We were in school together too, right?"

"I had a couple of classes with your brother Roark."

"We probably didn't run in the same circles, huh?"

"Not really."

For a silent moment that seemed an eternity, his brother glanced back and forth between him and Brooke. "All right. Well, good seeing you. Thanks for coming to the wedding and good luck with the prom. I better get back to work." Dev gave Trevor a sideways glance and strolled away.

"How did you manage to find us out here?" Trevor asked.

"Sophie said this is where you'd probably be."

So much for this being his perfect hiding spot.

"I wanted to talk to you about the prom."

"Good. Me too. I was going to call you today. I came up with a few ideas. Ways to make the whole thing different and memorable, but they shouldn't take a lot of time."

With a tight smile, Brooke moved across the clearing so the sun was at her back. "Actually, I'm here about the budget. I already have ideas and plans around how we're going to make it all work in time, but..."

"But?"

"I need you in order to discuss the money."

Trevor rocked back on his heels. "Right." She needed him for Honeywilde's half of the funds. Beyond that, she'd probably prefer a silent partner.

"You already have plans, huh? That's good. But, you know, the high school's prom committee will have plans and opinions too. I wouldn't get attached to anything until you meet with the committee chairs. When do you meet with them?"

She attempted to mask her reaction, but a flash of concern filled her gaze before she could chase it away. "Tomorrow. I thought I'd show them around. Present some of my ideas. Guide them in the right direction."

"Good thinking. Let's hear your ideas."

"What, now?"

"Sure." He sat back down on his blanket and patted the open spot next to him.

Beau obliged immediately.

Brooke remained standing.

"Come on. I want to hear all about these plans. And…" He reached into his backpack. "I have snacks. Trail mix, waters. I brought some cookies that Marco made yesterday."

"Cookies?"

That got Brooke's attention, and she slowly approached the blanket. "I've heard Honeywilde's cookies are to die for."

"These are s'mores cookies. So, if chocolate chunks and marshmallow are your thing, then you might like them. I guess."

"I'm willing to try and see." Brooke sat on the blanket, with Beau settling right beside her.

Half a cookie in, Trevor dusted the crumbs off his jeans. "These prom plans, let's hear 'em."

As proper as she could, with a cookie in one hand and petting a dog with another, Brooke listed off her ideas.

All fine and formal, fussy, and standard adult plans for the kind of party thrown at a chateau, but they weren't right.

There was nothing wrong with her ideas. They weren't awful, per se, but teenagers clearly weren't her usual target market.

Trevor stuffed the rest of his cookie into his mouth and chewed. And thought. "Okay," he said when finished. "Those aren't completely terrible, but for teenagers, everything you mentioned feels…staid."

"Staid?"

"Super staid."

Her plush lips opened in a perfect *O* of outrage.

"I didn't say your ideas sucked. They need more oomph though."

She crossed her arms, Beau whining at the sudden lack of contact. "Let me guess. You have the oomph to add."

"I've got all kinds of oomph." He crossed his arms too.

Brooke glanced away, but he saw her smile. "You're ridiculous."

"I've been told. But in all seriousness, these kids deserve the best. Isn't that what you want? This prom needs to be unexpectedly amazing, right? I'm good at the unexpected. After what they've gone through, these juniors and seniors need all that froufrou stuff you're familiar with, but they aren't a bunch of fifty-year-olds going to a charity ball. Kids need pizazz. A ball *and* a shindig. We've got to give them a mix of both."

Fighting another smile, she met his gaze.

After a long pause of bottom-lip chewing, releasing it pinker and plumper than before, driving him to distraction and utter madness, Brooke dropped her hands to her side. "Fine, you may have a point. I've done balls, but I don't think I've ever hosted a shindig."

"Not to worry. I've got the shindiggery on lock."

Finally, she lost her battle, and a pop of laughter escaped. "I guess we're in luck then. But there's something we have to discuss first."

"Please don't say a string quartet."

"Money."

"What about it?"

"I need the money from Honeywilde. If I'm going to move ahead with plans, I need to know what kind of budget we're working with."

"Oh, *that* money. You and I need to meet with the prom committee first, see what they have in mind and, split between the two hotels, tally up what we can give them."

She pinched her lips together again.

"You did say you're meeting the committee at Jolie tomorrow, right?"

"Yes, but—"

"Then let's meet with them first and then figure out the rest."

Her shoulders tensed. "I guess that makes sense."

"Trevor?" Sophie called out his name before she came into view. "Trev!" She skidded to a halt at the edge of the clearing. "Oh. Hey, Brooke. I'm sorry to interrupt, but Trev, I need you. We have to set up the tables on the patio for that book club's tea today. Well, knowing this book club, tea and a few bottles of wine too."

"Okay, but we're not done here."

A smile spread across Sophie's lips, taking up half her face underneath her ridiculously floppy hat. "Brooke can come too. Y'all can finish talking while you put up tables. You don't mind, do you, Brooke? We're serving Jolie's wine to the book club. You can make sure we pick out wines best paired with a southern gothic novel. Come on." Without waiting for a response from either of them, Sophie started back toward the inn.

"I guess we're setting up tables now."

"Apparently."

Trevor reached for his blanket and handed Brooke one end to help him fold. "Sophie's like a whirlpool. If you stand too close, you get sucked in."

"I see that. But I can't stay long."

"That's okay. We can do yoga some other day."

Brooke stopped short, eyes wide as she scrunched up her nose. "I didn't come here to—We weren't doing yoga."

Trevor plucked the corners of the blanket from her hands, his fingers brushing hers as he finished folding. "Not yet we weren't. Sheesh. Patience. We'll get to it."

Her complete bafflement gave way to a smile when she realized he was messing with her. "It's like that, huh?"

If by "that," she meant he couldn't resist flirting with her, then yes. It was exactly like that.

Chapter 8

Against all better judgment, Brooke followed Trevor back to Honeywilde and down into the basement where they kept all of their linens.

This was only to satisfy her sick curiosity about how the competition operated, the inner workings of their management team, and how much ivory-colored linen one place could own. Following him around had absolutely nothing to do with spending more time around him, or any amusement she might find at his playful disposition.

Chances were good he wouldn't be amused at all if she told him there'd be no way Jolie could go halvsies on this prom budget.

They'd be lucky if they could even go thirdsies.

Trevor rolled a cart from around the corner and tossed a stack of tablecloths on top of it "I meant to ask, how's your sister doing after the other night?"

"She's fine."

"She'll be even better after a little time away from Rex Richards."

"No kidding." She didn't want to get into her or her sister's personal lives with him, but she couldn't agree more.

"Will you grab that stack?" He pointed to another pile of linens behind her. "Didn't she date Tommy Bouharan back in the day too?"

"Ugh." Her sister had the worst taste in men. "I forgot all about him. Thanks a lot for the reminder."

"Between him and Rex and the guy who hooked up with the bartender at the Tavern, how many butts have you had to kick in the name of your sister?"

"Um, none?" Brooke busied herself straightening the tablecloths already on the cart.

"Sure you haven't."

Torn between sharing the chaos that came with being the oldest of three sisters and keeping her private life and past as far away from Trevor as possible, she went with splitting the difference. "I might have had a word of prayer with a few people over the years, but there's been no actual butt kicking."

"I still say you must be a sight to behold when you get on a roll."

He didn't know the half of it.

"What about your youngest sister? Is she as much work as Reagan?"

She stopped folding and refolding linens. "We're supposed to be focusing on the prom. Let's stick to talking about that."

With no lack of dramatic flair, Trevor dropped the cloth in his hands and leaned forward over the cart. "You mean to tell me, all you want to talk about for the next two weeks is the prom and nothing but the prom, so help you God? No can do, Sarge. I won't survive the monotony."

"Sarge?"

"Get it? Because your name is Sargent and you keep trying to give me orders."

"I do not." She tossed a tablecloth at him. "Don't call me that."

"You just made my point for me." He laughed.

Her resistance to conversation wasn't because she didn't like him and want to know more. Quite the opposite actually.

Trevor was a walking quirk. A lean, long-legged, walking eccentricity.

At Dev's wedding, he'd told her about the time he learned to crochet. Just to prove to himself he could. He'd taken up knot-tying and somehow, for him, that'd segued into crochet.

Because sure, why not?

Also, what in the world motivated him to do yoga? And how he could be so cheeky and yet charming at the same time? Why did her skin tingle every time his fingers brushed hers, and why did he always smell so good?

But the more she talked to him, the more things she found to like. And the more things she liked, the more the ground crumbled beneath her feet.

She needed that foundation solid, hard as a rock, so she'd never fall again.

"Let's just stay on the topic of the prom. I think that's for the best."

Trevor smirked, as though he knew exactly how full of it she really was. "Okay." With arms outstretched, he smoothed both hands over the linen she'd thrown at him. He hummed low in his throat. "Prom...hmm, let me think. Sticking to the topic of prom."

He studied the material, adjusting and smoothing, plucking something away from the pristine white, paying such close attention.

Prickly heat began to dance up the back of Brooke's neck.

He kept petting the damn square of linen, making it smoother with every pass of his hand, removing even the tiniest speck until it was perfect. What if he applied that same level of attention to a person?

Say, her, for example. Caressing her skin until she grew supple and soft beneath his touch.

"I know." He looked up, his gaze locking onto hers. "What was the best thing about your prom?"

The basement walls shrunk closer, her hearing drowned out by every other sensation warring for attention. "Wh-what?"

"Prom. You've restricted me to one topic, so what was your favorite part?"

"You know that's not what I meant. I don't even remember my prom."

Trevor rounded the cart and stood before her.

He was tall, but in her heels, she had to lift her chin only a little to meet his gaze.

"How do *you* not remember your prom? You were all about Windamere High back in the day."

"How do you know?"

"I was in school for a year with you. Everyone knew. Brooke Sargent ran Windamere High."

"I did not."

His laugh rolled out, full and close enough to warm her skin. "When I was a freshman, you were practically queen of the high school."

That wasn't how she remembered things. "I was more workhorse than queen. All I did was study and run student government. I'm pretty sure Shelly Mathis won prom queen *and* homecoming queen my senior year."

"But you were in charge of everything."

"Which made me a geek, not a social queen. By spring of my senior year, I'd been accepted at Wake and prom was…I don't know. I cared more about going to college than to a dance."

"Who'd you go with?"

"I don't remember."

"Liar."

"Excuse you." The urge to throw another tablecloth at him was strong.

"You do too remember. Everyone remembers who they went to prom with. I went with Julie Phillips."

"Of course you did."

"What's that supposed to mean?"

Julie and Trevor were behind her in school, but even as a freshman, Julie was one of the prettiest, most popular girls in Windamere's tiny corner of the universe. She was the type people remembered, not Brooke.

"Never mind. Don't answer that. Answer my first question. Who'd you go with?"

"I didn't take a date. I went with some of my friends."

Trevor considered her. "I'll interpret that to mean you turned a bunch of guys down or they were all too intimidated to ask. Either way, it's just as well. Prom dates are a lot of drama. You probably had more fun going in a group than anyone who went as a couple."

Maybe. But looking back, her lack of relationships should've been a sign.

Even back then, she was so focused on her goals, she didn't take the time to foster close friendships. She had two sisters and they were more than she could handle.

And there had been no boyfriends.

Boys were nothing but a distraction. Self-centered and energy sucking, they cared only about themselves and what they wanted. So she'd avoided them.

Sadly, marriage had only proven her seventeen-year-old self correct.

"Come to think of it, we should probably keep the group-date option in mind for our prom," Trevor kept talking, oblivious to the spiral she struggled to pull herself out of. "It's popular nowadays to go with friends in big groups, versus going in pairs. I think it's a millennial thing. We don't want the atmosphere to be over-the-top romantic or couple-y."

"There will still be couples though." There were always couples, successful pairings who somehow knew how to make and keep each other happy. Making everyone else feel like even more of a failure.

Wow, she needed to get a grip.

"We won't veto all of the romance, but we can keep it light. Focus on the fun."

Brooke shook loose the clutches of her past and tried to ignore the claw marks. "Focus on the fun. Right."

"This means I'm going to vote a hard no on your hurricane lamp centerpieces tomorrow when we meet with the prom committee chairs."

"Because they're staid."

"You got it, Sarge." Trevor winked at her.

She narrowed her eyes to glare at him.

"Uh-oh, the Sargent stare."

Her stare turned to a full-blown scowl.

"Now, now. Don't be mad. Come here." He took her hand and began walking toward the back of the basement.

His hand was warm and strong and he'd grabbed hers like holding hands was the most natural thing in the world.

Tingling heat went up her arm, spreading through each limb. "Why? What are you doing?"

"Relax. I'm not going to abduct you. I want to show you something." He led her to a small storage room in the back corner of the basement.

The room was dark as pitch, and he had to use the glow of his phone to find the light switch. Once on, the single bulb barely illuminated the room. Only enough to throw shadows everywhere and make the place spooky as all get out.

"You're right, Trevor. My ideas are too staid. Let's have the prom here instead."

"Ha-ha. The room is not what I'm showing you."

He left her there, in the creepiness, as he rummaged around on some of the shelves lining both sides.

At least she was no longer lost in thought about her failed marriage. Sadly, being abandoned in a musty storage room was only a few rungs higher on the ladder of life's calamities.

"Here it is." Trevor returned with something in his hands.

Metal and Moroccan in style, a decent-sized lamp with a small battery-powered candle cast more light around the room.

"We used a bunch of these for the Chamber of Commerce's party. You can still get the feel of candlelight, but this is more fun." Trevor held the lamp up, casting more light around the room. "See? Something like this is different. Not the same hurricane lamps these kids see every Thanksgiving on Mee-Maw's dining room table."

Brooke stifled a laugh and studied the patterns of illumination along the walls and floor. Admittedly, it was a much more stylish option than her idea.

"You look so good in this lighting," he said.

Her gaze jerked to his. "What?"

"You heard me."

She waved away the compliment and reached for the lamp to turn it off, but he moved it out of reach. "I mean it. At this point, I've seen you at a midday wedding, a late-night pizza joint, and now in a basement with piss-poor lighting. You look amazing."

She tried again for the lamp. "Flattery will get you nowhere, Mr. Bradley."

"Who said I was trying to get somewhere with you?" He clicked off the lamp, plunging them into darkness.

Brooke squinted, trying to make out his silhouette or see anything at all. Failing that, she stuck her hand out and found his arm. "Trevor."

"Just kidding." He turned on the lamp, the patterns of dots lighting their faces again. "I'm totally trying to get somewhere with you."

"You're nuts."

"I know."

"Thank you, though. For the compliment. Normally I have better manners. You caught me off guard."

Two lines crinkled his unfairly smooth forehead. "Off guard? You know I'm attracted to you."

Yes, but his attraction wasn't something she could wrap her head around. He was shiny and new. Carefree optimism and energy.

She was a salty old crone in comparison. "I know you're forthright and complimentary. I'm not used to it."

He made a show of contemplating her statement as he turned on the overhead light. "Not used to honesty and compliments. What the hell kind of crowd you been running with, Sarge?"

"The wrong kind," she muttered.

"Then it's a good thing you've started hanging out with me." Trevor grinned and led the way out of the storage room, back to the table linens. He grabbed an armful while Brooke scooped the other stack up in both arms.

"Take the lantern with you. See how it looks at Jolie." He balanced the lantern on top of her linens and headed up the basement steps.

She stopped at the top of the stairs and turned toward Trevor, her arms too full to open the door.

He joined her on the top step, crowding them in and reaching around, close enough that his body heat warmed her, his clean scent tempting her senses. With a long, strong arm, he practically engulfed her as he opened the door. "Thanks for helping me with these."

His breath tickled her ear, and her heart kicked demandingly in her chest.

"I…" Brooke swallowed hard. "You're welcome. But I really should head out now. I have meetings at Jolie this afternoon and you've got stuff to do here."

"No worries. I'll see you tomorrow morning."

Trevor's easygoing confidence continued to put her at ease, all while whittling away at the foundation beneath her.

They stepped out of the basement and back into the bright light of day.

No worries.

Yeah, right.

Chapter 9

During the day, Chateau Jolie appeared an ideal rendezvous for lovers and romantics.

Rolling acres of vineyard surrounded the back of the hotel in a semicircle. In front, a visitor had to travel down a long, gently winding road before reaching the parking area.

Trevor could imagine Edith Piaf's voice drifting through the air. At any moment, someone should ride by on a bike, with a basket. And a baguette.

He liked it.

A visit to Jolie would've come sooner if he'd known the chateau was so inviting. All he'd ever heard about was the winery. In the years since he'd been back in Windamere, the Sargent family had done little to promote the hotel.

"I think my sister spent some time here last summer," he said as soon as Brooke met him in the reception area. "With our chef, I believe."

A smile curled her lips. "Nice try."

"What?"

"I'm not dishing dirt on your sister."

"I know she and Wright spent the day here. I busted them on the way back."

"Sophie was here at an undisclosed point and time. That's all you'll get from me."

"Boo."

"How about I show you the ballroom before the prom committee gets here?"

A chirping sound cut through the air. "Oh, hang on. That's me." Brooke pulled her phone from the pocket of her gray dress pants.

She read the text, and the smile died on her lips.

"Sorry about that." She flipped the phone to vibrate and shoved it back into her pocket.

Her face went paler than her white blouse, and she led him through the lobby and across the hall.

He shouldn't ask.

He wanted to know, but he shouldn't ask.

The chateau was bright with natural light from the tall windows, the walls and décor all fair and airy in color. The main floor was the polar opposite of Honeywilde's rich warmth, but the effect opened the hotel up, making it welcoming and old-world. A guest could almost forget they were in North Carolina and think they had somehow stumbled into the Burgundy region of France.

Brooke pushed open two enormous French doors and he stepped into a long, mostly empty room, with honey-colored hardwood floors and tapestries draping the walls.

"Very nice." He moved past her to the center of the floor. One whole side of the room was lined with French doors that matched the entrance. "All of these open up to that garden?"

"Yes."

"You've got to be kidding. This place is perfect. How could the school not want this place as their first choice for prom? Have they seen it?"

She shrugged before opening one of the doors so he could check out the garden. "I doubt any of those kids have been here." Brooke muttered the rest under her breath. "And the Honeywilde name overshadows all."

"What's that?" he asked, though he'd made out every word.

"Nothing."

Trevor shook his head and stepped outside for a quick tour of the rose garden, taking in the myriad other flowers, a walking path, even a bench and arbor.

As much as he loved his family's inn, Jolie had it all over them when it came to being a prime prom location. Or any dance for that matter.

He returned to find a frowning Brooke staring at her phone, her forehead crinkling.

"What's up? What's wrong?"

"Huh?" She glanced up. "Nothing. Just…thinking about the prom. I'm a worrier."

"Don't worry." He stepped closer. Close enough that her hand was only a few inches from his. "You don't have to."

"What are you doing?"

"Because we are both consummate professionals in our field."

She laughed.

"We could plan this event with our eyes closed. Plus, this is supposed to be a fun, amazing event for the kids in our town. There's nothing for you to worry about." He took her hand and stepped back before pulling her toward him.

"Trevor."

"There will soon be laughter and dancing in this room. We're doing something nice for a bunch of kids, not planning an execution." He turned, maneuvering her in that direction.

"I am not dancing with you right now."

"Dancing?" He pretended to be shocked. "That's a great idea."

She continued to smile. "I'm serious. We don't have time. The committee chairs will be here any minute."

"Then we better make this quick before they show up and get in the way of my moves."

Brooke pinched her lips together before she spoke, humor making her voice crack. "Your moves?"

"Don't act like you don't remember my moves." Trevor swept her closer, a hand on the small of her back as he turned them again.

Something vibrated against him.

"Sadly, I think that's your phone and not your knees going weak," he said.

"I'm not answering."

"Suits me." He held her closer, her body pressed against his as they turned again. Her scent, the curve of her back, familiar, and sensations he'd missed.

"I'm not much of a dancer."

"Pffft." He stepped out and back in, maneuvering her to turn beneath his outstretched arm. "Don't forget, I've spent all night dancing with you already. You did great."

"That's because I let you lead."

"Then let me lead."

Trevor guided them, taking up the floor with long strides. Over the years, he'd picked up his share of dance steps. Between the parties at Honeywilde and his travels, he liked to think he could hold his own.

With a quick prayer that he didn't muck it up, he spun Brooke into him, before dipping her backward.

She inhaled sharply, and then cracked up laughing. "You did not just dip me."

"If you say so."

Dark lashes fanned against her skin as she blinked.

"Kind of feels like you're mid-dip though."

"Please don't drop me."

"Give me some credit. I'm not going to drop you." He straightened and brought her with him, still holding her close.

His smile had to be ear to ear. But Brooke was smiling too.

"Admit it. This is fun."

Lids lowered, she demurred for a moment, and then her gaze tangled with his. "Fine. This is fun. I needed a little fun, so thanks."

"You think the high schoolers would die of embarrassment if we danced at their prom?"

"*I* might die of embarrassment. We aren't eighteen anymore."

"We'll be there regardless. Think of how much fun we had at Dev's wedding. It could be like that, only funner."

Another laugh popped out. "Funner?"

"Super funner." Unable to resist, he brushed her hair back over her shoulder, his fingers getting lost in the soft, dark strands.

Brooke's gaze softened, her lips parted to answer.

Damn, he wanted to kiss her.

He'd told himself he was going to play this cool. Let her lead, play by her rules, plan a prom, and hope for the best. But his attraction hadn't waned since Devlin's wedding, and neither had their chemistry.

If anything, they'd both grown.

Seeing her here, in this place she called home and work, in her element, she was as impressive as she was vulnerable. The vulnerability was new, her walls not as tall as before.

"Are you asking me to prom, Trevor?" A playful smile touched her lips.

"You have restricted my conversational skills to one topic. What choice do I have?" He moved his hand across her back, his fingers brushing over the dip of her spine, her skin warm beneath the thin knit top.

A slight shiver ran through her, her gaze unwavering.

"If you'd loosen up the restrictions, a lot of things could be more fun right now."

"Things like?" The question fell from her lips, and she seemed as surprised as he was that she'd asked.

But her dark gaze took him in, daring him to answer, to put a name on what crackled between them.

"Oh, my God, this place is amazing!" A teenage girl bounded into the ballroom.

Had to be gravity-defying determination that kept Brooke from falling flat on her butt in her scramble to step away from him.

"I can't believe this. *This* is where we get to have prom?" The girl turned in circles, long braids flaring out and spinning with her.

"You must be Dorian." Brooke appeared shell-shocked. She waited for the girl to stop twirling before offering her hand.

"Yes. Sorry." She took Brooke's hand, everything about her oozing contagious joy. "I'm just beside myself. Look at this place!" She rushed over to the young man who was lingering near the door.

"This is Lance." She urged him forward. "We're the prom chairs."

Dorian's sidekick, a blond jock-looking fellow with a smile like he did chewing gum commercials, shook hands with them both. "Thank you for letting us use Jolie on short notice."

"We're delighted we can help."

Without waiting through any further niceties, Dorian took off, oohing and ahhing over every square inch of the room.

Brooke called after her. "As you can see, there's plenty of space here. We have tables and chairs for the room as well."

Trevor joined in, trying to channel all of his siblings, to provide some ideas that were fresh and unique for these kids. What would Devlin want? What would Sophie do? How would Roark make it happen?

"We were thinking some flowers would be nice. Since we've discussed having the doors open to the garden."

"Yes." Dorian clapped her hands together, her nodding fueled by pure enthusiasm and energy.

He liked the girl already.

"We could get the flowers from Brenda's, downtown," Trevor suggested. "Beyond that, you'll need food and drinks."

Brooke cleared her throat and stepped in. "Don't most people still go out to dinner before the prom?"

The wind went out of Dorian's sails. "Normally, yes."

"But we'd included dinner in the cost of tickets. So our classmates paid premium price because they thought they'd get a meal at prom," Lance said, shrugging.

Brooke's tone went flat. "I see."

"I don't," Trevor whispered from the side of his mouth.

"The juniors and seniors have already paid in a lot of money, expecting to get dinner at the prom. Some of them might not have the extra funds lying around to go out to eat next weekend."

"So, if possible, it'd be best if we have food here?" he clarified.

Dorian nodded. "At least heavy appetizers? But only if it's possible. We understand if it isn't."

Trevor shared a sympathetic glance with Brooke.

They couldn't let a bunch of kids go hungry at their prom because some business person didn't know how to manage their money.

Brooke spoke, but the words sounded like they were being pulled out of her by the roots. "We'll do something for food here. Don't worry."

"Yeah, we'll figure it out," Trevor added. "Other things to think about would be decorations, a DJ, prizes—"

"Only all of that?" This time, Brooke was the one muttering.

"That's all of the major things we'd included. Unless you guys know of something we forgot." Dorian smiled at them both.

"I think that about covers it. Here, why don't I show you the garden that we can incorporate into the event?" Brooke ushered Dorian to the doors, making her way outside like the room was on fire.

Lance wandered over to stand beside Trevor. "Do you work here or…"

"I'm with Honeywilde. So, what does your committee have in mind as far as music?"

For some reason, Brooke rushed right through what all they needed to organize for this prom. That was the whole point of this meeting, so if he needed to take the lead here, he would.

"Other than we've got to have some?" Lance stood there, not a trace of sarcasm, even as he refused to expound.

"Um…yeah. Other than you've got to have some. Any ideas, preferences?"

"I don't even know. If things are desperate enough, we batted around the idea of creating a playlist and borrowing some speakers to hook up to a phone. We're pretty limited on options, now that we have zero money."

"No, no, no. You can't use phones and a speaker," Trevor insisted. "This isn't a house party at the lake and you don't have zero money. That's where our help comes in. How do you feel about using the best DJ in the area?"

Lance's eyes widened for a split second. "DJ Knight?"

"That's the one."

"There's no way we can afford him. He's the best."

Brooke and Dorian returned as if on cue.

"I know the guy; he's a buddy of mine. If I can get a deal, would you like him to handle the music at your prom?"

Brooke's glare could've cut through steel. "He's the most expensive DJ around."

She would probably take great pleasure in throttling him as soon as Dorian and Lance were gone, but the kids were hooked on the idea, and Trevor could get him at discount. So long as DJ Knight was available.

"Do you think he's available on such short notice?" Lance asked.

Trevor nodded. "That'd be the catch, but I'll call him and see what I can do."

"What if this prom ends up being the best one ever?" Dorian positively glowed as she grabbed Lance's arm. "Come on, I want to show you the garden outside. You're going to die." She dragged Lance to the garden.

Brooke leaned in to Trevor's shoulder, her voice barely a hiss. "Now you've gotten their hopes up. What happens if you can't follow through?"

"Don't worry. I'll handle it."

"That's what worries me. You're filling their heads with all these grand ideas and we haven't discussed what kind of budget we're working with. You're talking about real flowers and in-demand DJs and who knows what else you offered up while I was gone. Four-course meal?"

Trevor turned to her. "Breathe. It's fine."

"We need to discuss the budget. You're talking about dinner and I'm worried we won't even be able to afford the good punch from Tanner's. You do know the school has *no* money. Zero dollars. Jolie and Honeywilde are footing this entire bill."

"You sound like my brother."

"Then your brother is a wise man."

"We'll have the money. As long as we aren't serving filet mignon or hiring Beyoncé to sing, the budget is there." He was pretty sure anyway. A little finagling might be necessary, but they'd be close enough.

Twin lines appeared between her dark eyebrows, a scowl marring that beautiful face.

"Seriously, it's fine. Honeywilde is giving more than enough to cover music and flowers, and I'm not even taking into account what Jolie contributes."

The color drained from Brooke's face again, the scowl slowly morphing into a look of mild terror.

"What is it? What's that look about?"

The Sargent stare was back, no words, just the shadow of panic in her eyes.

"You look like you're freaking out and that's freaking me out."

Finally, she spoke. "We need to discuss this budget, sooner rather than later. Like, as soon as they leave."

"Does this mean you're officially accepting my help?"

"I—Yes, of course. I asked you to help days ago."

He had to chuckle. "Actually, no, you didn't. I simply went ahead and started helping. If you'll remember, you didn't even invite me over today. I asked when the prom chairs were showing up and told you I'd be here."

"What? That's not—" Brooke froze midsentence, the slow realization playing out across her face. She glanced away, a faint pink coloring her cheeks. "I thought I'd asked."

He took her elbow and tugged her toward the garden. "Doesn't matter. Now that we've got this whole partnership thing in full swing, we can have our official meeting as soon as we're finished here. Everything is going to work out fine."

Brooke muttered under her breath again. "That's what you think."

Chapter 10

Trevor put on a smile and murmured from the side of his mouth as they approached Dorian and Lance. "There's something you're not telling me. What am I missing?"

Only the fact that Jolie's contribution was probably a quarter of what Honeywilde could donate. If that.

Trevor was running around with delusions of prom grandeur while she was wondering if they could get away with popcorn and punch for hors d'oeuvres.

She had no choice but to fess up. "Let's talk when they leave."

Dorian had Lance cornered near a trellis, hands flailing in animated gestures as she talked about something.

"Hey." She turned as they got near. "We were just talking. This is going to end up being more amazing than that other venue ever thought about being."

"I think so too." Brooke's insides twisted. That's what she wanted, from the moment she agreed to this project. Unfortunately, the reality of her situation crept closer and closer every day, its ugly friend—guilt— following close behind. "We'll touch base and meet again, say, the day after tomorrow?"

"Perfect. I'll give you my number and you can let us know if you get an answer on food and music before then."

That seemed highly unlikely.

Dorian flung out her arms to hug Brooke and Trevor. "I can't wait to hear. I never thought I'd be this excited about our prom again."

"Yes, thank you. Both of you." Lance offered his hand in another formal shake.

The two of them turned to go, both happy—in their own way. Cute and unjaded by life, even after losing thousands of dollars, and the faith of their classmates, in an instant.

Somehow, she and Trevor had to make this prom phenomenal for them. They were good kids who'd obviously put their heart and soul into the prom that died. They deserved their dream. Not popcorn and punch, but an actual formal function. If it meant having a yard sale to fund it, or selling her car, Brooke couldn't let them down.

"You guys are the best!" Dorian waved on the way out.

As soon as they were gone, Trevor took Brooke's arm and led her to the white arbor at the far end of the garden. "I get the feeling we should have that official meeting now, don't you? Let's talk budget."

Goody. Time to talk about how her side of the partnership had little to offer beyond a setting. Yay.

They sat and, for a moment, she worked very hard at smoothing out her slacks and avoiding Trevor's steady gaze.

But she couldn't deny reality forever. She'd tried it in her marriage, and the tactic hadn't worked then either.

"I...I don't think the funds that Chateau Jolie can contribute to this project will quite match what Honeywilde is contributing," she said.

Trevor lifted his eyebrows, urging her to continue.

"You know, depending on what Honeywilde plans to spend. When I met with Roark, he didn't speak exact numbers, so..." Maybe she'd luck out and they could keep everything vague, and Honeywilde would pay for most of it.

Miracles happened all the time.

"I've been given a budget of two thousand to work with," Trevor said.

So much for a miracle.

"Roark would prefer I not max that out, but he'll get over himself if I do. I know the kids lost almost eight grand from their ticket sales, but we don't have to pay for a location rental anymore—thanks to Jolie—and, if we have about a four-thousand-dollar total budget, that's more than enough to cover food, music, decorations, and everything else."

"Yeah. See...that's the thing. Jolie doesn't exactly have two thousand dollars to put in."

"You don't?"

"No. Not even close."

"Roark doesn't know this, does he?"

"He never asked. Like I said, exact numbers weren't mentioned at that first meeting. I think he assumed that we would go in dollar for dollar, and it's been a whirlwind since, and—"

"And you just let him believe whatever."

"Yes."

"How much were you planning to put in?"

"We can probably donate, I don't know, realistically? Somewhere around a thousand dollars. Probably."

"Probably?"

"Definitely." The chateau needed the money in its operating account, especially if she had to pay her attorney to stave off the wolf. "Less is better. If possible."

"Less?"

"Yes."

"Okay. Then, in that case, let's say we have under three grand to work with."

"Which is nowhere near enough for the things you were talking about today. Flowers and music and steak and lighting." She flailed her hands out, counting off all the things he'd mentioned. "I want these kids to have the best, but we can't afford all of that."

He took her hands, cradling them in his. "It's okay. Breathe. We don't need steak. We nix the flowers unless Brenda can cut us a deal, and we order some trays of chicken fingers instead of a sit-down meal."

How was he so calm about all of this? Sure, he didn't have an ex-husband looming in the wings, trying to take away a chunk of his family's business, but he was still preternaturally chill for someone who'd learned they have about half the budget he'd thought.

"Chicken fingers are a long fall from what they had planned at that place in Newton. And what you had planned five minutes ago. I want to give these kids more than chicken nuggets." The guilt chewed at her from the inside out.

"Yeah, well, that place in Newton shut down and these kids know that dream is gone. They'll be happy with whatever they get."

"But you heard Dorian. She thinks this is going to be even better. She used the word 'amazing' about a dozen times."

"And it can be amazing. But we're going to have to get real creative, real quick."

With a groan, she leaned forward, burying her head in her hands. "You're so calm and positive. Meanwhile I've been hiding the truth, but you're not even mad. It's making me dizzy."

"Hey." Trevor placed his hand on the center of her back. "This isn't your fault. You've got nothing to feel bad about. You're helping these kids out in a major way. They'd be dancing in a field somewhere if it weren't for Jolie. So what if you can't pitch in two or three grand on top of giving them this awesome place to have their dance? You're doing plenty."

"It's not that. It's…" Ugh. She couldn't blurt out her envy of Honeywilde, or that she didn't want them to overshadow Jolie or what she was doing. Her distress was for partially selfish reasons. She owned that, but she didn't want Trevor to know.

"What?" He leaned forward too, his face right beside hers. "How can you possibly feel guilty about offering up your hotel and pitching in almost a grand on top of that? We'll make it work. I promise."

"It's not that."

"Then what is it?"

She swallowed hard. The truth had to come out. Anything less made her appear neurotic. Which…maybe she was.

"I want to give these kids the best prom ever," she mumbled into her hands.

"I know, so do I."

"But I don't want Honeywilde hogging all the credit."

He put his hand under hers and gently tugged it away from her face. "What?"

With a heavy sigh, she sat up. Might as well face her shameful envy head-on. "I want to do all I can for these kids, not only because they deserve it—and they do—but also because I need for Jolie to be the hero for once. I don't want—jeez, this sounds awful and I can't believe I'm telling you—I don't want Honeywilde to get all the glory this time."

He blinked, probably trying to comprehend the incomprehensible.

"You guys always swoop in and save the day. For crying out loud, you're *known* for saving the day. That's great, for you. But Jolie could really use this opportunity to show we're committed to Windamere too." She leaned forward, locking her gaze with his, praying he'd understand without making her say it. "Chateau Jolie *needs* this chance."

Trevor remained still, intent.

"I'm afraid if you and Roark and the rest of the Bradleys do something like spend thousands while we can't, then we're completely overshadowed, and I know this sounds awful, but I don't want to be overshadowed. I'll work my ass off to make sure that doesn't happen. I can't throw a bunch of money at the problem, but I'll make up for it in sweat equity." She paused to catch her breath.

If Trevor laughed in her face or gave her a look of disgust, she'd completely understand. But spilling the truth to him was like two hundred pounds falling off her shoulders. Letting him in on her motivations made her want to throw up, but at least it was a less guilty nausea.

Instead of laughing, Trevor nodded thoughtfully. "I understand."

Brooke blinked. "You do?"

He chuckled. "Of course I do. Listen, no one gets how overwhelming and all-consuming my family can be more than me. They're great, I love them, Honeywilde is awesome, but when my family gets involved in something, it's like trying to work with the sun. I have felt exactly how you feel."

With a long sigh, she smiled. Being open was exhausting, his understanding baffling. But a little optimism bloomed somewhere way back in her mind. "Your family is great, but...you aren't wrong. You guys had that great rock-star wedding and so many weddings after that. We didn't even have a chance at getting the Chamber party last year. You pulled some Hallmark-movie-level heroics, saving the town with the Blueberry Festival, and I hear you're doing it again this year. I'm happy for all of you, but..." *You're playing a big part in cutting into Jolie's business.* "The Sargent sisters would like a chance to shine too."

"And it's hard to shine when you're up against the sun."

"Exactly."

"Is that why you didn't want my help to start with?"

"Yes." Also because when he looked at her, her limbs went all tingly and her head spun like she'd twirled around the ballroom, but she'd shared enough for one day.

With a quick shake of his head, Trevor angled himself toward her. "Brooke, I can help without stealing the spotlight. I don't like the spotlight. That's my brothers and sister. Jolie can be the hero of the day. Roark will want Honeywilde mentioned as a sponsor, but I'm the one he put in charge of this project. I'll remind him we're taking the passenger seat on this, even while we're shelling out a few grand."

"You'd do that?"

"He won't like it, and he's going to give me the cold shoulder for a few weeks, but that's nothing new. For those kids? I'll deal with his aggravation. All that matters is a great prom for the school. You give what you can, and what you can't give, you make up for in legwork. We'll have to come up with ways to stretch three grand 'til it screams, but if we put our heads together, I know we can. How's that for a solution?"

"I can do legwork. I won't rest until this prom is over and is a certified roaring success."

"Good. And if you want to shine a light on your hotel, you might consider contacting the local papers. Maybe some regional ones. Roark's girlfriend taught us all about that. Get the word out about this awesome thing that's happening at Jolie. Spread the word."

"Even before we pull it off?"

"After is too late. If word gets around, you might even end up with a TV spot."

He made an excellent point. If this prom was going to stand a chance of being good promo for Jolie, she needed to get the word out there. In addition to the actual planning. "I'll make some calls this afternoon."

"See?" Trevor sat back, tossing his arm across the back of the bench. "I'll talk to Brenda. See if she can meet us over here tomorrow and find out what kind of deal she can give us on flowers."

"I'll work on the food, try to find something quality at low cost. Talk with our distributor for the small plates we serve at tastings."

"I'll figure out the music."

"And I'll sort out any other miscellaneous items we're forgetting."

"We've got this. You're not in this alone anymore. We're partners. I'm here to deal with all this crap right along with you."

In her experience, when there was too much crap to deal with, guys didn't deal. They fell apart and blamed her.

"Everything is going to work out. You'll see."

And for the first time, she kind of believed it.

Chapter 11

"Trevor Bradley, get over here and give me a hug." Miss Brenda—early bird that she was—beat him to the chateau the next morning. She and Brooke were already midtour of the ballroom when he arrived.

Brenda crossed the floor and embraced him with both arms.

He'd called her as soon as he left Jolie yesterday and, like the loyal family friend she was, she hadn't hesitated to help.

Brooke joined them, a vision in snug white jeans and flowing top to match, but her gaze still carried the same weight from yesterday. Shoulders ratcheted up tight, she radiated stress. "We were discussing arrangement options and placement, and our budget."

That was his cue. He'd promised Brooke he could work out some kind of deal on flowers. Now to somehow deliver.

"Have you shown Brenda the garden?"

"Not yet." Brooke's shoulders lowered two notches.

"Allow me." Trevor offered Brenda his arm to escort her outside, to what would likely be her favorite part of the whole place.

"Why, aren't you a little charmer?" Brenda smiled. "Have you been taking notes from Devlin?"

"Maybe. And speaking of Dev, you know, you've worked with my family for years."

"I have."

"And we all try to look out for one another, help each other's businesses as we can. And the town. We all like to help the town."

"Mmm-hmm. Cut to the chase, charmer."

"I'm wondering, with this prom, if maybe you could give Jolie the same Bradley discount you give us."

"Maybe I could, but that all depends on—My goodness, would you look at this garden!" She squeezed Trevor's arm before basically shoving him away to flit toward the flowers.

"Look at this trellis. Is this a variation of clematis? This looks like purple clematis. And this right here—mmm, I wouldn't mind having some of this in the store for arrangements—this is Dusty Miller. Looks absolutely beautiful with pale roses. Hard to get. I haven't used any in ages. I need to order some." Brenda rambled on, talking more to herself and the flowers than to Trevor. Hands over her mouth in awe, then over her heart in adoration, she oohed and cooed as she toured the garden.

"Look at this Brunia!" Brenda knelt down to pet a silvery, textured plant.

"I thought you'd probably love it out here."

"This is a showpiece. Is this your work?" Brenda pushed herself up and hurried to Brooke's side as soon as she joined them.

"No, ma'am. My sister Laurel is the gardener. This is her baby."

"Well, honey, she deserves an award. This garden is beautiful. I wouldn't mind buying a few bundles from her sometime, for the shop."

"Really?"

Brenda dug into the side pocket of her cargo pants. "Yes, really. This is my card. Tell your sister to call me. I wouldn't hog a bunch. A few things here and there for unique pieces. I'd like to take a look at the roses when the blooms come in a bit more too. That is, if you aren't going to use them all here at the hotel. Wouldn't blame you if you did."

"That's..." Brooke closed and opened her mouth a couple of times. "I will tell her. She'll be thrilled. Thank you."

"No, thank you for showing me. Now, Trevor, honey, you were trying to sweet-talk me into something when we came out here. About the discount?"

"Yes, ma'am. The flowers are for the school's prom and, as you probably know, the kids lost all their money to a business that went under."

"That is some awful carrying on, isn't it?"

He shared a quick glance with Brooke. "Our thoughts exactly. Which is why we're doing all we can to help. But we're on a tight budget, and this whole prom is a good deed that Jolie and Honeywilde are partnering on. The ballroom needs to look great, but we don't have a bank to break on the event. If you know what I mean."

Brenda crossed her arms and tapped a finger against her lips. "I know exactly what you mean. You want the place to look like you dropped a load of cash, even though you didn't."

He tapped his nose and pointed at her.

"Hmmm." Brenda walked back inside, her voice low as she talked to herself again. More names of flowers and a bunch of florist-ese he didn't understand. "If we incorporated some of the flowers from outside, we could go with a more natural, vintage feel that would actually suit the chateau perfectly."

Brooke joined her. "Trevor offered up these rustic lanterns to use too. What if we did one on each table, maybe some of them in the garden and lobby, then a few flowers or greenery on the tables?"

"More accents than arrangements." Brenda nodded. "It would keep the price down, and I could cut you a really good deal on a couple of larger pieces. Do at least one spray of roses, and have them so the prom queen candidates could each get a rose to take home."

Brooke beamed, looking a bit like Dorian had yesterday. "That would be wonderful."

"That'd be about all you'd need with this place as pretty as it is. Keep the doors open and light the garden. I have some greenery for inside. I could loan it you at no cost. Voila. You've got a prom."

Brooke clasped her hands together. "Thank you. You're like a fairy godmother right now. You have no idea."

Brenda chuckled and patted her with a mothering touch. "Yes, honey, I do. I make things happen. Don't you worry, we'll have this room ready for prom royalty."

Thank you, Trevor mouthed.

"If you have one of those lamps, I'll take it with me and figure out a nice way to stage the tables."

"That would be lovely. I have the one here that Trevor gave me." Brooke left in a blur of white.

As soon as she was gone, Brenda peered up at Trevor. "That girl is a very nice, very pretty ball of stress."

"Not everyone can be cool cucumbers like us."

"Stop." She flapped her hand at him. "She's a hard worker though. I can tell. You sure you can keep up?"

"Hey." He did his best to look offended, but this was Brenda. "I'm a hard worker."

"I know. But not *that* hard." She pointed to the door Brooke had just exited.

He couldn't argue with her there.

"Seems like an intense personality, that's all I'm saying."

He shrugged. "You've met my family, right?"

"Too true, honey. Too true."

"Plus, I don't mind. Intensity has its perks."

"I bet." She swatted at his arm. "I know she's pretty, but you better behave."

"Don't I always?"

Brenda approached him and took his hands in hers. Small, with decades more mileage, her hands could barely hold his. "I adore you, but no. You rarely do. I'm only teasing about the hard work though. I know you work as hard as anyone. Even harder nowadays. Just be sure to keep it up. I think that girl needs you."

"That's why I'm here."

Apparently satisfied, she patted his hands. "Good. And I'm more than happy to help those Windamere High kids, and you and Brooke. I'm flattered you asked."

"I knew you'd come through." He wrapped his arms around her, swallowing her whole in a hug.

"Here's the lamp." Brooke returned in another rush.

Brenda gave him a wink and took the lamp. "I'll see what I can come up with and I'll be in touch. Y'all behave now."

As soon as Brenda cleared the doorway and was out of sight, Brooke latched onto his arm, a blinding smile on her face. "Did you hear her? She's going to cut us a deal!"

"I heard."

"That is the best news ever!"

"I know."

She shook the arm that she was holding. "How are *you* not more excited?"

Finally seeing excitement was more enjoyable.

While he had the chance, he looped her hand under that same arm and tugged her back toward the garden. "I knew she'd help us out. I knew she'd be impressed with you and this place. I wasn't worried. I told you not to be."

"I know, but all absence of my worry isn't realistic."

Brooke didn't pull away or remove her hand from his arm as they followed the stone path around the garden.

A week ago, he never would've guessed the put-together, take-charge woman who'd captivated him at Dev's wedding had just as many doubts and insecurities as anyone. The realization made her human. Projecting that kind of confidence in the face of uncertainty shone a different light on her. A softer light, but somehow even more brilliant.

Trevor stopped near the same trellis where they'd found Dorian and Lance yesterday. "Brenda is right about this garden. I bet the roses in full bloom are a guest pleaser."

Brooke tilted her head. "You'd think."

"You should talk up the garden aspect of the chateau in your advertising, if you don't already. That rose is already my favorite." He pointed to a peach-colored bloom, barely open.

Brooke walked toward the rose, but didn't let go of his arm. "Makes sense. The full bloom is a beautiful creamy peach. A lot like Honeywilde's signature shade. I can check with Laurel, she'd probably let you have a clipping if you want. She loves to share. You could take some back to the inn with you."

"Brooke Sargent, are you giving me flowers? I didn't think we were that serious yet."

Her mouth fell open, followed immediately by a grin. "I don't know how you do it, but I think we might actually pull this thing off."

"Because I'm awesome?"

"And so humble." She smiled, bumping the back of her hand against his chest.

He took her hand, clasping it in place.

She'd held his arm and she didn't resist him now. She was guarded, but she was human. Flesh and blood, with desires and a look of longing that matched his.

"I wanted to kiss you yesterday," he confessed. "Right inside that ballroom, before the prom committee rolled in on us."

"I know."

He moved in even closer, and he wasn't letting go. "I still want to kiss you."

Brooke swallowed hard, close enough he could almost see the fluttering of her pulse on the side of her neck. "I know. Me too."

Rather than discussing their desire any further, he did something about it. Instead of saying more, Trevor kissed her.

A small gasp escaped Brooke's lips, spilling into the kiss.

He brushed over hers, gentle, without expectation, though all he needed was the green light.

She curled her fingers into his t-shirt, her lips pliant against his. Then the softest bit of suction to his bottom lip.

Green light, granted.

Trevor pressed his lips fully against hers.

Yesterday, pressed against him as they danced, she'd finally softened, even allowing a little flirtation. To have her in his arms now was a boon.

Her kiss wasn't what he imagined. It was even better.

Without hesitation, Brooke kissed him back, parting her lips, allowing the brush of his tongue against the seam. Her breath hitched, pouring fuel on his need.

He wanted to do more than kiss her. He wanted to run his lips down her neck. Up the slender, sculpted arms revealed by her sleeveless top. Anywhere on the miles of leg hidden by the clingy denim.

He wanted to take her somewhere private. Away from the rush of planning and the pressure of business, and away from the stress that kept drawing clouds over her beautiful face.

All he needed was a stolen moment, one chance to get her away from it all, the two of them. Where she could let go of whatever troubled her and he would bring her such pleasure.

He could strip away all of these burdens, along with their clothes, and make her forget all about the mountains of responsibility waiting on her.

But he'd wait. He was nothing if not patient, and when they were together, everything would be perfect. Because nothing would matter in that moment, except the two of them, and the things he made her feel.

Brooke eased back, still in his arms and leaving his senses buzzing.

"Where are you going?" he asked, blinking his way back into reality.

"Nowhere." She did the same, her breathing still quick. "You go around kissing people in gardens like that?"

"I don't go around kissing people. I kissed you."

Again, she smiled. "You certainly did. But my sisters have a way of finding me at the worst times, so this might not be the best place."

"You weren't saying that a second ago."

"I was kind of busy."

"Then I'll kiss you again and you'll be too busy to come up with reasons to stop."

Her bubble of laughter filled his chest.

"Brooke, we've got a—Oh, hey, Trevor." Reagan stopped inside the door, a sly grin on her lips. "I'm sorry, did I interrupt?"

Chapter 12

"See what I mean?" Brooke said.

Reagan didn't look sorry in the least. "I'd come back, but—Ah!"

A small, wrinkled blur of fur ran past her, little toenails tapping across the floor as Beans headed straight toward Trevor.

"Well, hey there, little guy." Trevor bent and scooped up the wriggling, grunting bundle, and got a smattering of chin kisses in return. "Where'd you come from?"

Laurel ran out the door after her pug protégé. "Sorry. That's Beans. He's a little wound up." She glanced at Brooke, her eyes frantic. "He didn't scratch up the ballroom floor. I promise."

"I know; it's fine." Brooke moved closer to pet him. Beans looked completely satisfied with being in Trevor's arms.

She empathized.

"Is he yours?" Trevor asked.

"Goodness, no. This is Laurel's new baby."

"I got him from the Pug Rescue last month. He's still excited to check out the chateau every day, like it's the first time he's seen it."

Trevor rolled Beans over, cradling him as though he were a baby. "It is an exciting place, isn't it, buddy?"

"This is adorable and all, but we came to get you because…" Reagan paused and quirked her lips to the side. "We've got a teensy bit of a problem-slash-emergency."

All of Brooke's alarms went off at once. "What is it?"

"I think it's a leak."

Brooke had pushed past her sisters, on a direct course toward the emergency, though she had no idea where it was, before she even realized she'd moved. "Why didn't you say something? Where's the leak?"

"I did say something. Just now. It's the lobby's bathroom sink." Reagan followed, with Laurel and Trevor bringing up the rear, Beans still cradled in his arms.

"It's not leaking right now. I turned the water off."

"You did?" Complete shock colored her tone, but she couldn't help it.

"I'm not an idiot."

"I didn't say you were."

"Guys, stop bickering," Laurel called out. "We've got company."

They all reached the downstairs bathroom, the bathroom that the prom guests would use, to find sopping paper towels lined across the floor of the powder room and sink area.

"How did this mess happen?"

Laurel moved to stand between Brooke and Reagan. "A guest noticed it was leaking, but when I came in here, it was already a big puddle. I grabbed all I could find to soak up water and ran to find Reagan. She shut off the water."

"Where was the water coming from?"

Reagan opened the vanity and pointed underneath. "From this pipe. Like a mini geyser."

A growl of frustration bubbled into Brooke's throat.

"The place is old. There is no telling how old the plumbing is," Laurel tried, using a sweet voice. "These things happen."

"Mom and Dad had all of this renovated though." Brooke ran her hand over the piping, hoping she might find a giant hole or some obvious problem.

"Here." Trevor handed Beans to Laurel. "If it's a seal or a gasket, you'll have to turn the water back on to find the problem. You've all got on good shoes and Brooke is wearing all white. You'll get filthy. Let me take a look."

"So will you," Brooke argued. "We can call a plumber."

"I know more than a little about plumbing. And I'm right here. At least let me see if it's something simple. We have to fix the plumbing in our cabins all the time."

He shared a stare-off with her for a few seconds.

"Okay. But don't ruin your clothes either."

With a smile, he nodded. "What are the chances I could get a few towels?"

"On it." Reagan ran to get more.

"All right. I'm going to have to turn the water on to find the problem. Stand back a bit."

"A lot. Stand back a lot." Laurel pulled Brooke along with her and they backed up all the way to the doorway with Beans.

Trevor turned on the water and then the cold tap, but nothing. When he turned on the hot, though, water sprayed like a garden hose from the connection on the flexible supply line.

He shut off the water.

"Looks like the gasket up here. They dry out and crack sometimes, especially older ones. You guys wouldn't happen to have replacement parts lying around, would you?"

Brooke moved closer to see what he was talking about. "We have supplies in the basement, but we can handle it. I can't ask you to fix our plumbing."

Reagan returned with the towels and handed them to Trevor. "I've got a wine tasting in ten minutes. There's no way I'm doing plumbing work right now. For the love of God, let the man help."

Her gaze clung to Trevor's once more.

She and her sisters knew next to nothing about plumbing. The logical response would be to ask him for help. Yet, she hesitated.

Asking for something she needed was ridiculously difficult, even with Trevor.

She'd already kissed the man, let him hold her as she came to life like dancing flame in his arms. Relying on him any further was like stripping down naked and standing in the middle of town square.

Laurel shifted her wriggling pug to her hip. "Fixing this now is better than having an out of order sign up until we get around to it."

Trevor gave Brooke a knowing look before he forged ahead without waiting. "Come on, show me where the stuff is in the basement."

He wasn't going to make her ask. Somehow, without her saying anything, he recognized that telling him how desperately she needed his help with this emergency meant baring too much.

And to him, that was okay. He was going to help her anyway.

With a cursory glance toward her sisters, Brooke followed.

"I'll get the sink fixed up in no time and we can get back to the prom business of before."

She moved ahead, to show him the way to the basement.

The prom business of before included them making out in the garden, and kissing Trevor had been exactly as wonderful as she knew it would be.

Soothing, warm, and strong. Equal parts skill and unleashed enthusiasm. He made her feel like a teenager again. Or like the teenager she'd never been. Secret kisses in garden nooks, hoping they wouldn't get caught, wanting desperately for him to kiss her again.

Pulling away from the memory, and avoiding a tumble down the stairs in her utter distraction, she glanced back. "Thank you for doing this."

As they reached the bottom of the stairs, he winked playfully. "No worries. Have you noticed we keep ending up in basements? I'm kind of into it. I like basements. They're private."

She shook her head with a smile. He would be into something random like hanging around basements. "I'm not sure exactly where the plumbing supplies are, but they're down here somewhere." Her words got swept away with the touch of Trevor's hands on her waist as he stepped in close.

"I lied," he said. "Before, about fixing the sink and then getting back to what we were doing earlier. The sink can wait two or three more minutes, right?"

"I...um..."

"Or we can get straight to the plumbing and put a long pause on the kissing."

His eyes sparkled, bright blue, even in the dim basement shadows. Lips still full and pink. Lips that teased and tempted, tickling her senses until a longing she'd forgotten surged inside her.

Hands steady and sure, but demanding nothing.

"I don't want to pause the kissing yet," she said.

"Good. Me neither." Trevor slid his arm around her, his hand in the small of her back, bringing her closer. He pressed his lips to hers more fully. His lips were soft, his kiss gentle, and their bodies barely touched.

She longed for more.

All it took was mere inches. Brooke moved, stepping into him, her body touching his. Closer than when they were dancing, closer than they'd ever been at that wedding.

Trevor's touch warmed her more than the midday sun. His kiss soothed, but burned bright inside her.

Kissing him was everything she knew it would be, and more.

With a rough sigh, she curled her fingers into his shirt, dragging him down farther.

Trevor's noise of approval spread heat throughout her body. His gentle touch turned firm and he curved her body into his.

Reagan was going to wear a self-gratuitous smirk for days. Laurel would be hearing wedding bells, no matter how ridiculous the idea or how many times Brooke told her sisters she would never get married again.

"You, wearing all that white." He nipped at the skin where her neck met her shoulder, a raspy purr in his voice as he spoke. "All I can think is how I want to get you so dirty."

Heat flared through her body, her balance thrown off. She pulled away to catch her breath.

"What?" He steadied her, his expression one of such false innocence.

"You. Saying things like that."

"I was just being honest."

His honesty was overwhelming; his unbridled attraction and appetite more than she'd ever experienced.

"I know. I'm not complaining. I just...I need to catch my breath."

"Take your time." He grinned.

"It's been awhile, since I was kissed like that." The confession was out before she could self-edit.

"You should be kissed like that every day."

Warm and flushed, she leaned in, tucking her face into his neck.

His palm was a warm, steady pressure in the center of her back as he rubbed circles up her spine. He kept rubbing until her shoulders slumped, her weight against him.

If he kept rubbing her back, she'd stand in that musty basement forever.

"My sisters will come looking for us if we don't go back up soon."

"Wouldn't want the Sargent search party after us."

She laughed and, with a great deal of willpower, eased away. "We need to start looking for plumbing."

"You mean, that whole reason we came down here to start with?"

"Yes. As much as the duty pains me." A standing toolbox took up the space at the end of a countertop. "If you need tools, check inside there."

Trevor dug around in the toolbox before moving on to search the set of shelves along the far wall.

"You know another reason I like basements?" he called out.

Brooke barely lifted her head from her search under the cabinets. "This should be interesting. Why?"

"Because there's all this cool stuff in them."

The noise of shuffling plastic drew her upright.

Trevor had picked up a box, worn and covered in a thin layer of dust, but the drawing of the female face on the front could still be made out. "Cool stuff like this."

"Oh my word, put that down." Brooke rushed toward him.

"Is this ..." He held the box out of reach and turned it fully toward her. "Is this a Barbie box?"

"Yes. So?"

"I'm not judging. I'm admiring." Trevor set the box down and bumped around some more, moving items around on the shelf. "You don't happen to have the Barbie van, do you? My sister had one. I used to borrow it all the time for my missions."

"Missions?"

"My GI Joes had away missions and no transportation. The Barbie van was awesome. Sophie would get so mad when I took it. Eventually she gave up and let me have the thing."

"If you'd like to borrow ours, you can. But you can't keep it."

"Ha! I knew you'd have a—Holy crap, you have Power Rangers!"

"Would you like some alone time with the toys? Our mission is supposed to be fixing my sink."

Trevor turned toward her, a blue Power Ranger in one hand, a yellow in the other. "Admit it, you're a pack rat."

Brooke plucked the Rangers from his hands and set them back on the shelf. "I am not a pack rat."

"You plan on reselling these?"

"No."

"Got some kids around here I don't know about?"

"No."

"Then you're a pack rat."

"My sisters and I had those toys for years. We shared. I couldn't see throwing them out. And what if some kid stayed here and wanted something to play with?"

"So having these toys down here, in great, clean condition, I might add, is purely a practical business decision."

"Yes."

The truth was, she couldn't bear to part with the items down here. Some toys and things meant nothing, but she could still remember playing with the Power Rangers and cramming them all in the Barbie van. Laurel had played with them until the legs popped off and a few Barbies got bad haircuts. She'd created a whole romance between Ken and the pink Ranger. Malibu Barbie had been heartbroken.

Brooke went back to her search, ignoring Trevor, who'd picked the toys up again.

"Tell the truth. Which one is your favorite?" he asked.

"Which what?"

"Ranger?"

"The pink one," she answered without looking up. There was no debate. The pink Ranger had been her introduction to female empowerment. Before her, Brooke hadn't fully grasped that a girl could be hero. More than that, she could be her own hero.

Too bad she'd forgotten the lesson years later.

"I liked the green one." Trevor dug around, grabbing the pink and green Rangers and joined her.

"The free-spirited bad boy? Of course you did."

"So did every other five-year-old boy. If they deny it, they're lying."

"Give me that." She took the pink one off his hands, adjusting her legs so she could stand upright on an empty bit of shelving. "I loved them all though."

An unspeakable number of hours had gone into her Power Ranger's play time. She'd make Reagan watch the show with her, on Saturday mornings, and then reenact the show with her own figures while making up entire complex story lines of her own.

This had gone on for years. Enough years that she reached an age she felt it necessary to hide her playing from her younger sister.

Everything was so simple then. Joyous.

She'd do anything to have one more day of that kind of fun and innocence.

Trevor joined her, standing the green Ranger up as well. "You're secretly a sentimental softie, aren't you?"

She let go of her Ranger so fast she almost took off part of her elbow.

"There's no shame." He laughed. "I may or may not still have some of my favorite Hot Wheels and Beanie Babies in my possession, but that is neither here nor there."

Her laughter popped out loud enough she clamped her hands over her mouth.

An impish grin took over his face. "Hey, don't hate. I thought that floppy-eared dog was going to be worth millions someday. I might still retire on the spoils of my stuffed-animal collection. You never know."

Pain pricked her cheek and it was a couple of seconds before she realized it was a facial cramp from smiling hard. "Fine. I admit it. I might be a little sentimental sometimes."

But Trevor was the first person to ever notice that part of her.

In the back pocket of her jeans, her phone vibrated. Expecting Reagan and a call about the tasting, she grabbed it, ready to answer.

Then she saw the name on the screen.

Immediately, her cheeks went hot, even as the temperature around her seemed to drop twenty degrees.

"Brooke?" Trevor's concerned voice came from miles away.

Her ex-husband's phone number stared back at her.

She hadn't heard from Nick in over six months. She hadn't seen him in almost a year.

Yesterday, her attorney had filled her in on his claims. Nick alleged he was owed half of her holdings in Jolie. His claim was complete BS but she'd have to deal with his demands regardless.

Finally, her phone quit buzzing, the quiet stillness screaming in her head.

That he had the brass ones to contact her directly shouldn't have surprised her. He'd never lacked bravado or narcissism. But they were divorced now. Everything was official and final. He couldn't just call her up or contact her personally. That's what attorneys were for.

Who did he think he was? She had nothing to say to him.

"Brooke." Trevor touched her arm. "Is it your sisters? Are they looking for us?" Trevor asked.

Brooke flinched, remembering where she was, and that she wasn't alone.

Trevor, with his blue eyes, his wit and fun-loving disposition.

She should lie. Say the call was Reagan, pretend they needed to hurry and get back upstairs, and then run Trevor off. Get him out of there. Get him away because he made her consider things she'd written off years ago as impossible.

But she couldn't.

Denying her attraction to him was pointless now, and keeping this from him was deceitful in a way she'd never been before. If she was going to keep kissing Trevor—and she intended to do exactly that—she didn't want to lie to him.

Brooke tossed her phone on the shelf, resolved. If Trevor freaked out, he freaked out. She couldn't lie about her past or who she was anymore. "That was my ex-husband."

Chapter 13

Trevor fought it, but his eyes still bugged out. "Who?"

"My ex-husband. The man I was married to until last year. He's calling me, but he shouldn't be."

A million questions swirled around him at once. "You're—Wait, you were married?"

"For almost four years."

Trevor didn't say anything. What should he say? Instead, he nodded.

"I would've said something sooner, but I don't like talking about the past and there was no reason to mention it before, so…" Her explanation ended with a shrug.

"No, I…I understand not wanting to bring it up in casual conversation." He stared into the far reaches of the basement, his head spinning like he'd taken a knock upside the head. "I had no idea."

"Most people in Windamere don't know. That's intentional. But I…I wanted you to know."

Struck silent again, he stood there.

Prioritizing privacy was something he totally got. His own family didn't know half the stuff he'd done or did.

Of course, he'd never been married, but still, he didn't like people up in his business.

"I'm surprised I never heard a word about it though. Towns like Windamere? Keeping a secret is tough."

Brooke shrugged again.

Her being a divorcee didn't dim his interest. Divorce happened. Hell, his parents were divorced. But Brooke seemed the type to succeed at everything. He'd assumed, during the time she lived away from their town, she'd made a ton of money in some big city, and racked up all the experience she needed to kick butt at running a hotel and winery.

He couldn't imagine her falling in love, getting married, and then things going south.

"Please say something," she whispered.

His gaze jerked to hers.

Normally, Brooke was the quiet one. He was the ice breaker, the talker, the awkward-silence filler. His silence had to be killing her.

"Not so appealing now that I'm a divorcee, huh?"

"What? *No.* I mean, yes. You…Brooke, this doesn't make me any less interested. You caught me off guard is all. I think I'm more in shock that I never heard so much as a hint of a rumor about any of this."

"I'm a private person."

"So am I, but…"

"And I'm, I don't know, embarrassed. Divorce is still a big deal around here. I feel like I failed and let people down."

"What people? You don't owe a successful marriage to anyone."

"My parents."

"Oh."

"We're a really close family. They never liked him, but I still think I messed up."

"Is he from here? Do I know him?"

Her laugh was as dry as dust. "No. He's most definitely not from here. I met him after I moved to Richmond. He and I worked for the same company. That's how we met. I was an analyst, with all these aspirations and dreams. Hardworking, but with reasonable expectations. I thought we had a lot common. But I was wrong."

There was clearly more to the story, but Brooke glanced away, saying no more as she fiddled with the foot of a Ranger.

A few seconds ticked by, and they stood there like that, in the silence of the basement, two Power Ranger toys standing guard.

Brooke was the one to break the silence this time. "I don't know what else to say. I just wanted you to know."

"Why?"

"*Why?*" Her gaze widened. "I guess I felt like I was hiding something by not telling you. I don't know." She rushed through the rest in one quick sentence. "And in case you weren't interested in dealing with the baggage or something, I wanted you to know so you could back off now. Divorcees aren't always the most attractive option for good-looking young guys."

Trevor smiled with his entire body. "If anything, you're hotter now for having the guts to tell me something you don't like to talk about. And second, I believe you just called me good looking. So let's bring that into focus for a minute."

Brooke's laughed echoed across the basement. "This is news to you?"

"Maybe. You did turn me down last summer and then spent about eight months avoiding me."

"I did not avoid you for eight months."

"If I saw you in town, you'd throw me a quick wave and then avoid eye contact and take off."

"That's because I'd filed for divorce only a few months prior."

The coin dropped. "That's why you said no when I asked you out at Dev's wedding."

"Yes."

He moved to stand right in front of her. "I'm glad we're past that now."

"I haven't actually agreed to go out with you yet."

But she'd opened up about her past, and there was nothing to stop them from going out, again and again, and having the time of their lives for as long as it lasted. "I'm not worried. You'll go out with me. We've already gone out for pizza, had a picnic."

"When did we go on a picnic?"

"The other day. With Beau and the cookies."

With a slant of her gaze, she tucked a strand of her hair behind her ear. "Very sneaky. I'll have to check my schedule for a real date."

He took her hand, pulling her closer. "Then let's go check."

"We still have to find plumbing to fix the sink."

"The pipes are over there." He nodded toward the back corner. "Several of them, on a shelf. I saw them while I was poking through your toy collection."

"And you didn't say anything?"

"I was enjoying the moment. I like basements, remember?"

With a roll of her eyes, she took the piping from him and led the way from the basement.

Reagan and Laurel had disappeared to manage the reception area, leaving him and Brooke alone with the plumbing.

"I meant to tell you," Trevor said as he scooted out far enough from beneath the sink so he could see Brooke, "I called DJ Knight last night."

"And?"

"And he has an event out of town the Friday before the prom, but should be able to get back in plenty of time Saturday to hook us up. Hand me the wrench?"

"*Should* or *will* be able to? There's a difference." Brooke passed him a wrench.

"He's going to let me know today. All he has to do Saturday is drive back home and then to Windamere. He's based out of Asheville, so I'd say more will than should."

"What about a backup plan? Maybe we should book another DJ, just in case?"

With a huff of laughter, he passed her back the wrench. "With what money?"

"Good point."

"I'll know today. If he's a no-go, or even still on the fence, I'll find someone else. No worries. I've got this."

Once he finished tightening the connections, he eased his way out of the cramped space and stood.

Brooke had a look on her face like the whole bathroom was about to flood.

"I know what I'm doing. Relax."

"What?" Her gaze met his. "Oh, no. It's not that. It's this DJ thing. I'm just…concerned. Music is only the most important part of a prom—right after what to wear and who wins king and queen. A bad DJ and lame music can ruin everything."

"Lame music? I am not going to hire a DJ who plays lame music." Trevor closed up the toolbox and set everything aside.

"I know you wouldn't. Normally. But we're low on time. Most nonlame DJs aren't going to be available."

"Except for the one who is available and happens to be the best and happens to be a friend of mine." He turned on the tap. The air clearing the new piping caused a few spurts and burps, but within seconds, hot water flowed from the sink's faucet, without a single drip beneath the sink. "I'm telling you, I've got the music covered. Trust me."

She turned the water off and on and off again. "Thank you so much for fixing this." Her gaze locked with his. "And I'm trying, Trevor. I promise I am."

Chapter 14

An empty math classroom served as their meeting place with Dorian and Lance. Colorful trigonometry charts lined the side walls, an equation remained half erased on the whiteboard up front.

Trevor squeezed into one of the desks in the empty classroom. The plastic blue chair connected to a tiny desk top with *Class of '15* carved into the wood laminate.

A lifetime had passed since Brooke was a student at Windamere High, but the desks remained the same. While she was here, her parents were enjoying the height of their success. The winery growing and the hotel thriving. The Sargent girls were all in school and their oldest, the pride and future of the family business, was pulling straight As and running the student government.

She should've been happy, but with few friends outside of her sisters, and no life, her joy came from dreaming about getting out, going hundreds of miles away to learn and live on her own, before coming home as a raging success to take over the Jolie crown.

Jeez, she'd been such an idiot.

"Hey, sorry we're late." Dorian breezed into the classroom, Lance right behind her.

"No problem." Trevor shifted in the tiny desk, making it squeak.

Brooke stopped exploring the room and pulled her planner and notes from her bag. "We have a lot of information to share with you guys in a small amount of time though, so let's get started."

"Y'know, I was thinking last night." Trevor shifted again. "Have you guys heard anything from that place in Newton where you sank all your money?"

Brooke gave him a look. "I'm sorry, I'm sure he meant that to sound more sensitive."

Lance shook his head. "Nah, it's okay. That's exactly what happened. We lost our money like it'd gotten flushed down the toilet. But no, we haven't heard a word."

"And we can't get in contact with anyone at the location," Dorian added.

Lance leaned back against the teacher's desk, arms crossed. "We tried to reach out to the owners, even after we got the final letter telling us our money was gone. Pointless though. No one would call us back."

Dorian's dark braids were styled up today, and she smoothed a hand up the back and sighed, far more animated than her co-chair. "Did you hear how we found out there was a problem with the venue?"

"No," Trevor answered for them.

A huff of a laugh from Lance. "Dorian set up an appointment to meet their designer there. Since Zen, the place in Newton, did everything in house, she was going to discuss how we wanted things to look, because she's got great taste."

With a tilt of her head, Dorian gazed up Lance. "Aw, thank you."

He shrugged off the gratitude. "You do, and we didn't want them doing whatever and it sucking. She showed up to meet with their designer, and the place is, like, pitch dark. Doors locked, not a car in the lot, no one home."

"I panicked and called Lance."

"I drive all the way out there and there's Dorian, alone. She's upset, nobody showed up, we can't get anyone on the phone. Man, I was pissed."

Dorian patted Lance on the arm. "I had to convince him not to call the sheriff."

"You were all alone and it was getting dark," Lance said again.

With an understanding nod, she let go of his arm. "We called Mr. Cooper—our teacher sponsor who works with the committee—as soon as Lance got there. The next day, the principal did some digging and we found out the place went out of business."

"Some of our committee members thought we should sue."

"Like we can afford to pay for an attorney and a lawsuit," Lance scoffed.

Tell me about it, Brooke wanted to blurt, but she resisted.

"That money is long gone. We can't even afford to pay you guys anything."

Trevor's gaze caught Brooke's.

The full story made their situation even sadder.

"We're going to make sure you have the kind of meal you already paid for," Trevor promised.

"We've discussed the budget and the food for the prom, and we plan to do better than a few appetizers," Brooke added.

"Really?" Dorian clasped her hands together.

"That's our plan anyway."

"You've done so much already, but a sit-down meal would be... We'd be over the moon. Really." The girl appeared ready to hug her at any second.

Lance remained statue-still at the desk.

"We also talked to a florist, Brenda," Trevor added. "She's going to cut us a deal so you won't be dancing in a bare ballroom. There will be table centerpieces, a couple of large arrangements, some greenery—"

"You guys!" Dorian basically hugged Brooke then. She clung to one of Brooke's arms and leaned in. "You guys are the best. This is amazing. Thank you!"

"We're pretty stoked things are working out too." From his spot at the desk, Trevor stretched his legs out and leaned back, probably the exact same way he'd sat in class when he was a student here. Cool as a spring morning, he'd cruised into their meeting today in decent jeans and a T-shirt.

His attire was plenty appropriate for the day, seeing as how they were meeting with two teenagers dressed similarly, but Brooke still found it necessary to don a skirt and a blazer.

Even if she and Trevor had been closer together in high school, they wouldn't have been friends.

Trevor was jeans and flip-flops. Hiking and yoga and no worries.

She had on three-inch black heels without really knowing why.

"All we have to iron out now is the music and the food," Trevor said. "Other than that, we're good to go."

That wasn't really true. Music and food were two huge, important tasks to accomplish. She and Trevor were barely getting started, but she appreciated the enthusiasm that lifted her from the quagmire of details.

Dorian clapped her hands together. "Well, the prom committee met yesterday and they're super pleased with everything we told them. They were really excited about the prospect of getting DJ Knight, but we totally understand if that ends up being a no-go."

"As a matter of fact, I've got some news on exactly that topic."

Brooke's stomach rolled and flip-flopped like a Slinky.

"He's in! I booked him last night."

Dorian squealed her delight and Lance gave Trevor some kind of odd high five.

"I can't believe he's going to play our prom!" Dorian clapped her hands together. "Thank you."

"Glad to help." Trevor grinned.

As wonderful as the news was, Brooke felt more anxious than before. Delivering on a DJ of that level set precedence. They could not let these kids down.

If they let these kids down, they'd let down the whole town. She'd be letting down her family, and she'd never forgive herself.

"What about you guys?" Trevor asked. "Did you find someone at the school to do the announcements of the prom court king and queen?"

"Yes!" Dorian was a flurry of movement as she rounded the teacher's desk. She opened her book bag and dug inside. "I have everything here." She pulled her phone from the bag. "One of the vice principals, Mrs. Meadows, agreed to emcee that part. She's perfect. Great speaking voice. And we did manage to nominate a prom court in a hurry, because for a while there nothing got done. We'd all given up on everything. But anyway, six guys and six girls. Final voting is next week."

"Sounds good." Trevor gave Brooke an expectant look.

"Yes, very good," she said. "I think we're making amazing progress."

"Agreed." Dorian smiled. "Luckily, no one returned or sold their prom dresses, even when we thought all hope was lost." She gazed up at Lance, pink hearts practically dancing in her eyes.

Lance never moved from his spot, looking completely oblivious.

Brooke stopped staring at the two of them, only to find Trevor studying her. He pushed his way out of the desk. "I think that covers everything. We better let you guys get to your next class."

Dorian hoisted her book bag onto her shoulders. "Yeah, we better get to calculus."

"We'll reach out to you early next week."

Dorian waved on her way out with Lance, and the boy still looked upset about her ever being abandoned in a parking lot.

Once they were gone, Trevor slid up beside her. "You don't seem that excited about the music. I thought you'd be thrilled."

"I am thrilled," she said, and meant every word. "I'm just… You know me, I'll celebrate when it's all over and we've pulled everything off without a hitch."

A small frown caused a wrinkle between his eyebrows. "That's no fun. We should celebrate the little successes along the way. Yay us! Good job. Go team."

Brooke grabbed her purse. She didn't want to be a Debbie Downer, but her mind insisted on practicality. Worst-case scenarios and backup plans.

She'd gone into marriage with none of the above, and she was still paying for that mistake.

"How about you and Dorian and Lance celebrate as we go, and I'll save my backflips for when it's over."

Trevor opened the classroom door for her. "If I get to see you do a backflip, I'm one hundred percent okay with that plan."

They made their way down the hall, dodging a few students as they rushed to class.

Voice low, Trevor leaned closer. "Y'know, I get the feeling there might be something between Dorian and Lance."

Brooke turned. "I was thinking the same thing. I don't know if they'll ever be a couple, but I think she's into him."

"Why wouldn't they ever be a couple?"

"I don't know. I wouldn't say he's dull, but compared to her, he's pretty reserved. Those were the most words he's ever strung together around us."

"He's the strong silent type. Nothing wrong with that."

"No. But she's one of the bubbliest personalities I've ever met. They're completely different."

Trevor stopped walking. He quirked his lips to the side, mulling over her comment. "Different can be good though. And did you see how she looks at him?"

"Now *that* was obvious. It's adorable." Brooke looked beyond Trevor, to the bulletin board of school announcements beside him. "But Lance is oblivious. Probably all caught up in himself and baseball or football or whatever, and being chair of this prom. He wouldn't notice she liked him unless she grabbed him by the collar and kissed him."

Trevor leaned one shoulder against the wall. "Mmm. Getting grabbed by the collar and kissed. Sign me up."

"We're around minors. Behave." Brooke plucked one of the papers off the bulletin board. "Look at this."

On plain white paper, someone had printed colored image of Jolie— probably lifted straight from their website. Beneath it was an announcement for this year's senior prom. The font was nice, layout unfussy.

"That looks pretty damn good, actually."

"I know." Her head tilted toward him, she let out the smallest sigh through her nose. "It looks great."

"Are you getting sentimental on me again, Sargent?"

"Maybe. I don't know. You heard them in there. The committee is excited, and the juniors and seniors are freaking out. We're like their heroes." A new and unusual sensation for her.

She'd worked her tail off for years, trying to make everyone around her proud, including herself. But not once had she ever felt like a hero.

"You know what would be really heroic?"

She was afraid to ask.

"You and I should go out to that venue in Newton and see if we can get those kids any of their money back. See if we can find the owners, confront them, and get Windamere High some kind of restitution."

Chapter 15

Brooke's mouth fell open. "Have you lost your mind?"

"I don't think so. Why?"

"We can't—They're out of business. You heard Dorian. No one is out there."

"And you don't find the whole thing super shady?"

"Yes, I find it suspicious, but we aren't the police. We can't show up at that building, even if anyone is actually there, and demand money."

"I'm not saying demand. More like ask. With emphasis."

"Those owners are not going to be hanging out in the venue. Beyond that, the money is likely gone. They've probably filed for bankruptcy by now."

"That's bullshit—"

Brooke wide-eyed and shushed him simultaneously, jerking her chin toward a student passerby.

He lowered his voice. "That's bullshit and you know it. A place like that? Event locations. There's got to be money somewhere. And there's no one more deserving than these seniors."

"I know, but going after that venue is none of our business."

No, but when had that ever stopped anyone in his family?

"Someone should make it their business. Someone should stay on the place about getting some kind of refund."

"That's not our job. Our job is to plan the new prom."

"And not even to try? How bad would you feel if you could've gotten them some money back, and you didn't even try?"

He couldn't let that happen. Knowing the details of how abruptly the place went out of business, giving those kids no warning. Something was up.

"I'm sure the administration tried," Brooke said.

"Have you met the administration recently?"

"No."

"Well, I have. I'm telling you, they aren't the sort to go kicking down doors."

"We are not kicking—"

Trevor threw up his hands. "A figure of speech. I won't actually kick anything. We'll knock. And ask nicely. What's the worst that could happen?"

Brooke shook her head as she repinned the announcement to the board.

"Think about it. Me and you, we roll up in there. You've got on your power suit. If you can't get their money back, no one can."

She glanced down at herself. "This is not a power suit."

"Close enough for Newton."

"How would *I* get their money back?"

"I don't know. Tell them you're the attorney for the school district or something. An auditor. A regulator. Throw some legalese around and scare them. I don't know."

"You mean lie."

"Embellish. They'd believe it coming from you. You've got that boss air about you."

Her burst of laughter was more derision than humor.

"I'm serious. I stand up a little straighter every time you come into a room. So use it for good. Like a real superhero."

"This is certifiable."

Over the years, he'd been called weird, crazy, a kook, and worse. But she hadn't called him certifiable. She'd called this idea certifiable.

Which meant she was considering it.

"We should at least try," he urged.

She nibbled at her lip in silence and Trevor remembered what her sister Reagan had said about Brooke saying yes. All you had to do was patiently wait out the answer in purgatory. "You said you're free today, right?"

"Yes." Apprehension filled her answer.

"Great. We can go right now. Cruise by that place, Zen, and see if anyone is there. See what's what."

"I feel like this is something that could get us arrested."

"Tell you what; we don't even have to talk to anyone. Not necessarily. We can check it out and leave." He smiled, attempting to look as innocent as he possibly could.

"You don't, for one second, think I believe you, right? Check it out? Drive by, all sly and incognito, without stopping?"

Trevor shrugged. Some questions were best left unanswered.

"You're trouble."

"Sometimes."

"Tell me, when you went to this school, how many times did you get detention?"

"Not even once, thank you very much."

Brooke leaned back, looking as impressed as she did shocked.

"My brother Dev broke all the rules before I even got here. I didn't want to be predictable."

Tossing her hands up, she led the way to the double front doors of the school, right up to the passenger side of his truck.

"So you'll go with me?" he asked.

"I don't trust you to go alone."

Chapter 16

She was the furthest thing from a hero, yet here she was, in Trevor's truck, on her way to Newton.

The blame lay firmly with her sense of responsibility and Trevor's dimples.

"You got the address there?" Trevor asked as they drove into Newton.

She checked the website on her phone. "It's 303 Greenbriar Street. Newton, North Carolina."

"Greenbriar Street. Isn't that where the old cigar warehouse is?"

"I think so."

"Good. Then I know where I'm going."

"Frequent guest of the warehouse, were we?"

"No. Dev and his friends broke in there once. It sat vacant for years, and they couldn't resist. He told me they were going and I begged to go with them to see. I'll never forget sneaking out that night. I was in middle school and thought I was the big man, trespassing. Once we got there, though, place was pitch dark. Not going to lie, I got a bit paranoid thinking the law would show up at any second." He laughed. "That was the first and last outing I ever went on with Dev."

Trevor glanced at her and grinned. With one hand still on the wheel, he reached over and rubbed her arm, his hand warm and smooth. "Don't be alarmed. I gave up a life of crime right then and there. I love an adventure, but I don't have to break the law to have fun."

"I'm not alarmed." Though technically they may be breaking the law today, depending on what transpired, any alarm she expressed was due to her awe at even being in his truck at the moment.

Brooke Sargent of a month ago would've never kissed Trevor in gardens or basements. And she absolutely would not be on her way, with no clue what the afternoon might hold, to confront a business about a prom.

Brooke of a month ago would be in her office, stressing out over spreadsheets and profits and losses. She'd fight her bitterness and resentment with a giant cup of black coffee every morning and a big ole glass of Cabernet at night.

But today, she was cruising around with an undeniably gorgeous man, who dangerously viewed her as some kind of Wonder Woman, living his adventure with him while basking in his admiration.

Explaining away his interest came easy. She was merely another adventure for Trevor, another carefree way for him to pass his time. Regardless, once she'd stop fighting his attention, she began to enjoy it, even looking forward to any time spent with him.

How long had it been since someone wanted her? How long since she wanted to be with someone else?

Maybe Reagan was right. Maybe the only way to truly move on and heal was to find someone new. Not in the way of a relationship or commitment, but finding someone to have fun with, enjoy.

What harm could come if she and Trevor simply spent time together?

He couldn't disappoint her, because she'd never again rely on anyone enough to let her down. He wouldn't hurt her because that required love, and now, all she had to give was like.

And perhaps a heavy dose of lust.

"Son of—" Trevor hit the brakes and Brooke threw her arms out reflexively.

"What? What is it?"

He pulled into a freshly paved and painted parking lot and took a spot up front. "Correct me if I'm wrong, but that isn't at all what the cigar warehouse used to look like."

Brooke stared at the expansive brick building with an additional Spanish-influenced masonry entrance and a tin roof that looked brand new. Shallow, cobbled steps and edging, a ramp, and beautiful landscaping led to tall double doors of solid glass.

"The only thing this place and the warehouse have in common is the brick itself. This place is gorgeous."

"It is." Trevor jumped out of the truck.

"They must've completely renovated to reopen as Zen."

"For the record, I think that's the stupidest name for an event location."

"That's not why they went bankrupt though. Someone poured way too much money into this place. There's no telling what this cost."

"Come on." Trevor climbed the stairs with wrought-iron railings. "This entryway alone probably cost thousands."

More like tens of thousands.

Trevor tried the door. "Locked."

Both of them cupped their hands on the glass doors and peered in.

Brooke gasped. "Would you look at those chandeliers? And the exposed brick."

"Not to mention that flooring. The original floor was plain concrete, not whatever that is. They spent a damn fortune renovating." Trevor knocked on the door.

"What are you doing?"

"Seeing if anyone is home."

"You said we were only going to look."

"And you knew I was lying." He kept knocking.

Brooke jumped away from the doors as the lock turned from inside.

"If you're a collector, you're trespassing." A tall, balding man with a paunch opened the door wide enough to glare at Trevor.

"We aren't collectors," he said.

"But if we were, and we had liens on the place, we would not be trespassing," Brooke added.

The man sneered at her and tried to close the door, but Trevor wedged his foot in the opening and grabbed the handle.

Paunch's face began to turn scarlet as he tugged harder, and Brooke blurted the first thing that came to her mind. "We're interested in buying Zen and wanted to speak with you."

Trevor turned and gaped at her blatant lie, but Paunch immediately ceased his tug-of-war to push the door open. "Why didn't you say so?" He backed up and waved them in before trudging toward the main room.

Still wide-eyed, Trevor stared as she walked passed him. "You're full of surprises, huh?" he whispered.

"I'm improvising. You wanted an adventure."

"I am so turned on right now."

"Shhhh."

The two of them joined Paunch in the center of the main room.

"I'm...Sally." Brooke stuck out her hand. "Sally McElhaney."

"And I'm David, of McElhaney and Associates." Trevor went along with the lie, seamlessly.

"Walter," the man said.

Brooke straightened her blazer and looked around, buying herself a moment. "We own a capital investment firm in Charlotte and we heard this place might be available. Our firm specializes in property investments, and we wanted to see if Zen might be a location of interest."

Barely moving, Trevor bumped his arm against hers.

Yes, she was extraordinarily good at making this crap up, because this was exactly the sort of thing she used to do for a living.

"That—Yeah, that'd be great if it was. What, um, what all would you like to know?"

Brooke strolled away from Walt, putting on her best unimpressed expression. "We'd like to take a look around first, if that's all right."

"By all means."

Brooke's heels clicked across the artfully painted concrete floors. The exposed-brick walls stood in stark contrast to the crisp white of the table linens and the white, wooden folding chairs.

Trevor appeared at her side as she inspected the floor-to-ceiling windows along the back of the building. "Look at you," he whispered. "You're scary good at this, and it's working."

"You're the one who wanted to come here and decided to confront someone. We had to have some kind of story to get in the door."

"I'm not criticizing. I like it. What's our next move, partner?"

"I have no idea. We're improvising, so…" She waved her hand forward.

"Got it." Trevor stood a little straighter and spun around to face Walter. "What's the asking price on the place?"

"Negotiable, but we're looking for seven fifty."

Brooke tried not to choke on her breath. Three-quarters of a million dollars? In Newton?

Trevor's gaze locked with hers. The price was absurd. "That's asking a lot for a place in Newton, Walt," he said.

Walt shrugged like it was no big deal. "I said the price was negotiable."

"What's the total amount of the liens on the property?" Brooke asked.

"I don't see how that's any of your business, miss."

"If we invest or choose to buy, it is."

"I don't see how."

"A $750,000 price tag is grossly inflated. It's my business because I suspect the price reflects your need to crawl out of whatever hole you've dug for yourself."

"And seven fifty is a mighty deep hole," Trevor added.

"As investors, we aren't interested in paying for your mistakes. We're interested in paying for the property. Which, off the top of my head, I would say has an estimated value more in the ball park of right under $500,000. Any additional loss on Zen is yours to negotiate with your creditors."

"In other words," Trevor crossed his arms, "you're asking way too much for this place, Walt."

"What's the name of your firm again?"

"McElhaney." Trevor grinned.

As Walter stood there, his mouth opening and closing like a fish, Brooke took another look around. There was no way the venue would be worth that much. Not at this location, not even if the tables and all the setup came with it.

Wait a minute.

She studied the room again, the hairs on the back of her neck prickling up. Why were the tables and chairs set up? As though for an event.

"Why are these tables out and decorated?" She took a few steps closer to Walter. "Are you still booking events?"

"Wha—No." Walt's cheeks puffed out, color rising in them.

"Holy sh—" Trevor breathed. "You're still booking events, aren't you? You're taking people's money." He moved forward to stand right beside her.

Walt didn't answer, but his face went even redder.

Trevor's volume went up a notch. "You're supposed to be out of business. Supposedly, you went bankrupt. At least that's what you've been telling people."

Fury and indignation flamed up inside Brooke, quickly spreading like fire. "They were told you went out of business. You...you lied to them!"

"Who? What them?" Walt asked. But he didn't deny lying.

Beside her, Trevor bristled, his voice twice as loud. "You lied to a bunch of kids. You're the reason they almost didn't have prom. You stole from them and then you lied."

"And you give honest business owners, like us, a bad name," Brooke added, her heart thundering in her chest. "You're a liar and scam artist."

"Preach," Trevor said. "Did the ten thousand you took from those kids over at Windamere High even manage to cover what you spent on this sound system?" He pointed to the speakers all around the room and the command center at the far end. "Or how about the landscaping outside? You know you could sell back any of this equipment and at least do right by a bunch of kids who lost their prom because of you."

"Get out. Both of you!" Walt bellowed.

Trevor stood his ground. "The school district might not have the time or interest in coming after you, but we do."

Brooke pointed her finger at Walt. "You're going to regret the day you ever scammed a bunch of kids."

"I said get out. Or I'm calling the cops."

Trevor grabbed Brooke's hand. He shoved open the door for her and called back as they left, "You'll be seeing the cops, all right."

They ran to Trevor's truck, her hand in his.

Through her anger, even after such a confrontation, her heart flew. Light. Alive. She jumped into the passenger side, trying to catch her breath as he sped out of the parking lot. "What did we just do?"

"We confronted the beast."

She tugged on her seat belt and he headed into downtown Newton. "My heart is pounding."

Trevor laughed, the sound filling the inside of his truck. "Now *that* was an adventure."

"I've never done anything like that."

"I don't know why not. You're great at reading people the riot act. Ole Walt looked about ready to mess his drawers."

With a laugh, she touched her cheeks, warm and flushed with adrenaline. "That side of me isn't exactly something I'm proud of."

"You save it all for Reagan's ex-boyfriends?"

"No. Well...I guess so." The truth was, she hadn't confronted anyone at all until her divorce. She'd barely confronted her ex. Until the day came she had no choice.

Her ability to stand firm and take no crap had grown from that experience. Her tolerance for nonsense was nonexistent. Any capacity to remain passive long gone.

She'd only ever had to use it on Reagan's string of dating misfits. Using it on someone doubly deserving, like Walt, felt...felt amazing.

"I have to say, that felt really good." Brooke smiled.

"Yeah, it did."

"Do you think we should go after Zen?" she asked. Jolie certainly didn't have the resources, and the idea of more legality and attorneys and lawsuits made her stomach churn, but right was right.

"I don't know all of the options, but after seeing that place, something has to be done."

"Who knows how many other people they've deliberately misled?"

"True. But they could've sold off that sound system or any of that other stuff in there to at least give those kids some of their money back. This isn't a matter of them not being able to refund money; they're choosing not to."

"I feel like kicking that Walter guy's butt. Even in these heels."

Trevor grinned from ear to ear. "I'd turn this truck around right now to see that."

"He'd call the cops on us."

"Definitely." He turned into a shopping center parking lot and killed the engine.

"What are you—"

He was already out of his seat and circling to her side of the truck before she could finish her question. He jerked her door open, stepped up on the runner, leaned in, and kissed her.

His kiss wasn't the sweet, tentative one from the garden. Not the deliberate, thorough kiss from the basement either.

This kiss demanded attention.

Trevor cupped her face, the tips of his fingers threading through her hair. He slanted his mouth over hers, hungry. Though she was sitting down, her world spun.

Brooke reached for him, clung to his arms, opened for more. Heat spread through her body and she gasped.

With one final tug against her lips, Trevor parted. "That was awesome. *You* were awesome."

Her pulse flying and her breathing coming entirely too quick, Brooke took his offered hand and he helped her down from the truck.

"Those kids are lucky to have you on their side," he said.

"Us. They're lucky to have us."

"I'll talk to my brother Dev about what we found out today. He has friends down at County Square now—which still cracks me up—and he might've made buddies with someone in the school district. If there's something more we can do, we have to try." He tugged on her hand. "Come on."

"What are we doing now?"

"This adventure has made me hungry. Let's eat."

Chapter 17

"You like Thai, I hope." Trevor marched toward a glass-front restaurant with decorative ceramic elephants outside.

"I wasn't expecting to have some right now, but sure." Brooke held on to his hand as they hurried inside.

Trevor chose a booth by the windows and sat, willing his heart rate to go down. Their foray into scam-busting had his blood pumping faster, the colors of the Thai restaurant shining brighter.

"I can't believe we did that, but I'm so glad," Brooke said, echoing his sentiment.

"Told ya. Adventure is fun."

A waitress brought over water and menus and left them to decide.

Brooke studied the tall page for a second, and then slapped the menu down. "Order whatever you like," she said. "Let the adventure continue."

Trevor ordered Tom Yum Gai soup, and two Panang dishes.

"Sounds promising." Brooke rubbed her hands together and leaned forward. "I think my mom and dad still drive all the way out here when they're in town and get a Thai craving, but I've never been."

"Then you're in for a treat."

Brooke sipped her water while his mind caught on the mention of her parents. His mom and dad were long separated. His mom was the only one to still come to Windamere. She'd visit Honeywilde too, but only if Trevor invited her.

"Where are your folks?" he asked.

"Right this second? Who knows? They're retired in a RV somewhere, seeing the country."

"Seriously? That's great." Miles of open road and the freedom to take your time while traveling. "Good for them. I'm jealous."

"Jealous of spending month after month, being cooped up in that small RV?"

He balked. "They aren't cooped up. Not if they're doing things right. They're probably out seeing waterfalls, lakes, purple mountains majesty, and the like."

Their soup arrived and he dipped into the covered bowl to serve up two smaller, steaming cups. "Getting out and seeing the world beyond Windamere is important. I mean, spending a year in Peru might not be for everyone, but still. Getting out and going beyond our town can be life changing."

"You spent a year in Peru?"

He nodded. "Right before I moved back to work at Honeywilde."

"How did I not know this?"

"You aren't the only one who keeps your private life private."

Brooke swallowed her spoonful of soup and smirked. "Touché. But you guys were already running Honeywilde then. Didn't your family miss you? Seems like they would've needed you at the inn."

He sipped the spicy, sweet broth and shook his head. "They *wanted* me here. They didn't *need* me. Looking back, I do feel kind of bad about my timing, but when I left, I had no other choice. Staying at Honeywilde would've been the worst thing. For everyone."

Not long before, his parents had abandoned the family business, leaving his oldest brother, Roark, to take over the operation of the inn. Devlin was still drinking, Sophie was overworked and anxious, and Trevor was unhappier than he'd ever been.

He blamed Honeywilde for his parents' failed marriage, blamed Roark for working him and his brother and sister too hard, and blamed any and every one for all of the other problems in his life.

Rather than cope and deal, he'd been a silently seething bitter pill. He'd hated Honeywilde back then, and the resentment was spreading to his family.

"If you say so." Brooke poked her spoon around in the soup.

"Definitely so."

The best thing he ever did for himself and his siblings was to go away. Going away helped him think, prioritize. When he returned, he could appreciate his family and the inn in a way that was impossible before.

That's why he planned to go away again.

His place in the family chain might be clearer now, but his fulfillment within that chain was another matter. He loved his family, and Honeywilde, but life could shrink down to something too small when it completely revolved around one place and three other people.

He needed…more.

"That's why I'm going back to Peru in the fall."

Brooke coughed, trying to swallow her soup. "You are?"

"Not for a year. Obviously. But I'll be visiting for a few weeks in late summer with the same volunteer group."

"Your family doesn't need you here?"

Trevor shook his head. "Roark has everything under control now. Dev is his go-to guy for events at the inn; Sophie could run the place blindfolded. They've got everything under control. I'm really more extra help than anything. I'll be a lot more use in Peru, helping build houses and working in hospitals.

Focusing on her empty spoon, Brooke frowned. "I doubt you're extra anything. I couldn't plan this prom without you and I'm sure your family feels the same."

Trevor brushed off the comment. "Regardless, Dev took a couple of weeks off to go on his honeymoon to Canada. I figure I can have a couple of weeks to help out a good cause."

"Yes, of course. I'm not disagreeing. That's commendable work and I admire you for doing it. I just…I can't imagine leaving Jolie, or my sisters. I can't imagine leaving at all."

"I'm not leaving forever. You're frowning like I'm hopping on a plane tomorrow, never to return."

"I don't think that." Her face had drained of color, her jaw held tight, concern coloring the dark depths of her eyes.

He knew that look. He'd seen it hundreds of times before. "Sure you do. At least a little. My family thought the same thing, after I got back. They thought for sure I'd take off again. Maybe you're wondering the same thing."

"No, I'm not—"

"I'm not going to abandon you with this prom. I would never do that. Getting away when all the sh—the you-know-what hit the fan made the whole situation better. After my parents divorced and Dad gave up the inn, the place was in constant turmoil. I can't…I mean, let's just say I don't do well in that environment."

To say the least.

He'd never told anyone that, but if Brooke trusted him enough to talk about her divorce, maybe he could trust her with how rocky things had gotten at home.

"Truth is, I wouldn't be here now, helping you, helping out at Honeywilde, if it weren't for my time abroad."

"Okay."

"And I'm not going away for a year again, to anywhere. You can count on me."

They'd spent only a few days together, but he already knew how important reliability was to her. Brooke didn't want to count on anyone, and she wasn't one to throw her trust around. He'd had to maneuver his way into being her partner on a damn prom project.

Maybe her lowered expectations were because of the divorce. Or maybe her defenses went deeper. Whatever the reason, he knew what it was to be let down by loved ones, and to be the one who let them down.

He wasn't going down that road again.

This time, his family would know all about his plans, his intentions, and he'd return in a few weeks, with an idea of what came next in life.

The waitress brought their food, the rich aroma filling the air. "Here's your Panang."

His mouth watered, the hint of pepper tickling his tongue. He stirred his bowl, adding some rice to the broth to taste that first steaming hot bite. But first, he watched and waited for Brooke's reaction to his choice.

She brought the spoonful of chicken and broth to her lips and her eyes rolled back into her head as she chewed.

"You like?"

"Delicious." She drew the word out, sending prickly heat up and down his body.

Trevor focused on his dinner.

Not on Brooke or how much he willingly shared with her, how good he felt when he made her happy, or how incredible she'd been today dealing with that blowhard.

He definitely wasn't focusing on the noise she made as she savored her meal or the look of pleasure on her face.

Prom. He needed to think about the prom and get her talking again.

"So, which friends did you go with?" he asked.

Brooke blew on her next spoonful. "Go with where?"

"To your prom. The other day, you said you went with a bunch of friends. Who were they? I probably know them."

"Just other student government people. What about you? You went with Julie Phillips. Was that senior and junior year?"

She'd wasted no time changing the subject off of herself, like he wasn't going to notice.

"I went with Cindy Gandolfo my sophomore year, Brandy Kline my junior—"

"Your *sophomore* year?" Brooke interrupted him with her spoon suspended in midair. "Cindy Gandolfo would've been a senior."

"What can I say? I like women with some life experience." He cocked an eyebrow as he ate.

She tried to dismiss his comment with a roll of her eyes, but color flooded her cheeks.

They continued eating their late lunch, a companionable silence between them, but he wasn't letting the mysterious stone of her high school love life go unturned. "Did you ever take a date to prom? Like, say, Troy Richenbacher?"

Brooke plopped her spoon down and brought her napkin to her mouth. "Where in the world would you have gotten that idea?"

"Come on. Everyone had that idea. Rumors about the two of you were big news my freshman year. Troy was a basketball god and, like I said, you were Miss Windamere High, but you never dated anyone. Like, ever."

"Thanks a lot."

"Well? Did you or didn't you date Troy Richenbacher?"

"We went out a few times my senior year, yes."

"But he didn't make the prom cut?"

"If you must know, he broke up with me shortly before prom."

"Why?"

"Because I wouldn't have sex with him."

"Ah, classic high school move." Trevor stabbed a piece of broccoli with his fork. "At eighteen, there's really little hope for us. Luckily, we grow up and, I like to think, improve."

"Not all of you."

"Ouch."

"No!" Brooke put her spoon down again. "I don't mean you. I was referring to my ex."

"That bad?"

With her hands busy adjusting and readjusting the position of her bowl of food, she looked everywhere except at him. "Kind of. Yes."

So much more of her story lay behind that "kind of."

He kept quiet, refusing to pry but wanting to know everything.

"I guess at first things weren't bad," she finally said. "But…later, things went south. Fast."

Trevor nodded, remaining silent.

"When I met Nick, my ex, I thought he was the perfect guy. Successful, smart, good looking, driven. He wanted it all. I should've known, anything too good to be true usually is. But I thought we had a lot in common. He had goals and determination, like me."

"Young and hungry?"

"Yes. We dated for a while—not long enough—and got married. I was so stupid and eager. I could see our whole lives mapped out ahead of us. Our futures were bright, life would be ideal. My parents would be so proud. I knew this with every fiber of my being."

"What happened?"

"Life was not ideal." A derisive laugh punctuated the sentence. "Life just…happens. Bumps in the road, struggles. A lot happened or didn't happen, and while I kept going and staying positive, he gave up. Every little setback was the end of the world for him. Then he started taking it out on me and…we just weren't right for each other. I'd been in such a hurry and so sure we'd make the perfect pair, but I was wrong."

"I'm sorry."

Finally, she met his gaze. "Thank you, but it's not your fault. If anything, it's mine. I should've known."

Trevor scowled, an underlying sentiment of what she said tying a knot in his stomach. "What do you mean, you should have known?"

"If I'd been patient, waited and dated him longer and not been so damn sure of myself, I would've seen how manipulative and mean he could be."

"How is—Hold on. That is not your fault. People get blinded by love or whatever. You couldn't have known."

Her noise of derision indicated otherwise. "The end wasn't amicable. Let's put it that way. I left him last year. Our relationship was over long before then, but I stayed. And staying made things worse."

"What finally made you leave?"

"You aren't going to ask why I stayed? My sisters still ask me that to this day."

"You obviously had your reasons for trying to make it work. I'm more interested in why you left."

"I couldn't take the turmoil and misery anymore. He became hateful. I was barely surviving in an unhappy marriage, and I woke up one day wondering, What are you doing?

Trevor was quiet for a while.

"But I didn't want to give up on this man who I promised to love and honor. I guess I thought it would get better or…I don't know."

"But it didn't."

"No." Her raw, scratchy laugh tied a knot in his throat. "About a year and a half before I left, Nick lost his job. He found another one, but he never got over being fired. Things weren't great before then, but after that, he spiraled. I think he felt like a failure. He couldn't get past it. He had a strong personality and I thought that was a good thing, but really he was temperamental. Once we were married, he took all of his stress and unhappiness out on me."

"What's that mean? Did he hit you or—"

"No. He never laid a hand on me, but the stuff he would say, the way he treated me when he got mad...I can't even explain how bad it got."

Trevor screwed up his face.

"You have some experience with this?"

Trevor nodded, a time when his own father cursed his name and told Trevor he wished he'd never been born, all because one of the heating units broke at the inn. Trevor had spent the night in one of the cabins that night, just to get away from the anger. "My father started drinking when stuff went south at the inn," he confessed. "He'd yell or be downright hateful. He never hit any of us, but his words were like fists. I got in a fight once that didn't hurt anywhere near as much as some of the stuff he'd say."

Brooke twisted her napkin around her finger, her dark eyes sadder than he'd ever seen them. "I know. And I'm sorry you went through that."

When she finally glanced up, his gaze caught with hers. "I'm sorry too. For you," he said.

He reached across the table, offering his hand.

She placed her palm against his and he held on tight.

"One day, I realized there'd be no apology from him," she said. "Nick was never going to ask forgiveness or make amends. He didn't recognize he had a problem. I tried and tried. I asked him to go to counseling, to stop taking his anger out on me and insulting me. But he wouldn't. I was worried his words might turn to fists and I...I couldn't stay and allow myself to be treated that way. Especially when he saw no issue with his behavior. So, I woke up one morning, early, and while he was still asleep, I threw everything I needed and really cared about in a bag, got in my car, and drove all the way to Chateau Jolie. I never went back."

"Good for you."

She shook her head. "Is it? I know leaving was the right thing to do, but I still carry guilt for it."

"You're a devoted person. I think that's natural given how loyal you are to your sisters and anyone you care about. But his misery wasn't your fault. His unhappiness and refusal to get help, also not your fault. You had no choice. You had to leave."

Again, she glanced away. "I know."

Heat flashed up the back of his neck. He knew something about what she'd gone through, and right now, she was lying to herself. "Do you?"

Chapter 18

When she glanced up, Trevor's intent gaze stared right inside her, trying to see even the darkest parts of her life that she kept hidden. She didn't want him to see.

He wouldn't like what he saw.

He made no secret of his interest in her, but he'd mainly seen the woman she portrayed herself to be. If he knew the real her, the Brooke who couldn't put her past behind her, a woman who'd allowed herself to be verbally and emotionally abused, the doubts and dark thoughts she'd entertained...

And she wasn't finished with any of it yet. Her ex-husband was still around, trying to take from her what she held most dear.

Her stomach turned, a wave of nausea sweeping over her.

Who was that woman she'd become? A woman who'd been demeaned, yelled at, and now sued. She wished she could say she didn't know this woman. Being a victim angered her in ways she never thought she'd feel.

Insecure, scared, and the furthest thing from heroic.

A hero would never allow herself to be treated that way. She'd fancied herself as independent, strong—and she was when it came to other people—but she'd let someone, who supposedly loved her, treat her in ways she'd never allow her sisters to be treated.

And to this day, she had no idea why.

Trevor shifted in his chair, leaning forward. Closer. "Your silence is answer enough."

"What?"

"When my dad started drinking all the time and my mom was depressed, I claimed I knew it wasn't my fault. But I guess I said that only to have something to say. Deep down, I blamed myself for their fighting, my parents' hurt and anger, our family falling apart."

Brooke clung to her napkin. "I knew your folks separated, but I didn't know things were that bad."

"Surprise. The Bradleys aren't a perfect family. Never were. I told myself all the time that my parents' misery wasn't my fault. But deep down, I thought somehow my brothers and sister and I held blame."

"What finally convinced you otherwise?"

"Talking to my mom."

She flinched, the idea of ever hearing Nick's voice again bringing on another wave of sickness.

"I am in no way advising you to talk to your ex." Trevor put his free hand out for emphasis. "Absolutely not. But, for me and my situation, when I finally reached out to my mom last spring and slowly kind of opened up communications, I gained perspective. I realized she and my dad had their own issues long before us kids ever came along. It wasn't until then that I finally knew, in my soul, their problems weren't our fault."

She shook her head. "I don't think I'm there yet."

"I don't think you are either. But that's okay. Takes time. Looking back, maybe that's part of why I needed to go away for a while. I couldn't see the bigger picture. I was still hurting, and so were my brothers and sister. We aren't completely better now, but we're getting there."

She knew a little about the Bradleys' hard times with their parents and the inn. Most folks in town knew a little. But she hadn't expected Trevor to speak of it. He was as private as Brooke, and seemed unfazed by so much, she never would've guessed how much he'd struggled.

He might play it off like talking about his family's issues was no big deal, but sharing that kind of truth mattered. And it took trust, and guts.

"You're going to be okay," he said.

"I wish I was so sure."

"Eventually you will be. It's okay if you aren't there yet, but you don't have to go around telling yourself you are."

"Is that what you did?"

"Totally. Don't do what I did. Spare yourself. Or you could end up barely talking for a year."

"You did that?"

He nodded.

"Yeah, right." The notion of a silent Trevor was inconceivable.

With a noncommittal grunt, Trevor poked what was left of his rice around the plate.

"Wait. You're being serious."

"Sadly, yes. I didn't talk for most of my freshman year of high school. Which might explain why you don't remember me." He smiled, attempting to make light of his situation.

But she wasn't having it. "I never knew. I'm so sorry."

"Freshman year, when my parents were at their worst. Their marriage was a wreck, the inn continued to tumble downhill. None of this was new, but my brother Roark had left for college and Dev was acting out in spectacular fashion. Roark was the one who held the place together for us. Without him, everything went to hell and, long story short, I couldn't cope. I didn't want to deal with any of it. Running away wasn't a viable option, until later, so I…withdrew."

A quiet Trevor, all alone, not making friends easily or laughing or putting people at ease with his mere presence. To imagine that time was depressing, even though she hadn't known him.

"I went to school. Passed, barely. But that was it. Spent most days alone in my room. I think the only person I ever said more than two words to was Sophie. I'm not sure anyone really noticed at the time."

"I wish I'd known you were going through that. I would've helped."

"We didn't exist in the same circle then. Helping me wasn't an option."

"I know, but—"

"Your job isn't saving everyone. Anyway, I saved myself. One day, after Sophie totally freaked out because I wouldn't tell her where I'd been all weekend, I realized I was hurting myself, and her, because of the actions and moods of other people. Home sucked big time, so I got out as much as I could. Started hiking and walking, wandering around a lot, just so I didn't have to be at home. And here's the funny thing about wandering. You're alone, but not really. I'd meet random people while I was out, and they loved to talk. I didn't have to talk about myself or my messed-up family. I found this one guy, taking pictures of plants, and talked to him for hours about his thesis on wetlands. One lady was out every day with her shih tzus. She'd happily talk for hours about nothing but her dogs. It got me out of my head."

"Maybe I should start wandering." She smiled.

"I'm serious. Getting out, maybe even getting lost, it helps."

"Does one have to wander alone, or can she bring a buddy?"

Trevor gave her a soft smile, his dimples faint but undeniable. "I think a combo is good, if *I'm* that buddy."

She laughed and squeezed his hand, feeling surprisingly light for having discussed such heavy topics.

But then, that was being with Trevor. He just made things…easier. He put her at ease.

With a quick kiss dropped on the back of her hand, he let go. "You ready to go?"

No.

She didn't want to go anywhere. In that moment, all she wanted was to stay with him.

When she first met him, very little about Trevor spoke of long term. Being with him would be exciting, adventuresome, even healing, but temporary. But he kept revealing unexpected depth. He insisted on being so much more than met the eye.

And, as risky as her situation was, with the worst possible timing ever, she liked him. Not temporarily, but really and truly growing to care for him.

Right now, there was nothing more terrifying.

Chapter 19

He stared at the tall, locked gate surrounding the school's back parking lot, Brooke's Toyota sitting all alone inside. "I don't think you're getting your car today."

Next to him, Brooke leaned forward, peering around as though there might be some secret entrance, hidden behind a bush. "There's absolutely no way in?"

"Unless you want to climb that fence, no. I'll gladly give you a boost, but you're on your own if you try to yee-haw your way through the front gate."

"Dang it."

"I'll take you home. Reagan or Laurel can give you lift back tomorrow."

A couple of days ago, she would've resisted. Argued that she didn't want to put him out or make him go out of his way. Today, she simply agreed. "Sounds good. I'm too tired to climb a fence right now."

By the time they made it back to Chateau Jolie, night had fallen.

"You want to come in for a minute?" Brooke asked.

Trevor was out of the car and walking her to the door before the question was completely out of her mouth.

Heck yeah, he'd come in for a minute.

Inside, the warmly lit lobby sat empty, until her sister Laurel popped her head out of the office. "Hey." She looked them over. "Long day?"

"Little bit. You'll have to take me to get my car tomorrow. It's locked up behind the school gate."

Laurel's expression never changed, but she studied them both intently. "Okay. I'll expect the full story behind why when I take you to get your car tomorrow. 'Night." She waved, her shrewd gaze lingering until she turned and left.

For all her sweet, dog-loving, fluffy ways, there was a lot more to that Sargent sister.

Brooke headed toward the back of the chateau, nearing the ballroom, and Trevor followed.

"Didn't Sophie and Wright come here before Dev got married?" he asked. "To try the wine." He put the last part in little air quotes.

"You've already asked me that."

"And you wouldn't answer."

"Exactly."

"But that was before we kissed."

Exhaustion laced through her laughter, but the sound warmed something deep inside him. "Kissing me won't make me talk."

"Careful. I might take that as a challenge."

Brooke stopped at the bottom of the grand staircase and turned to him. Her hair was less perfect than when they'd started the day. The power suit was wrinkled and she looked due a good night's sleep, but the woman still stunned him.

Turned out, Brooke Sargent went beyond being a challenging adventure. She compelled him, made him want to step up, not only for her but for himself. Being there for her, whether she was stressed or needed to talk about her past, held value. He didn't want to let her down; he didn't want to let Windamere High down.

He had the kind of motivation and focus he hadn't felt since Peru.

Trevor made a point of strolling casually to a higher spot on the other side of the staircase banister. He leaned forward, resting his chin on his forearms. "For what it's worth, I already know she and Wright came here last summer. And they were a lot more than friends when they visited. Unlike some people, my sister isn't Fort Knox."

"If you already knew, why ask me?" Brooke moved closer, one foot on the bottom step, then the other.

"I don't know. Because I like poking around. And messing with you."

"I've noticed."

"And I don't want today to end."

Her smile was soft and fond, and her looking at him like that was everything.

"As tired as I am, I don't want today to end either," she said. "I had fun. For the first time in a long time."

"Don't look now, but I think today may have qualified as a date."

She tilted her head.

"We went out, had a meal, I brought you home, walked you in."

"You may have a point."

"I should kiss you and make it official."

Trevor leaned forward and cupped her jaw. Her lips were soft, searching, giving in to the kiss immediately.

This was something he could get used to, way too easily.

"What if..." Brooke's gaze danced away as she pinched her lips together. "What if you didn't say good night?"

His heart thundered in his chest.

"What if you stayed?"

"I'll stay if you want me to." He wanted to stay; all he needed was the word.

"I'm not ready to say good night but I..." She studied him, the weight of what she wanted to say heavy in her gaze.

He tucked a knuckle beneath her chin, lifting her face again. "What? You can tell me."

"I want you to stay, but I'm not ready for...more. Not yet. I know I don't want to stop kissing you, but sex is a big step for me right now."

He stopped her worry with another kiss. "Hey. I'm not Troy Richenbacher. I would love to stay, and we aren't going to do anything you don't want. I could stay here and do nothing but this." He pressed his lips to hers again. "I'll still be the happiest man in the tri-county area."

She took Trevor's hand. "Really?"

Was she kidding? A few weeks ago he could barely get a wave from her in the grocery store. Staying with her tonight was more than he'd ever hoped for. "Yeah. Really."

Brooke grew quiet, the expressionless mask all of the Sargents had seemed to master firmly in place. Then she tugged on his hand.

Together, they climbed the stairs. Her room was on the third floor, in the far west corner. He didn't say a word on the way there, refusing to break the spell.

She let him in and closed the door.

The room was dark except for a small night-light left on in the bathroom.

Her face in shadows, she turned to him, her back to the bed. "Would you be okay just spending the night? Here with me?"

In answer, he took her hands in his and led her to the bed. He eased her back on the bed and slipped off the high heels she'd worn all day. Then he stepped out of his shoes and climbed on top of the covers with her. At the foot of her bed was a folded quilt. He pulled it over them and drew her close.

"I feel guilty asking you to sleep over. Like I'm some—"

He stopped her by covering her lips with his once more. He kissed her until her shoulders melted free of tension, the air around them growing heated enough to burn off all doubt. Then he leaned up to look her right in the eyes. "You're not there yet and I'm not going to rush. Don't get me wrong, I want to have sex with you. *So* much sex."

She tucked her face into his chest and laughed.

"But we're not going to ruin everything by being in a hurry."

With a nod, she rolled over with him, nestling into the nook between his shoulder and chin. "Thank you."

He liked Brooke. *Really* liked her.

He'd been attracted to her for months, but physical attraction wasn't the same thing as connecting with her the way he had over the past few days.

His brothers might laugh—then again they were both in love now, so maybe not. But now he knew Brooke in a way that went deeper than need and desire. He understood some of what she was going through and the more he got to know her, the more he wanted to know.

The possibility, the promise of what they could share, sent a shiver through his body.

"Are you cold?" Brooke cuddled closer, her arm a welcome weight against his chest.

He was the furthest thing from cold.

He was warm and wanted. She'd asked him to be here, trusted him enough to be vulnerable, and he would do everything in his power to prove worthy of that trust.

Chapter 20

Locks of dark hair tickled his arm and chin. Trevor woke to the sight of inky lashes against ivory skin, Brooke's face smooth and relaxed in sleep.

The morning sun crept up, her bedroom still cast in the blueish light of early dawn.

Unreal. Like something from a dream. He smiled, because this was reality. *His* reality. Practically perfect.

Then his stomach growled.

He slid from Brooke's bed as quietly and carefully as possible and crept downstairs.

Food.

Holy hell, he needed food.

Jolie didn't have a full-service restaurant like Honeywilde, but Sophie had said they served tapas with their fancier wine tastings. Surely they put out Danish or donuts for their guests in the morning.

As he reached the bottom of the main staircase, the scent of coffee greeted him.

A quick check of his watch. Barely six AM. Someone was an early riser, God bless them.

He wandered toward the lobby area, following the coffee trail and the unmistakable smell of chocolate baked goods.

"Oh." Brooke's sister Laurel drew up short as she came around the corner.

Beans the pug circled her feet, paying him zero attention.

"Well, good morning." Her sweet naiveté didn't prevent a knowing smile from dancing across her lips. "I wasn't expecting anyone to be up yet. Or, you know, for you to be here at all this morning."

More important than the awkwardness of the moment was the tray of chocolate croissants in Laurel's hands.

He returned her smile and pointed to the tray. "Let me get that for you."

She passed the croissants over and directed him to a seating area by one of the windows. "You can put that on the ottoman, thank you. Would you like some coffee?"

"I'd love some."

While she left to get coffee, Beans remained, eye-balling the platter of croissants with a hungry black gaze.

"I don't think those are for you," Trevor told him.

Beans spared him a glance that said he wasn't interested in Trevor's opinion.

Laurel quickly returned with two cups, served on saucers. "Here you go. I guessed black."

"You guessed right. Thank you."

"Have a croissant." Laurel folded herself into the wing-backed chair opposite him, her legs crossed.

Trevor didn't hesitate or bother with a plate. He bit into a flaky, hot croissant. "Holy chocolate," he muttered over a mouthful.

"Why do you think I get up so early to put them in the oven? Ensures I get to enjoy mine before they all get picked over. I don't like to share sweets."

Beans wiggled and grunted until he was centered on her lap, his face right in Laurel's face.

"I don't mean you." Laurel tore off some of her croissant. She put the small bite of food on the floor, and Beans followed every movement with precision vision, jumping down to get his treat. "What's mine is his. That's how we roll."

"I know exactly what you mean."

"You have a dog?"

"Beau. Big bushy brown baby."

Laurel smiled, understanding warming her expression in a way only another dog lover understood. "You should bring him over sometime. Beans and Beau."

"He's mad at me right now for being busy over here so much. I'll probably get the cold shoulder for being gone last night."

"Speaking of, you were gone all day yesterday with my sister."

"Is that a question or a statement?"

Laurel sipped her coffee, her expression giving nothing away.

Another Sargent stare. The look had to be hereditary.

"Yes, I was gone all day with your sister. We had some work to do, and then a date."

"And then you spent the night here?"

"Yes, I did. And I have to say, I admire your complete lack of beating around the bush."

She seemed to consider this over another bite of her breakfast.

The details about his time with Brooke weren't anyone's business and, thus far, the two of them hadn't defined their relationship. If Laurel asked him the nature of it, he wasn't sure he had an answer.

"I'm not looking for details," she said. "Just confirmation of facts."

Thank goodness.

Beans jumped back into Laurel's lap, and she shifted him over her side. She tore off another bite of her croissant. Folding the food between her fingers, she hesitated. Her actions were driving the pug crazy. His big black eyes followed her every moment, his wrinkly face looking like he might open his mouth at any moment and beg her to drop the food already.

"She seems happy."

Trevor pulled his attention away from the dog.

"Brooke, I mean. Planning this prom with you. She seems happy. I like seeing her happy. But, you know, don't screw her over." Laurel shoved the bite of croissant into her mouth.

Trevor gaped while Beans looked heartbroken.

"I have no intentions of screwing her over. Actually, I'd like to take her on another date, if she'll say yes."

"Good. Then I won't have to sic Beans on you."

He laughed, but Laurel didn't appear to be kidding.

"Y'know, Brooke says she's protective, but I don't think she's the only one."

"Oh no, she's definitely the protective one, but she's my sister and I love her. She deserves only good things from now on."

"Understood. I have a sister. I'd feel exactly the same way."

They finished their croissants in silence, Beans getting his last nibble before Laurel set her plate on the ottoman. "How's the prom planning going?"

"Very well. Your sister worries, but she shouldn't. Brooke is amazing. I think we're doing great."

"That's good to hear." She scratched and pet Beans, focusing on her dog as she spoke. "I've had to take over hotel reservations because of this prom. Not my favorite thing in the world and particularly boring when no one is checking in, but if the prom is going to be great, then the suffering is worth it."

"No one checking in? It's early May. Almost peak tourism season. You guys should be packed."

Laurel's gaze went wide. "I...I meant this week. We don't have many guests checking in this week." She quickly made a production of studying one of Beans's ears.

He waited for her to make eye contact, confirm that she was, in fact, lying her tail off to cover for her slip up.

Nothing.

Beans continued to stare while Laurel refused to look up.

"I guess the dog and I can keep having a stare-off 'til tumbleweeds roll by, *or* you can tell me what you mean about no one checking in."

With a heavy sigh, she finally looked up. "Brooke will kill me."

"I won't let her."

"I thought maybe you knew already."

"Clearly I don't. You're stalling. Tell me."

"It's nothing, just... our hotel business has been off. Slow. Business is slow. Has been for the past year or two. Brooke didn't tell you?"

"She mentioned money was tight due to investing so much into the winery."

"That's true. But the other part is the hotel is sucking money down its gullet to stay alive."

Trevor fought not to grin. Smiling now would be in bad form, but the girl had quite a way with words.

He couldn't blame Brooke for not telling him every detail about Jolie's business, but after everything they'd talked about and shared, it surprised him that she hadn't.

Probably shouldn't. Brooke played things close to the vest and he empathized. Still, in this, she could trust him.

Chateau Jolie was beautiful, the winery one of kind around their parts. Business should be booming, not in a slump. Then again, Honeywilde had had its share of struggles for years too.

The inn's resurgence wasn't exactly his doing, but he was involved. He'd learned some invaluable lessons over the last couple of years, and he'd gladly share anything he could to help Brooke and Chateau Jolie.

Trevor settled back, pondering solutions.

Seemingly satisfied with his scratches and that there'd be no more croissant for now, the pug snuggled down into the narrow space between Laurel's leg and the arm of the chair.

And just like that, an idea came to Trevor. Something that might help Chateau Jolie with its lagging reservation rates. His notion wasn't so unusual, but might be a hundred yards left of field from what Brooke wanted.

Still, he'd toss his idea out there and see what she thought. He was also going to ask her out on another date.

Why not? The worst that could happen was she'd say no to both.

Chapter 21

"What time is it?" With her leg stretched out, Brooke expected to find a warm, slightly longer leg next to hers.

All she found were cold sheets.

"Trevor?" she called, and sat up.

No answer.

His shoes still sat by her bed. He couldn't have gone far.

Or maybe he could've. Knowing him, he'd wander almost anywhere, shoeless.

She grabbed her phone and texted him, only for a vibrating sound to come from her dresser.

Of course he didn't have his phone with him. That'd be too easy.

"Uh-oh." Brooke jumped from her bed.

The sun was coming up, and it was almost seven in the morning. If Trevor was traipsing about the chateau, he was bound to run into Laurel. Better Laurel than Reagan, but still.

Brooke pulled a sweatshirt on over the pajamas she'd changed into and took off downstairs.

She wasn't ashamed of spending the night with Trevor. Not in any way.

But sharing this tenuous step with her sisters?

Severely unprepared for that leap.

She'd shared a special kind of intimacy with Trevor last night. Not sex, but the night meant as much to her as if they had.

After her divorce, she'd been so certain she'd never want to be with anyone again. Definitely not anytime soon. Perhaps never.

But Trevor had strolled into her life, carefree yet steadfast, and altered her view.

The load of a serious relationship remained off the table. However, dating…Hanging out, having fun, that option held a lot of possibilities.

"Good morning." Legs crossed, snuggled into one of the winged-back chairs, a lap full of pug, Laurel sipped her coffee as if it were any other morning.

Brooke approached slowly. "Good morning." She eased down to the edge of the other chair. "Coffee smells good."

An empty cup and a croissant-crumb-covered plate sat on the side table.

Laurel wouldn't come right out and poke into other people's business. That was Reagan's style, not hers. But unless one of their few guests was an extremely early riser, even on vacation, Trevor had sat here and had coffee and pastry with Laurel. Who knew where he might be right now, but the bigger question was, who would crack first, her or Laurel?

"You want some?" Laurel asked.

"No, I'm good."

"You sure? I figured you'd be hungry. After last night." Her sister smirked.

"Ha-ha. Where is he?"

"Who?"

"Your breakfast buddy. I know he was here. Where did he go?"

"You mean Trevor Bradley? Your good-looking prom partner, with the floppy bedhead and sleepy smile? Trevor Bradley, who I ran into before six a.m.? *That* breakfast buddy?"

A growl of frustration filled her throat. "Yes. Him."

A triumphant smile filled her sister's face. "I don't know."

"Laurel."

"I don't."

Beans woofed to back up her claim.

"I like him though."

Ignoring the editorial, Brooke leaned forward to scratch the top of Beans's head.

"Trevor seems like a really good guy, and he's obviously into you. Do you feel the same?"

Brooke kept petting the dog.

"I mean it." Laurel scooped Beans up to move him away. "I know Reagan gives you a hard time about getting back out there, and getting on the horse or whatever, but that's not what I'm talking about. I'm talking about him. Trevor, as an individual. He's a good guy. Beans and I are excellent judges of character."

With a sigh, Brooke leaned back. "I know."

"Then why aren't you saying anything?"

"I don't know."

A lie. Her reason was fear.

Admitting the tangle of feelings she had right now would make them real. She barely understood them herself.

"I think it's a bit too early to be thinking about how I feel."

Another lie.

She liked Trevor, admired him, cared for him. He was good looking, made her laugh, made her feel stronger.

Before Nick, she would've been able to admit she was falling for Trevor, hook, line, and sinker. Now, attraction automatically came with mountains of doubt.

Four years ago, her ex-husband had been the bee's knees. And then everything was a disaster.

"I don't think it's too early for him. He acted like he was pretty much done thinking. I think his mind was made up. He called you amazing."

He'd said as much to her face too.

What if he did fall in love with her? What if he was able to love fully and she was incapable of giving that to him in return? She was damaged goods. He was still young and fresh and new.

"Part of me thinks he'd be better suited with someone like you," Brooke confessed.

Her sister's response included cackling in her face. "Whatever."

"I'm serious. He's adventurous, unpredictable, loves to be outside. The two of you would have a lot in common."

Laurel scoffed. "Liking nature and being a bit of a spaz does not a suitable pair make. Mr. Hubbard, the barber in town, likes the outdoors and is quirky as heck, but you don't see us hooking up, do you?"

"Mr. Hubbard is seventy-eight years old."

"So? If he were twenty-eight, we still wouldn't be a good match. You need to understand one another. Trevor gets you."

"How do you know after one croissant together?"

"Because, believe it or not, *I* get you, and I know when someone else does too. Nick never did. Your ex wanted to win. He wanted kudos and prizes to stroke his pride, the best of everything, and that included having you. Trevor likes you for you. Bossiness, neurosis, and all."

"Gee, thanks."

"He's got a family and a family business that he's committed to. He's supportive and caring and successful. The two of you have a lot more in common than you know."

Brooke swallowed the raw knot in her throat. "You think I'm all those things?"

"Duh."

She laughed over her urge to cry at the compliment. "You're a lot of trouble when you're profound."

Laurel grinned. "I know. Brings me such joy."

They shared a smile and Laurel moved Beans back within Brooke's reach.

"Trevor's still here, by the way. I don't know where he went, but he borrowed a quilt and went outside about fifteen minutes ago. I doubt he went far, seeing as how he didn't have on any shoes."

"I don't know. Knowing him, he could be hiking right now."

"But I bet you could catch him, if you tried."

"You're right. Thanks, sis." Brooke hurried out the front doors of Jolie, the morning mist beginning to burn off with the rising sun.

Trevor could be in the vineyard, strolling around, eating grapes. Or down by Laurel's barn, chasing chickens around the pen. Or stopping to smell the roses somewhere because that'd be a very Trevor thing to do.

Rounding the side of the hotel, she caught sight of a brightly colored quilt on the ground, beyond the garden, underneath a couple of oak trees.

In the center of the quilt sat Trevor, his back to her.

She approached, but he didn't turn around. Not until her shoes hit the edge of the quilt did he turn, opening his eyes. "Morning, sunshine." He smiled, blue eyes twinkling.

Brooke slid off her shoes and joined him on the quilt. "You must've missed the memo about me not being a morning person. You're out here before seven a.m. You're the sunshine."

As soon as she sat down, he leaned over and pressed his lips to hers, tasting of chocolate and coffee and Trevor.

She shivered and pulled her hands inside the sleeves of her sweatshirt. "What are you doing out here?"

"A little quiet time, watching the sun rise." He moved closer and rubbed her arms to warm them.

Before, the affection would've put her on guard. Now, she welcomed his touch.

"I slept like a baby last night," he said.

"Me too." Surprising, but true.

"I enjoyed talking to your sister this morning. Nothing like you or Reagan, but still decidedly a Sargent."

"Uh-oh. What did she say?"

Trevor kept rubbing. "Don't worry. Nothing bad."

Her shoulders relaxed a smidge more. For a moment, she enjoyed the early-morning quiet, the sun growing warmer on her face with each passing second.

"She did say something about Chateau Jolie's struggling room sales though, which you've failed to mention."

Immediately, the stiffness returned. With a groan, Brooke bent forward to bury her face in her hands.

"So it's true?"

What if she simply didn't answer? The route of no reply or no eye contact had a lot of appeal right now.

Trevor tugged on her shoulders, urging her to sit up. "Come on. Your reaction is pretty much all the answer I need. No point in avoiding the topic."

He was right. Again.

Brooke eased herself up.

"You could've told me. I understand why you didn't, at first, but there's no reason not to discuss it now."

"No, I know. I hate that we're in this position though. And I don't want to dump my problems all over you.

"You're not dumping." He bumped his elbow against hers. "We're partners, remember? You know me. I'm not going to judge."

He wouldn't. Of this, she was certain. So she took a deep breath and trusted him.

"We've been struggling. Since right before my parents retired. They bought this place decades ago because of the vineyard. They wanted to grow that part of the business and eventually they did. But, because that was their passion, they let the hotel side of things drop off. Didn't matter at first because business was good regardless. We didn't have much competition. Then Honeywilde hit its renaissance phase."

"And took business away."

"A lot of business. We still book a few rooms, but not nearly enough. You guys are bigger and have the capacity. We've had to dip into the winery to cover costs and that's no way to operate. It's not sustainable. I didn't tell your brother, or you, because I'd hoped our financial situation wouldn't be an issue for the prom. And it won't. Not with the plan we've got going. But long term, I don't know what we're going to do to fix things."

"There's enough business to go around though. Maybe your issue is visibility."

"Maybe. Maybe it's all too much to juggle. What if we'd be better off selling the hotel portion and focusing on the winery? Or maybe the best option is to bring a sommelier on staff, and a manager to split off the winery. Or do we hire someone to manage the hotel? I don't know. I don't know if my sisters and I can manage it all and sometimes…sometimes I feel like I'm going to smother under the weight."

He nodded, never once interrupting and waiting until she finished before he angled himself toward her. "You've got a lot on you right now."

She groaned and wanted to crumple again, but his hold on her kept her upright.

"But you will sort this all out over the next few months. You have your sisters to help, and you and I can bounce around ideas. This will work out in the long run."

"How can you be so sure?"

"Because, I've been there with my family. And I've met the Sargent sisters. I've worked with you. If anyone has the resolve to sort out problems, it's you."

A pang twisted her heart at the vote of confidence.

"But, if I may, a thought came to me while I was talking to Laurel earlier about the slowdown in bookings."

"I'm listening."

"What about making Jolie pet friendly?"

Brooke scrunched her nose. "We're already pet friendly."

"Then you're making my point about visibility. See, I didn't know this place was pet friendly. I bet most folks don't know that. Pet friendliness isn't something you do any kind of special promotion on."

"We list the feature on our website and print advertising."

"Nowadays, that's not enough. That's what worked for your parents, but you need to think outside of traditional. Go left where they went right."

An image came to mind of Beans, tucked in the small space between Laurel's leg and the arm of the wingback chair. Of Trevor and his bushy brown dog, Beau, following him all around the lake. A memory of her childhood pet, a feisty little terrier mix that was the love of her life in elementary school.

People loved their dogs, and many would travel with them if given an option. Particularly a luxurious option when nine times out of ten pet friendly meant the motor inn.

"I could make some changes to our website," Brooke said. "Highlight the pet friendliness more. Reagan could do some stuff with social media. She's all about that. Maybe tweak our magazine and brochure ads."

"Exactly. What about some target-market advertising?"

"Oh, like ads at pet-lover events like that wag-a-thon fundraiser for the Humane Society."

Brooke bounced on the quilt. "And Bark in the Park. They have huge turnouts every year."

"Now you're thinking."

"Honeywilde isn't pet friendly, is it?"

"No, and I don't think anywhere up on the mountain is, except y'all. I've got Beau, but he's only allowed in the great room and our private quarters. Occasionally Roark's office. Allowing pets is too much of an issue with the restaurant, but here you've got the winery separate and downstairs, closed kitchen and no full-service restaurant."

The idea made her want to scream with glee. It was brilliant and would set Jolie apart from the competition. Between targeting pet owners and getting some PR from the prom, maybe their hotel would get a shot in the arm.

She turned to Trevor. "I love this plan. Thank you so much."

With a flash of dimples, he shrugged. "Not a problem. These are your ideas. Sometimes you only need a second set of eyes to see something that's already there. Feel better?"

"A lot."

"Good, then let's take it to the next level." He scooted over a bit and bobbled around on his bottom until he sat up straight. Then he looked at her. "Sit up a little straighter and cross your legs like this."

Warning bells went off in the back of her mind. He'd already said he came out here this morning for some quiet. Trevor was trying to get her to do yoga.

"I'm fine sitting here like this."

"This will have you feeling better than fine. Come on, sit like this."

There'd be no point in arguing and she kind of owed him enough to at least try. "Okay, I'll sit up. *But* I am not going to stand on my head or do something crazy."

"You won't have to stand on your head. We're going to sit here and breathe. We might stand up, but let's not get ahead of ourselves."

"Sit and breathe. You promise?"

"Yes." Trevor leaned over to bump playfully against her. "Now. Sit like this."

He repositioned himself next to her, legs crossed but with both ankles loosely lying on the blanket instead of tucked under him.

Easy enough.

Brooke mimicked his posture, her eye lids drifting down.

"Good." His voice eased over her skin, even and low. "Relax your shoulders. Back straight. Chest lifted. Breathe. Keep yourself lifted and straight. Head over your heart."

She opened one eye. "Do what?"

Trevor glanced over and put his palm to his sternum. "If you're sitting up, shoulders back and chest lifted, your head will be over your heart, your heart over your pelvis. Aligned."

With only the one eye, she stared.

"Hush, and do it."

"I didn't say anything."

"Your right eye said plenty."

"Fine." She closed her eyes and shifted around, sitting up, nice and straight like her yogi said.

"Inhale. Slow, steady breath. And out."

Brook sat on the floral quilt, in the middle of their side yard, breathing in and out. And somehow, in the midst of all the breathing, her mind slowed in its bounce from topic to topic. Fretting over her sisters, worrying about the hotel and their future, stressing about the prom. Instead, she found herself focused on Trevor's voice, telling her to breathe in and out. Then she thought only of her breathing.

Her deep breaths were pitifully shallow, but she tried. "I'm not sure I'm doing this right."

"You're breathing. There's no wrong way. You're doing great. This time, arms out as you inhale." Trevor stretched his arms in front of him, palms facing out, fingers laced. "And down as you exhale."

Brooke followed suit.

They did that three times, and each time the tightness in her shoulders loosened a little bit.

"Right hand on your left knee," he instructed, showing her how. "Turn your body. Not too far. It's not a flexibility contest; you only need to feel the stretch. Keep your back straight. Head over heart, remember."

From behind her, he put his hands on her sides, angling her into a more comfortable position. "Like that. Good. You want to keep your chest lifted. Drop your shoulders down, don't bunch up. There. Wonderful."

He got into the same position next to her. "Slowly to the other side. Same thing."

She turned, placing her left hand on her right knee, her mind fully occupied with keeping her head over her heart and breathing. They sat that way for a long moment, and she began to study the back of Trevor's head.

The fluffy top of his hair, mussed into soft, chocolatey waves. The back and sides were clipped and well kept, his flop of hair on the top a total juxtaposition.

She'd never really noticed the difference until now.

He probably had to get his hair cut once a month to keep the back neat. His neck was tan too, from a life spent outside. A life of adventure.

How had she never noticed the beautiful color of his neck until now?

She'd noticed and appreciated plenty about him, but little things...

The little things had escaped her.

Like how his voice, when pitched low, was one of the most soothing sounds on earth. Right up there with rippling water and rain.

She needed to take the time to soak all of this in, because Trevor wouldn't always be here with her, every day, all day. He had a life and responsibilities at Honeywilde. He had a trek to Peru to make.

He wouldn't be hers forever.

Remaining in one place for too long would be torture for him anyway.

Why would she want him to stay when he'd made clear his love of changes, his frustrations with boredom and being tied down?

"Back to center," he said, turning in time to catch her staring.

"Oops, sorry."

"Don't worry about it. If the position feels good, keep going. There's no time limit or rule, and you won't get in trouble if you aren't perfect."

That was an interesting concept.

"Now. Right arm up. Inhale. Stretch up to the sky and gently over to the left."

She did as he did. "Like this?"

"Yes. Great. You can move a little. Roll forward or back. Do what feels good. Now, let's stretch out. Lay back. All the way down, flat on the quilt. Arms over your head."

Brooke lay down, the stretch pulling up her ribs, a pleasurable tightness and then release of tension along her sides.

Trevor lay down beside her in a similar pose. He remained quiet, eyes closed for minute after minute.

Finally, she worked up the nerve to whisper, "Is that it? Are we done?"

He whispered back, without opening his eyes, "Yes, we're done. Nice work. Did you like?"

"I did, actually."

"Good. Told you yoga would make you feel even better." He rolled over onto his stomach, placing his hands against the blanket and crawling forward. Slowly, he bent his arms and tucked his head.

"Uh...what are you doing?"

"What does it look like? I'm going to stand on my head."

Brooke lifted her head and peered across the yard to ensure no one else was outside.

Trevor had both knees on his elbows, with his butt in the air.

Laughter bubbled up from inside her as she curled onto her side. "You're going to fall." She laughed. "Stop."

"You're going to make me fall. Stop giggling."

"But you're trying to stand on your head!"

"Not trying. Doing." With a little wobbling, he extended one leg into the air, the other quickly following. His T-shirt drooped down, revealing the tan skin of his abdomen and a peek of his chest.

Last night, she'd slept with an arm over that chest and stomach. Solid and strong. Part of her, the portion that didn't harbor all of her fear and uncertainty, had wanted to slide a hand under his shirt. In the middle of the night, skate fingertips across his bare skin to test the softness over the hard muscle.

He had that same lean strength in his back too. No doubt as tan.

And he'd gladly let her see it too. All of him. As a matter of fact, knowing Trevor, if she said the word, he'd do more than make out with her right here on this blanket in light of morning, on the side lawn.

Heat rushed her body, pooling between her legs.

Times like this, her attraction and desire for him far outweighed any reluctance. Or common sense. She wanted him.

What was the worst that could happen?

"Jealous?"

Not exactly the emotion she struggled with at the moment. "Of what? All the blood that's rushing to your head?"

"It's good for circulation. And perspective."

She pushed her passion aside for a moment, staring at his upside-down face. "Were you always like this?"

"Like what?"

Laughter tickled her throat as she waved one hand up toward his feet. "Like this."

"Maybe. You are jealous, aren't you?"

"Honestly? Yes." To have the freedom to be impulsive. To be that comfortable and at ease in her own body.

Trevor knew who he was and he was happy he had the kind of confidence that you couldn't fake. A genuine assuredness she envied. Because even if Trevor didn't know what he was doing, even if he didn't have all of his bases covered, he believed everything would be okay.

That kind of thinking was foreign to her.

He lowered his legs and his bare feet back onto the blanket. "If you really are jealous, I can teach you how to do this."

"That's not what I meant."

Trevor leaned over and kissed her. He kept leaning and kissing until he toppled her over, rolling on the blanket until his body covered hers.

"We can't make out with you on the front lawn," she said between kisses.

"Boo."

Their legs intertwined, she tried to hook an ankle over his leg and use leverage to roll them over.

Her plan didn't work.

Trevor chuckled and, with his fingers laced with hers, pinned her hands against the blanket. "You keep wriggling around like that, we won't be going anywhere for a long time."

As improper as it may be, as much as she'd fuss at her sisters if it was one of them rolling around on the lawn with a guy, she didn't want him to stop.

If Nick—or any other guy for that matter—had ever attempted to pin her down, she would've been annoyed. Turned off. Possibly even irate.

But the heat in Trevor's gaze, the teasing grin upon his lips, her certainty that he'd never do this unless he knew she'd be into it, the fact that he *did* know, that changed everything.

Trevor wasn't some domineering blowhard. She'd been married to one long enough to know.

Life wasn't a competition for him, and she wasn't something to be conquered. He baited her for their pleasure, making her feel. She wanted things from Trevor she'd never considered before. Things *with* Trevor that'd been written off years ago.

A mischievous grin curled his lips as he leaned back, propping his weight up with a hand on either side of her head. "Hey, I have a great idea."

Expecting a random urge to go hike a mountain or run off somewhere to get it on, she grinned. "Shoot."

"Come to a birthday party with me tonight."

Chapter 22

Brooke's mouth fell open. "A birthday party? We don't have time. The prom is next week. We still have too much to do."

"I'm not inviting you to a weekend-long rave. Marco, our new chef at Honeywilde, his niece is having a huge birthday party tonight. Food, music, dancing, the whole nine yards."

She quirked her lips as she pondered his invite. Clearly this was going to take a little more convincing.

"Think of it as research for the prom. You could probably use a little help in the partying department anyway."

She bumped her knee against him. "Excuse you, I know how to party."

"Then you'll fit right in. Starts at six."

"I didn't say I'd go."

They'd been working hard, and he'd been more singularly focused on this prom than anything he had in a while. "Come on. We need to get out and have some fun."

"Last night wasn't fun?"

Leaning in, he brushed his nose against her cheek before kissing her again. "More than fun, but this is one little party. Say you'll go with me."

With a sigh, Brooke smiled. "Fine. I'll go with you."

Talking her into things took about half the effort it used to.

A blur of beige darted past his peripheral. Next thing he knew, he had a lap full of pug.

"Hey, sorry!" Laurel approached a moment later. "I know y'all are having some quality time or whatever, but Brooke, I need you. I have a guest who wants early checkout, but the software locked up or something."

"That happens. You have to close out of the room profile and log out completely. I'll show you." Brooke pushed herself up from the quilt.

Trevor rose to his feet as well and began folding up the blanket he'd dragged outside. "I'm going to head away home. I need to check in with Brenda about the flowers. Can Laurel take you back to your car?"

"Of course I can." Laurel looked back and forth between them, all smiles as she waited. Beans happily sniffed and snuffled around the grass.

Brooke bent to give him a scratch behind the ears. "Good, that will give me time to tell you about an idea Trevor and I had about boosting room sales here. I think you, in particular, are going to love it." She gazed up at Trevor, looking entirely too beautiful for such an early morning. "I need to follow up with the caterer as well. Make sure we're on budget."

"I guess I'll see you tonight then."

He got another smile. "Yes, you will."

As he handed over the quilt, Laurel cleared her throat and chuckled. "Um, you might want to get your shoes before you go."

* * * *

As soon as he returned to Honeywilde, Trevor underwent microscopic inspection. Both by Beau's nose and his sister's astute stare.

"Where have you been?" Sophie asked, Beau almost pulling her arm off in his haste to get to Trevor and sniff every inch of him.

"I believe you call it Nunya." He bent and scratched behind Beau's ear, showering him with attention. "Nunya business."

"Ha-ha. No really. You were gone all night. Where were you?"

"Working late."

With an annoyed puff, she tugged Beau away. "Uh-huh. And that's why the dog is losing his mind?"

"I reek of pug puppy."

Sophie shook her head. "I'm not sure I want to know."

"Of course you do. You're the nosiest person in our family."

"Thanks a lot."

"Brooke's sister has a rescue pug—a puppy—and obviously."

His sister's jaw dropped. Eventually, she managed to scoop it off the ground. "You spent the night with Brooke?"

"I spent the night at Jolie. There's a difference."

"Not really. You're—Are you two hooking up?"

"Aren't you the same woman who once told me to mind my business? Pretty sure you even let an elevator door close in my face."

"Maybe. But did that make any difference? You still didn't listen."

He stuck out his hand. "Give me back my dog."

Sophie clutched the handle of the leash against her chest. "You left your dog last night. When you decided to spend the night at Jolie, he was here, alone, and I took care of him."

"Nice try with the dramatics. He stays with you a third of the time, even when I'm here."

"Not the point. You can't have him back until we finish talking about your sleepover."

"There's nothing to talk about."

"Uh-huh. If you and Brooke Sargent are involved—not that I object, I think the world of Brooke, but if you're staying over…" With a quirk of her mouth, she tilted her head to the side.

"What?"

"You should tell me."

"Like how you told me everything about you and Wright?"

Sophie's mouth fell open, her inquisition falling silent.

Trevor froze. *What?* his mind yelled, but nothing came out.

"Eventually, yes, you dope. I did tell you everything about me and Wright. I told only you."

Crap. She had. "My bad. You did talk to me." His sister confided in him alone, and now he'd thrown that in her face.

Trevor turned, ready to walk away from the conversation if that was the only way out.

"Wait." Sophie grabbed his arm, turning him back. "So does that mean Brooke and you are as serious as Wright and I were?"

Ah hell. "That is not what I said."

"Then you're not?"

"I didn't say that either. Y'know what? Let's just change the subject."

"Don't get defensive. I'm not against you. I'm surprised, that's all. You're both so…different." Sophie stared up at him with big green eyes.

She didn't mean anything harmful by her curiosity, but her reasoning behind her surprise still stung.

Brooke was the reliable, secure one. Or so most people thought. They didn't know everything about her. They didn't know she had a million different facets other than the one or two she showed the world.

Trevor, on the other hand, was impetuous. Quiet and unpredictable, liable to take off at any moment.

That's exactly who he used to be, but that wasn't the sum total of Trevor Bradley.

People didn't know or understand who he was now. He couldn't blame them. Most people didn't get him, because he didn't want to get got. Even his brothers and sisters were given a little distance. Why should he open up and spill all of his business?

Nothing about that sounded like a good idea.

Unless he was talking to Brooke. Brooke, he'd told almost everything.

"Here." Sophie handed Beau's leash over. "I don't mean different in a bad way. But she's the manager of a hotel and winery who's practically anchored to her job and you're…you. You've never wanted to be tied down. You like to wander without warning."

"One time. I went one time without getting the family's executive-level approval. Let it go."

Sophie stared him down. "Don't be snide. You know I'm not judging. I'm just saying Brooke is business suits and heels, and you're…jeans and old hiking boots. I'm allowed to be a little surprised."

"I bet Brooke likes me in jeans."

His sister rolled her eyes. "I'm sure she does."

Truth be told, he understood his sister's surprise. But he was getting to know the real Brooke, the side of her she'd admitted to never sharing. Deep down, the two of them weren't so different.

Trevor tugged Beau a little closer and scowled as he scratched the top of Beau's head. "And she happens to own flip-flops too. I saw them in her room."

With a high-pitched noise, Sophie rushed over, wrapping her arms around him, squeezing him in a hug. "I know I'm being nosey, but only because I care. If you're happy, I'm happy. And I'll butt out. Maybe."

He patted her back and muttered as she hugged him. "You know, I'm not the first Bradley to stay over at Jolie."

She leaned back enough that he could see her face, and gave him the side eye. "You see how that turned out for me, don't you?"

Sophie's jaunt to Chateau Jolie with Wright had ended up with the two of them dating, falling in love, and becoming a bona fide couple. Likely to be married within a year.

Marriage had never been a part of his life plan.

Then again, he'd never had a life plan.

Dating Brooke was exactly what he wanted. Anything more had never occurred to him. He wasn't opposed; he simply hadn't considered that path.

When he turned to address Sophie, she'd already moved on to something else. Her attention on the entrance of Honeywilde, she stood back, her arms crossed, and looked the entryway alcove and double doors up and down, then side to side, and back again.

"Now what are you doing?"

"I'm butting out and, knowing my self-control, I'm changing the subject. Quickly." She held her hands up as if holding a large painting. "I want to do something different out here for the wedding next weekend. Something we can keep up through Mother's Day. Maybe even into June if possible. I'm tired of these same old plants and those black urn things."

"I think they look great."

"They've been there every spring for the last three years."

"We're tired of looking at them." Dev strolled up. "They're boring."

Trevor jerked around. "Where'd you come from?"

"Lakeside. We've talked about needing something different. Memorable."

"What about a lamppost?" Trevor suggested. "You could hang plants from it if you want. Or not."

Sophie slapped her hands together. "Yes! That's perfect."

Dev scrubbed a hand over his chin and stood there for a solid sixty seconds before agreeing. "Nice. I like it."

A bubble of pride rose in Trevor's chest. As much as he didn't need anyone's validation, a little approval was nice.

"How's the prom going?" Dev asked while Sophie began fussing with the plants and black urn things.

"Great so far. We've got Brenda handling flowers; we're renting the tables and chairs. Brooke is working on catering, and I got DJ Knight to handle the music."

"Nice!" Sophie popped up from behind a potted plant. "Did you get a deal?"

"You know it."

Dev clapped him on the shoulder. "Good work. I knew you had this in you."

"Yeah...but I have a couple of questions for you. Not about the prom, but semirelated."

With a low humming sound, Dev widened his stance and crossed his arms. "Okay. Shoot."

"First off, the stuff with the school losing their money to a venue that went out of business? That wasn't accurate. That was a pile of BS. We have good reason to believe that Zen mismanaged the students' funds and is still operating."

Dev scowled. "How could they? People would find out. That's fraud."

"I don't know how, but I'm telling you, they're still booking events. Maybe on the quiet or for known parties? Or they could just be taking their chances. The guy we ran into yesterday sure had the brass ones to try. I'm not sure what they're doing, but that place definitely wasn't shut down like the school thinks."

His brother scrubbed a hand over his mouth, muttering some choice words.

"I don't have documented proof, but Brooke and I were there. Something shady is going on, I know it."

His brother nodded. "Oh, I believe you. I've seen my share of shadiness before. Not much surprises me anymore."

A weight lifted from Trevor's shoulders, held up by Dev's support. "Maybe you know someone on the school board or someone at county who can look into them?"

"I don't know anyone on the board, directly, but I know people who do. Let me make some calls. See what can be done."

"Perfect." He'd figured his brother would be the best person to help. Knowing the kids might get some justice brought a smile to his face.

"What was the other question?"

Right. His other question. Here went nothing. "The party for Marco's niece tonight…we can bring a guest, right?"

"As far as I know, we can. Why?"

"I invited Brooke."

His brother's eyebrows went up a notch.

"I figured it was cool to bring someone."

"Sure. Should be fine if you bring a date." Dev rocked back and forth on his heels, clearly waiting for Trevor to say more.

Maybe Dev expected him to deny Brooke was his date. He'd shunned enough relationship talk over the years that Dev's expectation made sense.

"Cool." Trevor grinned wider instead. "I'll bring her."

He wasn't going to deny Brooke or his interest in her. If his family wanted to tease the last single Bradley about it, let them.

But Dev didn't give him a hard time. Rather, he waited until Sophie left with one of the urns before he spoke again. "I have a question for you too. I was wondering, did you ever end up calling Mom?"

"Not with this prom stuff going on. Still planning to though."

His brother's gaze darted away.

If he didn't know better, he'd swear Dev looked disappointed.

"Why?"

"No reason. I mean, Mother's Day is coming up and...I don't know. Only if you want to call. I know she said she wanted to make amends and come around some, but—"

"She does," Trevor said, stopping him. "She definitely does, but she's not going to come up uninvited. Not after last time. I was thinking I'd go see her, maybe weekend after next, after the prom is over."

"You could do that..." His brother let the sentence drift with a slight lift to his shoulders.

"*Or*"—Trevor went out on the limb Dev offered—"maybe I could invite her over for Mother's Day?"

Dev began a slow nod. "That'd be a nice gesture. You don't think it'd be too much?"

"Not if the four of us are in agreement. She wouldn't be staying here for a week or anything, just lunch. Everything went well at your wedding."

"True."

"And we'd talk this over with Roark and Sophie first, of course, instead of springing a get-together on everyone again."

"Yeah, let's don't go that route again. I'll check with Roark and Soph. Make sure everyone is okay with Mother's Day."

"And once you get the go-ahead, I'll call and invite her up."

Dev nodded again.

He'd been the most upset about their mother's unannounced appearance at an event last spring, and he held the most resentment. But, like all of the Bradleys, he was growing. He'd allowed their mother to come to his wedding and now had an interest in seeing her again. Progress.

If Devlin could open himself up enough to trust again, or at least try, anyone could.

Maybe even Brooke.

Chapter 23

Marco's niece's birthday party was anything but little.

Brooke took Trevor's arm, their walk into the reception hall of St. Mary's reminding her of walking into a museum gala in Richmond. Only with more glitter and teenage girls.

An array of white tulle, turquoise and white balloons, and silver, sparkly ribbon filled the room.

"I see two open seats over there." Trevor took her hand and led her to a table covered in white linen, the chairs all tied with a big silver bow on the back. A centerpiece of bold, brightly colored flowers sat at every table, giving the hall a feeling of undeniable joy.

A stage was set up as though ready for a band, and everyone looked as if they'd come from a wedding. There were several women in formal gowns.

Moments later, a man in a white suit stood in the center of the stage, a group of bolero-jacketed musicians taking positions behind him. "Ladies and gentlemen, if I may have your attention please. Allow me to introduce, the young lady of the evening, Camila Reyes, and her court of honor."

The reception hall erupted into cheers and applause.

In pairs, teenage girls and boys entered; the boys wearing white dinner jackets, the girls in matching cocktail dresses of pale turquoise and silver, with tiny bouquets of white roses in their hands. They formed a small *V*, and then Camila made her entrance.

She floated in on the arm of the man Brooke guessed was her father. She wore a floor-length, full-skirt gown of turquoise taffeta with a bodice of sequins. A tiara that'd make a beauty queen weep sat elegantly atop her head, her dark hair a cascade of curls.

Brooke's mouth fell open.

Her toy obsession as a child wasn't limited to Power Rangers. She'd also loved princesses and fairies. That is precisely what Camila looked like. A princess.

"Some entrance, huh?" Trevor touched Brooke's elbow, drawing her out of the trance.

"Amazing."

Camila's father said a few words and the band began to play a waltz for the two of them.

Trevor eased his hand down Brooke's arm, intertwining their fingers as he whispered. "I'll remind our DJ to do an announcement and special dance like that for the prom king and queen."

The waltz went on and led to another waltz, with Camila taking a moment to dance with each young man in her court.

The music eventually wound down. People began to find their seats, but Brooke remained enchanted.

"Trevor. Good, you're here." A tall man, with hair darker than Trevor's, greeted them. "I didn't know if you'd make the reception. Sophie said you've been really busy."

"I wouldn't miss this. Marco, this is Brooke Sargent. She owns Chateau Jolie, with her sisters. Brooke this is Marco Reyes. Honeywilde's chef."

Marco offered his hand. "Brooke. You're not the poor soul who's been working with Trevor the last few days."

"The very one."

"Then by all means, enjoy my niece's quince. You need to get some food; we have plenty. Get something to drink. Refuel yourselves. Both of you. Trev, I think all of your family is over on that side of the stage."

As Marco left to greet other guests, Brooke's stomach busied itself doing jumping jacks. "Your whole family is here?"

Trevor nodded, peering across the room. "Marco has been at Honeywilde for a while now. He wanted everyone to come."

"Then who's running the inn?" The idea of her and her sisters leaving Jolie in the hands of someone else made her heart thump faster. Images of the place spontaneously crumbling down to rubble drifted through her mind.

"We have a great staff. They can manage. And one of us can run back if there's an emergency."

Maybe she'd luck out and they'd have an emergency right now. Mixing and mingling with Trevor's family brought a pinch of pain to her temples, heat rising up her back. They were nice people, but around them, the pressure to perform jumped on her, full force.

After spending time with Trevor, she realized her reaction made little sense. She didn't have to be perfect, and the Bradleys were business competition, not an enemy. But she was here with Trevor, and that brought on a whole different kind of reaction.

Great. Now she was sweating in her good dress.

"Come on. I see Sophie."

"There you are." Roark Bradley intercepted them as they crossed the room, embracing Trevor in a one-armed hug. "I was wondering if I'd ever see you again."

"You're the one who stays cooped up in his office."

"Brooke." Roark might've been trying not to look befuddled, but he failed. "Hello."

She put on her best meet-the-family smile. "How are you?"

"Doing well. I didn't know we'd see you here."

"Yeah, me either." That was the only brilliant comeback she could muster.

"Hey." Devlin joined them, sipping pink punch from a little glass cup. "Y'all have to go check out the spread of food. It looks incredible."

Roark shifted to stand closer to her and Trevor. "How are things going with the prom? Any issues?"

"Everything is going great."

"No problems? You're all set?"

"Yep. All set." Trevor worked his jaw.

"Did you check in with Brenda?"

"I did."

Dev groaned into his punch. "Trev and Brooke have got things under control and we're at a party. Relax."

"Okay, but if you need help, I—"

"Roark." Trevor's tone came out stiffer than she'd ever heard before. "Thank you, but we've got it."

With a nod, his eldest brother backed off and greeted one of the other guests. While he was occupied, Dev moved closer. "I wanted to let y'all know, I spoke to a member of tourism who's married to a woman on the school board. I should hear from her soon and I'll let you know how far I get."

Brooke's gaze bounced from Dev to Trevor.

"I told my brother about Zen. He's going to help us go after them," Trevor said.

Dev held his punch up. "I can't promise all that, but we'll do our best."

"That's…" Brooke blinked, a stinging sensation behind her eyes. They'd already made more progress than she'd dreamed possible. "Thank you," she said.

"Brooke!" Sophie shoved her brothers aside and grabbed Brooke with the kind of strength she looked too small to muster. "I'm so glad you're here. I haven't seen you in weeks. Anna and Madison are out of town and I'm so tired of talking to these guys all the time. Come on, let's get something to eat." She dragged Brooke from the middle of the circle.

Brooke glanced back to find Trevor.

"I'll find you before the dancing starts," he promised.

"How have you been? *Where* have you been? Other than planning this prom, what have you been up to? Tell me everything."

Heat surrounded her as though she were curled against Trevor again, pressed to his chest. Warm, safe. "Nothing, except the planning. And working. That's us. Only working and planning."

"Ugh. Tell me about it. I haven't had a day off in two weeks and Wright's schedule is insane. But…" She drew the word out unnecessarily long. "We're taking a couple of days next month though. Got to mix some fun in with work, right?" She waited with an expectant gleam in her eyes.

Sophie knew about her and Trevor.

Brooke peered to where Trevor was speaking intently with his brothers. Were they talking about the prom or were they discussing her? Did his brothers have the same insight as Sophie?

She looked back toward Sophie to find she'd followed her gaze.

"You and my brother," she said. It wasn't a question. "I suspected he was into you at Dev's wedding, but honestly, I didn't think he stood a chance. Guess I was wrong."

"What do you mean? Trevor and I aren't—"

"Oh please. Look at him." Sophie nodded to her bundle of brothers.

Trevor smiled as his gaze met Brooke's, affection playing all across his face.

"I know. But we aren't…" What? Brooke had no descriptor for them. He meant a lot to her, but she couldn't define what. "We aren't dating or anything."

"You're clearly not just friends though."

"No, we're not that either." She didn't know what they were, but she enjoyed it the same.

"Listen, I love nosing into Trevor's business, if only to give him a hard time, the way he does me, but I don't want you to think I'm all up in yours.

I'm happy you guys are hanging out or whatever. A little surprised, but happy."

A wave of relief washed over her. If this were her sister Reagan talking to Trevor, the conversation would go a lot differently.

They reached the food line and two long tables stretched out, filled with platters of empanadas, fish, chicken, corn on the cob, vegetable skewers, beans, rice, and fresh fruit.

Brooke's stomach growled at the sight, timed perfectly with Sophie groaning aloud. "I'm about to eat my weight in corn and empanadas."

They worked their way down the line, piling their plates. The scent of seasoned chicken and aromatic rice made Brooke's mouth water.

Sophie stopped at the fruit, making room on her plate for more.

"All right, I lied earlier," she said. "I need to be up in your business a teensy bit."

Brooke bit back a knowing smile. "Does it matter if I say it's not okay?"

"Not really. I only want to say, I hope you really do like Trevor. He tries to hide the fact that he's super into you, because he keeps to himself like that, but it's obvious to me. And he may act all chill and casual, but he's not. When he cares about people, when it matters, he cares a lot. Maybe too much. And I don't want to see him get hurt. That's all."

Brooke stared down at Sophie's heart-shaped face, the cute little kewpie doll nose.

At first sight, no one would ever call Sophie formidable. Brooke knew better, after getting to know her the night she and Wright almost ended their relationship.

Sophie liked Brooke, but she'd never stand by and let someone hurt her brother.

Brooke would never willingly do that though. Trevor had earned a degree of trust and reliance, when she'd been sure that'd never happen again. She let Trevor kiss her, and touch her, and still she wanted more.

"I like your brother," Brooke said, admitting the truth aloud for the first time. An odd, tingling sensation rippled across her skin.

Sophie took a deep breath, her shoulders relaxing so much they almost sagged. "Good."

Brooke didn't answer to Sophie. She didn't answer to anyone anymore, but confessing her feelings gave her freedom.

Plus, she understood the protectiveness of family. How many guys had she wanted to quiz when they dated her sisters? How many had she wanted to throttle when they hurt them?

"I mean, you don't owe me an explanation or anything, but he's my brother. I care about him. And I like you. I don't want him getting his heart stomped."

"No one wants their heart stomped." Didn't stop it from happening, but still. "I can't promise we'll get serious or ever be a couple. Trevor and I are—I don't know what we are, but I don't want to hurt him or be hurt. We're enjoying each other's company and that's enough for now. I never thought I'd meet a guy I wanted to be around. I want to be around him, get to know him more."

And that's all she knew right now.

"Awww." Sophie shrugged her shoulders up to her ears as they made their way back to the corner of Bradleys.

"No, not aww. I said I don't know what we are."

"I know, but you want to get to know him more and he really is so awesome. A little all over the place sometimes, but he tries harder than anyone and cares more than everyone. He's the one who finally reached out to our mother last year. None of us would've done that."

"I know. He told me."

Sophie stopped dead in her tracks. "He told you about our mom?"

"Yes."

Her mouth fell open.

"Should he not have?"

"No, it's fine. I'm just surprised. He's usually very private. He must trust you." Sophie turned, continuing on to find a seat.

They found the Bradley brothers exactly where they had left them.

"You three better hurry up and get something to eat," Sophie called. "We aren't waiting on y'all."

Trevor hovered near Brooke, close enough to give off body heat as he checked out her plate of food. "That looks so good." He patted his flat stomach. "Got to fill up for dancing fuel."

"You really think you're going to get me to dance tonight."

He plucked a cherry tomato off of one of her skewers and popped it into his mouth. "I don't think. I know." With a quick wink, he was off to get in line with his brothers.

A slight pep in his step, he seemed lighter than air.

Trevor not only trusted her, he liked her. And he wasn't the least bit scared to show it.

An odd awareness began to wash over her. Clarity and understanding.

Deep down, at the center of a heart she'd thought hardened like cold steel, she felt the same.

Dinner passed in a flash, and as soon as the band started up again, Trevor leaned over. "Are your dancing shoes ready?"

"No, but somehow I'm betting that won't stop you."

He took her hand, helping her stand. "Remember Dev's wedding? Follow my lead and we'll look like professionals."

She let him lead her to the dance floor, where several teenagers and adult couples were already dancing. A mirrored ball hung suspended in midair, and a pair of twirling lights created the vision of stars on the parquet floor. The lights glittered off the sparkling ribbon and white tulle, weaving a magical thread through the night.

Trevor held her close, his eyes bright while his smile held a heavy hint of mischief.

"What are you thinking about?" she asked.

"That obvious?"

"Yes. Very."

"I'm thinking about how good you look tonight. And trying not to think about how good you feel."

"I was thinking something similar about you."

"Brooke Sargent, you minx!" He winked.

"Shh!" She turned her face into his.

"No, I love it. Tell me more."

Brooke leaned closer, her lips inches from his. "This whole party is like a fairy tale. I feel…I'm not sure what I feel. Like I can let go."

"Pretty sure that's the point. Keeping tradition and introducing Camila to the community, first. But as an adult, this is also some fairy-tale-level fun. Every day, working, day after day, can be a grind. This isn't." He nodded to where Marco twirled his niece under his arm. "Yesterday, Marco was covered in flour and had some kind of balsamic glaze all over him. Pretty sure he was wiping up broken egg yolk from the refrigerator unit the day before that. But tonight, look at him. He looks like royalty."

Trevor spun them in a turn and Brooke's gaze clung to his.

She'd forgotten how important fun was. Letting go of all the practicalities sometimes to simply enjoy life, maybe remember what it means to dream, believe in the romantic and the magical.

The same was true for the kids at Windamere High.

"Every day is school, school, school or work, work, work," she said.

"Exactly. How often do any of us get to dress up and be kings and queens? Princes or princesses? Especially after you get out of school. In the last six years, I've only gotten spruced up for Dev's wedding. I can see why people enjoy big weddings, quinceañeras, and proms. Why the kids get into it. If you got to be royalty for the day, why wouldn't you?"

As she watched the court, the girls beaming, absolutely beautiful in their joy, the young men debonair, every adult at the party bursting with pride, she couldn't come up with a valid reason why not.

"You're right." She and Trevor were going to do the same for Windamere High's prom. Not the basics that would barely count, but the magical moment those kids would remember forever. Afterward, they could look back on that night and remember the magic and freedom. When reality and responsibility weighed them down, they'd be able to say, "Remember our prom senior year? How much fun we had? How special those people made it for us when we thought we weren't going to have one at all?"

Trevor stepped even closer, fingers caressing the bare skin of her back. "I'm sorry, could you say that again?"

"The daily grind gets to be too much and—"

"No, I meant the part about me being right."

She rolled her eyes.

The band cranked up with a fast-paced song she recognized from the radio, and the dance floor was soon packed with almost every guest there.

Sophie and Dev joined them, cracking up at each other as they danced.

She and Trevor danced and laughed and the evening was exactly like Devlin's wedding.

Even back then, she'd been rejuvenated simply by being around Trevor. Whether she wanted to admit it or not, they had chemistry and connected. She'd tried ignoring those feelings, concentrating instead on her status and label as a divorcee.

Her isolation was punishment. Self-inflicted imprisonment for what she'd allowed herself to be put through. Her journey through divorce wasn't over, but she was tired of punishing herself. Tired of hiding her story away in shame.

Trevor offered everything that she wanted—the spark and adventure, passion and excitement—all with the understanding of what she'd been through and who she was.

And tonight, she wanted to accept.

Chapter 24

"Tonight was like a fairy tale. The music, the princess dresses, the decorations. There was even a crown." Brooke turned her head, her eyes glistening and dark as they walked to his truck. "Thank you for inviting me."

Trevor opened the truck door for her. "You're welcome. You deserve some fairy-tale time."

She climbed in, silent and still as they drove out of town. "I never let myself enjoy the fairy tale before," she eventually whispered.

He nodded, but kept quiet.

"Except maybe as a child, but once I hit high school, even middle school…I was too busy chasing perfection. Working hard to have the best grades, be the best at all I did. Maybe that's why I kept all those toys. Deep down, I missed the fun. The dreaming."

"Makes sense."

"I thought if I found the perfect job and the perfect guy, with the perfect ambition, everything would magically be…"

"Perfect."

With a sniff, she nodded. "But that is not how it works. Not at all."

Trevor's stomach knotted at the raw pain in her voice.

"And as much as I know I can't blame myself for what our marriage turned into, I do blame myself for not paying attention to what really matters. What seems like a perfect guy can be a perfect monster if you aren't looking for what's important in a person."

"But you learned that. The lesson was painful, but you learned."

Brooke brushed her cheek. "Another one of life's experiences, huh?"

He reached for her hand, holding her tight. "A rough one, but yes."

She took his hand in both of hers. "I'm so glad I went to that beautiful party. You keep making me step outside of my comfort zone. Making me have more adventures, and that helps more than you'll ever know. I know I fought you at first."

Trevor laughed, the memory of her stiff-armed dancing, alone in Jolie's ballroom, one he'd never forget.

"But you didn't give up on me. You've taken me out of my comfort zone and made me feel safe."

"And you've done the same for me."

Her nose scrunched. "But everything is your comfort zone."

"This is probably true, but that's not what I'm talking about. You make me feel comfortable and, as hard as it may be to believe, that's no easy feat."

With a tilt of her head, Brooke studied him. "I don't under—"

"Believe it or not, I'm not superconventional."

Brooke gave him a soft smile. "No."

"And it took me a really long time to figure out what I wanted to do with my life. In a family full of these driven types, I was…I don't know, kind of all over the place. I didn't have Dev's passion or Roark and Sophie's focus. My family thought I was nuts for going to Peru. I'm pretty sure they still think I'm nuts. But when I told you, when I talk to you about how I feel, you understand."

She leaned forward, kissing him on the cheek as he drove. "I do understand. As different as we are, learning more about your history and your family, I get it."

They started up the mountain and Brooke tugged on his hand, drawing his gaze to hers.

"I don't want to go back to Jolie right now. I don't want to go back to reality and people yet."

He didn't either. They'd shared an amazing night, a fairy-tale date. He wanted this moment to never end. "I happen to know a place. And I won't make you walk far in those heels."

"My feet and I thank you."

Trevor headed straight for Honeywilde, but his destination wasn't the inn.

Brooke wanted to be alone, except for him. He wasn't going to examine his satisfaction too closely. Instead, he took a right, around the inn, and headed up the hillside to the handful of yurts on their property.

The area was almost pitch black, most of them vacant, and the only one occupied already had lights out.

"I know I said I didn't want to see people, but I also don't want to be taken into the woods and left for dead," Brooke joked.

He pulled up to the yurt farthest from the rest. "You're going to love this. Trust me."

"As crazy as it sounds, I do."

"Hang on a sec." Grabbing his Mag light from under his seat, he lit the short pathway to the yurt and unlocked the narrow door. Inside, he felt around for the lantern by the door and turned it on. As he switched on the lanterns that hung every two feet in the circular tent, a quaint little setting emerged.

A queen-sized bed, wood stove, woven rug, and two rocking chairs filled the space. On his rare day off, he'd come out here with Beau. Take a break from everything, as much as possible, and spend the night away from the inn and bustle.

By now, Beau was back at the inn, probably shacked up with Sophie, but tonight, he still wanted a break from the eyes and ears of the inn, and so did Brooke. His favorite yurt was perfect.

He returned to the truck and opened Brooke's door.

"What's this?" she asked with a smile on her face.

"A surprise. Follow me and you'll see."

A few steps led up to the yurt's entrance and Brooke gasped as they entered. "This is adorable. Look at this place." She passed him and went to the rocking chairs, running her fingers across the stained wood. "I love it."

"This is our best yurt, in my opinion. Nicer amenities for guests who want to be adventurous, but not too rustic."

The night air was cool enough for a fire, so Trevor grabbed a few of the chopped logs stacked beside the stove, a bit of newspaper, and the long lighter Honeywilde provided their guests. "Give me a minute or two and I'll unlock some next-level coziness."

Behind him, Brooke laughed and one of the rocking chairs began to creak. "I've never cared about camping, but I could get used to this."

Once satisfied the fire was going, he closed up the stove and joined her.

Brooke gently rocked her chair, her head tilted back, eyes closed. She'd taken her heels off and wiggled her toes into the faux fur carpet. "This is amazing."

"My pleasure."

She tilted her face in his direction, her eyes barely open to slits. "I mean it. No one's ever—I really appreciate this."

No one had ever done something like this for her.

But how could they resist? After being with her a few short days, surprising her, getting her to try something new and step out, brought him a kind of joy he'd never known.

His gaze locked with hers. Screw it. He let his cards show. "Seeing you happy makes me happy."

Her dark eyes glistened and he moved on pure instinct.

"Come here." He stood and she hurried into his arms.

She moved fast enough to knock some of the air from his lungs as she embraced him. He held her close. She didn't cry, but she clung to him, her face buried in his neck. They stayed that way forever, nothing but the sound of the crackling fire to fill the silence.

Brooke finally spoke, the words muffled against his chest. "You always smell so good."

"Yeah? I don't wear cologne."

A muffled laughed vibrated his chest. "Of course you don't."

He leaned back so he could see her face. "Could be my soap. I use this homemade stuff a lady in town makes."

"Of course you do." Brooke's smile was unmistakably fond, her gaze laced with desire. A man could melt into that look and live forever.

Trevor kissed her.

All the things he thought he'd never had, at once possible, even probable. He kissed her long and deep, hoping to push away the past, drive out the demons, until all that remained was the two of them.

Chapter 25

The idea of making Trevor as weak-kneed as he'd made her was a boon. Sucking at his bottom lip, a thrill of pride filled her when he groaned again. He pulled her closer, his hand in the small of her back, tilting her into him.

He kissed her cheek and along her jaw until he reached her neck. That same falling feeling returned. She hung on to him and reveled in the plunge.

"I want to stay the night," she managed to whisper. "Here. With you."

"Wasn't planning on leaving. Unless you kick me out."

Curling her fingers into his arm, she kissed him again. "No. I mean…I want us to be together tonight."

Trevor's blue eyes shined in the soft light. "I want that too." He placed a kiss low on her neck, then her shoulder.

"I wasn't ready before. Now I am."

"You tell me if it gets to be too much. If I need to slow down."

"I will."

He moved his lips lower. Kissing along her collar bone, into the dip of her dress. With one capable hand, he slid the zipper of her dress down, baring one shoulder completely.

Brooke tugged at his shirt frantically. Unsurprisingly less patient and lacking his finesse. A sudden need to touch him, skin against skin, took hold. As if he knew, Trevor chuckled, pulling away so that she could take his shirt off. She tossed it onto the floor of the yurt.

He reached for her, deftly unzipping her dress all the way, until the silk fell in an emerald pool at her feet.

A small place inside remained stunned with disbelief. She was undressing with a man. She was going to have sex. After all that had happened. After knowing what pain intimacy could bring.

A much louder voice reminded her she was with Trevor.

He wasn't like her ex. He wasn't like any man she'd ever met. Kind, compassionate, full of quirks and humor, and being built like an Adonis wasn't a drawback either.

Standing there, exposed and vulnerable, should have filled her with doubt and panic. But the heat in his gaze fired up completely different sensations.

Heat spread through her body, the promise of things to come bringing her senses to life.

Trevor skimmed the back of his hand across her collarbone, a content hum as he did. "You're exquisite, Brooke. And you should've never been made to feel like you aren't." He slid his hand up to cup her jaw and behind her ear. "I'm going to help you remember," he said, and crushed his lips against hers.

She clung to him, her arms around his waist, touching as much of that hot skin as she could.

There was no way all men felt this amazing. Nick certainly hadn't. The smooth skin of Trevor's back, covering taut muscle, was addictive. She didn't just want to touch; she wanted to taste him there. She wanted to kiss her way up his back and watch him shiver, because she knew he would.

The realization made her shiver. Trevor took a step away and then scooped her up into his arms.

A squeak of surprise before she giggled. "I never thought I'd be carried anywhere."

"Why?"

"I'm almost as tall as you. Tall girls don't get picked up."

He placed her gently on the bed. "Well, my tall girl does."

Her heart tripped up in its beating.

Trevor's gaze held a special something, a reflection of how she felt when she saw a beautiful sunrise. His girl.

The realization made her swallow down an ache in her throat. He meant exactly what he'd said.

Her skin grew warmer, probably flushing with color, and the corner of his mouth crooked up in response. He put a knee on the bed and leaned down to kiss her. Hooking a hand under each arm, he slid her farther back onto the bed.

His hands were warm and strong along her sides. She lay down, wanting to do the same to him, needing to touch more of him. She ran her hands up his bare chest, loving the hard muscle beneath her fingers. Smooth and strong, like his kisses. A shiver ran through him, and she triumphed. She did that.

Trevor eased back, his lips leaving hers. His gaze was so certain and reassuring. He let his hand drift from her chin, down the line of her neck as the shiver raced up her back. He took his time, the warm pads of his fingers branding her bare skin. Across her collar bone, over her shoulder, to lower one strap of her bra, his mouth followed, taking that brand to the bone.

He kissed over the crest of her breast, between her cleavage, using his hands to mold her taut. Her analytical mind suspended, she allowed all of her senses to take him in. The strength of his body against her, the sound of his lips against her skin, the feel as he sucked at her through the satin material, gently nipping.

She reached for the back of his head, threading her fingers through his thick hair, encouraging him, because *dear God*, that felt good.

Reaching the place where her neck met her shoulder, he paid special attention there, licking and sucking until she thought she'd arch right off of her spine. He slid his hands beneath her, maneuvering until the clasp of her bra gave and he slipped the garment off, tossing it aside.

Going against the doubt that always tortured her mind, she didn't hide herself from him. Trevor thought she was beautiful and she felt it.

He kissed her breasts again; this time sucking the bare skin, taunting with his tongue until the sensation coursed through to her core, making her squirm.

She reached for him, tilting his head up. She'd go mad if he kept at that sensitive area. He pulled away and bent lower.

His lips were hot against her stomach, dipping lower again. Part of her still couldn't believe she was doing this, but she wanted him. All of him.

The silk fabric of her panties brushed her thighs as Trevor slid them off. She was completely naked and she made herself look him in the eyes.

His gaze hooded with heat, his touch strong, the last of her nerves dissolved to leave only desire.

Trevor slid lower on the bed, dragging his lips down her body in a heated trail. She moved her legs to accommodate him. He kissed her hip, over her tummy. At the first heated pass of his tongue, right over her core, she tensed.

He eased back. "You okay?"

"Yes." She made herself take a deep breath.

"I can go slower. Or stop."

"No!" She laughed at her empathic response. "No, it's not that."

His expression softened. "Then tell me."

She looked away. "It's been a long time since…I wasn't with someone who liked…"

"He didn't want to go down on you?" Trevor came right out and said it, like they were talking about the weather. Except someone just said they didn't like seventy-five-degree days with low humidity and a light breeze.

Brooke touched her flaming hot cheek. "No, he did not."

"Well, we've already established he's made of wrongness, so..." Trevor leaned up and kissed her stomach, then her hip. "Relax. I want this. You want this. Don't overthink it. I'll try to help you stop thinking at all."

With a laugh, she lay back. She wasn't a virgin, but with him, she understood desire and true pleasure for the first time. Sad, but true. Trevor bathed her with such attention and affection. It was an overload. But it felt like the overload she'd always wanted. The one she'd been missing.

His shoulders bumped her thighs as he lifted her knee and angled her legs. Then his lips touched her and—

"Oh God." Brooke arched her lower back.

The world and everything in it was suddenly...*amazing*.

She dug her fingers into the down comforter.

Trevor's tongue was warm and insistent. Long strokes and quick sucks and then he stopped to nip at the inside of each thigh before starting again. She wasn't completely sure all that he was doing down there and she didn't care. Because she was going to lose her *Ever*. Loving. Mind.

When his mouth descended upon her the third time, Brooke squeezed her eyes closed. She wanted to moan, her legs stiffening. She wanted to squirm. She wanted more. Less? No. More. Definitely more. The pleasure inside her built again like before.

He didn't let up, even as she brushed her hand across the back of his head.

"Trevor, I..." She couldn't finish her sentence.

Her. Unable to speak. Instead, she moaned. Loud. She sounded so needy, so carnal, a sensual shock to her ears.

She never would've guessed.

Trevor made his now familiar humming noise against her, and she gasped. Every sensation focused down on the bundle of nerves inside her that he coaxed relentlessly.

The wave began to crest and her orgasm crashed down. She dug her fingers into his shoulder, riding out the bliss.

The last trills of her climax passed while Trevor pressed kisses up her leg, across her stomach, and over her breasts until finally his gaze met hers.

She bit at her bottom lip, gazing up at him as tremors still shook her legs. "I can't believe I grabbed you like that."

He grinned, his hair a tossed mess of dark waves. "Does it look like I mind?"

* * * *

Trevor leaned back, kneeling between her legs so he could take in the view of the woman before him. Lying there, relaxed yet still sensually regal, and smiling up at him like she couldn't be more pleased. Or satisfied.

Maybe it made him a heel, but a wave of pride washed over him from causing that look.

He kissed his way up her body to brace his hands on either side of her head. "You good?"

A wicked twinkle lit her eyes as she shook her head. "Good is not the word I'd use." She danced her fingers up his sides, making him twitch. She explored his chest and arms. "I want to touch you."

"You are touching me. And driving me crazy, I might add."

"No, I mean *touch* you."

One of her hands disappeared. His breath left him as she tentatively cupped her hand against him. He closed his eyes because they were rolling back into his head.

"Brooke," he moaned as she stroked along his length. "You're going to kill me."

Her exploration was gentle and just enough to torture him. When he could take no more, he pressed her hand firm against his erection. "But you won't break me."

Her wisp of laughter filled his head as she stroked him harder, longer. She wrestled with the button and zipper, and he helped her slip his pants down, over his hips, until he was naked beside her.

Brooke looked down at him and bit her bottom lip with a grin. "My goodness."

A chuckle bubbled up in his throat. "You say the nicest things."

She touched him, running her fingertips all the way down his length.

The pleasure in her expression was a high. He had to look away or risk racing to the finish line. Being with her was more daring and adventurous than anything he'd done over the years. Because he cared. This meant more than one or two nights, or even a few weeks of exploration and pleasure. She mattered.

It was a new feeling, and his blood sang at the prospect.

This was more than he'd ever hoped for, but not all that he wanted.

Brooke leaned up to kiss him full on the mouth. "I want to feel you inside of me. Do you have—"

"I do." Trevor jumped up, digging for his wallet. He climbed back onto the bed.

Brooke opened the foil square and helped him put the condom on with the same delicate touch from before. The way she bit at her lip in concentration, showing him even more intense attention than she gave everything else. She finished and lay back, pulling him forward with her, kissing him, her tongue a sweeping, open invitation. Her legs rubbed against him, cradling him, welcoming him to ravish.

"Just go slow, okay?" she asked. "It's been a while."

He kissed her and guided himself inside her. He leaned back and eased in as slowly as he could.

Her lids fluttered before she squeezed them shut. "Trevor," she whispered on an exhale.

He loved hearing his name like that. Like she didn't know what to do and couldn't be bothered to care. Running a hand up her body, he brushed his thumb against her cheek, prompting her to open her eyes. He wanted to see her as he buried himself inside of her, wanted her to see him as he pushed forward. She surrounded him and leaned forward, kissing the places his thumb touched.

Inside her, he remained perfectly still.

Brooke's eyes sparkled. This time it was his laugh that was full of nerves.

She moved her hips, taking him all the way in. That simple friction shook him. She was so tight and perfect; there was no way he'd last if she got it in her mind to move about and help.

He touched her hips as he pulled back and into her again. Intent with his movement, he rocked into her again and again, until the tension in her body melted and she moved with him. She moaned, reaching up to hold on to his arms, fingers digging into his biceps.

"More," she said in a breathy exhale.

He lost what little restraint he'd clung to.

Shifting, he steadied himself with his hands on either side of her shoulders and thrust into her. He kept moving, the pleasure building until he had to bank it by biting down on his lip. Brooke moved too, wrapping her legs around him. Those long legs that looked too good in heels. Trevor tilted his head back, forcing himself not to think much about it. She already felt too good. If he started envisioning those heels still on...

She arched against him again, the same hungry moan from before. He didn't want it to end, but with how she felt and those noises, his body didn't care for waiting. He lifted one hand to touch her, searching for the bundle of nerves that would send her over the edge with him. He couldn't stop what was about to run over him like a runaway freight train, but by God, he wasn't going alone. He leaned over, increasing the angle of her hips. Surrounded by her, the feel, the smell, the look, her gentle moans rising up like blessings, he pinched his eyes shut, his body starting to shake.

"Trevor," she inhaled sharply, her body going taut so he knew what was coming. He felt it too. Her legs tightened around him, urging him on. When she started making indiscernible noises, he swore to himself that he wouldn't stop until she cried out.

Her body clenched and shook with her climax as her nails bit into his skin.

Trevor let himself go. His orgasm didn't just hit him. It jumped the tracks and took him with it, rocking him to his spine. Pretty sure he went blind for a moment, he held on to Brooke and the bed.

Moments later, she spoke. "That was…" Her voice came out raspy. "*Wow.*"

He managed a shaky laugh. "My thoughts exactly."

Chapter 26

This time, when she stretched her leg out beneath the covers, her toes came in contact with one toasty warm, muscular calf. Brooke tried to wriggle her feet underneath Trevor's leg.

"Good God, your feet are cold," he mumbled, rolling from his back to face her.

"Sorry." Not really, she wasn't.

He rubbed the side of his face against the pillow, eyes still closed. The action made his hair fluff up with static, his face unfairly youthful in sleep. "S'okay. Remind me to start keeping extra socks in my truck though."

Brooke's chest tightened, a longing in her heart stretching toward something warm and safe, yet terrifying.

He said the words so casually, like it'd be no big deal for him to start carrying around articles of clothing for her. For whenever her feet got cold, any time they were together. He said it as though this would happen frequently, both them spending the night together and her icicle toes.

His comment was offhand, his voice still raspy with dreams. Trevor didn't speak with any significant intentions—he was just being Trevor—but her heart held onto his heavy words, and relished the weight.

"Hey." He stirred again, pulling the pile of covers up to tuck under his chin. "I'm hungry. How do you feel about breakfast?"

"I'm a big, big breakfast fan."

"Best meal of the day." He grinned. "Let's run up to the inn. It's still early enough to beat the crowd."

Brooke sat up, suddenly wide awake. "Um…no. I'm not going into your family's restaurant for early-morning breakfast in the same dress I had on last night."

"Why not?"

"Trevor."

"Have I told you how much I love it when you say my name all outragey and indignant?"

"My dress is rumpled. You've got…sex hair. It'd be wildly inappropriate."

"If we went to breakfast naked, *that* would be wildly inappropriate."

She shook her head, not unlike a petulant child.

"I don't care if they know we spent the night together. I want them to know."

Brooke rubbed her eyes, blinking his words into focus. "You do?"

Private, casual-about-everything Trevor wanted his family to know, without question, that they were together.

"Yeah. I do. And need I to remind you that my sister and her not-yet-boyfriend Wright came over to Jolie for, and I quote, business, and ended up having to check in so they could get it on? All of which you bore witness to. I don't think my family is worried about what's appropriate. They're not going to judge us and I'm really, really hungry."

Defiant, her stomach chose that moment to growl. Loudly.

"Uh-huh. See? Breakfast. You know you want some."

Guilty as charged. She could eat half a dozen pieces of bacon right now. And waffles. So many waffles.

Even her strong sense of pride took a backseat to morning hunger and her love of breakfast food. "I'm not saying yes, but I *am* hungry. I'd need to wash up first. I don't want to look like I spent the night in a yurt."

"Even though we did."

"And I don't want to wear this dress and heels."

His eyes glinted mischievously.

"I don't mean go naked," she interjected before he could say it.

"We can swing by my room to freshen up, and I'll get Sophie to loan you some clothes."

"I'm at least half a foot taller than your sister."

"Then Madison's clothes. She'll have something you can wear. Sophie can get them for us. Leave the logistics up to me and let's get breakfast. Bacon." He dragged out the word. "Mmm. Bacon, bacon, bacon."

Brooke shoved him until he fell over in the bed, both of them laughing.

After returning to the inn and finding Sophie, Brooke was comfortably dressed in yoga pants and a T-shirt for some marathon she would never run in a million years.

"That's the best I could do while stealing clothes." Sophie handed her a pair of flip-flops. "And these should work. Trevor said you like flip-flops." She winked.

"That'll be enough, sis. Thanks."

"Yes. These are great, Sophie. Thank you." She prayed her cheeks didn't flush while Sophie bobbed on the balls of her feet, radiating satisfaction.

"You going to have breakfast with us, sis? Or are you going to keep standing there, looking like Roark after he balanced a checkbook?"

With a roll of her eyes, Sophie led the way to Bradley's, Honeywilde's renowned restaurant.

The crowd blessedly sparse this early in the morning, they found a prime table in the corner, by the windows.

Brooke ordered the waffles and a side of bacon. Sophie ditto-ed her order while Trevor got the special.

Slapping his hands together, he eagerly glanced around the restaurant. "Not many people here yet. Our food will be out in no time."

"Eh, I wouldn't get too excited." Sophie picked up her coffee mug, the steam rising in front of her face. "After the big party last night, Marco has the morning off. Our backup chef is working. I don't know how speedy she'll be."

"I have faith." Trevor reached for the basket in the center of the table, holding it out for Brooke. "And biscuits."

Her stomach cut a cartwheel in celebration. "Yes, please." This morning, she was going to carbo-load like she might actually train for that half marathon her t-shirt advertised.

Trevor and Sophie took a biscuit as well, and they were halfway through them when Sophie smacked her lips together and turned all of her attention toward Brooke.

"So are you two going to go to prom together?"

Brooke almost choked on her coffee.

"Sophie," Trevor warned.

"What? That's a legitimate question. You guys have planned the thing. I'm assuming you're going to be there anyway, and now y'all are..." She bobbed her shoulders up and down.

"What the hell is that?" Trevor bit into the second half of his biscuit, mimicking her shoulder shrugging.

"You know."

"We haven't discussed attending the prom." Brooke attempted to save them both.

"You should," Sophie said, with the certainty of an expert. "It'd be so romantic and fun. I guarantee you proms are more fun as an adult than they ever were as a teenager. I'd go if I could."

Brooke shook her head, but her gaze locked with Trevor's as she lifted her coffee mug.

"We'll think about it," he said.

"You're up early." Roark appeared at their table, focusing on Trevor, until his gaze fell upon the non-Bradley at the table. "Oh. Good morning."

She had nothing to be ashamed of. All the same, she wanted the floor to open up and swallow her whole.

The morning was too new for any sane business meeting, and she was sitting there in Roark's girlfriend's T-shirt with her hair in a ponytail. Didn't require a rocket scientist to solve the reason for her early-morning presence.

To his credit, Roark took only half a second to measure his reaction and plant a placid smile on his lips. Anything he said would only make the moment more awkward, but they were all adults. Let the awkwardness fly.

"I guess the prom planning *is* going well." As soon as the words were out of his mouth, he grimaced. "I didn't mean—"

"Sit down." Trevor pushed out the empty chair. "We know what you meant. You tried and it's the thought that counts. And yes, Brooke and I had a slumber party last night."

Brooke hid behind her coffee mug as their food arrived.

Roark sat and nodded for some coffee. "Not everyone has your Teflon self-confidence, Trev. Don't embarrass your guest."

"Are you embarrassed?" Trevor huddled close, his hand on her arm.

"Not really, which is shocking." She dropped her hands. "But it is a little awkward, seeing everyone like this."

"Please." Sophie waved a fork in her general direction. "No makeup and a T-shirt on and you're still more glamorous than me."

"And that's one of my favorite T-shirts. First marathon Madison and I ran together." Roark smirked as he sipped his coffee.

"We're family here. It's fine." Trevor rubbed her arm before letting go.

Brooke concentrated on eating her waffles.

Dev was the last to join them, with a casual smile in her direction. "I just got off the phone with the treasurer of the school board."

Brooke dropped her fork.

"And?" Trevor asked.

"I told her about you and Brooke and what you found out, and she's going to get someone to look into it. I don't know what all that means or how long it'll take, but I do know that was one angry lady when she found out. But she said to tell you both thank you, and she'll keep me posted."

Brooke sat back, a weird, warm sensation washing over her.

With a huff of laughter, Trevor sat back too. "Newton is a small town like Windamere. Even smaller. I bet they'll have the full scoop in no time. Somebody around there knows all."

"Nice work," Roark said. "If you got all of that money back, you guys might be the heroes of Windamere High."

Brooke couldn't imagine. Helping right that wrong was a different kind of success, a fulfillment she hadn't experienced in years. It wouldn't even matter if anyone recognized her as heroic.

"I was telling them earlier, they should go to the prom together." Sophie bit into a strip of bacon with a smile.

"That's a great idea," Roark said, echoing her sentiment.

"And we're thinking about it." Trevor gave them both a barbed stare. "But right now, we have a lot more work to do."

His entire family appeared stunned. Brooke probably wore a similar expression.

That was her line!

The Bradleys quickly moved on to the subject of the Blueberry Festival and all it entailed. The Sargents and Chateau Jolie had never done much with the festival. The event brought in a few more guests, but that's where their involvement ended.

"You guys should do a booth this year." Sophie clapped her hands together at her own suggestion. "Yes! You have to. You could do, like, a wine and cheese booth with promotional stuff for the hotel and winery."

The price of a booth had likely increased to something out of their price range. She'd love to do something for Jolie, but right now wasn't the time to spend hundreds on a booth with no return on investment. And she didn't want to sound rude.

Trevor came to her rescue. "Let us get through the prom first. Then Brooke can give the Festival some thought. There will still be booth opportunities available then, right?"

"Of course." Sophie's warm-natured smile radiated the kind of positivity Brooke envied. "Brooke gets the friends-and-family deal."

Friends and family.

A year ago, she never would've imagined a world in which the Bradleys would be either.

Chapter 27

"I can't believe you guys pulled this off." Even Lance, with all his restraint and deadpan delivery, appeared impressed.

"With a couple of days to spare," Trevor pointed out.

He and Brooke had worked tirelessly on Monday and Tuesday to get as much done as possible.

The tables were arranged in the ballroom, fully set up with centerpieces and chairs. The stage was up, lanterns out. Brenda had already brought over the artificial greenery, with the real flowers arriving Saturday around lunch.

Brooke had convinced a local restaurant to do the catering, at cost. Splitting the difference between fancy and chicken fingers, they were going to have skewers, a carving station, and a hot buffet line of side dish options. They'd also have nonalcoholic drinks and a creative punch to match the "Enchanted Garden" theme.

The morning after Brooke spent the night, they'd managed to sweet-talk Sophie into having Honeywilde provide their famous cookies, along with a few cakes as dessert.

Everything was coming together, but only because he and Brooke had worked their butts off.

All of that butt-working left precious little time for him to even touch Brooke since Saturday. They'd been in full professional mode for days.

Not that there was anything wrong with professional Brooke.

He admired and respected her. But he missed barefoot-yoga Brooke, almost as much as he missed naked-in-the-yurt Brooke.

"The prom is going to look magical." Dorian clutched her hands to her chest with no small amount of dramatic flair.

They hadn't told Dorian or Lance about what they'd found at Zen. No point in getting their hopes up if justice couldn't prevail and they weren't going to dump news of a scam on these kids right before their prom.

"That's our goal," Trevor said. "Mrs. Brenda is bringing in roses on Saturday and, with the lighting and tulle garland, you should have your perfect enchanted evening."

"Are you ready for the big night?" Brooke asked.

Dorian practically vibrated with excitement. "Yes! You have no idea. My mom and I went to Atlanta in February to find my dress. Mrs. Brenda's daughter is doing my hair." She tucked her hands under her braids as though to demonstrate. "And Lance got the best-looking tux you've ever seen."

Lance took Dorian's hand and weaved their fingers together. "I told her she better pace herself or she'll crash before the prom even gets here."

Trevor gaped at the PDA coming from the conservative jock.

"And I reminded him this *is* my pace. All day, every day." Dorian smiled up at him like he'd hung the moon.

"So, you two are each other's dates?"

"Now we are." Dorian swatted Lance's arm, good-naturedly. "It took him a little while to get the hint."

"I had no idea you were interested in me. Not like that, anyway."

Trevor laughed. "I did."

Both teenagers turned to him.

"It's true," Brooke said, backing him up. "He said something the very first day you guys were here."

"I saw how he looked at you." Trevor pointed at Lance. "And I caught Dorian giving you heart eyes when she thought no one was paying attention."

"Okay, embarrassing much?" Dorian buried her face in her hands and laughed.

"What about you two?" Lance turned the tables on him. "You're coming to the prom too, right?"

"Yes," Dorian added, emphatically. "You have to join us, all dressed up and prom-appropriate."

He and Brooke shared a knowing glance.

"We'll be around if you need us, but—"

"*No.* We want you guys to really come. Together. As prom guests."

Brooke's bottom lip pulled sideways like it was caught on a hook. "I don't know about all that."

"Come on. Please? We couldn't have done this without you. You have to come. You deserve to celebrate this as much as us. You can get dressed up. It'll be fun. Lance, tell them."

"Yeah, you have to come."

Trevor was in one hundred percent agreement. Never in his life had he turned down an invitation to a party. He might not own a tux, but he could find one on short notice if need be. All Brooke had to do was say the word.

"We'll think about it," she said instead. "But Saturday is your night. Not ours."

Also true. Mostly. Then again, he and Brooke, all decked out and cutting up the dance floor? Twist his arm.

"Saturday can be everyone's night." Dorian's smile filled the ballroom. "None of this would even be happening without you two. Promise you'll really think about it."

Brooke's gaze glanced off his once more. "We promise," she said.

As soon as the two teens left the ballroom, Trevor took her hand, tugging her closer. "Finally, a moment alone."

Brooke leaned into him, effortlessly. "A moment is all we have. I have a call with a woman from the tourism office. We're updating the print advertising in all of the travel brochures and booklets, to highlight our pet-friendliness. Thanks to you."

"A moment is all I need." He brushed his lips over hers and she opened to his kiss.

With a hand in the small of her back, he moved closer, until her body pressed against him.

He swept his tongue against hers, eliciting a groan before she pulled away. "This only leads to more than a moment."

"Boo," he whispered. "You're being so practical and responsible. Boo."

Brooke's laughter chimed like bells, making his heart grow heavy. "After this prom, we'll have plenty of time to kiss in ballrooms and dance and—"

"Spend the night in yurts?"

"Yes, that too."

He hadn't let go and he leaned his forehead against hers. "Good. I'm going to hold you to all of this, you know?"

"I'm sure."

"Slumber parties in yurts, the occasional morning of yoga and lunch of Larb, perhaps I'll even get you to go on a trip with me."

Her laughter shook her ribs against the palm of his hand. "If I ever have the time to travel, as unlikely as that is to happen, then sure. I will go on a trip with you."

"Don't be so doubtful. I foresee great things ahead for Jolie and you and your sisters. You never know, you might be spending a couple of weeks in South America with me before the year is out."

This time her entire body shook with laughter. "If you say so." She kissed him again. Quick and playfully on the lips. "Until then, I'm going to meet with this marketing rep and try to drum up some business. I'll see you tomorrow to meet with the DJ and make sure he's all set."

"You will indeed." Trevor returned her flirtatious affection, but he wasn't kidding.

He wanted more with Brooke. Possibly even a future.

The future wasn't something he often considered.

With a wave he left Jolie and headed back to Honeywilde and Beau.

His poor dog was surviving on only about fifty percent of the usual attention and affection Trevor gave him, and this afternoon he had some time to right that wrong.

He'd pulled into a parking space at Honeywilde when his phone rang. He thought nothing of it when he saw his buddy Bobby's, aka DJ Knight's, number come up.

"Hey, Bobby," he answered.

A hoarse, hacking cough had Trevor jerking his phone away from his ear. "Hey, man," Bobby finally managed.

Uh-oh.

DJ Knight sounded like he was dying, sinuses first.

"You okay?" Trevor put his truck in park, silently praying that this was not happening.

"Not good, man. Not good at all." Bobby started hacking again, his voice sounding like he had about a pound of cotton balls shoved up both nostrils. "I got the flu."

"No, Bobby. *No.*" His tone came out a lot harsher than he'd anticipated. "How can you have the flu? Flu season is over."

"I don't know. I'm not a doctor. But today, the nurse said flu season ain't over until May. I had to cancel my out-of-town gig. And this prom. Everything hurts, man. Everything."

"I know. I'm sorry. I didn't mean to yell, just…" This was a big deal. The seniors of Windamere were counting on him.

Brooke was counting on him.

"I'm sorry," Bobby said. "I even called a friend of mine in the business, but he's booked already."

Trevor scrubbed a hand over his face.

Think, think, think.

He had to fix this. Brooke was going to freak out.

But how?

"You know I'd do it if I could. Doc put me on Tamiflu, but it ain't doing jack that I can tell. If I feel better in the next couple of days—"

"No, you won't feel better that fast, Bobby. You just came down with it today?"

"Like out of nowhere. I've never been run over, but I woke up feeling like I had."

"Yeah, you're going to be down for the count for a least a week. Unfortunately, I've been there. You puke yet?"

"Oh God, dude. I feel like I'm going to right now."

Trevor closed his eyes and pressed the back of his head against the headrest.

The words "backup plan" marched through his mind in a military formation.

The notion was ludicrous. They didn't have the money for that, but Brooke was right. He'd celebrated too soon.

"Is there anything I can do?" Bobby asked.

"No, I wish. Right now you just have to concentrate on getting better."

But Trevor couldn't wait and hope DJ Knight might emerge victorious from Bobby's influenza within a few days, ready to DJ a prom.

Only in his dreams.

"Go rest," Trevor told him. "Lots of water and sleep and Tylenol. That's about all you can do."

"Thanks. Again, I'm sorry."

As he said goodbye, he told Bobby, once more, this wasn't his fault.

This was Trevor's fault.

He ran inside and called every good DJ he could think of. Then every halfway decent one.

Nothing. Even crap DJs were booked.

The prom was two days away, and he'd failed.

Chapter 28

Brooke's office bordered on arctic and she cupped both hands around her coffee as she waited on her computer to wake up.

Two days until the prom and everything was lined up and ready to go. At least she could breathe easier about that, because there was no breathing at all when it came to the hotel's finances.

As she entered her password, Beans scampered into her office, helping himself to her lap.

The chateau's accounts stared back at her from the monitor, in all their gaunt glory.

"Things don't look too good, Beans." She scratched the center of his head.

Beans was decidedly more optimistic, his curly tail wagging as much as it could.

The prom this weekend would drum up some publicity, but that wouldn't be enough. The local paper was running an article on what Jolie was doing for the school—Honeywilde included, though that didn't bother her quite as much as before—and she'd gotten one of the regional TV news channels to do a segment on it. Still, buzz took a while to build and they needed the income sooner rather than later.

"Maybe pooch people will start noticing our ads and checking in." Brooke scratched behind one ear, glancing down into his soulful black eyes.

He tilted his head back and forth, as if trying to understand.

She'd run the promo for a pet-friendly Jolie too, but so far, no bump in bookings.

"There he is." Laurel approached her desk and tilted her head, looking a bit like a confused puppy herself. "Were you talking to the dog?"

"No."

Laurel stared, expressionless.

"Maybe."

"Awwww."

"Don't start."

"You're bonding."

Brooke handed Beans over. "I can't help it. He's cute and comforting."

Laurel cradled Beans like a baby, and then spoke to him like one. "You are cute and comforting, aren't you? Are you as cute and comforting as Trevor Bradley? I think you are. Yes, I do. Yes, I do."

"Laurel."

"I'm surprised he was with you, is all. And call me crazy, but you looked like you were enjoying the quality Beans time. Last month, he wouldn't have set foot in here without me." Laurel studied Brooke, understanding in her steady gaze. An awareness that was far too keen for comfort. "Dogs sense a lot, you know."

"So you've told me."

"Because it's true."

Another long, unnerving silence. Is this what Trevor meant by the Sargent stare?

Laurel bounced Beans over to her hip. "You're happy, and Beans can sense that. Happiness suits you, sis."

"Thank you."

She turned to go, but pointed to Brooke's inbox. "And please go through your mail. It's slowly taking over the office."

A potential avalanche of envelopes filled the decorative metal bin.

Brooke gave the pile of papers the side-eye. Her focus needed to be on chateau financials, not dozens of solicitations, catalogs, and inescapable invoices.

She poked at the pile like she was poking at a bear. The tower toppled to the side, glossy postcards and stock paper envelopes sliding across the mahogany top of her desk.

One envelope stood out among the rest. Creamy white, high-quality stock, with gold embossing on the envelope.

She knew that look well. Her attorney was the only contact she had who'd spend that kind of money on mail.

As she reached for the thick envelope, a crater opened up in her stomach.

For days she'd avoided her attorney's calls and voice mails. She'd called the Barracuda back once and the short conversation was more than enough. Nick wanted more. He wanted Jolie. He wanted her soul, and

Brooke refused to let him have it, no matter how much she had to pay her attorney to fight him.

What more was there to say on the matter?

With her mother's old letter opener, she sliced through the top of the envelope and tried to steady her breathing with a sip of coffee.

She read a few key words and set her coffee down to keep from dropping it.

Definition of marital property.

Defendant seeks negotiation.

Acquired asset.

Equitable distribution of property.

This whole ordeal was only about money. She had to remember that. More precisely, who ended up with the most money in the end.

Like everything else with him, this was a competition for Nick and he didn't want Brooke to win. She might've been the one to leave, but he'd be the one triumphant.

Trevor's words pushed through her mind. Her ex's bitterness and anger weren't her fault. This had nothing to do with her, and Nick's misery wasn't because she was a bad person.

She knew that now.

Still, the attack stung. Even though she knew it was coming, his destructive greed hurt.

Her ex-husband's attorney's signature filled the bottom corner of the last page, scrawled in in inky, jagged lines.

She hated that signature. Hated the stupid, pompous twenty-four-pound paper he used and its cream color, because twenty-one pound in ivory wasn't fancy enough. She hated that this paper and these letters were the last bastion of communication she had with a man she struggled not to despise, the last link to a part of her life that she wanted to leave far behind.

But Nick wouldn't let her.

Brooke's gaze caught on the words *Equitable distribution of property.* "Equitable distribution, my patoot."

Nick only cared about winning, and that meant getting more money. She had precious little money. All she had was Jolie and he could *not* have it.

Paying her ex alimony was ludicrous to begin with. The judge didn't think so, but it wasn't her fault Nick had scuttled his career and she'd been successful.

She removed the do not disturb flag on her phone and finally forced herself to scan through Nick's texts.

We're not done. If you don't want this to get worse, you'll call me.

She opened her mouth to scream. But there could be guests in the lobby.

She grabbed the nearest thing. Her planner. And launched it across the room. The space was wide enough that the planner didn't hit anything except the floor. Dozens of notes and memos flew out, scattering across the floor.

He couldn't have Jolie. Her attorney would never let that happen. But in his attempt, he kept stopping her from moving on. He kept his claws dug into her life.

She was finally moving on. Trevor had strolled into her life and brought some calm and contentment. A chance at happiness was something she believed in again, but true happiness remained out of reach, because Brooke would be dealing with this...with her ex...forever.

Nick won, even if he was awarded nothing.

And she hated him.

It was wrong to hate. Bad for the soul. But hate him, she did.

Grinding down on her back teeth, she clenched her fists until her nails bit into the skin of her palm.

Maybe she would scream after all. Who cared what the guests thought? Not like there were a ton of them checked into the chateau anyway.

Nick brought out her absolute worst.

Four years she'd put up with living like this. The accusations, the cruel comments. Now that she'd finally fought back, the situation kept getting worse.

Brooke crumpled and threw the letter.

She should burn it.

Nick's attorney claimed that Chateau Jolie was worth more than reported, and that the property was Brooke's while they were married.

She'd never worked for Jolie or had any part of it while they were married. He couldn't come after her family's hotel and vineyard.

But he could try.

She remembered thanking God that they never had children; otherwise she'd never be rid of him. Now it seemed he was going to stay in her life forever anyway.

Finally, she did scream.

The agonizing sound had to come out.

She screamed at the monster he'd become, or maybe he'd always been one. She screamed for the life she wanted without him but couldn't attain. And she screamed at the young woman she'd been. The woman who was stupid enough to let him into her life.

Moments later, Reagan was in her office, panic stricken. "Are you okay? If you saw a rat, I'm going to die."

Brooke fought back the tears.

Not of hurt. She'd gotten over being hurt years ago.

Fury. She wanted to punch somebody.

"Uh-oh." Reagan's face fell. "Nick."

Brooke nodded and swallowed the knot in her throat. "His attorney has filed a motion. I got a letter from my attorney. He's going through with trying to take part of Jolie."

"That's bullshit!"

"I know."

"He won't win."

"I know."

"Everything was in Mom and Dad's name until last year."

"I know."

"You have to fight him."

"Reagan," she snapped, "I know. But fighting him will cost money. Money that we don't have."

"I don't care." Her sister, always "ready, fire, aim," thrust out her chin and pointed her finger at no one in particular. "If we have to sell off everything that isn't vital and live off beans for a year, we'll do it. We are not giving up any part of Jolie to that a-hole. If I need to start dating the honorable old Herbert Allen to get some free court costs, I'll do it," Reagan said, referring to the ancient judge who ruled over the city courthouse downtown. "I mean, he's about ninety, but whatever."

The knot returned to Brooke's throat as she laughed.

Reagan was bossy and overdramatic, but fiercely loyal. She meant every word she said. Ninety-year-old boyfriend and all.

But they weren't going to starve or date Herbert Allen.

Brooke sighed.

She didn't have the answer, but somehow, she'd save Jolie.

Chapter 29

Trevor's guard went up the moment he walked into Jolie.

A thick sense of dread filled the air, and not just because he was walking to the gallows.

Something dire had already gone down at the chateau.

He made his way to Brooke's office. The door was closed. He knocked.

"What?" With a jerky motion, the door opened. Brooke stood, grim, on the other side. "Oh, hey." Her planner clutched to her chest, she grabbed a handful of papers off the floor.

"Hey." He eased into the room like easing around a snake. "Everything okay?"

His bad news about the DJ needed to wait for another day. Except, they didn't have other days.

"Just dandy. You?" Brooke's tone was tight, her posture rigid, as she stood and returned to her desk to put down everything in her hands.

Trevor cut through the bullshit rather than dance around the pile. "You're upset. What's going on?"

She searched her office with the most hopeless, lost gaze he'd ever seen on her face.

"Brooke." He moved closer and placed his hand on her arm. "Seriously. Are you okay?"

"Not really." She tossed a hand up in the air, dislodging his touch. "Same stuff as always. Can't get away from it, no matter what I do or how hard I try." With a glance toward him, she laughed, but the sound held no humor. "No matter who I meet."

He rubbed the arm he touched. "Okay. I might need a little more to go on. I'm not following."

"I'm trying to run a business and…I can't."

"What are you talking about? You aren't trying; you're doing it."

"No. I'm failing. I'm failing my family and myself, Jolie is struggling, and all of this on top of trying to leave a life behind that won't let me go. My sisters want to help and they love me, but this is my fault. I should be able to clean up the mess I made, but I can't. It's too much, Trevor."

"I know." He held her arms again, rubbing them as he led her toward the chairs that faced her desk.

Brooke was spiraling.

He wasn't clear on exactly what she meant or what catalyst caused this whirlpool, but he had to figure it out if he was going to help.

Finally, she sat and he took the seat next to her.

"What's going on?" he tried again.

Brooke simply shook her head, her glassy-eyed gaze a thousand miles away.

"You know I'll listen. I'm here for you."

This brought her gaze to his. "I know. You're…" She reached over, sliding her fingers across his forearm to hold on. "You've been nothing but good to me. You don't need to get dragged into all this."

"This what?" He placed his hand over hers.

"Jolie. The mess we're in. Things are only going to get harder around here."

"I've been through hard times. For a long time."

"I know, but if you think I'm a lot to deal with now, there's no telling how bad I'll be in the next few months."

"Who said I think you're a lot to deal with now?"

Brooke Sargent's stare bore into his skull. "I know I'm a lot to deal with."

"So?"

"The new pet-friendly advertising isn't working. The publicity from sponsoring the prom isn't working. Nothing is working. We're still losing money left and right because we can't book rooms."

"You need more time. The promo only hit recently. Seeing results takes a few weeks, at least. You know this."

"Doesn't matter what I know. I don't have a few weeks."

He had no response. Unless Jolie's situation was a lot direr than she initially let on, they should be able to wait a few weeks or even a few months for the buzz and promo to kick in.

"What can I do?" he asked.

"Nothing. I could use a hug though."

"Of course." He stood, opening his arms. He embraced her in the warmest hug he'd ever offered. If he could chase away her problem he would.

"At least the prom is progressing without a hitch," she said.

His stomach dropped. "Um. I do have some bad news about the DJ."

Brooke stiffened in his arms.

"Still fixable, somehow, but the guy I booked has the flu. He canceled on me last night."

She lurched away. "Last night. Are you freaking kidding me? And you're only telling me now?"

"Because I was trying to find someone else. Literally all night long."

"I knew this would happen." With a squint and pursed lips, Brooke appeared ready to choke someone.

That someone didn't need to be him.

Brooke turned, digging her hands into her hair as she put several feet between them. "What are we going to do?"

"I don't know, but I'm working on it. I'll figure something out."

"How? You said you stayed up all night looking for someone else. Did you find anyone?"

"No." He grimaced.

"Then there you go." She threw her hands up. "We're screwed."

"No, we aren't. Very worst-case scenario, I'll get some speakers and a Spotify list. I have great taste in music."

"No!" she snapped. "That's exactly what Lance was going to do before, and we told them we would do better."

"But in a worst-case scenario, we'll have to do whatever we can. Those kids won't be upset. Not with everything else they're getting."

"*I* will be upset." Brooke jabbed her finger against her chest. "*I* care. We have to fix this."

"I'm trying," he promised.

Instead of a vote of confidence, Brooke scoffed, walking away to pace her office.

"I am."

"I told you we needed a backup plan. I told you we couldn't celebrate too soon."

"I know. But I couldn't predict the flu. What was I supposed to do?"

"Your job, Trevor."

He refused to flinch at the edge in her voice or the jab at his competence. No way was this all about him and a DJ emergency. Something more was going wrong here.

A pile of papers filled her desk, all of them folded as if from envelopes.

He stepped closer to her desk, getting a better look. There were letters, formal looking, not invoices or advertisements. He couldn't make out all of the words, but he saw enough.

"What's all this?"

Brooke shrugged and didn't answer.

In the corner, by her desk, one letter sat wadded up.

He was almost as nosy as Sophie and now was not a time to fight the compulsion.

Trevor bent and grabbed the wad. Smoothing out the paper, he began reading as soon as he saw the names at the top.

Nick Moretti

v.

Brooke Sargent

The plaintiff, Nick, was seeking damages. Code for more money. And something about Chateau Jolie.

He didn't need to read every word to know all of it was complete and utter bull. And the date on the letter was over a week ago.

"What is this?"

"*That* is none of your business." She picked up the letter, but he'd already seen all he needed.

"Your ex is suing you?"

She didn't answer.

"Did you know he was going to do this?"

"Maybe."

Sharp pain penetrated his heart. "And you never said anything?"

"How is it your business?"

"*How?*" he asked, his defenses prickling up like Beau's hair when he caught a whiff of a predator. "Because I care about you."

Instead of answering, she tromped to the window by her desk. Arms crossed, she glared at whatever lay beyond.

"Now isn't the time to be bullheaded, Brooke. What is going on?"

"You don't need to be involved in this."

Was she serious? He wanted to be involved. "I *am* involved. The guy's a jerk. You told me all about him. Or at least, I thought you had."

Her finger like a dagger, she pointed straight at him. "Don't. Don't you dare use that against me. You know how hard it was for me to tell you about him and everything that happened."

"I'm not using anything against you. I'm trying to understand. You could've told me about that." He pointed at the letter.

"I told you enough. More than I've told anyone else. But how does that help us now? We've got no music and you promised. You promised me."

The pain in her voice stole his breath.

He had promised and he meant to keep that promise.

But he didn't know how.

"This prom will be a flop, and you don't even care."

"I do care. Don't try to say that I don't. But you're not just upset over prom music. You've got the weight of this place on your shoulders and that"—Trevor pointed at the legal document—"to worry about, and you've been worrying alone. If you'd told me, I could've helped and you wouldn't be in this situation."

She scoffed again, turning her back on him.

"What's that supposed to mean?"

"You don't think I've tried to fix this mess? How could you possibly fix any of this? I could lose my family's hotel in a divorce that I thought was behind me. A mistake that *I* made, and all I want to do is move on from it and I can't. I could lose *everything*."

"I won't let that happen."

"I can't even count on you to get a DJ."

"This isn't about some stupid DJ."

"*Stupid* DJ? Just—just get out. Go home, Trevor. I'll figure something out myself. Like I always do." She walked to her office door and jerked it open.

Everything within him screamed against what was coming. "You can't throw me out because you're upset about your ex and a lawsuit. We can fix the DJ issue first and then figure out some way to deal with your ex."

Her beautiful dark eyes held no spark. Lifeless black holes as she looked past him. "There is no *we*. I will deal with my ex and, somehow, I'll deal with not having a DJ. Alone."

He approached her, but didn't walk out the door. With a deep breath and a focus on all he'd learned from yoga, he willed himself calmer. This wasn't about him or the two of them or a DJ. This was about her ex and her past, and the blame she carried around, like weights chained to her ankles. He kept his voice even and low. "Why didn't you tell me your ex was coming after you and Jolie?"

"What difference does that make?"

To him, the difference was huge. He'd believed she trusted him, in all things. That they were open with each other in ways they'd never been with others. But still, there was this huge thing she'd kept from him.

Big and threatening enough that she'd probably been hiding from it all along.

Perhaps it wasn't his place to be the hero here, but that didn't stop the desire.

"The difference is, there's being low on income and then there is your ex-husband lurking about, threatening to take part of your family business."

"But there's nothing you can do. I need something I can count on, and right now."

That isn't you.

She didn't say the words out loud.

She didn't need to.

He'd heard them plenty of times before. Seen the same look on her face on every single one of his family members.

His insides twisted, knotting into a ball of frustration like he hadn't felt in years. He could yell in frustration or anger, but yelling was something he never did. He hated the yelling and screaming and hurt feelings. He'd had enough of that to last him two lifetimes.

Plus, Brooke was already hurting. Arguing with her, forcing his point, wouldn't help that pain. "I'm telling you, I will figure something out for the music."

Her gaze remained on something he couldn't see.

"Brooke. At least look at me."

She refused, staring at some faraway point. Away from him. Away from them. "For now, Jolie is still my hotel and I'd like to be alone," she said. "Please leave."

He wasn't her ex.

He was nothing like that guy, so he wasn't going to act like it and force his point. If he stayed, any words they shared would disintegrate into harsh accusations and blame they couldn't take back.

He hated that path as much as Brooke, so he left.

But he refused to be gone for good.

Chapter 30

Trevor trudged around the lake's beach area, hauling four umbrellas along.

"Good Lord, you're wrecking my raking job from this morning. I'm going to have to go over the sand again." Sophie snatched the two umbrellas from his left arm.

"That's what you get for raking a lakeside."

"All the high-end resorts do it. Especially in the Caribbean."

"We aren't in the Caribbean."

Sophie tilted her face up to the sun and sighed. "Tell me about it. I'd burn like toast, but I like a nice beach, so lay off my sand."

The day was beautiful: sunny with a cool breeze, low humidity, and a forecast of the midseventies.

But he could find nothing delightful about the day. A storm cloud hung over him, ugly and dark, isolating him from everything except what'd gone down yesterday.

Brooke threw him out of Jolie. Through all of his adventures and experiences over the years, he'd never been thrown out of anywhere.

She would've permanently thrown him out of helping with the prom too, if it were her call to make.

"Trev? You all right?"

"Not at all." He trudged farther down the beach, dropped one umbrella, and began setting up the other.

Behind him, his sister fought with the two umbrellas she had, before catching up with him.

"Might as well spill your guts," she said. "That's some Roark-level moping you got going on and you never mope. So what's up?"

He shook his head. Where to begin? "For starters, we don't have a DJ for the prom. But that's a small hurdle compared to Brooke tossing me out of Jolie yesterday and refusing to talk to me."

"Holy—What?" Sophie dropped her umbrellas where she stood and circled around to face him.

"DJ Knight. Bobby? He's got the flu."

With big eyes, she blinked. "Not. Good."

"Nope. And Brooke is upset, stressed out, but she sure as hell won't let me help."

"Have you offered to help?"

Hackles raised, he scowled at his sister. "Of course I've offered. Have you met me?"

"Yes, I have. That's why I'm asking. How did you offer to help?"

"What do you mean, how?"

"*How,* Trev? What did you suggest to fix this DJ thing with the prom? Were you the Trevor who gets things done, hunts down our mom and reaches out to her so we can all work through things, goes to Dev to track down Zen and get a school its money back? *Or* were you the Trev who is all, 'It's cool, man. No worries. Everything will work out fine'?"

Unease washed over him. "The former?"

Sophie cocked an eyebrow.

"I didn't get a chance to suggest many solutions, but I told her I would fix it. I could DJ for the prom. It'd be fine." He left out his suggestion about a playlist.

"How are *you* going to DJ?"

"I don't know. It's music. I'd figure something out."

In standard sister fashion, she rolled her eyes. "Trev. For the love. Do you have some turntables and a sound system I don't know about?"

"No. I could rent that though. Or something. I don't know."

"That is exactly my point. You mean well, Trev. You always do. Full-throttle enthusiasm and, here lately, you get stuff done. But you're still super laid-back about most stuff. There's nothing wrong with that, but when someone is freaking out, you need to show some sense of urgency. Freak out a little bit too. Like you did with Zen."

He'd wasted little time in finding a way to go after that venue, and he'd kept Brooke in the loop the whole way. Because he knew how much it meant to her.

"Brooke isn't made like you. Most people aren't. You can roll with whatever and keep a cool head without panicking. Other people can't."

"But Brooke likes that I'm laid-back."

"I'm sure she loves it. I saw the two of you at the quinceañera, all giddy and dancing. She needs someone who knows how to relax and won't worry about every little thing. But with matters like this, you can't simply say things will be fine and expect her to feel all better and not be in a panic. You've got to *make* things fine."

Sophie was right.

Brooke was already torn up about the letter from her ex's attorney. Yesterday's argument was a powder keg of her past and present. The DJ just lit the wick. Brooke was cracking under the financial pressures—anyone would—but she refused to accept any help.

Sophie drove one of the umbrellas into the sand and leaned her weight against it. "Once you sort out this prom hurdle and pull the whole thing off, she'll be fine. Everyone gets snippy when under pressure."

"Yeah, but this isn't really about the prom."

"What do you mean?"

"I…." Brooke had said most people in Windamere didn't know about her marriage or her divorce. She'd like to keep things that way.

This was his sister, but still. Brooke's past wasn't his to share.

"Sorry." He focused on planting one of the other umbrellas in the sand. "It's not my place to say."

"Is it about her being married before?"

With a flinch, his mouth fell open and he turned to his sister. "How the—You knew?"

"I might've pulled her up online."

Trevor shook his head like he was shaking off sand. "Unbelievable."

"All that stuff is public record if you look."

"You mean, if you stalk."

"I was not stalking. I googled her, one time, last year, and saw she'd gotten a divorce."

"Wait. Why were you googling her last year?"

With a one shoulder shrug, Sophie bent to pop open the striped umbrella. "I met her after Wright and I fessed up about dating, and I thought she was awesome. Then she came to Dev's wedding and you were making moony eyes at her. I look out for y'all whether you know it or not, so I figured I'd pull her up and make sure she really was awesome. Turns out, she is."

"I wasn't making moony eyes at her during Dev's wedding."

His sister laughed and laughed. "Okay, sure."

Trevor resisted the urge to jab his sister with an umbrella.

"But I know she's divorced. Is that what you thought wasn't your place to say?"

"Yes. So much for privacy. Her ex is trying to bleed more money out of her and he's trying to take away her part of Jolie."

Sophie's *"What?"* bounced across the lake water. "That will never happen."

"I know. But I don't think that's the issue. He can make Brooke's life hell while he tries. Cost her a ton of money in attorney fees, that I guess she could countersue him later, but right now all of this costs money she doesn't have."

"And she can't borrow it off her sisters or the hotel?"

"Definitely not." Trevor dug the heel of his shoe back into the sand. "Thing is, I've seen how hard she works, how hard she tries. Everything matters to her, Soph. Everything. She wants this prom to be perfect. She wants her hotel and the winery to be the best, for her sisters to be taken care of. She doesn't deserve this. She should be treated like gold."

"Have you told her that?"

"I think she knows."

"Why don't you make sure she knows? She needs someone who will be there for her. Someone she can count on. Prove to her that you're that person."

Was he?

Was he the kind of guy who'd be there through good times and bad? When the going got tough, would he stay put and push through the hard times?

A couple of years ago? No. But now...

Images of all he'd done since he'd returned home scrolled through his mind. The work at Honeywilde, even when he'd had his scattered moments, was worthwhile and quality. Reconnecting with his mom. All he'd done at Chateau Jolie with Brooke.

No, *for* Brooke. He wanted to help the high school, but he'd worked his hardest because of her. She motivated him to do more. Be more. For her and for himself.

He was that guy now, and she could always count on him. Even when she was upset about a DJ and mad at him.

"You're right," Trevor told his sister.

But how? How did he fix this? There was little he could do about her ex. He had more control over the DJ situation, but limited time.

"You know, if the price was right, you could probably get someone to do the music on short notice." His sister echoed his thoughts. "With all the bands and DJs we've used over the years, surely there's someone who's available."

Trevor made more shoe prints in the sand. "I tried everyone we've ever used. All booked. And beyond that, we can't afford the 'right price.' We're on a budget, with only so much for music. I can't exactly fly in a band."

"I'm assuming Jolie can't supplement?"

"No." He could go to Roark. Swallow his pride and tell his brother this was important and they needed to help. Running to big brother was something the old Trevor would do. Sliding down the path of least resistance was fine back then. But he'd grown past that.

This was his prom, his partnership with Brooke. He wanted to fix this.

"What you need is a big ole chunk of change," Sophie said. "I know money isn't everything, but it wouldn't hurt."

Their budget meant limitations, but...

If he had access to additional funds, maybe some money stashed away for a rainy day.

Or a trip abroad.

"I've got an idea. I've got to go." He jammed the last umbrella into the sand and turned to his sister.

"O-kay."

He grabbed her, giving her a quick peck on her forehead. "Thanks for the help."

"How did I help?" she called out as he hurried from the lakeside.

Her voice faded as he rushed away, but he didn't have time to explain it all now.

He had a lot of work to do but, for the first time in his life, he knew exactly what he wanted, where he was going, and how he'd get there.

Chapter 31

Maybe the lack of guests for the coming weekend would be a blessing. A couple hundred teenagers dancing and singing until almost midnight might turn a few grownups off of Chateau Jolie for life.

Brooke stared at her computer screen.

Who was she kidding?

She needed people in rooms, even if they disliked teenagers, and the prom wasn't having the effect she'd hoped for. Things would only get worse too, as soon as the kids realized they had no DJ and the only prom music they'd be hearing was a phone and a playlist hooked up to some Bluetooth speaker.

If tale of this fiasco made the rounds, Jolie would be even more pitiful than it already was.

"We're screwed without music." Brooke crossed her arms on her desk and buried her head. "We are so, so screwed."

Except, there was no *we* anymore.

Thanks to her.

She'd made sure to run Trevor off good and proper this time. If playing the ice princess didn't work, acting like a snide shrew certainly did the trick.

Now she was neck deep in disaster, without Trevor to help pull her out.

Getting mad at him hadn't been fair, but he didn't get it. Nothing about her situation was going to be fine, and no amount of saying so would make it so.

There had to be some other way to kick up room sales, and fast. They couldn't use any more money from the winery, but maybe they could still use the winery. Give away more free tastings or packages. Perhaps even a drawing for a case of wine...or a bottle of wine every month for a year.

She'd batted these ideas around with her PR lady, and promos like that took time to bear fruit.

Time she didn't have. The bank refused to increase their line at the moment. Her parents would dip into their retirement if need be, but that was a last resort.

A last resort she was quickly approaching.

"I really don't want to go there," she said to no one.

The family business was hers now, and no, her parents wouldn't let the place go under, but they shouldn't have to bail her out. Again.

She banged her head against her arms.

All of this had been easier to shoulder with Trevor around. No denying that fact.

He'd let her down with the DJ debacle, but she'd been a fool to run him off. *We'll figure something out*, he'd say. *Everything will be awesome. Just you wait and see.*

The whole time they were planning, he'd assured her of success and, as much as she hated to admit, true or not, his words worked.

She'd believed him. Maybe that's why this hurt so much.

But still, with all of her fretting and perfectionism, she'd been more confident in planning this prom than she'd been with anything in years.

All this time she'd doubted that there would ever be anyone there for her, but Trevor had been there from day one. No matter how many times she tried to keep him at a distance or shut him out, regardless of how difficult she'd been, he was there.

Tiny tapping sounds made her lift her head. She expected Beans to scamper into her office. Instead, a mature female voice called out above the pitter-patter.

"Hello? Is anyone here?"

Brooke was upright, face swiped, and hair smoothed before she made it to her office door. "May I help you?"

Standing in the lobby was a petite woman dressed in jeans, a soft pink sweater, and pink and green floral Wellingtons. She was probably in her sixties or seventies, and her hair was platinum white as she shook out the raindrops. At her feet stood two of the cutest squat little corgis Brooke had ever seen.

"This is Chateau Jolie, yes?" she asked.

"Yes, it is, welcome."

"Thank goodness," the woman exclaimed. "You popped up on my phone as a hotel near me."

"Please, allow me." Brooke took the umbrella from her hand and set it in their umbrella holder."

"Thank you. It is pouring out."

The corgis pranced about on their dual leash, their fur and feet damp.

"I have something to dry them off. Hold on a moment." Brooke darted into the downstairs bathroom and grabbed a couple of hand towels. "Here," she said, returning and offering them to the lady.

"Perfect. Reggie and Roscoe cannot stand to be wet. Can you, boys?" the woman cooed to her dogs as she dried them.

"I'm Brooke Sargent by the way. The manager."

Once done, the woman straightened and offered her hand. "I'm Clarissa, and I cannot tell you how glad I am we found you." She patted her dogs. "The boys and I were on our way to Tennessee, when all of a sudden, out of nowhere, the sky just opens up. Well, I'm not big on driving at night anyway, but we got a late start—you know how these things are—but I refuse to drive near dusk and it's raining cats and dogs. Plus, Reggie and Roscoe do not care for thunder, so I am *done*. I don't care that it's only another hour or two, we're stopping. I'll call my friends and tell them we'll be there tomorrow. But I can't stop any old place, you know? Not with the boys. So, I asked my phone—my grandson taught me how to talk to my phone—I said, phone, find a pet-friendly hotel near me. And voila. Here you are. You are pet friendly? Please say you are."

"Yes, ma'am. Very much so."

"And gorgeous! This place is gorgeous." Clarissa wandered across the lobby, her dogs following her.

"Thank you. We like to think so."

She left the sitting area and headed toward one of the windows. "And did I see a sign that mentioned a vineyard?"

"Yes, ma'am. We're a hotel and winery, with our own vineyard."

That got Clarissa's undivided attention as she faced Brooke. "A winery. And do you serve?"

"Yes, the winery is in the cellar with a seating downstairs and out back."

She clasped her hands together, drawing her corgis' attention. "Marvelous. Absolutely marvelous. I would be forever indebted to you for the teensiest bit of cabernet right now."

"Of course."

"Or maybe not so teensy. I'm not driving anywhere in this weather anyhow. You know how it is."

"I do indeed."

"Then join me, dear." Clarissa was already headed toward the stairs.

"I'd love to, but I have so much to do and—"

With a flick of her hand, Clarissa dismissed her objection without even turning around. "Come on now. You can't expect a little old lady to drink alone. You said downstairs, yes? Reggie and Roscoe can come too?"

Brooke followed, having no choice. "Yes."

"You have made my week, my dear. Let's have a not so teensy glass of red, and I will check in and all will be right with the world."

This is what Trevor's sister, Sophie, would be like in about fifty years. A tornado in a teacup, but Brooke welcomed the sense of being overwhelmed. A glass of cab sounded ideal right now, and her new guest wasn't entertaining a no for an answer.

They found a seat in the empty tasting area of the winery. There were no tastings this late, so Brooke did the honors and poured.

Clarissa was a talker, and all Brooke had to do was nod. Clarissa's command of the conversation allowed Brooke a reprieve from thinking about Jolie or the prom or Trevor.

Fine with her.

"You don't know how nice it is to have a pet-friendly place that's still a high-end hotel. I can't tell you how many times the boys and I have stayed in roadside motels because I am not leaving them at a kennel."

"I'm so glad you found us."

"Well, can you imagine how it'd look if a board member didn't bring her babies to the regional meeting?"

"Meeting for what?" Brooke asked.

"Humane Society, dear. We have our regional meeting tomorrow. No one leaves their pets at home. We rent pet-friendly houses and sitters for while we're out."

"You're…you're on the board of the Humane Society."

"Yes, I am." Clarissa clinked her glass against Brooke's.

Their one glass turned into a bottle and when they finally made it back upstairs, Laurel was checking in two gentlemen and their sweater-wearing greyhound.

She gave Clarissa and the gentlemen their room keys. They all left with their luggage and fur babies.

Laurel turned to her as soon as they passed the sitting area. "I think this pet thing is really going to take off," she force whispered.

Brooke smiled. "I think so too. Maybe even bigger than we imagined."

"Those guys saw our ad on the Bark in the Park flyer. And they were saying a lot of people travel for that Wag-a-thon, and we'll probably get a ton of bookings since it's near here."

"And the lady you checked in is a board member of the Humane Society."

"Shut up." Laurel gaped. "Advertising this more was such a great idea, sis."

And it wasn't Brooke's. "The pet-friendly promo was Trevor's idea. Remember?"

Laurel bobbed her shoulders as she stacked some papers. "Yeah, but y'all came up with the details together. It's awesome, and not only because Beans is bound to make new friends. Speaking of, where is Trevor? I figured you two would be inseparable and he'd be camped out here, what with the prom two days away."

"I don't know where he is. Maybe he's got some Honeywilde stuff to take care of." Brooke cringed at her lie and cowardice. "That's not true."

Laurel did a double take, one eye brow twitching into a comical wrinkle. "Do what?"

"Trevor. I do know where he is. He's probably at Honeywilde, but only because I ran him off."

The papers in Laurel's hands hit the reception desk. "Dang it, Brooke. What did you do?"

Her sister didn't ask, *What did* he *do?*

"Do you want to talk about what happened?" Laurel asked instead.

With a heavy sigh, the story came pouring out, about the attorney's letter, the DJ, everything.

"You didn't have to run him off though, sis. The two of you working together are more likely to fix a little DJ problem than you alone."

"I realize this. I know I messed up. I don't need a lecture now."

"Really? Because sometimes I think you do."

Brooke peered over at her typically more forgiving and patient sister.

"I mean it. You're awesome and you do a great job of keeping me and Reagan straight and all, but sometimes you can bulldoze straight ahead without the patience to think."

"I was upset."

"The DJ bailed on him. So what? Y'all should get out there and find another one. You don't kick Trevor out of the hotel and your life, definitely not out of the prom partnership. That's not even your call to make."

"I know."

"Do you?"

Their gazes clashed.

"You're so accustomed to being in charge, to being responsible for any and everything, that you feel you have to go it alone. Especially when the going gets tough. But you don't. You're surrounded by people who love you and can help. Me, Reagan. And now Trevor."

"I doubt Trevor loves me, especially now."

Laurel nailed her with a look. "I don't. I'm not sure if you're aware, but you tend to shut people out when you get overwhelmed."

"I...I know."

"Then do something to change that habit. You don't have go it alone, sis. Not even when the dog poo hits the fan. You don't have to *be* alone, either."

Brooke's vision blurred as she blinked.

Laurel was right. Admitting she put up walls was one thing, tearing them down was another.

But Trevor had been beyond her walls and done no harm. She trusted him. But she'd gotten scared.

And more than anything, she missed him.

She still didn't have a solution for the prom music, or a quick injection of income, but these weren't problems she had to solve on her own.

Her sisters were there for her. And so was Trevor. They'd known each other mere days, but he'd been there. When she'd freaked out over the budget, he was there; when she'd launched onto her soapbox at one of the owners of Zen, Trevor had had her back. When she'd confessed the truth about her marriage, Trevor hadn't batted an eye.

She'd kept the full truth from him anyway.

She could've told him about Nick's attempts to take Jolie. Trevor wouldn't have judged her. More than likely, he would've tried to help.

That's all he'd done since this whole thing had started. He'd never given her any reason to think he wouldn't stand right beside her while she sorted out this latest legal mess.

But telling him about the lawsuit would've meant accepting it was real.

As long as she hid from her past, denied what haunted her and pretended none of this was an issue, then it wasn't real.

Trevor would've wanted to tackle the problem like heroes, even if they failed. But he never would've ignored it.

The problem wasn't Trevor. The problem was her.

"I have to talk to him."

Laurel smiled. "Yeah, you do."

This was too much to handle on the phone though. Instead, she'd call Honeywilde and make sure he was there. Then she'd go and speak with him in person. She owed Trevor an apology and, as long as he accepted, they had to figure out a fix for the prom music.

"I can keep an eye on the front while you try to call from the office. I have a feeling you'll want the privacy."

Brooke hurried to the office, her mind a flurry. As soon as she got her thoughts together and sat down to dial Honeywilde's number, Laurel called out. "Um, *Brooke?*"

"Hold on. I'm about to call the inn."

"I know, but you need to come back out here first."

With a grumble, Brooke got up. Maybe she should write some of her thoughts down, so as not to forget anything.

"Brooke!"

"I'm coming!" She begrudgingly rushed back to the reception desk.

There, standing across from Laurel, were five dark-haired men. All vaguely familiar.

"They said they're here to see you," her sister whispered.

"Why are you whispering?" Brooke looked at the group of men again.

"Ms. Sargent? Brooke Sargent?" One of them stepped forward.

"Yes, that's me."

"We were told to come by and see you about a performance Saturday night."

"A what?" She glanced at Laurel.

Her sister shook her head and shrugged.

"For your dance. We wanted to talk to you about what kind of music you might like, maybe have a look at the room and setup so we'll know what to do with our instruments and equipment."

Brooke stared, words spinning around in her mind, but none coming out. She knew she recognized them. They were the band from Camila's quinceañera.

"Wait, are you guys going to play for the prom?" Laurel asked for her.

"Yes. We play all the top forty, classics. Pretty much anything you want."

Brooke's brain finally found the right gear. "I—I'm sorry. Evidently I've missed something."

"Trevor Bradley called us today. An emergency he said. For your dance."

The man next to him nodded. "Please tell me you're available, he said."

"Normally we wouldn't be free on a Saturday night, but our bass player is out of the country, so we didn't book any shows. Señor Bradley said he'd find us a stand-in to play bass though, not to worry."

That sounded exactly like something Señor Bradley would say.

"I…That's…But there's no way we can afford you."

"We have already been paid. Evidently someone can afford us." The leader of the group grinned.

Laurel bounced on the balls of her feet. "Are you telling us you're going to play the prom tomorrow? Trevor Bradley already arranged everything and paid you?"

"Sí."

Brooke gaped.

She'd seen them live; they were phenomenal and probably charged an arm and a leg, because they were worth it, so how in the world could Trevor afford to have already paid them?

With him, he could've done anything from taken out a loan to robbing a bank.

"Never mind her. She's in shock." Laurel patted Brooke's arm and stepped forward to shake hands with the band's leader. "I'm Laurel. Please, come in. I'll show you around the ballroom and the stage. You can check out the layout and decide how you'll set up." She turned back and smiled as she led the solution to at least one big problem to their ballroom. "My sister Brooke has another matter to take care of."

Chapter 32

The damp, foggy dusk fit his mood better than the bright sun of yesterday morning.

His shoulders refused to relax, his neck insistently tense. He wasn't in a bad mood, per se, but he could do hours of yoga right now, and it'd barely make a dent.

Trevor planted his hands on the dock, leaning back as his feet dangled in the lake.

A chill from the water crept up his legs, doing little to cool or calm the restlessness inside.

His heart and mind galloped, with no place to go. The racing wasn't because he'd given up thousands of dollars this morning. That was all for a good reason and the right thing to do. He didn't need that money to survive, and Peru could wait another year or two.

His disquiet had everything to do with Brooke.

He'd let her down, true. But his misstep was only a spark that ignited the real issue between them.

Whether or not they could work through that issue wasn't up to just him.

He was ready and willing, but Brooke had to be too. She had to trust him, and more than that, she had to learn to trust herself.

A mighty tall order given what she'd been through.

What if she wasn't ready? Maybe she couldn't.

There'd been a time, in the not so distant past, he'd thought he could never truly be open or vulnerable or trust anyone again. He'd been so certain that the best way to protect himself was to remain aloof, distant, carefree.

You never worried if you didn't care about anything.

But along came Brooke and her sisters and the kids at Windamere High, and he couldn't help but care.

His carefree attitude had morphed into not caring at all. And that was a lonely way to live.

Brooke wasn't any different. Except instead of adopting an air of cool nonchalance, she kept everyone at arm's length. Sometimes even her sisters.

By keeping people at a distance, they only hurt themselves. Trevor knew that now. And he wanted Brooke to know.

The big question was, would she understand?

He'd do everything he could to help her understand. Tomorrow morning, the morning of the prom, he'd go to Jolie and stay there until they made amends. He refused to let their pride and apprehension ruin what they had.

"Trevor?"

He glanced up, and Brooke appeared from the fog like some mystical goddess.

Without another word, she sat down beside him. She slipped off her flats and swung her feet over the side of the dock, letting her toes dangle in the water.

"Hey," she said.

"Hey." He sat up, both of them moving their feet around, the only sound one of swirling water.

"Guess who came to see me today," she finally said.

Trevor shook his head and shrugged.

"The band from Camila's quince."

He nodded.

"They're going to perform at the prom tomorrow." She tilted her head to glance at him from the corner of her eyes. "But you already knew that, didn't you?"

He shrugged again. "Maybe."

Brooke's smile was soft, dare he say, fond. "How did you manage to pull it off? Where'd you get the money? From Honeywilde?"

"No."

"Then how?"

Trevor pulled his feet out of the water and turned to face her. "That's for me to worry about. I took care of our DJ problem and now those kids are going to have the best prom this town has ever seen."

Brooke's nose crinkled, her Sargent stare firmly in place as she studied him. "But the money had to come from somewh—Wait. Your trip to Peru. You spent that money. Trevor, no."

"I said don't worry about it."

"But Trev."

A smile started at his toes and grew until it reached his lips. "That is the first time you've ever called me Trev. Say it again."

"That is your trip money. I can't let you do that."

"Already done. And it's *my* money. I can do whatever I want. I happen to want a great live band for tomorrow night."

"Trev—" she began, but he reached over and took her hand, effectively stopping her.

"I fixed the issue, okay? And you can argue until you're blue in the face, but you ain't winning this round, Sarge. Accept it."

With a squeeze of his hand, she smiled again. "I...I didn't know what we were going to do, and now? Now, I can't believe we're going to pull this prom off."

He leaned forward. "We? Does this mean we're a 'we' again?"

Brooke shook her head. "We were always a 'we.' I'm so sorry for the other day. For the way I acted, for not telling you about my ex. For everything. I...I was upset about the chateau's finances and him and then the prom on top of it and...you didn't deserve what I said. And none of it was true."

"Eh. Some of it was true."

"But—"

He put his free hand up. "No, I can admit my faults. You were upset. This prom means a lot, on a lot of different levels, and I can be a little too laid-back when I need to step up. But more than anything, it's my fault I haven't been completely honest with you."

Brooke frowned. "What do you mean?"

"The reason I kept insisting things were no big deal and everything was fine isn't because I don't care. I realized, it's because I care too much. About this project, but mostly about you."

She blinked rapidly, pinching her lips together.

"I tried to play it cool, but I've known all along. From the moment we started planning this prom—No, actually from the moment I met you at Dev's wedding, I started falling for you."

Her smile wobbled.

"After my parent's marriage and what we're still going through with my mom, I don't know. I try to keep things casual. But my feelings for you are anything but cool and laid-back. And I should've told you."

Brooke took his other hand and scooted closer. "I should've told you too. I resisted letting you in and then I blamed you for everything when things started going sideways. You've never let me down and I started falling for you too. And that scares me. Your relaxed way of doing so might drive me crazy sometimes, but that shouldn't matter. You've always kept your promise. I should've trusted you."

He leaned in, brushing his lips against hers.

"And yes, my ex is threatening the hotel, but I know he won't win. He's manipulative and mean but until I cut him out of my life completely, I'll never have any peace. The best thing I can do is let my attorney handle him and move on."

"Maybe I can help there too," he offered. "I didn't spend all of my savings on the band."

"Trevor, no. Absolutely not."

He'd seen her objection coming a mile away. "Just hear me out—"

"The pet ads are starting to work," she interrupted him.

His jaw dropped. "They are?"

"Yes, and it didn't even take that long. Business isn't up much, but…I believe, for the first time in forever, I believe. In your idea and in Jolie. I know things are going to be okay. Business will pick up and I'll be able to pay my attorney. She has enough of my money, she can wait a few months on getting more. What matters is I believe in my sisters, in the hotel, and in myself, thanks to you."

"I have no doubts about any it." He kissed her again. "But if you need my help, you know I'm here."

"I do," she said. "I know I can always count on you."

Chest tight, he smiled around the warm joy about to burst out.

"But first, we have a prom to attend."

"Yes." Trevor smiled. "Maybe there's even a chance I'll get a dance with my favorite person."

"I can't agree to a dance with you." Brook caught her bottom lip between her teeth.

"Why?"

"Because I want to dance every dance with you. The whole night." Brooke took his hands in hers. "Trevor Bradley, will you go to prom with m—"

Trevor kissed her firmly on the lips. "Heck yeah, I will."

Her laughter danced across the lake.

"But what are you going to wear?" he asked.

"I'm not telling you. It has to be a surprise."

"I need some idea though. Formal? Semiformal? Should I wear my tux or a dinner jacket or what?"

"*You* own a tuxedo?"

"You should know by now, I'm full of surprises."

Chapter 33

The soft scent of roses floated on the air, the lobby of Chateau Jolie glowed with candlelight, and, for the first time in her life, Brooke felt like a princess—no, that wasn't right. She'd lived too long and been through too much to ever be a wide-eyed princess.

Duchess.

Duchess was more like it.

She was a duchess, awaiting her duke.

"Holy shine, sis!" Laurel jumped in front of her as she rounded the stairs. "You look beautiful."

"Thank you." Brooke touched the low knot of her updo. "Not too much?"

"Exactly the right amount. You're like…the lady in red. You remember that really old song?"

"The song is not that old." She smoothed her hands over her hips, the chiffon tickling her palms.

On a wing and a prayer, and a whole lot of sucking in, she'd put on a formal gown from her college senior year. Astoundingly, the dress still fit.

There'd be very little eating and no sitting down in her future, but by gosh, the thing zipped and that's what mattered.

Reagan joined them and eyeballed the dress and Brooke's hair. "You look pretty good. Not bad on your hair either."

Laurel rolled her eyes. "Don't pull a muscle being nice, Reagan."

"Whatever. Brooke knows she looks great. Always does. Meanwhile we're over here in basic black."

"By choice," Laurel pointed out. "We agreed. Tonight is about the Windamere High seniors, and Trevor and Brooke." She touched the lace on the cap sleeves of the gown. "Trevor is going to die when he sees you."

As if summoned, Trevor appeared in the doorway from the lobby. He approached the stairs and almost tripped over his feet. "Wow. You look—Wow!"

Heat filled Brooke's cheeks. Her sisters made a hasty exit toward the ballroom.

"And you look incredibly debonair for a man who's an expert at standing on his head." She stepped off the last stair and touched the lapel of his tux.

His smile lit the room. "Pssh. You think this is debonair? I'm barely getting started." He lifted his hand. In it was a clear plastic box. Inside was a cluster of stephanotis, tied with white satin ribbon. *"This* is for you."

"You did not."

"Of course I did. How could I not? If we're doing this, we're doing things right. Come on, let me put it on your wrist."

Brooke offered her wrist and Trevor slid on the corsage.

"Brenda said to be careful because these stephanotis bruise easily."

Not unlike Brooke. At least, before she had Trevor.

The old Brooke was hurt, broken. And she carried the bruises around, refusing to let them heal. She kept them, hiding them, almost coveting them, as a reminder of how much people could hurt her, disappoint and misuse her, if she let them.

So she didn't let them. Instead, she kept everyone away, never letting them know the real her.

With Trevor, she'd finally let the bruises heal. She let him in, and her life was all the better for it.

There would always be people who'd do harm. But that didn't have to define you.

Being a divorcee, even if everyone knew, and knew all about what she'd been through, didn't make her who she was. Her past and her marriage were but a small part of the whole person. And she had so much more ahead.

She hadn't given much thought to the future in years, when all it held was doubt and darkness.

Now, she looked forward eagerly, and she didn't look back in anger.

Brooke adjusted the elastic band so the flowers lay just so. "There. Now I can look back at who I was and I'm not angry with her anymore. I'm me because of her." She blinked at Trevor, realizing she'd said the last bit out loud. "Sorry. I probably sound like a crazy lady."

"Not at all. You sound wise. And happy."

Trevor offered his arm. "Now, shall we?"

"We'll be the first ones in the ballroom, you know?"

"I know, but I still want to make an entrance. Maybe we can get Beans to watch us."

Brooke laughed, floating on air.

"And don't worry. We'll make enough of an impression. I plan to wow some teenagers with our old-folk's moves."

"Oh no." Brooke covered her face with her free hand. "You aren't going to ask the band to play the 'Electric Slide' or 'Macarena,' are you?"

"I am now!"

"Trevor."

"You know I love to dance." He gave her a cheeky grin, his dimples on full display, still taking her breath away.

"And I love you," she said, her heart pounding in sync with each word.

Trevor's bright eyes glistened as he placed his hand over hers. "I love you too." He leaned down and placed a gentle kiss on her lips. "Come on, let's go to our prom."

Epilogue

One month later

"The verandah looks amazing." Brooke squeezed his arm, her smile brilliant. "And this was all your idea?"

"Most of it." Trevor took in the sight of the woman beside him, dark hair worn down, set off by her white dress and sweater. No tension marred her brow, her shoulders loose and relaxed as she leaned forward in her chair.

"Good job."

"I told you I work best under pressure. Sophie said we had a few weeks and Mother's Day brunch needed to be special. Now, here we are."

He'd worked with his sister to bring his Italian villa idea to life for this brunch. Marco had prepared a northern-Italian-inspired menu, they'd ordered wine from Jolie to complement, the décor was rustic, fresh and classic. All white flowers, greenery, white candles, and some awesome carved wooden bowls for the breads.

"I mean it though. You really have a knack for this," Brooke said.

His chest swelled and his face cramped from smiling.

He did have a knack for this. The prom had been a roaring success. So much so, Brooke had been approached by Dorian's mom to host her law firm's Christmas party.

And she'd asked if Trevor would consult.

Things were happening for him. Plans.

He'd always avoided plans like the plague, but now, opportunities lay before him and he welcomed the option of making plans.

Roark joined them at their table, and he pulled out a chair for Madison.

On one side of Trevor was his brother, Dev, on the other, a woman he never could've predicted would be the one for him. Across from him sat his mother. Another prediction he never would've made. Their mother, and all the Bradley siblings, together on Mother's Day.

Everyone in a good mood, everyone flourishing.

"They're here!" Brooke all but jumped from her chair. She waved to Dorian and Lance and grabbed the manila envelope she'd laid on the table.

Trevor was right behind her.

Dorian and Brooke shared a hug. "Thank you so much for coming up here on Mother's Day," Brooke said. "We really wanted to see you guys."

"You brought your folks, I hope." Trevor shook hands with Lance.

"They're behind us. They ran into someone they knew in the lobby and got distracted."

Brooke beamed, almost at a Dorian level of enthusiasm. "That's okay. We have some news for both of you first."

"You're getting married," Dorian blurted.

"What?" Brooke paled.

"No," Trevor said at the same time. "I mean, not *no* as in never. Right?" He looked to Brooke.

Brooke gazed at him, her affection completely transparent. "Right." She turned to Dorian. "Just not now."

In that moment, he wanted to grab her and kiss her.

But they had business to attend to first.

"Our surprise has to do with you," he said.

"Here." Brooke passed Dorian the envelope.

Dorian opened it and pulled out a piece of a paper.

"What's this?"

"That is a copy of a filing. The filing of a lawsuit," Brooke said. "Sadly, I know way too much about these. But this is a good one."

Dorian read the paper, Lance leaning over to see too. They both scowled in confusion.

Brooke clapped her hands together, lacking the patience to wait on such good news. "The school district is suing the owners of Zen."

"What?" They both lit up, staring with wide eyes.

"To get your money. The school district is going after them to have the court award your money back."

"Plus damages," Trevor added.

"You're..." Dorian blinked. "You're lying."

"Nope." Brooke's smile was infectious. Trevor's face began to hurt.

"Oh my—You think it will work?"

"Most likely. It is the school district, after all."

"Oh, my God!" Dorian jumped up and down, and went in for another hug.

"We should all know by the summer."

"That is awesome." Lance took the paper to look it over.

"That's why we wanted you guys here for Mother's Day. We all need to celebrate. Your brunch and your parents' brunch is on the house."

"You guys are the best." Dorian clasped her hands together in front of her chest. "Thank you."

"It was our pleasure," Brooke said. "Truly."

"And then we can turn around and pay you guys for the best prom ever."

"No, no. We couldn't accept payment. We wanted to do the right thing."

"We'll have to give you something. The senior class would kill the committee if they knew we didn't give something back to Chateau Jolie and Honeywilde."

He shared a look with Brooke.

Well… they wouldn't say no to a little something.

"Come on." Trevor held out an arm. "We have a table for you and your folks right over here."

They got Dorian and Lance and their parents seated and made their way back to their spots.

"They were so happy. Did you see their faces?" Brooke whispered.

"I did." He held his hand out for a small high-five, as he pulled out her chair.

"We are kind of heroic, huh?"

Trevor sat down, surrounded by family and friends and the woman he loved. And all of them believed in him.

He leaned over and gave Brooke a quick kiss on the cheek. "Turns out, we make a pretty great team."

About the Author

Heather McGovern writes contemporary romance in swoony, southern settings. While her love of travel and adventure takes her far, there is no place quite like home. She lives in South Carolina with her husband and son, and a collection of Legos that's threatening to take over the house. When she isn't writing, she's working out, or binging on books and Netflix.

She is a member of Romance Writers of America, as well as Carolina Romance Writers, and she's represented by Nicole Resciniti of The Seymour Agency.

Connect with Heather on her website, Facebook, Twitter, or her group blog. She'd love to hear to from you!

www.heathermcgovernnovels.com
www.facebook.com/Heather.McGovern.Novels
www.twitter.com/heathermcgovern
www.badgirlzwrite.com

Books by Laura Browning

Winning Heart

Mountain Meadow Homecomings
Special Delivery, Book One
Lost & Found Love, Book Two

The Barlow-Barretts: An American Dynasty
Bittersweet, Book One
Balancing Act, Book Two
Remember Me, Book Three
Broken Heart, Book Four

Published by Kensington Publishing Corporation

Welcome to Mountain Meadow, Virginia, where homecomings lead to happily ever after...

Tabitha MacVie has come to Mountain Meadow to meet the sister she never knew, and find the family she longs for. What she discovers is a close-knit community determined to close ranks against the new art teacher, especially once she catches the eye of the town's most eligible bachelor. Tabby tries hard to keep Joe Taylor at a distance. But staying away from the handsome preacher isn't easy once he opens his arms to her....

Tabby is the answer to Joe's prayers. Too bad the spirited beauty believes she doesn't belong in Mountain Meadow—or with him. Still, Joe can't resist offering her shelter against the local gossips, or giving her a strong shoulder to lean on when her family hopes are dashed. And when Tabby's life is suddenly on the line, Joe will do anything to save the woman who stole his heart.

Lost & Found Love

A Mountain Meadow Homecomings Novel

Laura Browning

LYRICAL PRESS
Kensington Publishing Corp.
www.kensingtonbooks.com

First Electronic Edition: February 2016
eISBN-13: 978-1-60183-572-7
eISBN-10: 1-60183-572-8

First Print Edition: February 2016
ISBN-13: 978-1-60183-574-1
ISBN-10: 1-60183-574-4

Printed in the United States of America

During the edits on this manuscript, life changed for me. My eldest brother, John, passed away quite suddenly. He was the first of the four kids in our family, but John was so much more.

He was my hero. The big brother, who was there to help when I was hurt or sick. He was my protector when it came to getting picked on by the sibling closest to me in age. He was left-handed, like me. I don't know if I ever thanked him for that hand-me-down baseball glove, but it sure made life easier.

He sat next to me when Jaws first came out, putting up with my clawing him in the arm with my fingernails. Then the next day he went swimming in the ocean with me.

He gave me my first ride on a motorcycle. Later on, he encouraged my interest in bicycling, and even slowed down enough to take rides with me. It didn't matter that he was a competitive cyclist and I just liked to ride. He was willing to take the time to share that interest with me.

He served his country in the Navy. He was loyal, and responsible, yet he still knew how to have fun. He had a wicked sense of humor and a laugh that could make everyone smile. He loved to travel, but he also loved coming home again.

In a story where finding family is so important, it only makes sense to dedicate it to a man who knew the true value of family. This happily ever after is for you, John.

Chapter 1

For a girl who'd grown up in a rundown millhouse, what Tabby stood in front of now was a dream. Best of all, it was hers. The house was a unique blend of colors. A rich, rusty red exterior with creamy yellow shutters and lacy wood trim, which betrayed its Victorian origins. The rounded left front, with its big bay windows on the first and second floors, reminded Tabby of the tower on a castle. The third floor was tucked under a steeply pitched roof, and at ground level, a wide, covered veranda wrapped around the front and side. Tabby gazed at it with a smile. It was exactly like the picture the real estate agent had sent her. Good thing. She'd bought it, sight unseen, in an Internet auction.

The purchase was a win-win situation for Tabby and the former owner. The elderly woman had taken the proceeds and moved into the Mountain Meadow Retirement Community. She was free from caring for such a huge home, and Tabby had gotten a great deal.

With her cat carrier in her left hand, Tabby unlocked the heavy front door and wandered inside. Her artist's eye quickly circled the high-ceilinged front hall, the living room on one side, and the dining room on the other. The house had possibilities. Even the furnishings would work with a colorful throw here and a few accent pillows there. Since the previous owner had little use in her new patio home for most of the furniture, she had thrown what she didn't need into the deal.

At a sound behind her, Tabby turned. A leggy boy with long, dark brown hair shifted from foot to foot. His grin alone was enough to light up the room, even without the sunshine streaming through the lacy curtains.

"Who are you?" she asked. "My one-man welcoming committee?"

"Tyler Morgan. I do odd jobs at Tarpley's…uh…Mountain Meadow General Store, but most folks around here call it Tarpley's. They—that's Mr. and Mrs. Tarpley—sent me over with a box of groceries for you. Said it should get you started till you have a chance to stop in."

Tabby glanced from the box to the boy with his warm brown eyes. *Was this place for real?* She'd grown up around Asheville, North Carolina where folks were friendly, but not like this.

"Thanks, Tyler. That was thoughtful of you and the…Tarpleys was it?"

"Yeah." He smiled with a trace of shyness. "You're Miss MacVie, aren't you? The new art teacher?"

Tabby nodded. It seemed a quiet, unobtrusive arrival was out of the question. Another difference to keep in mind about such a small community. Someone new around here was news. Not exactly what she wanted to be. "Yes."

"Cool." He grinned, the shyness disappearing. "I like art way better than math and science, but not as good as English."

Tabby laughed. "Maybe I can change your mind."

"What's in the pet carrier?" He craned his neck to see.

Tabby held it so he could. "My cat. Katie Scarlett…Katie for short."

Tyler's eyes rounded, and he laughed. "She looks like you—black hair and gold eyes too. Can I take the groceries back to the kitchen for you?"

While doing her student teaching, Tabby had gotten used to the lightning fast conversational changes children always seemed to make.

"If you don't mind. You caught me just walking in for the first time." She followed him, since he already seemed to know his way around the house. If all her welcomes were this warm, then the task her mother had given her should be easy. Tabby sucked in a deep, cleansing breath of relief.

They put the groceries away. Tyler pointed to the kitchen door that led out to the back corner of the veranda. "It will be easier to unload your car and come in this door. You can go up the back stairs. I can help."

"That's mighty nice. Thank you."

"You sure don't have much stuff," he commented as he looked at her open trunk.

Tabby laughed again, finding it so much easier to relax here. "I just got out of college, so no, I don't. Just my clothes, my bike, and my art supplies." As Tyler made a move to grab a stack of canvases, Tabby stopped him with a smile and a gentle hand on his shoulder. "I'll get those. You carry my case there with my paints and brushes. We'll take everything to the top floor."

After they'd unloaded, she opened her wallet, but Tyler shook his head. "Holly and Jake, my sister and her husband, would kill me if I took money for being neighborly."

Tabby's eyes widened. This place couldn't be for real. She felt like she'd walked into *The Andy Griffith Show* with Tyler as a cuter, twenty-first century version of Opie. "Well thanks then, Tyler. I guess I'll see you in a week, or sooner."

With a wave, the boy sprinted out the door and down the walk, no doubt on his way to tell everyone, including the mysterious Tarpleys, that he had actually met the new art teacher. Tabby smiled. She could get to like this town if Tyler and the Tarpleys were any example of what to expect. If the one welcome she really wanted was just as warm, Tabby could easily call Mountain Meadow home.

* * * *

Joe studied the two sulky combatants as they faced him from the other side of his desk. As Pastor Joe, head of the town's largest Baptist church, he had mediated many disagreements. This one between Hannah Hairston and Charlie Gardner was just the latest in a long line. The two had been at each other since the Christmas pageant last year when Charlie had knocked Hannah's halo off. The latest problem was a dispute over glue and scissors in the first grade vacation bible school group. The teenager in charge of the class called Joe in for help when it looked as if the problem was escalating.

"Let me see if I understand this. Charlie, you want the glue, and Hannah won't give it to you... And Hannah, you want the scissors, and Charlie won't give those to you. Is that correct?"

They both nodded. Joe worked hard to keep the smile off his face.

"Well, you give me the scissors, Charlie, and Hannah, you give me the glue." They dutifully handed them over. "I'll give the glue to Charlie and give Hannah the scissors. Does everyone have what they want now?"

Charlie nodded, and Hannah did, too, but then she asked suspiciously, "What if I want the glue back, Pastor Joe?"

Joe looked at Molly Saunders and said gently, "Well then you give it to Molly, and she will help you exchange it. How about that?"

Molly's look of gratitude also revealed a bit of the crush he feared she still harbored. "Thanks, Pastor Joe."

"No problem, Molly."

It was opening day of a week's worth of vacation bible school. Joe recruited his high school students to assist with the younger kids during the day, and in the evenings, he met with the teenagers. Joe watched Molly leave with the two children in tow. He loved his job, and he loved the area, but lately discontent nagged him. It had started last Christmas right after the ceasefire between the Presbyterian and Baptist church ladies.

He'd watched Jake, the town's police chief, and Holly Allred settle into their marriage, and seen the love and trust restored to Evan Richardson and Jenny Owens, one of the rural area's few doctors. The two couples had forged strong, loving relationships, even marrying in a double ceremony. The wedding had been short notice, but the Allreds had been out in force. Jenny had no family, and Evan was alienated from his. Still, it had been a joyous affair.

What Joe suffered now, he tried to reassure himself, was not so much a crisis in faith as simple loneliness. Sure he had parishioners all around him. In fact, he spent a lot of time surrounded by people—just not someone with whom he could share his feelings or concerns.

It was hard enough as a single man in a community like Mountain Meadow. It was almost impossible when you were also the minister of the Baptist church. Women, he found, fell into two categories when it came to ministers. They either turned tail as fast as they could, or they instantly envisioned remodeling the parsonage. It didn't matter that all he might want was company for dinner and a movie. Joe might be a man of God, but he was still a man. He'd like to be able to enjoy the company of an attractive woman once in a while without her obsessing over how the parsonage would look with a woman's touch or, conversely, trying to end the evening early.

Lately, he'd even wondered if he'd made a mistake choosing the path he had. Joe closed his eyes for a moment. A crisis of confidence wasn't what he needed right now. He'd grown up in a small community like this, farther west, and the path he'd chosen as a kid and a teen had been anything but holy. Seeing his best friend killed in a knife fight had been a wake-up call. No, he hadn't chosen wrong. It just wasn't always an easy or a comfortable choice. Having someone he could talk to would help. His monthly clandestine card games with Evan, Jake, and Sam provided some outlet, but not the intimacy he craved.

The last of the teens left, and Joe locked the church before walking through the parking lot and across to the backyard of the parsonage. In the house next door, a light on the third floor glowed, but otherwise, the house was dark and nearly as empty looking as it had been the past few months. He jumped slightly as a dark shadow dashed back toward the house and up onto the veranda railing. Two glowing eyes glared at him. A cat?

Joe didn't have anything against cats, but he definitely did not want paw prints all over his prized possession, a vintage, cherry-red Mustang convertible. He'd gotten it his first year in college and spent years restoring it to mint condition. He didn't need to drive it often with work right beyond his backyard, but he enjoyed it this time of year for the odd afternoon drive along the Blue Ridge Parkway.

That was one of the attractions of living in Mountain Meadow, one he couldn't lightly dismiss. He knew the car raised the eyebrows of a few of his more conservative flock, but this was one area where he wouldn't compromise. It was a way to relax, one of his few vices other than the odd poker game. He grinned.

As he walked by, he saw the car was still pristine, and he glanced back at the veranda railing, but the cat was gone. He spotted a bike leaning against the wall of the house. He'd heard the rumor his neighbor was the new art teacher, and he'd already half formed a picture of a motherly woman with paint stained fingers and Birkenstocks. The bike didn't quite fit that image. It screamed serious bicyclist. He might have to readjust his mental image of his new neighbor.

Before he settled down to work on his sermon, Joe reached for his guitar. Music had always been an important outlet for him. Sure, being able to sing was a tremendous bonus for the guy who had to stand up in front of a congregation, but Joe loved classical and pop music too. So that's what he launched into from the privacy of his own living room. With the evening breeze fluttering the curtains at the windows, it was the perfect way to spend the bit of free time he allowed himself.

He heard a window slam next door. The light in the neighbor's third floor window was still burning, but the window had been firmly shut. Had he disturbed her with his singing? They would have an uneasy relationship if that were the case because Joe not only loved to sing, he loved to listen to music. Still he tried to be thoughtful. That was part of who he was. The angry, defiant teen had disappeared long ago.

He closed his own windows on that side of the house before turning up his stereo while he made a snack. With plate and glass in hand, he went to his study to work on his schedule for the week. Even with the addition of vacation bible school, he still needed to fit in the visits he made to the nursing homes and members of his congregation who were unable to get out and about much. And there was a sermon still to write.

He started on the sermon first. Joe found that once he had an idea the words flowed. He thought about Hannah and Charlie. The two children had wanted to share, but had simply been unable to move past their differences until they were shown how. He smiled and began to write.

When he stretched and stood up a couple hours later, he noticed the house next door was dark. He wondered again about his new neighbor. Of course he knew she was the new art teacher for the Mountain Meadow Public Schools. How could he not? It was a small town where everyone seemed to know everything. His parishioners also enjoyed sharing whatever news they had.

What bothered Joe was the comments weren't always well-intentioned, or didn't seem to be.

The town's Facebook page had several comments about the fact that the new teacher had put a sizable down payment on the house next door, and they were already wondering how a new teacher could afford that. Joe shook his head. Facebook, phones, or face-to-face—Mountain Meadow loved to gossip.

If this teacher was like the last few new teachers to move here, she was nearing retirement and simply seeking a place where she could work for a few years until she could draw a second pension after working to retirement age in a neighboring state. Joe contented himself with his picture of a kindly, matronly woman who would have kids working on papier-mâché and macramé, maybe some clay projects for the older kids. He had modified his vision somewhat to make her lean and athletic after getting a glimpse of the bike, but in his imagination she still had Birkenstocks. He smiled as he turned the lights off and went to bed.

* * * *

The singing from next door, beautiful as it was, didn't help Tabby's attempts to work. She continued half-heartedly trying to translate her first impressions of Mountain Meadow to the canvas in front of her, but it wasn't easy. Too perfect. The whole town seemed too perfect. Bright, Rockwell-esque art wasn't her forte, although she was trying to stretch herself. She slapped her brush and palette onto the small table next to her easel. Who was she trying to kid? She was attempting to create art that was a bit more marketable than her normal subject matter, but Normal Rockwell she wasn't.

Turned against the opposite wall were the rest of her paintings, some so dark Tabby didn't look at them again once they were done. She also couldn't get rid of them. They were part of who she was, part of her personality. She had always painted darker images. Disturbing, some of her instructors had called them. Other teachers hadn't been so kind. While she knew, logically, there was nothing wrong with her art, she also recognized, with the same logic, that it made some people uncomfortable.

People didn't look at the work of Edvard Munch and smile. The drawings Kathe Kollwitz produced weren't hanging behind people's couches. Tabby knew her work was unlikely to head a list of popular artists. She had accepted that, but it didn't mean she couldn't create some commercially viable pieces. She hoped Mountain Meadow would be the inspiration for that. A new start that would give her a fresh perspective on life.

She paused and rolled her shoulders as Katie Scarlett glided into the room. The cat picked her way daintily through the canvases, hopped up into the window seat, and curled up.

"I know. I know. I should go to bed. What kind of artist am I that I paint at night rather than taking advantage of all that marvelous daylight?" Tabby set the brush down and sat next to the closed window, her hand absently stroking Katie's sleek coat. She examined the house next door, like hers in a lot of ways. There were lights on there, down on the first floor in what would be the equivalent of her dining room. Was he still singing in that lilting tenor voice? Tabby closed her eyes, hearing it again in her head. It had been beautiful, mournful, and a bit lonely.

The beautiful voice from below had soothed and seduced her. Peace was a fantasy she had never found. The rich, male voice had rolled over her like a cool mountain breeze or a dip in a quiet pond. It had also given her a feeling of loneliness. However, unless she changed her approach to life, she would become as lonely here as she had always been. Had the singer below been sharing his talent with his family? His girlfriend?

That was why she'd slammed the window shut.

She wanted life to be different here, hoped she would have a new start. Dropping her head forward, Tabby sighed in resignation. Just once it would be nice not to have people look at her as if she were a freak. Just once it would be nice to feel normal. Did people look at Stephen King or Dean Koontz as weirdos because they wrote stories that often plumbed the worst of what man was capable of?

Tabby turned off the lights. It was time for bed. She was here to find her sister, to start a new life that she hoped would provide a chance to be like everyone else. Surely, the darker side of her art could be kept under wraps.

Tabby rose before dawn. It was her first workday of a week she knew would fly by. As the only art teacher in the town's small school system, she had two rooms to set up—one at the elementary school and another for both middle and high school, since the two schools shared a campus. She was pleased to see plenty of supplies. The upper grades' room boasted not only a kiln, but also a great supply of clay and two electric pottery wheels.

There were paints, mostly tempera and watercolors, but she did find a small supply of canvas and acrylics. No oils, which was what she preferred to work in, but this would be a great start for all the kids. Drawing boards were neatly stacked at the back of the room where there were also rolls and rolls of paper, from plain newsprint to bright colors. Tabby was beside herself with happiness.

She'd worried when she accepted the job with such a small system that it would also be impoverished, but it appeared to her the folks in Mountain Meadow did not take arts education for granted. She had already met the music teacher, who also served both younger and older students, and the band director, a bit of a stuffy, fussy man who looked at Tabby's long flowing skirt and blouse and her Birkenstock sandals and simply raised his brows superciliously.

Tabby sighed when he walked away. Disapproval rolled off him so obviously, even a complete idiot would have felt it. Had he expected June Cleaver complete with sweater sets and pearls? Tabby was sure he wouldn't be the last to treat her with censure. People often ridiculed or disapproved anything or anyone different. It would probably be best if she kept most of her best artwork to herself.

Images from her childhood flashed before her, but she pushed them away. She was gone. It was over, and other than finding her sister, Tabby wanted no reminders of her past. She had been careful to leave no forwarding address with her college. She had arranged for everything to go to a post office box and hoped that would be enough to prevent anyone tracking her down. Her art had made her a target since she first picked up crayons as a child. Over the years, she had learned to be careful.

Tabby deliberately busied her hands and her brain setting up class rolls and portfolios to take her mind off her childhood. The nightmare images were sometimes too easy to allow back in. The pictures stayed, though, and by the time she stumbled through her kitchen door that afternoon, she flew straight up the stairs to her studio. Painting had always been her outlet, and as long as she kept it to herself, surely she would be safe here.

She set aside her Norman Rockwell-like vision of Mountain Meadow. This time when she painted, the images flowed dark and disturbing. She worked without stopping through the afternoon and evening and on into the night. She didn't eat, didn't drink, intent only on getting the pictures out of her head and onto the canvas where she could control them.

* * * *

Joe's gaze narrowed on the light high up in his neighbor's house when he arrived home. He had yet to see the new teacher, just her cat, which dozed during the mornings on the wide veranda as Joe went out for his morning run. The cat was a sleek, black-coated animal with the most amazing golden eyes that followed him wherever he went. Joe knew from Tyler that rather than fitting his image of the matronly teacher, Miss

MacVie was young and she looked like her cat, whatever that meant. Tyler wasn't quite at the age yet where he paid attention to females. Either way, he had one advantage over Joe—Tyler had actually seen the mysterious Miss MacVie.

Joe fixed dinner, listening to some classic rock while he hummed along. As he sat down at the kitchen table, he glanced out and saw once again that the only light came from the third floor window. After dinner, he worked in his study, polishing his sermon. When he stopped for a snack around eleven, the same light still burned in the house next door. In the middle of the night, he went downstairs to get a drink of water, pausing as he looked out and saw the light was still on. Was she all right? His brow furrowed as he stared at that window. Weren't artists always going on about needing natural light? That must mean they painted during the day. So what was she doing?

He stepped out onto his back porch. The sash was open, and for a moment, he thought he heard soft sobs. Joe frowned and started to cross the drive to her house, but then the light went off. He watched the window for several minutes, but no other light came on. He was torn between wanting to find out if she was okay, and not wanting to intrude on someone he had never met at one o'clock in the morning.

* * * *

Tabby felt drained and glad it was Friday. The school year started Tuesday, right after Labor Day. Although she looked forward to it, today she simply wanted to get her work done and go home. She'd finished last night's painting, and if she could help it, she wouldn't look at it again. Maybe someday she would find a market for her work, but not now. It was too personal.

Tabby decided she would use the weekend to get things in order in the house and finally go to Tarpley's to stock the kitchen. When she arrived home a little after noon, she spotted a tall, lean figure with broad shoulders and a tight butt headed through the backyard next to hers over to the Baptist church. His caramel-colored hair glinted with golden highlights in the sun. No way was that the minister. She had pictured an older man with slicked back hair and a bit of a paunch when the real estate agent mentioned she would be living next to the parsonage. Tabby was surprised to find out he was not married, having assumed he was an older, widowed man. Maybe this guy was a parishioner.

Well, no matter. Minister or not, she had no intention of making his acquaintance. Tabby made a point of staying as far as possible from organized religion. Some of the biggest hypocrites hid behind the pages of Bibles they made a habit of thumping. In her experience, the more of a hypocrite they were, the louder they thumped.

Tabby retreated inside her house to assess what she'd need from the store. When that was done, she changed her skirt and long-sleeved shirt for a pair of biking pants and shoes. As hot as it was, she still slipped a long-sleeved shirt over her head so her arms and torso were covered from her wrists to her neck. She scraped her hair back into a ponytail, put on her helmet, and went for a ride.

Heading out of town quickly, she enjoyed the wind and the sun on her face as she rode along a narrow, twisting back road. She had a specific destination in mind, at least an address she wanted to check out, and was vaguely disappointed when she pushed her bike up the long, drive to find not the house her mother had described, but a newer, log home, and it appeared deserted.

Tabby studied the small grove of trees at the top of the hill behind the house and left her bike near the drive as she climbed to the top. Mama had told her she used to sit there, and Tabby wanted to see it close up. She was surprised when she reached the summit to find a tiny headstone there inscribed with the name Hope Richardson and a date thirteen years earlier. There was also a quote, "Like our love, born too soon. You will always be our best and brightest Hope."

The stone didn't look weathered enough to be thirteen years old, but it also wasn't brand new. Why would a stone with the name Richardson be here on this land? Tabby's fingers tingled as she touched the cool stone. The edges around the engraving were rough. Tabby frowned. She looked at the quote again, overcome with the feeling that she didn't know nearly enough about the woman she had come to find.

All at once, she felt as though she were intruding, which in fact, she was. A nervousness she couldn't explain overwhelmed her, and she leaped to her feet before running down the hill back toward her bike.

"Whoa!" A voice like a whip cracked, and strong hands grabbed her arms. Tabby froze. She fought back the urge to struggle away from the firm grasp as mental images of another man in another time flooded her brain. She had to fight the panic nearly blinding her, but it was a losing battle.

Chapter 2

"Let me go!"

The tall man's scowl deepened. "Who are you? And what are you doing here? You do realize you're on private property, don't you?"

As soon as he released her, Tabby took a deep breath and brushed her hair off her face. Back under control, she looked up, not that she had to tilt her head far. He paused for a moment, his thick brows still drawn together over dark gray eyes.

"Who are you?" he asked again, now with an underlying curiosity that bordered on intense. He wore authority like a well-worn coat, an obviously complex man who, right now, was frowning ferociously.

"Tabitha MacVie," she whispered, desperately trying to think of an excuse for why she was there. She cleared her throat. "The new art teacher in Mountain Meadow. I—I'm sorry. I was riding and thought this was a road, and then—then I got up here and saw the trees, and…"

"…And you're a very bad liar," the man said. While she no longer sensed any real hostility from him, persistence burned in his gaze. "Let me introduce myself. I'm Evan Richardson, the commonwealth's attorney. Now, maybe you could tell me who you really are?"

Tabby's chin jutted. "Tabitha MacVie, and I *am* the new art teacher."

"But you didn't just stumble on this place, did you? Are you from here?"

"No." She tilted her head at him. "You said your name is Richardson." She glanced over her shoulder, deciding to take a stab in the dark. "Like the baby?"

He nodded, still watching her with narrowed gray eyes. "Why are you here, Miss MacVie?"

"I came here because my mother used to live here, and I came because I was hoping to find my sister. Maybe you know her."

"Why don't you tell me who you believe this sister is?" Caution shadowed his words as if he somehow already knew what she would say, but wasn't sure he wanted to hear her actually voice it.

"Her name's Jenny. Jenny Owens. Mama said I would find her here. This was where she grew up, but it looks deserted. Has she moved, Mr. Richardson? I would like to find her, to tell her about Mama. I have a letter for her."

"Jenny's my wife." His eyes narrowed. "She's expecting our child in less than a month. I don't want her upset at this point, so what's in this letter?" His gaze shifted to the tiny gravestone on the hill. "We've already had our share of troubles—then and now."

"Mama's dead," Tabby said. "She died last year of cancer, but she wanted Jenny to know why she left. I—I came to tell her." Her voice died as she, too, looked up the hill and her brow furrowed. "Never mind, Mr. Richardson. It's been my secret for the last year. I can keep it a while longer."

Worry darkened his expression, making it obvious how much he cared for his wife. Tabby wondered if Jenny knew how lucky she was. This was the kind of man who would always look after her first, even before himself. Tabby smiled. "My sister's lucky to have you. I'll go. I'm sorry I trespassed."

"Wait." He reached out to touch her arm, but Tabby avoided the contact without making it obvious. She didn't liked to be touched, a holdover from her childhood that she couldn't seem to shake. "I could give you a ride."

She shook her head. "No. I need the exercise to clear my head."

Evan nodded as if he understood. "We live on Maple Street. If you'd like to come by this weekend, we'll be around."

Hope stirred, but Tabby had learned long ago to be cautious. With a shift and a tug at the long sleeves of her shirt, she asked uncertainly, "Are you sure?"

Evan smiled. "Jenny would have my hide if I kept you away. In fact, why don't we make it for dinner tomorrow night? Nothing fancy. We'll throw something on the grill and invite our neighbors, Holly and Jake. Holly's brother, Tyler, might even be one of your students."

"Tyler Morgan?" At Evan's nod, she smiled. "I've met him. I'd like to meet some other people, if you're sure."

"Four-twenty-four Maple Street. Around six tomorrow."

He slipped behind the wheel of the big SUV he was driving, reversed, and headed down the drive. Tabby twisted her hair into its ponytail, put her helmet on, and mounted her bike to head home. She would meet her sister. She could give her the letter Mama had dictated to her. Then she would be done. Tabby had purposely kept herself from forming any expectations beyond that.

* * * *

Joe couldn't stop smiling. Vacation bible school finished Friday night with a big, noisy cookout in the back of the church. Joe watched all the younger kids running around playing on the swing sets and the jungle gym while the older kids engaged in a spirited game of volleyball. He moved from group to group, spending time not only with the kids but also with the parents who were invited to this final night.

As he locked up the church and walked home, he reflected on where he was. A full year in Mountain Meadow and his ministry was paying off, particularly with the kids, which was exactly where he wanted to have an impact. Membership was up among younger families, but even the older members were content with some of the changes he'd introduced.

Things had turned a little sticky last year when Jake and Holly first showed up, but since the entire town soon fell in love with Holly and her baby, Noelle, that awkwardness was long forgotten. The only unsettling moments from his point of view were the constant invitations to dinners where someone's unmarried sister, cousin, or best friend from high school suddenly showed up. He wouldn't mind a date now and then, but he'd prefer to do the choosing on his own. He'd also prefer to eat something other than spaghetti or meatloaf.

Joe's glance slid to the house next to his. He glimpsed a tall, slim woman lifting a bike and setting it on the veranda before she disappeared indoors. Ah. That must be the elusive Tabitha MacVie, not at all old it seemed. In fact, what he'd so briefly glimpsed had made his breath catch. Though her hair had been back in a braid, Joseph could tell that Tyler hadn't exaggerated, it was long and nearly as black as her cat.

He wondered if Miss MacVie ate spaghetti or meatloaf. He hoped not.

As the evening wound down, his eyes strayed to the house more and more. When darkness fell and he saw the only light was once again in the third floor room, he was disappointed. What was she doing up there? He was tempted to grill Tyler, but that would be a bit too obvious. Not to mention pathetic.

With effort, Joe put her from his mind and returned to his house. He had a lot to get done Saturday, plus rehearsing his sermon one more time, and he didn't need to be thinking about the mystery woman. But despite his promise to himself, when he got up the following morning to run, his eyes settled on her back door. The first thing he noticed was the bike was gone. Was she out riding again?

Joe stretched and began the longer run he normally saved for Saturday mornings. Five miles before he came home, showered, then stopped in at Tarpley's to do his grocery shopping. It was a weekly ritual.

While he ran, he amused himself with ways in which he could meet his new neighbor. He envisioned offering her help getting settled, but she'd probably already done that. He pictured heroically rescuing her from something—maybe a burning house. No. He certainly didn't want to see her house burn down. Maybe…

In the end, he met her in an aisle in Tarpley's when they both reached for the same box of macaroni and cheese. It should have been the most mundane of ways in which to encounter an attractive woman, except that as soon as their hands touched, she stumbled back with a startled gasp and clutched her hand within her other as if she'd been burned.

Joe got that. He felt the same way as he stared into eyes as wide and golden as his next door neighbor's cat. Her hair was only a shade lighter than the cat's. This was the elusive Miss MacVie. She was tall, he noted, nearly eye-to-eye with him, and he was a shade over six feet. He smiled, but received only that shocked look in return.

Resisting the temptation to see if he'd spilled something on himself or had a smudge of grease on his face, he held out his hand. She didn't take it.

"I'm Joseph Taylor." He persevered, hoping to high heaven he didn't blush. "Most folks call me Joe. I believe we live next door to each other." When she still didn't say anything, he continued. "Most of the time people say their name back to me. Have I upset you in some way?"

Finally, as if she pulled herself out of a trance, she shook her head. "No. I'm Tabitha MacVie—Tabby."

He was still smiling, he realized, feeling awkward, but she had such a wary, watchful look on her face that he suspected she already knew most people called him Joe, just with Pastor with a capital P in front of it. It looked like she fit firmly in the first category of women, the ones who wanted to run like hell. "I'm sorry we didn't meet sooner. Every time I stopped by, you were gone or it was late. It's been a busy week."

She seemed to shake herself, and a myriad of emotions flickered over her face, but when warmth and hope were once more overshadowed by wariness, Joe sighed.

"It was a busy week for me too. I've haven't even had time to shop until today. Tyler brought me food the first day, and I've lived on that until now."

She had spoken to him. That was a shade better than some encounters he'd had during seminary.

"Now I feel guilty for not making more of an effort to meet you sooner," Joe said. "Why don't I cook dinner for you tonight—welcome you to the neighborhood? I was going to throw a couple of burgers on the grill."

Her smile was regretful. He was already getting the avoid-the-pastor two-step. "I already have a dinner engagement," she said. "Evan and Jenny Richardson."

Not a date. Maybe there was still hope. "You've met them?"

She was wary again. He saw it in the inscrutable look blanketing her eyes, almost as veiled as a cat's. "I met Evan yesterday."

He wanted to prolong their conversation, but couldn't see any way to do so, especially when she was so obviously uncomfortable. He handed her the mac and cheese, and noticed she was careful not to touch him again. "Here. Take this. I can get a different box."

Joe finished shopping, berating himself the entire time for mishandling the encounter. He was also overly conscious of Tabby's tall form gliding up and down the aisles. She wore jeans and a long-sleeved man's shirt with the cuffs turned back. Her dark hair was pulled back into a neat braid. Heaven help him, she was beautiful. And every inch of her screamed hands off.

He should have been more assertive. She hadn't been rude. He'd encountered that as well from women who obviously didn't even consider him human. She just hadn't been encouraging.

He finished shopping first and hurried home, careful to keep one eye on her drive as he put away his groceries. He would offer to help, that way they could talk some more. It would buy him some time.

* * * *

Tabby still tingled from where her hand had brushed Joe Taylor's. For an instant, his touch had felt overwhelmingly right, a little zing of electricity that had made other parts of her zing too. She cringed at the thought. How could her own mind betray her in such a way? A preacher? She shuddered. It brought back horrible visions of her childhood. Still, Joe's touch was different than those holier-than-thou men who had made her life hell.

He was different with his tawny hair and warm blue eyes. Many people thought blue eyes cool, but Joe's were as warm as a summer afternoon when the sun heated her skin and the insects buzzed lazily around the flowers. Tabby shook her head. It wouldn't do to start spinning fantasies about her neighbor, the *minister*. Artists who dated ministers probably painted landscapes or kids' portraits. Better to stay away and avoid the disillusionment.

Up front, Tyler helped an older woman bag customers' groceries. When he spotted Tabby, he grinned. "Hi, Miss MacVie. Mrs. Tarpley, this is Miss MacVie, the new art teacher."

The older woman smiled kindly. "Good morning. Welcome to Mountain Meadow. Are you settling in all right?"

Tabby returned her smile. "Very well, thank you. Call me, Tabby, please. I really appreciate the groceries you sent over. How much do I owe you?"

Mrs. Tarpley looked startled. "Oh, there's no charge, dear. It's our welcome to the community."

"Thank you." As they continued to talk, Tabby carefully avoided answering most of Mrs. Tarpley's questions. While she knew the woman was simply curious, Tabby felt she had to be cautious. Until she'd accomplished what her mother wanted, she didn't dare arouse too much curiosity. She'd prefer not to arouse any at all.

She drove home with the car packed. She was bent inside the hatchback looking for the frozen items when the man already occupying too much of her thoughts spoke from behind her.

"Allow me to help."

Tabby bumped her head as she abruptly straightened, rubbed the bruised spot, and said, "Oh, that's not necessary…" but Joseph Taylor had already grabbed bags and strode up the steps to her porch. She frowned, but followed, opening the door to allow him into the big, airy kitchen. She was way, way too conscious of him as he continued to bring in bags and she unpacked them. Even when he finished, he didn't leave. Instead, he began removing things from the remaining bags and setting them on the counter, so she could decide where to put them.

He made her nervous, but Tabby couldn't ask him to leave. He had helped her. Besides, she had never met a man that made her insides flutter. He did. Why was that? A small, cynical voice reminded her that he would never stick around once he got to know her better. All her life people had turned tail once she had either trusted them enough to show them some of her art work, or they had discovered it on their own. Why should this man be any different?

When they finished, she smiled tightly. "I—I have some iced tea made. Would you like a glass?"

"I thought you'd never ask." He grinned. "And I'd run out of groceries to unpack."

Her gaze slipped to his generous mouth. His grin affected her more than anything she'd seen so far. It brought out fascinating dimples in his lean cheeks. Tabby realized she was staring and spun away with a blush. She would like to paint him. Not only was he beautiful, but for the first time that she could remember, he inspired images in her mind that were warm and bright. She felt like a moth to his flame. She had to get him out of the confines of the kitchen. "We could take it out on the porch in the shade."

And so, a few minutes later, Tabby found herself curled up on a porch swing, sipping tea while the minister of the Baptist church sat nearby. But it was hard to think of him that way when he didn't fit any of her previously conceived notions about what ministers should look like.

"I appreciate your help," Tabby said.

Joe smiled. "But you'd like me to go home now?"

Tabby flushed and her gaze skittered away. "I didn't say that."

He leaned back in his chair and set his glass on the table next to it, idly watching as a bead of sweat ran down the outside of the glass. "You didn't have to. Some people are very effective at getting a point across without saying anything at all. It's there in your voice and your body language. Do you think I haven't encountered reactions like yours before?"

She didn't want to be lumped in with other people. More than that, she didn't want him to see how much he scared her. Tabby stuck her chin out. "Why would I have any reaction? I hardly know you."

He smiled, but beneath it, she glimpsed weariness and disillusionment. "Yet you do. Have a reaction, that is. Is it me personally or the fact that I'm a minister?"

Tabby set her glass aside. She met his steady gaze squarely, though inside her stomach fluttered with nerves. "You're very direct."

"Sometimes you have to be, and while I'm being direct, I'll tell you that I'm attracted to you, Tabby, and I don't think that attraction's all one-sided."

Tabby shook her head, trying to convince herself with the same words she said to him. "No. But not in the way you mean. I'm an artist. I'd like to paint you. You—you have an air about you I would like to capture on canvas."

"It's my halo."

Tabby gaped a moment, then burst out laughing. "I can't believe you said that. Won't you get struck by lightning or something?"

"No more so than you for saying your only interest was in painting me." He lifted one brow and grinned.

She opened and closed her mouth a couple of times then said, "I don't date ministers. I don't do the whole church thing."

Joe gazed at her with his impossibly patient blue eyes. He tilted his head a little, and one dimple appeared when he lifted the corner of his mouth. "I'm not asking you to marry me, nor am I even asking you to 'do the whole church thing'—though I wouldn't kick you out if you showed up. Could we try neighbors, maybe even friends first?" When Tabby hesitated, he arched one thick golden brow. "I'll let you paint me."

"Really?" Her eyes lit up. "Are you bribing me, Pastor?"

His smile expanded. "Whatever works, and call me Joe or Joseph. You'll have to add the bribery to my list of sins."

Tabby stood up. "Now?"

"You want to get started right now?"

"Yes. I'd like to get my sketchpad. It's upstairs in my studio."

Tabby didn't realize he'd followed until she turned from picking up the heavy sketchbook and the zippered bag that held her pencils. Joe's eyes were riveted on the painting still sitting on the easel, a violent flaring of dark colors intermixed with flashes of vivid fiery lights and glimpses of tortured souls. Tabby pivoted and covered the painting with an oilcloth. When she faced him again, her chin jutted and her shoulders were stiff.

Without looking at her, he said quietly, "It's what you were painting the night I heard you...."

If anything, her body stiffened even more. "Heard me what?"

He looked at her. "Crying."

She turned away with a shrug of her shoulders. "It's just a painting."

"It's like being inside Dante's *Inferno*."

She turned back and smiled at him challengingly. "Then let me paint an angel instead, and I have one more request."

"What's that?"

"I want to sketch you while you sing."

He blew his breath out with an embarrassed laugh. "Seriously? You slammed your window the last time."

"I want to hear you. We can do it here or at your house. You pick."

He looked around the cluttered room with its high ceiling and the gentle whirr of a ceiling fan. "Here's fine. Where do you want me?"

For an instant the words *naked and in my bed* came to mind. Heat flashed through her in what felt like an entire body blush. She needed some control.

"Near the window. I want to see the light on your face. That way I can capture the cascade of sparkles from your halo."

Joe laughed and relaxed. He half sat on a stool near the window, while she perched at the far side of it on the window seat, her sketchbook open.

She had drawn plenty of models in her life drawing classes, but this was different. What she was trying to do was different, and Tabby had no idea at all how, or if, it would work.

As she watched, he closed his eyes for a moment and began in the clear tenor she remembered so well, and she found it was as enthralling as it had been the first time she heard it. Only now, watching him as well as hearing him, she felt warmed inside. He glowed, almost as if he did indeed have a halo. Somehow, Tabby knew that would make him laugh if she told him, but it was true. He was light and warmth, and he fascinated her.

She sketched quickly, catching his face from different angles, and when she finished, she simply listened to the breathtaking pull of his voice. She knew the song he sang now, a song that never failed to touch her heart—"Thankful."

* * * *

Joe finished the last note and focused on Tabby. She sat with her sketchbook closed and her face angled toward the window. "Tabby?" he questioned softly. "What is it?"

"That was beautiful, Joseph," she whispered. "You have no idea. And… And I can't tell you." She blinked as if trying to clear her head.

With a sudden burst of energy, she stood up, took the dark painting from the easel, set it facing the wall with other canvases that had been similarly stacked so all that was visible were the backs of them, and replaced it with a fresh canvas. Joe watched, knowing that for the moment at least she had forgotten him. He kept quiet, curious as to what he would see, feeling somewhat like an eavesdropper. She began what looked like another sketch, only this time using a brush and thinned paint to lay out the basic composition.

He looked at his watch, vaguely remembering Tabby mentioning dinner with Evan and Jenny Richardson, but she was so intent on what she did he hated to interrupt her. As she finished outlining her composition and sat back for a moment, he finally spoke, "Tabby, it's a little after five. Aren't you going to the Richardson's house?"

She started. He smiled at a concentration so intense she could forget he was there. If he were a more egotistical man, he might be offended, but strangely enough he understood her absorption. He experienced it in his singing and often in writing a sermon, and he was flattered she allowed him to share hers. She stared at him, and the intensity of those golden eyes changed to panic as she glanced down at the paint smearing her hands.

"I—I have to get ready. I don't even know where I'm going or how long it will take to get there."

"It's okay. It's a couple of streets over. No more than a five or ten minute walk. I can show you the way."

"Would you really?"

"It would be my pleasure."

He waited for her on the veranda, rising slowly to his feet as she came back through the door a quarter hour later. She wore a long, flowing skirt that left little more than her ankles bare, but made of a material light enough it seemed to caress her body each time she moved. The top was the same way, covering her from wrists to neck. He wondered that someone as free-spirited as she seemed to be was also almost excessively modest. The most revealing thing he'd seen her wear were bicycling shorts, and even then those were capris, falling to around mid-calf.

"Are you ready?" he asked with a smile he hoped would allay some of her nervousness, and she nodded. They walked companionably next to each other, people greeting him with a wave that Joe happily returned. Too soon, he stopped in front of Evan and Jenny's huge Victorian home. "There you are. Think you can find your way back home?"

The response he felt coming died on her lips as a young voice piped, "Pastor Joe! Miss MacVie!"

Tyler dashed over to them, his long hair flying around his head. Behind him came Mountain Meadow's Police Chief and his wife, carrying their daughter, Noelle.

Tyler skidded to a halt next to Tabby, and flushed. "I—I want you to meet Jake and my sister, Holly, Miss MacVie." His dark brown eyes swiveled to Joe. "Are you eating at Evan and Jenny's too?"

Joe shook his head. "No. I walked over to show Miss MacVie the way."

Holly and Jake reached them, and Jake spoke up, "Well, I'm sure you'd be more than welcome, Joe."

He saw the uneasy shift in Tabby's expression. Better not to press things too far, since she was already spooked by his profession. He smiled. "Thanks, but not this time. I still have a few kinks to work out of tomorrow's sermon. I'll see y'all tomorrow." He turned to Tabby and murmured, "There, I've delivered you safe and sound and didn't even try to convert you on the way."

The uneasiness fled from her expression, and she laughed, "Thank you, Joseph."

* * * *

With mixed feelings, Tabby watched Joseph leave. While she might be reluctant to call a preacher friend, the fact remained he was the closest thing to a friend she had so far in this town. She turned her head in time to see Jake open Evan and Jenny's front door as if he belonged there. Tabby envied that kind of easy familiarity.

"Evan? Jenny?" Holly called as they all entered the front hall. To one side, a double set of sliding doors parted. "Oh, there you are." Holly continued. "We're here, and we've brought Tabby with us. Come on, step up. Don't be shy."

Tabby's heart thudded to the point she feared it would beat right out of her throat. For a moment, all she saw was Evan's towering form. He didn't look entirely happy, and his expression appeared guarded. From behind him stepped a petite, blond-haired woman, her belly swollen with advanced pregnancy. However, that wasn't what grabbed Tabby's attention.

She stared into eyes as golden as her own. Looking at her elder sister felt as though she'd taken a step back in time. Only her mother had never looked as confident as Jenny Richardson did. Tabby took a half step forward, uncertain what she was about to do or say, but then she halted.

Jenny's smile of welcome had faded as Tabby stepped from Jake's shadow. The color left Jenny's face. Tabby was sure it must have fled hers too. Despite her pregnancy, Jenny was still quick on her feet. She turned to Evan in such a way that he actually took a step back.

"You should have told me," she snapped at her husband. "You should have asked." She turned a hostile gaze on Tabby.

From the corner of her eye, Tabby was aware of Holly and Jake hurrying Tyler down the hall to the kitchen. Tabby wished Joseph had stayed. Somehow, she had a feeling he would bring calm to this situation because it always seemed to surround him.

"Who are you?" Jenny hissed after the door swung shut behind Tyler and his family. Tabby raised her chin and saw Jenny do the same thing.

With a deep breath, she began, "Tabitha MacVie, from Asheville, North Carolina. My mother…"

Jenny's eyes shot sparks. "I don't want to hear *anything* about your mother," she interrupted. She looked Tabby up and down. "How old are you?"

Tabby shook, and even Evan took a half-step back from the anger and pain in Jenny's voice and expression.

"Twenty-three," Tabby whispered.

"Why don't we go into the living room?" Evan suggested, no doubt hoping to move this confrontation away from the hallway that led straight back to the kitchen. He attempted to take Jenny's elbow, only to be shaken off furiously.

Jenny's gaze swept Tabby from head to foot. "For all his faults, and for everything else he lied about, it seems my father did tell the truth on one count. My mother was a slut."

"Jenny!" Evan snapped. "Stop it. Tabby is a guest in our home."

"She is your guest, not mine," and with that, Jenny stomped up the stairs.

Evan stared after his wife, then looked at Tabby with embarrassment. He spread his hands wide in a frustrated and helpless gesture. "I'm sorry. She's usually not... Maybe it's the pregnancy...."

Tabby smiled thinly. Why had she ever imagined this would be easy, that in an instant she would gain the family she had always dreamed of having? "You should go to her. She needs you even if she is angry at you."

Evan spared her one quizzical glance before he sprinted up the steps.

Tabby studied the beautiful house. Her mother had told Tabby what childhood had been like for Jenny, and how it had probably continued even after Mama had run away. The light and furnishings in this house made it obvious that her sister's life was far different now. And even if she was angry with her husband at the moment, anyone could see how devoted Evan was to her.

Tabby had known her reception might not be a warm one, but she hadn't anticipated the extent to which Jenny would reject her. She probably should have. Rejection was certainly not a new experience.

Head tilted, she listened for a moment to the laughter floating down the hallway from the kitchen. Giggles from Tyler and Noelle, easygoing rumbles from Jake, and Holly's gentle chuckle...all the sounds of a happy family. She had no right to be here. Family had never been happy for her.

After reaching into the deep pocket of her skirt, Tabby removed the envelope she had carried with her for more than a year. She knew its contents because she had written them as her mother dictated to her. It was the explanation Jenny Richardson wasn't ready to hear. She would be, at some point, so Tabby propped the envelope against the drawer of the hall tree and quietly let herself out. She retraced the steps she and Joe had taken just a few minutes ago.

After letting herself into her house, Tabby allowed the screen door to bang shut and ran for her studio, but she didn't turn on the lights. She curled up in the corner of the window seat and wrapped her arms around her bent knees, rocking and remembering.

Chapter 3

Tabby swiped a tear from the corner of her eye. So much for the fairy tale ending. She should be used to it. Conflict and fear were two things she was way too familiar with. As Tabby stared out the window, raised voices echoed down the long years separating memory from reality. Mama had tried to protect her from Tommy MacVie, largely succeeding up until the time Tabby started school. It was easy enough to hide the artistic talent that had shown up the moment she had first picked up a crayon. Most children weren't putting together complex compositions, especially ones that already revealed an understanding of life's harsher realities.

As dusk transitioned into darkness, Tabby continued to sit in the window seat. The memories of a childhood filled with rejection battered her.

Within a week of starting kindergarten, the school was already on the phone. They had samples of her drawings they wanted her parents to see. Her daddy had beaten her black and blue that night, stripping her room of every crayon, marker, and watercolor. He had thrown out every blank piece of paper in the house.

"You are not to draw," he'd ordered. "Not here. Not anywhere. I've talked to the school. If you draw anything other than what the teacher tells you to, I'll break your fingers. Then you won't be able to draw."

She had been five years old. Eighteen years later didn't make handling rejection any easier. Whatever grounded, realistic self-talk she'd created about her sister—about how they were really strangers to each other, and would have to get to know each other—in her heart she had hoped there would be some instant communion. Instead, Jenny seemed to hate her.

Tabby's daddy hated her, but she hadn't understood why. It wasn't until she'd grown a few years older that she realized drawing pictures of children and women being beaten made adults nervous.

For Tabby it had simply been reality. A reality she was trapped in.

Her art had been her only outlet. Not drawing wasn't a choice. It didn't matter that her father thought she was possessed. He followed his own upbringing and tried to beat the evil out of Tabby. With each whack, he told her he would "break" her from her sneaking around, drawing pictures that had to be from the devil. Only the devil would draw such lies.

Except, they weren't lies. They were the truth that Tabby lived, and she still didn't understand why her daddy seemed to hate her so. When Mary tried to stop him, he shoved her against the wall and continued thrashing Tabby until she passed out.

Sometimes Tommy's beatings left welts and bruises. More often they drew blood, but never in places where it showed. Oh no. Tommy was far too smart for that. If Mary tried to interfere or stop him, then he beat her too.

Tabby rested her cheek on her knees as she rocked back and forth in the window seat. She wished Jenny had known just how bravely their mama had tried to defend Tabby. She swallowed, though her throat felt thick and tight.

No matter how her daddy tried to keep her from drawing, Tabby couldn't stop, not even for her mama. She used the dirt on the playground, any scrap of paper she could sneak out of school. Tabby couldn't make her unusual artistic ability go away, so she learned to hide it and the horror she lived through at home.

Tabby scrubbed her cheeks, but the tears kept coming as she mourned not only her mother but the relationship it now appeared she would never have with her older sister.

Tabby and her mama had been enablers as well as victims. She knew that now. She understood that she should have spoken up. She had tried to get her message out several times through her pictures, but Tommy had already convinced everyone in the school system that she was simply a disturbed girl they were trying to help.

She didn't want that following her now. She wanted a new life without the garbage of her past.

And she wanted her sister.

* * * *

Jenny stared at the envelope in her hands as if she had caught hold of a copperhead. Opening it would change everything. She had yet to unseal it, though she'd carried it with her all evening. Evan had talked her into coming back down, but when they did, it was to find the envelope propped against the hall tree and no sign of Tabby. Evan made excuses that she was feeling ill and had decided to go home, but Tyler was the only one still young enough to believe it.

Jenny felt like an idiot, and for the first time since her reunion with Evan last Christmas, she felt his censure. It was there in the tightness of his mouth, the shadows around his gray eyes.

"Are you going to open it?" he asked her now as they lay side by side in their big bed. Evan skimmed through the latest *Law Review* and didn't even glance over as he asked the question.

Jenny sighed. She had propped several pillows around herself in an attempt to get comfortable, but with little success. She tapped her fingers on the envelope, seeing the creases in it that showed it had been carried around for quite some time. "It's not her handwriting," she said stiffly.

"Whose?" Evan asked mildly, finally closing his magazine.

"My mother's. I saw some letters she wrote when I was going through my father's things. This isn't her handwriting. This is too bold."

Evan slid his arm around her shoulders and gently squeezed. "There's only one way to find out what it says and who it's from. Open it."

Jenny turned her gaze to him, pleading for understanding. "I—I can't, Ev. Would you?"

He took the envelope and slid one long finger beneath the flap. His elegant hands were steady as he removed the two sheets of paper. "You want me to read it to you?" At Jenny's nod, he unfolded the sheets. "It's dated summer a year ago. Tabby must have carried it with her all that time."

"Just read it."

He began:

My Dearest Jenny,

Tabitha is writing this for me because I can no longer write. I'm dying. It began as breast cancer, and I found the lump early on, but I was too afraid to see the doctor. When I did, the cancer had spread to my lymph nodes and beyond. By the time Tabby finds you, I know I'll be gone. I know you probably won't have a good opinion of me—after all, what Mama runs off and leaves her young daughter behind? And I'm sure your daddy made sure to point that out.

But I kept track of you, honey. I know you're a doctor, and I'm so proud of you because I know you'll be able to take care of yourself. You won't have to depend on any man for food and shelter. I made sure Tabby was looked after, too, so she can get away from here and never come back. I want her to find you. I want you to find each other. Sisters should stick together.

Tabby is finding out about you as she writes this for me, and I expect she's as shocked right now as you'll be when you read it, but you both need to know what happened.

Jenny, as I'm sure you already know, your daddy was a moonshiner. I was still in high school when I first met Billy at the harvest dance there in Mountain Meadow. Do they still have that at Halloween? I was a good girl, but your daddy caught my eye. He was a classic bad boy with his long hair and his fast cars. I guess we were drawn to each other. I was looking for excitement, and he was looking for—I don't know—maybe someone to corrupt. At any rate, we married against the wishes of my family. When you came along eight months after our marriage, there was talk. A lot of folks around Mountain Meadow and Castle County turned their backs on me. They had already turned them on your daddy and the rest of the Owens family a long time before.

Things went along fairly smooth at first. I pretended I didn't know how your daddy made his money, and he was content to let me think it was from farming. Then along about the time you turned seven, things got rough. A new sheriff in the county vowed to crack down on what some folks called the Moonshine Capital of the South. Your daddy moved his still off his land onto another man's farm, but he got caught, and the man was threatening to expose him. Your daddy couldn't afford to ignore the threat because the man was rich and powerful, so he offered him a deal. What I didn't know was I was the deal. Your daddy traded my body to keep his still.

"Jesus!" Evan stopped reading and cleared his throat. He looked over at Jenny. "You're awfully pale, Jen. You want me to quit?"

"No. I want to hear it."

"All right." So he continued:

I was too frightened to do anything but what I was told. My family had turned their backs on me, and if your daddy went to jail, I didn't know what I would do or how I would take care of you, so to my shame, I slept with this man. It went on for several months until I couldn't take it anymore. I felt like a whore and knew I had to get out. You see, I was silly enough to fall in love with my lover, but I knew he would never leave his own family. As much as I didn't want to leave you, I was also afraid to take you. I had no way to support myself, let alone a bright little girl like you. It tore me apart inside, but I knew your daddy would take care of you. Billy might not have been good for much, but he would do that.

Jenny's hands clenched into fists. Oh, her daddy had taken care of her all right. He had set her and Evan up so that Evan believed she'd slept with half the high school basketball team. It destroyed their relationship to the point it took twelve years for them to find each other again.

So I left. I ended up in Asheville, North Carolina where I met Thomas MacVie. He was a handsome man, a couple of years younger than me, but he was determined to have me. I was anxious too, but for a whole different reason. I realized I was pregnant with my lover's child. Your daddy wouldn't touch me while I slept with another man. He kept calling me slut, though he was the one who'd pushed me into his bed. Tommy seemed like the perfect solution at the time.

I didn't lie to him. I told him I was pregnant, and it didn't seem to matter to him. He seemed happy about it. He was controlling and strict in his religious beliefs, but I could live with that. He was about as far removed from your daddy as I thought a man could be. And I thought that had to be a good thing.

All I will tell you about that is I was wrong, but I won't tell you more than that. That's Tabby's story to tell if she chooses. If Tommy shows up around Mountain Meadow though, you call the police. I will only ask two things of you, Jenny. Forgive me for not finding you, and I beg you to watch over your sister.

Your Mama,
Mary

There was silence in the bedroom as Evan finished reading the letter. It sat on his lap, beneath his hands. "I wonder why Tabby waited a year to find you? She even mentioned that when I caught her at the farm."

Jenny shrugged, trying to feign indifference, but the letter left her feeling uneasy and disturbed. Her mother implied Tommy MacVie was not so different from her daddy. Had he done something to Tabby? "Maybe she had to finish school."

Evan tapped the paper with his fingertips. "Maybe," he agreed, but she could see the puzzle it presented in his mind. "I wonder what the story is your mother felt was Tabby's to tell?"

Jenny sat up. She had to pee again. Just one of the inconveniences of advanced pregnancy. "I'm sure I don't know." When she came back to the room, Evan was looking over the letter once more.

"You know, the day I met her at the farm, she was running down the hill from Hope's grave as if the hounds of hell were behind her."

Jenny wasn't ready to bend. "Perhaps she saw you and was trying to get away."

"No. I did dismiss it to begin with as just due to her concern over being caught trespassing, but it was more than that."

"So she's got a guilt complex. Maybe she should have."

"Jenny, it's more than that. I've seen guilt. This was fear. I think your sister's childhood might make yours look like a walk in the park, and we know how bad yours was."

Jenny, who was ever practical, shook her head. "I think you're reading things into it that are simply not there. She's managed to graduate from college. She had to have some support from home."

Evan shook his head. "I don't think so. I'm going to do a little digging and see what I can find out about her."

"Well, I, for one, am going to get what sleep this baby will allow me."

* * * *

Joe stood at the door to shake hands with everyone as they filed out following Sunday service. He was anxious, for once, to get home. He thought he'd heard Tabby return early yesterday evening, but her house had remained dark. For now, he'd have to be patient and hide his anxiety with a smile.

Betty Gatewood, one of the most stiff-necked of his parishioners, pumped his hand.

"That was a wonderful sermon, Pastor Joe. What a wonderful illustration using the children from vacation Bible school. I guess we've all had to learn a little more about helping each other over the past year, haven't we?"

"Yes, ma'am," he agreed with a grin, thinking back to the truce he and the Presbyterian minister managed to forge between two congregations that had battled for decades. He noticed as the congregation filed out that Tyler hung back, even making some excuse to Jake and Holly about walking home. After everyone else cleared the sanctuary, Joe looked at his young parishioner. "Something on your mind, Tyler?"

The boy shuffled his feet and blushed. "I-I was wondering if you'd seen M-Miss MacVie?"

Joe shook his head. "Not since last evening when I left her with y'all. Did you have a nice cookout?"

The boy dug his hands into his pants pockets. "Well now, that's the thing, Pastor Joe. Miss MacVie didn't stay. She left right after she got there. Evan said she wasn't feeling well, but all the adults looked nervous and wouldn't look at me, like they do when they're lying to you. Doc was actin' funny all evening, too, like she was pi—I mean mad at someone." Tyler shifted again. "I walked to church this morning so I could knock on her door to see if she was okay, but no one answered. All I saw was the cat."

Joe squeezed Tyler's shoulder comfortingly even though another frisson of unease went down his spine. "I'll check on her when I get everything wrapped up here. Will that suit you?"

Tyler grinned. "Sure. Thanks, Pastor."

The boy dashed down the steps and ran along the sidewalk. Joe shut the door and headed back to his office. The church treasurer and secretary had totaled the offering and were preparing the deposit. They acknowledged him with a smile as he waved to them before entering his office and shutting the door. Joe looked out the window toward the back of his house and Tabitha's. Nothing stirred in the thick heat of early September, but he saw the window on the third floor was open to whatever breeze there might be.

Was she working in her studio and hadn't heard the boy? He'd like to think that, but he couldn't get his mind off the fact something made her flee Evan and Jenny's house last night. Thinking of the slam of the screen door he'd heard, Joe realized it must have been Tabby. But she hadn't been working. There hadn't been a light on in the house all evening. Unease changed to worry, and he couldn't explain even to himself why this woman had touched him more than any other.

He tossed his coat and tie over the veranda railing near her back door and rolled back the sleeves on his dress shirt before unbuttoning the collar. He had already banged on the door, but the only thing stirring was the cat. The black feline took one look at him with her golden eyes and disappeared into the bushes around the front of the house. He shook his head. It was downright spooky how much that cat's eyes looked like Tabby's.

Joe waited a few minutes more and knocked again. When there was still no response, he swallowed and pushed open the unlocked door, knowing he might well destroy any headway he'd made with her on a personal level by intruding on her privacy now. The kitchen was dark and cool.

"Tabby?" he called. He tried again at the bottom of the stairs, pausing for a moment as he went over things in his mind. Her bicycle was on the porch, and her car was in the drive. He supposed it was possible she'd gone for a walk, but deep in his gut, he didn't think that was the case. After taking the stairs two at a time, he checked the second floor where he found what was obviously her room from the personal touches: a skirt tossed over a chair back, a brush, and hair bands scattered on a vanity. The bed was neat as a pin, like it hadn't been slept in.

He ran up to the third floor and slowly pushed open the door of the studio. He hadn't felt quite this much trepidation since he'd served as a medic in the military. There'd been plenty of times they'd had to enter situations where they had no idea what they might find on the opposite side of a door.

The studio was a mess. A handful of canvases were ripped, their frames broken, and her easel lay on its side. However, the painting of him she had started was carefully propped on the window seat, above the huddled, sleeping form of Tabitha MacVie. She was still dressed in what she'd left the house in last night. Hair that had once been neatly braided now cascaded in tangled strands around a face almost deathly pale in comparison.

"Tabby!" he whispered urgently, rushing over to her side. Calling on his past military training, he put his fingers to the side of her neck. Her pulse was normal. Breathing appeared fine. He felt her forehead only to find it cool to the touch. Relief coursed through him. It appeared she was doing nothing more than sleeping. "Come on, darling," he coaxed, barely wondering at how easily the endearment slipped off his tongue. "Wake up."

Her lids fluttered. "Joseph?" her voice was hoarse and her eyes unfocused. "You sound worried. You shouldn't worry about me. You should always be joyful."

His gaze skittered around the room again. "What happened, Tabby? Are you all right? Did… Did someone break in? Did anyone bother you?"

At his words she finally struggled to sit up and focus. As her eyes took in the canvases, they widened, panic reflected in them until she assessed what was actually destroyed. "Oh thank God," she whispered. "It's only those. Not the ones that matter."

A trio of canvases lay torn and splintered, and they didn't matter? Joe looked around again. He spied the one he'd seen yesterday, the one he'd commented looked like Dante's vision of hell. Its frame was broken and the canvas slashed. Yes, it was a dark painting, but it was brilliant—*and it didn't matter?*

He looked into her pale face, into tawny eyes that burned so brightly, and gently stroked the hair from her face. "Tabby, shall I call Doc?"

She shook her head, then did something that shook him to the core. Her hand covered his where it rested against her cheek and she closed her eyes, as if she were trying to absorb his touch into her skin. For a moment, he would swear she purred like a cat. "No. No. I'm fine, Joseph."

"The police? Jake can get an investigation rolling. We don't normally have a lot of crime around here."

"No. There's no need."

Confused, he looked around the mess in the studio. Had she done this? But she'd talked almost as if it were a surprise. If she did do it, wouldn't she know what was destroyed? And why would she destroy her own work? He swallowed, sensing he hovered on sensitive ground. He helped her to her feet, his hands on her arms to steady her as she swayed. His brow furrowed.

"How long has it been since you've eaten?" he asked quietly, sure she hadn't had supper or anything since then.

"I don't know. What day is it?"

"It's Sunday, Tabby."

"Oh. Good."

He pulled her against him and wrapped his arms around her so she wouldn't see the shock on his face. She didn't know what day it was? As his hands stroked her back, he rested his cheek against the side of her head. "I think we should call Doc."

She shook her head again. "I—I don't want to see her, Joseph. Not Jenny. It will hurt her."

He continued to hold her and rub her back. It felt right. "Why will it hurt her, Tabby?" he probed gently.

"It hurt her to see me last night. It makes her remember things that hurt her. I get that."

His eyes narrowed in confusion and concern. She wasn't making sense. "Did you already know Evan and Jenny?"

She leaned her forehead against his shoulder. "No. I knew of Jenny, but she didn't know about me. She's—she's my sister, Joseph, but she didn't know. She doesn't want to know."

A sob shook her, and his arms tightened. "Ah, Tabby," he murmured and rocked her. He didn't probe, didn't ask questions. He had figured out long ago that silence often elicited more information. But in this, Tabby surprised him once again because she volunteered nothing else. Instead, her arms crept around his waist, and he wondered again at how right it felt to hold her. Her body curved into his as if it had been made to do exactly that. He leaned his cheek against her silky hair. He wanted to do so much more than simply comfort her that it scared him. He'd managed to stay clear of getting entangled into any kind of relationship, and a relationship with this woman wouldn't be easy or simple.

"You're so peaceful, Joseph," Tabby whispered. "I heard it in your voice the first night here. But you sounded lonely too. You don't seem that way now. You must have found what you were looking for."

His fingers stroked through her dark hair and tilted her face to his. "You heard all that in my voice?"

She withdrew from him and grimaced. "Don't mind me. I'm tired, I guess." She looked around the studio. "Don't worry about this. I was exorcising some demons I guess you might say."

Whatever the moment, he realized it was gone. He turned her loose, shoved his hands into his pockets, and swallowed. "Those must be some pretty powerful demons. I'll help you clean up, then why don't you get a shower and a change of clothes? I'll go down to your kitchen and cook some brunch—that is if you don't mind sharing a meal with me?"

Tabby glanced around the studio. "I—I can do that." She glanced back at him, and Joseph nearly took a step back at the loneliness he saw in the depths of her gaze. "Would you—do you have time—I mean I know it's Sunday, and you've probably got another service later, but could you sit for me again? Just for an hour?"

"Sure." When he saw the relief in her expression, he knew he would do almost anything to keep that haunted look off her face. Together they began to straighten the mess. Joseph noticed she was careful to avoid showing him any of her other paintings, but big deal. Some people were superstitious about that kind of thing.

"Would you sing to me again?" she asked as she set her jar of brushes back on the table next to her now upright easel.

"Yes," he replied in a voice suddenly gone husky. *All day and all night, if need be.*

They parted ways on the second floor, Tabby to her room and Joe to the back stairs leading into the kitchen. A few minutes later, Joe glanced around the airy room as he finished the scrambled cheese and tofu he'd sautéed with mushrooms and basil.

It had taken no more than a quick glance in her refrigerator to figure out she didn't eat meat.... And he had tried to tempt her with burgers on the grill. Way to go, Taylor. For a man who truly appreciated the finer points of a good cheeseburger, this could be a problem. Tabby leaned against the counter nearby, watching him cook.

They took their plates to the kitchen table, the occasional tinkle of utensils against dishes the only sound.

"Where is your cat? I never see her when you're around."

Tabby shrugged. "Here and there," she said vaguely. "Probably perched in a tree. Katie Scarlett is an observer of the world. She was dropped at the shelter. I think she'd been abused."

"You named your cat after Scarlett O'Hara?" Joe asked with a chuckle.

Tabby grinned. "I had an old tom I picked up off the streets. He had one eye and a rather rakish air about him, so I named him Rhett." She shrugged. "It seemed to fit."

"Shadow might be as fitting for her, as invisible as she always seems to be."

Tabby smiled slightly. "Katie is a creature of the night."

"Like her mistress?" Joe asked, arching a thick brow. "I see you burning a lot of midnight oil."

Tabby shifted, suddenly seeming a little ill at ease. Joe was sorry for that. "I paint when the mood strikes me." She jumped up and put their plates into the sink. "Speaking of which, you promised to sit…and sing."

He followed her upstairs, his gaze locked appreciatively on the gentle sway of her hips beneath the filmy mid-calf length skirt she had on. Her hair hung loose, still damp from her shower, falling sleek and straight to just below her waist. Such long hair was rare these days. Most women chopped it off short. Joe gulped, wondering what it would feel like spread out over him.

When they reached the studio, she casually replaced her painting of him on the easel before she picked up a portion of canvas frame they must have missed. When she caught him watching her, she blushed.

"I'm sorry you saw this. I would have eventually stripped them and painted over them."

"Tabby, the one I saw was very, very good," he commented.

She paused and looked at him steadily. "They would never be for sale. They were personal. Call them therapy if you like. It helps me work out things, you know? And this," she threw out, swinging her elegant hand in an arc to encompass the ruined pictures, "was simply the final part of that therapy."

He could see the subject was closed. He had yet to gain her trust, but he got that. "Where do you want me?"

She glanced up from where she was already mixing colors on her palette. "The stool where you were the other day is fine." She tossed her hair back over her shoulders and began to fill in the canvas with broad strokes. She stared at him intently, but not in a way that made him uncomfortable. "Sing for me," she prompted softly. "I want to hear angels."

He felt himself blush and she laughed. It was a beautiful sound, and the effect on her expression was startling, turning her classic beauty into something earthy and sensual. Joe could only stare.

After an hour, she smiled. "Thank you. I don't want to keep you any longer. You must have evening service to prepare for."

"I do. Can I ask you a stupid question?"

Tabby smiled quizzically. "Sure."

"Just what were you going to eat last night if you had stayed at Evan and Jenny's house? I mean, it's obvious you're a vegetarian."

Tabby shrugged. "Salad, potatoes...then as soon as I got home a big bowl of hummus and crackers."

"Hummus?"

She laughed. "It's a mixture of chick peas, sesame paste, and a few other ingredients all mashed together. Lots of protein and healthy fat."

"Mmm. Kinda partial to cheeseburgers, myself."

Tabby tilted her head. "You did all right with the tofu earlier."

"I was trying to impress you, and I didn't want my halo to slip." He was unrolling his sleeves and trying to button his cuffs again when she put down her palette and came around to help him.

"Here," she offered quietly, "let me."

He watched her bent head as she quickly fastened his cuffs. Acting on instinct and the urge overwhelming him, Joe lifted her chin with his fingers, but while his eyes lingered on her soft lips, he simply leaned forward and pressed a kiss against her forehead. Slowly, he reminded himself.

"Thanks," he murmured. She nodded and turned away from him to go back to her painting. He puffed his lips in frustration, unable to tell if it had affected her at all. But why should it? All he'd done was kiss her forehead. Smooth. He watched her a moment longer. Tabby was back in her own world. Was it even a place she would allow someone else to see?

He shook his head and walked quickly down the steps. When he stepped out onto the veranda, Katie Scarlett opened her eyes from her resting place on his suit coat, uttered one last purr, and leaped down onto the porch to rub gently around his legs. Joe smiled at the cat as he picked up his coat and tie. The nagging feeling he was being watched made him glance toward the street where two ladies in flowered dresses now scurried down the sidewalk. Joe closed his eyes briefly and groaned. It looked like the church ladies were already on full alert.

* * * *

Tabby stared at the emerging portrait of Joseph and smiled. It did almost appear that he had a halo. She hadn't seen Joe at all on Monday but chalked it up to him already having plans for Labor Day. For her part, it gave her time to work on his painting as well as go over her lesson plans for the upcoming week. She would be at the elementary school all day on Tuesdays and Thursdays, and the other three days of the week would be split between middle and high school classes since both shared the same campus.

Nerves made it difficult to get to sleep Monday night. Her student teaching hadn't been nearly as nerve-wracking because she'd always worked with a veteran teacher, but now she was on her own. What if the kids didn't like her? Tabby shook her head. That was silly. She had gotten along just fine with the students during her student teaching, particularly the younger ones. Everything would be fine.

But everything was not fine. When she hurried outside in the morning, her car wouldn't start. It was too far to walk. She looked at her bike and her watch. She had time to ride. It would mean being on time instead of early. With a resigned sigh, she ran back upstairs, pulled on her cycling pants, stuffed her no wrinkle skirt into her backpack, grabbed her helmet, and rode her bicycle to school. Since there was no bicycle rack at the elementary school, Tabby had to go in and ask the principal if it was permissible to bring her bike into the building. Mr. Underwood's eyes popped at her arriving in cycling pants.

"Certainly, Miss MacVie, but I do hope you have more suitable attire for the school day?"

Tabby held her book bag in front of her, feeling suddenly indecent and embarrassed. "Yes sir."

"Very well. Use the staff restroom to change before you leave this office."

She felt humiliated. It set the tone for most of her day. While the students seemed to adore her, many of the teachers, older women who were themselves mothers, looked at her askance. A few even glared, and Tabby began to wonder if she had committed some horrible breach of etiquette during her workdays the previous week, but she couldn't remember any of the women acting hostile toward her then. They had been a little reserved, but she had expected that. She was new and not from around Mountain Meadow, but today she was even getting a cold shoulder from the new kindergarten teacher. About the only one who did treat her normally was Mr. Powers, the P.E. teacher, who had seen her arrive on her bicycle, and Tabby noticed his eyes kept straying toward her butt.

By the end of the day, she was exhausted and frustrated. It was frightening to think that her third, fourth, and fifth grade students behaved more maturely than her colleagues. When she noticed Mr. Powers lingering around the front door, probably waiting for her to come out with her bike so he could see her dressed in her cycling pants, Tabby sneaked out a back door and took the long way around. She arrived home hot, sweaty, and tired. She carried her bike up onto the veranda and took off her helmet.

Hearing someone behind her, she spun around, trying to control the stab of panic that hit her. Joe stood there with a can of Coke in each hand.

"You looked like you could use this," he commented dryly. He was dressed casually in khaki shorts and a polo shirt, his eyes hidden behind sunglasses. "How was your first day?"

Tabby started to say fine automatically, then let her book bag fall to the porch.

"Terrible."

Chapter 4

Joe's heart missed a beat at the devastation in Tabby's expression. He set the two cans of Coke on the porch railing and opened his arms to her, as if it were the most natural thing in the world, and suddenly it was, for Tabby stepped into his embrace. He patted her back and closed his eyes, savoring the warm scent of her and praying she wouldn't feel the effect she was having on him. After a minute, he felt her relax. He set her away from him, handed her coke back to her, and picked up his own. "Wanna tell me? Sometimes that helps."

He guided her to the chairs on the veranda and thought it was a sign of how worn out she was that she made no protest.

"Well first, my car wouldn't start, so I rode my bike to the elementary school. Then Mr. Underwood looked at me like I was naked when I walked inside in my cycling pants to ask if I could store my bike in my classroom."

Joe groaned mentally. He had forgotten Dennis Underwood was the principal there and one of his more conservative church members. Remembering his own view of Tabby in her cycling pants, he could understand where Dennis might have overreacted.

"All of the teachers treated me like I smelled bad, even the new kindergarten teacher."

Joe closed his eyes for an instant. Another one of his church members. She'd done her student teaching at the end of last school year and was one of those women ready to redecorate the parsonage if he winked at her wrong. Many of the other teachers were also members of his church. Bless their gossiping little hearts. Joe had a feeling the ladies' worship committee was already hard at work. He had turned down no less than three invitations to supper for tonight. Now he knew what motivation lay behind the sudden spurt of invitations.

"The only teacher who was nice to me was Mr. Powers, the new P.E. teacher. After seeing me arrive this morning, he spent the entire lunch period staring at my butt. I had to sneak out a back door this afternoon because he was still hanging around the front door."

Joe's eyes narrowed to slits behind his sunglasses as an unaccustomed shaft of jealousy sliced through him. Staring at her butt? What kind of man would do that? Then he realized with chagrin he'd done the same thing the first time he watched her walk up the steps in those cycling pants. In fact, he'd done it a few minutes ago. It was a nice butt from his perspective. He could imagine…Lord! He better not think in those directions. He needed to stick with something practical he might be able to handle but thinking of her delicious derriere was not it.

"I work on my own car a lot. I could take a look at yours," he offered. Cars. There. That was safe.

"Would you? I'll get the keys, then if you don't mind, I'll leave you to it. I need a shower and a change of clothes."

He smiled, and from behind the lenses of his dark glasses, he allowed himself the luxury of letting his eyes drift over her figure. She was certainly tall and slender, but the curves were in all the right places. As she walked past his chair, his eyes drifted down to the butt the P.E. teacher found so interesting, and Joe smothered a groan. It was definitely worth a second glance, even a third or a fourth. The door slammed behind her, and a discreet cough came from the direction of his porch.

Joe glanced over his shoulder to find Jake Allred standing there in uniform. Joe sprang to his feet, feeling suddenly awkward, even if Jake was one of his poker buddies.

"I see there is some grist to the rumor mill," Jake remarked.

Joe shoved his glasses onto his tousled hair as he came down Tabby's steps and popped the hood on her car. "Do I dare ask what the rumor mill is saying?"

Jake joined him, leaning casually against Tabby's car as Joe methodically checked belts and hoses.

"If you'd get on Facebook, you'd know."

Joe rolled his eyes. "We've had this conversation before. I refuse to encourage gossiping, and that's all the town's Facebook page has become."

Jake snorted. "There's a general consensus you're succumbing to the wiles of your neighbor. While some describe her as young and free-spirited, the less charitable are already bandying the words 'jezebel' and 'witch' around."

Joe straightened abruptly and bumped the back of his head on the hood of Tabby's car. "Oh for heaven's sake. This town's got more ears than a field full of corn."

"And more tongues than the tower of Babel?" Jake finished. He patted Joe on the back. "Between Facebook and what I'm sure is going on behind the scenes over the phone, it could get ugly fast. Trust me, I know. I came by to offer some friendly advice if you don't mind, Joe."

He looked at Jake warily. "Advice from you I'll take. There are a few, now, I don't have a mind to be so charitable toward."

Jake grinned lazily. "If the lady is worth it, then stand up for her early on and be damned to all of them. 'Scuse me. Holly would have my hide if she heard me cuss in front of the preacher."

Joe laughed at that. "Trust me, Jake. You won't say anything I haven't already heard. I haven't always been a preacher. Besides, it's not me you have to worry about. It's the guy up there... And he hears it no matter where you say it."

Jake glanced at the car's engine compartment. "See her publicly. Make all the gossips go public, too, so you can get it out in the open before it festers. And I'm telling you again, you need to get on Facebook. Read what's there so you can put a stop to it. Good luck to you. She's a real pretty lady. Classy."

With that, Jake sauntered back out to his car and drove slowly down the street, waving to some of the neighbors out working in their yards. Joe stared after him. See Tabby publicly? He was having a tough time seeing her at all. She was more skittish than her cat.

Joe looked back at the car. All the belts and hoses were fine. Fluid levels were fine. He checked the battery connections and found corrosion around the terminals. He disconnected them, then went to his toolbox in the trunk of his Mustang for a wire brush. After cleaning the terminals and checking the wires, he reconnected everything as Tabby was coming back outside. He tossed her the keys.

"Get in and try her. Let's see if she'll start. You still might need a boost."

The car started, a little reluctantly, but it started. Tabby grinned.

"Let it run for a few minutes. Chances are your battery is a little low."

Tabby got out of the car and smiled. Joe couldn't help himself. He tucked a strand of hair behind her ear, and their eyes met for a long moment.

"Thanks," Tabby said a little breathlessly. "You saved me calling a mechanic. Can I make you dinner to say thank you?"

Joe shook his head, thinking of Jake's advice, not to mention the prospect of more tofu. "No, but you could let me take you out to dinner. That way I can have my cheeseburger and you can munch on rabbit food."

Her face grew wary. Sure, it was easy for Jake to talk about going public, but Joe not only had to contend with his parishioners, he had to contend with Tabby's own reluctance. He sighed, knowing he needed to deal with it head-on.

"It's dinner, Tabby, not a lifetime commitment or an altar call."

She blinked and chewed on her lower lip. "Joe...I..."

"I won't even denounce you as a heathen." He kept his tone light. Why was he bothering? Any other woman he would have already cut his losses and moved on, but Tabby was different. Special.

Her breath huffed out on a strangled laugh, and she looked down at her jeans and long-sleeved T-shirt. "Do I need to change?"

Joe felt a surge of relief. He noted she was covered once again from ankle to neck. "Not at all. Go grab your purse or whatever you need. We'll take my car."

Tabby's eyes went to the Mustang and suddenly glowed. "With the top down?"

"Sure."

"I've never ridden in a convertible before."

What the devil? Where had she grown up?

"Then hop in."

Joe's red Mustang convertible no sooner pulled out onto the street than he could have sworn he saw curtains twitching in several windows on both sides. Jake was getting to him, making him paranoid.

* * * *

Evan tucked the information he'd uncovered into an envelope and shoved it into his briefcase. He was breaking every ethical rule in the book, but by God, he would take this home for Jenny to see. He'd called in a few favors from former college classmates to get some of it, but the last fax arrived just a few minutes ago. From what he could see, there was plenty of reason for Mary Owens MacVie to warn Jenny about Thomas MacVie.

As he left his office, Wanda Sue Gardner, one of his paralegals, looked up and smiled. "Leaving early, aren't you, sir?"

Just a year ago, he knew his staff would never have dared to comment on what time he left, but that was before Jenny came back into his life. He smiled. "Jenny wasn't feeling too well today. These last few weeks are making her miserable."

"Still waiting to be surprised?"

Evan grinned now. "Yes. Faith if it's a girl. Peter if it's a boy."

Jenny's BMW was parked on the square in front of the courthouse. He'd taken to driving it lately because she could no longer fit comfortably behind the wheel of the sports car. As he tossed his briefcase into the passenger seat, he saw Joe's red Mustang. The pastor's tawny hair glinted gold in the afternoon sunlight, but that wasn't what attracted Evan's attention. It was the laughing face and the dark hair of the woman next to him. Tabby.

He felt a surge of protectiveness toward her after what he'd pieced together of her past, and relief that she'd chosen someone as rock solid as Joe Taylor for a friend followed quickly. His eyes narrowed as Joe pulled up in front of Mercer's and Evan watched the preacher offer Tabby a hand out of the low-slung car. He wondered if the two of them knew how they looked together. Already like a couple.

Evan slid behind the wheel, still smiling, and drove home. The Tahoe was where it sat when he'd left that morning, so it seemed reasonable to assume Jenny decided not to go into the clinic today. In recent weeks, she had begun to shift many of her patients to Dr. Razawi at the hospital. He'd agreed to cover for her, but Evan knew it would be only temporarily. The area was short on doctors. They needed Jenny as much as she needed them. She'd completed additional surgery work that meant she was often called on to help in the OR, especially with emergencies.

When Evan entered the house, he heard her in the kitchen. It never failed to make his breath catch a little when she smiled at him. He'd first fallen in love with her when they were fourteen years old. They'd dated all through high school until their fathers conspired to tear them apart. Evan shoved that back. That was behind them now.

Her father was long dead, and his father was on house arrest for the next two years for his part not only in what had happened thirteen years ago, but also an attempt on Jenny's life last year. Evan hadn't spoken to him since then and had no plans to begin any time soon. Evan had Jenny back, and to Evan that was the only thing that mattered.

He took her into his arms, his hands going automatically and protectively to her swollen belly. "How are you feeling?" he whispered into her ear.

"Uncomfortable, but better than this morning. How was your day?"

Evan set his briefcase on the table. "Productive. I have some information on Tabby and Thomas MacVie I think you should read."

Jenny arched a delicate brow, and her golden eyes twinkled. "Well if Facebook's to be believed, she's already seduced the minister, bewitched the P.E. teacher at the elementary school, and has a cat some folks believe is her familiar."

Evan paused in the act of opening his briefcase. "Oh for Christ's sake! Has someone actually posted that kind of shit?"

"Not sure. You know I try to avoid looking at the town's page, but it's other places too." Jenny held up her hand and began ticking off on her fingers. "My nurse practitioner, Sara, heard it from her brother, Jim, who heard it from his wife who heard it from Sally Concannon who heard it from both Betty Gatewood and Jeanie Underwood. One of those two supposedly saw Pastor Joe's clothes strewn all over Tabby's veranda and heard him singing love songs to her in an upstairs bedroom."

Evan's mouth had dropped open halfway through Jenny's recitation. When his wife finished, he stood there stunned for a moment, then began laughing until he clutched his stomach in both of his hands.

"It's not funny, Evan," Jenny said stiffly. "She's my sister."

Evan's face sobered. He'd known she'd come around, particularly if there was a threat. They had both struggled to rebuild their concept of family in the wake of their parents' betrayals. Jenny was probably a little further along than him in that.

"Damn right," he agreed. "That's exactly why you need to take a look at this. Start with Thomas MacVie's rap sheet."

Jenny lowered herself awkwardly into the chair Evan pulled out for her and took the envelope he offered. As she slowly examined the contents, her brows drew together. "How did you get all this information, Evan?" she asked as she continued to sift through it, reading between the lines as he had.

"A few friends from law school who owed me favors. Plus, Tommy MacVie appears unpopular with not only law enforcement, but also his neighbors. People were more than willing to spill their guts over the phone."

She looked up at him, her golden eyes concerned. "You called people?"

Evan shrugged. "A couple of neighbors. I didn't tell them where I was from."

Jenny ran her finger down the paper. "There are a lot of abuse arrests here, all dismissed."

Evan nodded. "Lack of evidence. I talked to the D.A. in that area who referred me to the former district attorney, who's now retired. He said they could never get your mother or Tabby to testify against him. The guy was slick. Even social services couldn't find enough evidence of abuse. The house was always neat as a pin. Tabby never seemed to want for anything. She was always clean and well fed. One thing did keep coming up...how modest Tabby was. No one ever saw her in a bathing suit, shorts, or even a short-sleeved shirt."

Jenny tapped her finger on the medical records he had somehow accessed. "She appears to have been very accident prone," she said in a dubious tone. "A broken arm at five, a wrist at seven, the other arm at eleven, and several ribs a year later. That alone should have been enough to launch a thorough investigation."

Jenny looked up at her husband. "I want to meet her."

"You can't right now."

"Why?"

"She's having dinner with Pastor Joe at Mercer's."

Jenny's mouth dropped open. "So the rumors are true?"

Evan chuckled. "Well, I seriously doubt the pastor's clothes were all over her porch or that they were in a bedroom while he sang love songs to her, but they are neighbors, he does sing—beautifully so Holly tells me—and when you see the two of them together…"

Jenny grinned and finished for him, "They already look like a couple."

"Exactly."

* * * *

"What did Jake Allred come by to tell you this afternoon?" Tabby asked Joe curiously over the noise of the wind rushing by the open top and windows of his Mustang.

After dinner, Joe had suggested a drive along a stretch of the Blue Ridge Parkway, leaving the top down so she could enjoy the warm, evening breeze.

"You saw him?" he asked with a quick glance in her direction just as he slowed and pulled off the road. They stopped at a place where they could get out and sit on a large rock overlooking the valley below them.

"Yes." She kept her gaze on the patchwork quilt of farmland still visible in the waning light as she carefully seated herself, thinking that if she painted landscapes, this would certainly be a view worth capturing. "I glanced out the window and saw him talking to you."

Joe, who had stretched out beside her, took her hand. Instantly, warmth flooded through her, and she closed her eyes briefly in surprised enjoyment. His thumb rubbed along the back. "He told me if I cared about you, I should take you out publicly and not worry about what anyone might say."

She stiffened slightly. "Is that what this is all about?" she asked without looking at him. Joe released her hand to touch her hair and her cheek.

"Partly. Tabby, I have to be honest with you. I would have gotten around to this anyway. Jake's visit just spurred me to act more quickly than I might have."

"And the fact that I told you right up front that I don't date ministers makes no difference?" Tabby wasn't sure whether she was angry or scared by his persistence. Having always kept her distance from men, she wasn't sure what to do with one who was ignoring the keep off signals.

His fingers cupped her chin. "I can't help what I feel, Tabby. If I were a lawyer, a doctor, or a musician would you even worry about going out with me?"

Sadness tightened her chest. He was so beautiful, and when he touched her, it felt right. It felt good. She wanted to touch him back. Instead she looked down, breaking eye contact. "But you're not any of those things, Joseph. You *are* a minister."

"Why does it make such a difference?" he demanded. "Yes, I am a minister. It's what I *do*, but can't you look beyond that to who I *am*? Beneath it, I'm still a man."

He bent his head then and kissed her. Although she sensed his frustration, his kiss was pure gentleness, asking not taking. Tabby's hand rested against his shoulder. Waves of heat and desire coursed through her. She wanted him like she'd never wanted anyone. Yes, he was a minister, so what would happen when he got a good look at her standard paintings? Sure, he'd seen one, but he didn't realize that was the norm for her. His portrait was the departure, not the scene he'd compared to Dante's *Inferno*.

Her mind raced ahead to a future where she was mindlessly painting flower arrangements or seascapes complete with lighthouses and seagulls, just to make sure she didn't upset anyone. Panic followed quickly. She couldn't breathe. She felt as stymied and hemmed in as she had around Tommy and his ultra-conservative view of religion.

She couldn't do this. They couldn't do this.

She pushed him away. "Stop, Joseph."

He vaulted to his feet and stepped away from her as he raked his hands through his hair. "Sorry."

"Don't apologize. It's not you. It's not anything you've done. It's me."

He laughed, but with no real amusement. "I have to tell you, that sounds way too close to a classic dump the loser line."

"Except I'm about to give you some truths I don't often share." Tabby sucked in a shaky breath. "Please, sit down. I need you to understand, so maybe we can find some way through this."

Joe came back and dropped down at her side. Wrists balanced loosely on his knees and hands hanging, he tilted his head to look at her. "Okay. I'm listening."

Tabby drew her knees up and rested her chin on them. After taking another deep breath to calm herself, she began. "My…father…was a rigid, religious man. I grew up in a small church that believed in a very literal interpretation of the Bible. The man was the head of the household in all things. Spare the rod, spoil the child, and all of that. Ever since I can remember, we were in church on Wednesday evening and, it seemed to me, all day on Sunday between morning services, Sunday school, and the evening preaching. Women and girls wore dresses. We were not to cut our hair. If that were all there was to it, Joseph, I could've dealt with it and moved on with life."

She touched his cheek and saw such tenderness in his expression that it made her ache. "Do you like what you've seen so far of my painting of you?" she whispered.

"The sketches are incredible," he acknowledged.

Tabby shifted and worried her lower lip. "You saw the other painting, right?"

"The one that looked like Dante's vision of hell." Joe stared at her intently in the waning light. "The one you tore up."

"Yes. Joseph, I don't paint pretty pictures. Every artist has an eye—I guess you'd call it. For writers, it would be their voice. What you saw on the easel that first day? That's my voice. It's been my voice my entire life, and my father made me pay the price for that every day I lived there. "

Joe took her hand in his again. She couldn't mask its trembling. "Tabby, I believe we are all given gifts, like your art and my singing, and it's up to each of us to choose how we use those gifts. What I believe *is* wrong is to deny what God gives us. If your muse inspires those paintings, then there must be a reason for it."

Tabby felt like a door had opened in front of her, but it was so hard to take that first step. She stared into the warmth of his blue, blue eyes and wondered if she was about to lose something precious before she'd even held it in her hand. "I can't change my art," she whispered. "It's part of me, and I have to get it out on canvas."

"Is that why I heard you crying that one night?" Joe asked.

She nodded, realizing now she hadn't fooled him. "Yes," she replied, then rushed on. "As long as I can remember, I've had the most fantastic images in my head and the overpowering urge to get them on paper. What I didn't understand then was how regimented everybody seemed to be about what was appropriate for children to draw."

"This sounds a little like that Harry Chapin song."

Tabby tilted her head. "What song is that?"

"'Flowers are Red.'" Joseph hummed the tune, but Tabby had never heard it and shook her head. He sang the refrain. "Flowers are red young man/ Green leaves are green/ There's no need to see flowers any other way/ Than the way they always have been seen...."

He stopped and laughed a little self-consciously. "It's a story of a little boy who goes to school. He draws with all sorts of colors all over his paper, but because his colors don't fit everyone's expectations, he's punished and forced to conform. Eventually, he stops seeing things in his own unique way."

He reached over and took her hand. "Is that what everyone tried to do to you?"

She nodded. He understood. For the first time in her life, she felt like someone actually got what it was that drove her.

But the fact remained. He was a minister. People had expectations of him.

"It's okay, Tabby," he reassured her.

"I didn't understand what was wrong to begin with. Between the school thinking I was some sort of psychotic mess and my father believing I must be in league with the devil to draw such dark images, I began to feel I was defective." She took a deep breath. "My father thought I was evil. He brought the preacher and all the deacons to pray the demons from me. It started when I was six."

His arm tightened around her shoulders. "When did it stop?"

She ducked her head. "When I was twelve. When I hit puberty. I think they just decided I belonged to the devil, or maybe I finally convinced them they'd succeeded in purging my demons. I had become adept at hiding what I considered to be my 'real' art. I did the standard landscapes and pottery projects at school, like everybody else."

"Just like that little boy?" Joseph turned his head, a slight, understanding smile on his face as he gazed at her.

"Pretty much. So the minister and the deacons quit coming by each week, but that didn't stop my father from dragging me to church. No one would sit near me. None of the other children were allowed to play with me or even talk to me. I guess their parents thought I would corrupt them or contaminate them in some way. How stupid is that? I should be ostracized because I paint what comes from my heart?"

She lifted her chin and stared at him defiantly. "It's hypocritical, Joseph. I won't set foot in a church. Not any church, not even if you're the man in the pulpit. So you can see why I don't date ministers. You have a certain code you must live by. People have expectations not only of you but of anyone you're linked to. I understand that, but I can't live up to those expectations. I *won't* live up to them."

Joseph twined his fingers with hers, lifted her hand to his mouth, and kissed the back of it. "I can understand how traumatizing what you went through must have been. You want people to see you for you: a person who, while certainly an artist, is not only an artist. Your art is a part of you, but you are not only your art. Would that about sum it up?"

Again she nodded. He gently squeezed her hand.

"May I not also ask the same of you in return?" His voice was quiet, his tone gentle.

His softly spoken question hung in the air between them. At once, Tabby realized that in his own, quiet way, Joseph had brought her own logic to bear on his situation.

She let her head fall forward, and closed her eyes briefly. "Why me?" she finally whispered.

His chuckle was a breath on the night air. "I'm not sure I have a choice in this, Tabby. It's simply what I feel. I am in awe of your talent. I enjoy your company." He twisted so he could tuck a loose wisp of hair behind her ear. "You are beautiful, and I just want to get to know you better. Look at me, Tabby. See me with that keen artist's eye of yours and know that what I feel will only lift you up, not judge you or confine you in any way."

She trembled. He had opened a doorway that all she needed to do was step into. Could someone accept her as she was, without trying to change her? The lure of that, the temptation, was overwhelming. Her mother had accepted her unconditionally, some of her art professors had, but no one else. Now Joseph offered it with open arms.

And she could no longer resist. He pulled her into his lap. She closed her eyes and leaned her forehead against his cheek. Peace filled her. Tabby leaned back, and her gaze met his warm blue eyes.

"I have nothing to hide from you, darling," he murmured. "Let me in. Give us a chance." He touched his lips to hers, one hand softly cupping her cheek as he explored. Tabby trembled at the feelings that gently probing kiss aroused. He didn't take, he invited, offering her an amazing gift of himself.

Her belly tightened in wonder and fear. In addition to the heat she saw in his eyes, was the stubbornness in his chin. This was a man who would neither give her up nor allow her to be taken from him. The door had opened wide, and all she could see was warmth and welcome.

"Joseph, you barely know me."

"I know enough."

This time when they kissed, the gentleness was gone. Passion replaced it. As his tongue traced the outline of her lips, Tabby moaned softly. His kiss was more than she had ever imagined, and it made her insides flutter.

He smoothed her hair and brushed along the length of her jean-covered thigh. Her heart raced, and her breath erupted in shallow gasps at the heat and heaviness his touch produced. Tabby's fingers slipped beneath the open collar of his polo shirt to touch the heated skin beneath. This time it was Joe who groaned.

They stretched out on the warmth of the granite boulder. Tabby burned where they touched, not at all sure she was ready for the feelings Joseph had awakened. The rigid pressure of his erection pressed against her leg, and she began to shake. What if he didn't like what he saw? What if he figured out she had no idea what she was doing? She had barely even kissed anyone.

As if he sensed her fears, Joe leaned over her in the darkness and gently kissed her one more time. "I won't push, Tabby. I should take you home before we can't stop," he murmured. "You have school in the morning."

His concern warmed her and frustrated her at the same time. Just how did that happen?

Chapter 5

Memories of Joseph's kisses still lingered the next morning as Tabby warily entered the main building of Mountain Meadow's middle and high school campus. She sent up a silent prayer that the middle and high school classes would turn out to be better than the elementary classes. While her colleagues were more liberal in their views, Tabby discovered some parents had already called to have their children removed from her classes.

Was this all because she'd arrived at school the first day in her bicycling pants? There had to be something else going on, but if there were, she wished she knew what it was so that she could fix it.

She had a wonderful chance here to start over.

At least one familiar and friendly face greeted her. Tyler was in her third period class, a mixture of sixth and seventh graders. She started them off with her own version of pre-testing by having them complete pencil sketches of several geometric figures, then a line drawing of a still life. It gave her an idea of how developed their fine motor skills were for the first unit she planned to teach. She was pleased to see Tyler had a good eye for both line and perspective. He needed work in learning how to shade and finish a sketch.

"Good job, Tyler," she praised as she walked by.

"Thanks, Miss MacVie."

She heard another kid murmur, "Brown noser," before Tyler whispered back, "Kiss my a—"

"Tyler…" she interrupted quietly.

"Sorry, Miss MacVie."

At the end of the day, Tabby wasn't sure whether things truly had gone better, or if she was still basking in the afterglow of her evening with Joseph. She had thought about him several times during the day. Even now, her hand shook slightly when she thought of his kisses, and how he'd patiently drawn her out. It was that, even more than the kisses, that made her blush. He'd been a perfect gentleman bringing her home. He'd held her hand in the car. After they pulled into his drive, he walked her to her door, kissed her on the cheek, and told her good night. His actions were as polite and circumspect as anyone might want from the town's most eligible minister. However, Tabby had felt the heat of his gaze, heard his whisper against her ear that he couldn't wait to see her again. And the way he made her feel wasn't circumspect at all.

As she tidied up the room for the day, her principal knocked at the door. He was a tall, spare man who had years with the school system and laughter lines around his eyes and mouth. Tabby admired the rapport he had with the students.

"Good afternoon, Miss MacVie. How was your first day on our campus?"

Tabby flushed. "I was pleased with how things went overall. I hope you were too."

He smiled. "I have no complaints." He picked up one of the drawings that her high school students had completed and arched a thick brow at her. "Pre-testing in art? I like it." He drew up a chair and sat down as he flipped through the sketches. "Tell me some of what you've learned about your students."

Tabby's fingers knotted nervously in her lap. She did not come from a background that allowed her to talk to men, any men, with confidence, so it was always a struggle. "I have a lot of students who have some excellent technical skills. They have a wonderful eye for perspective and basic line drawing, but are not well grounded in shading and filling in nuances that make a sketch come to life."

"How will you address that?" he inquired.

"I plan to set up objects in arrangements that use strong artificial light from one direction. That will provide excellent contrasts between light and dark to teach them to see the light and shadows. Then I'll demonstrate some specific shading techniques for them to try."

Dr. James set the sketches down and smiled at her. "You have some sound ideas, Miss MacVie."

"Thank you."

He glanced sideways at her. "I suppose you know I'm not in here just to make conversation."

Tabby swallowed, clenching her fists in her lap. "I guessed as much," she whispered.

Dr. James leaned forward, resting his forearms on the table and clasping his hands. "We are a small school system in a small community. People sometimes have a difficult time adjusting to anything or anyone they perceive as different. Unfortunately, you have already gained that reputation. I would hate to see it affect your work. Please understand, as long as your work within the walls of *this* school is above reproach, you have my complete support. In my opinion, who you choose to entertain or date is your business. The students are my only concern."

Tabby met Dr. James's steady gaze. "Thank you, sir."

He squeezed her shoulder briefly, then left the room.

Apparently, the cycling pants weren't the problem. People were already talking about her and Joseph. Tabby frowned and bit her lip as she looked out the window into the courtyard. Had Joseph already heard any of these rumors? It seemed they would have to talk about that.

Her first concern, though, had to be her job. She knew she'd made a bad impression at the elementary school, but perhaps she could change that tomorrow. After packing her belongings and tidying her desk, she headed home. A big black Tahoe was parked out front when Tabby pulled into the drive. In the shadows of the porch, she saw someone curled on the swing.

Blond-haired and petite. For a heart-stopping moment, the woman reminded her so much of her mother Tabby nearly fainted thinking she was seeing ghosts. But she was cautious this time around and stopped several feet away from Jenny Richardson.

"Your cat was keeping me company until right before your car turned the corner, then she disappeared."

Tabby stared at Jenny before blurting, "Wh-why are you here?"

Jenny ran her hands over her stomach with a faint grimace. "To apologize. I read the letter from Mama. It's hard to readjust my feelings about her in such a short time after thinking about her in a certain way over the last twenty-three years, so I hope you can understand that. However, I also realized I was pushing those feelings about her on to you, and you're the most blameless in all this mess."

Tabby thought about how often her mother had tried to protect her from Tommy, clutched the porch railing, and transferred her gaze to the front yard as she muttered, "Maybe not as blameless as you might think."

Jenny shifted her position as if trying to ease the ache in her back. Tabby looked at her sister again, noting the curiosity, but also the fatigue in her older sister's face. How different her life might have been had someone as assertive as Jenny been there to help Mama and her.

"When's the baby due?" Tabby asked.

"Not long." Jenny smiled wanly. "Not soon enough."

Tabby cast around for something to say to ease the awkwardness she felt. "Mama used to say when women carried low like you they were having a boy. Are you?"

Jenny's expression changed to one of surprise. She patted the seat next to her. "Sit down, Tabby. Mama used to say that, huh? She'd be right in this case. I've known all along we're having a son. I just didn't tell Evan. We were both going to be surprised, but the ultrasound tech accidentally left a picture in the file that left no doubt about little Peter's identity. Don't say anything to Evan, though. Okay?"

Tabby nodded. Silence stretched between them, not the comfortable silence of long acquaintance, but the faintly awkward one of strangers unsure of where to take the conversation.

"Are you always this talkative?" Jenny asked in some amusement.

Tabby blushed. "I-I'm sorry. I'm not very good at conversation. I'm sure you gathered from Mama's letter that my upbringing was...different."

"Would you like to talk about it?"

Tabby shook her head. "I don't mean to offend you, but I'm not ready for that."

"Would you at least tell me why Mama said I should call the police if Tommy MacVie showed up in town?"

"He's threatened to kill me if he ever finds me."

Tabby said it matter-of-factly because she truly believed that was his intention. Too much bad blood lay between them. For years she hadn't understood. Not until that letter, when Mama admitted Tommy wasn't her father. By then, all Tabby had felt was relief.

Jenny's shock, though, was obvious, but there was something else too. Her sister rubbed her forehead, as though her head ached. Tabby glanced her way, trying not to make it obvious. Her sister looked like she'd gained weight in just the couple days since she'd seen her so briefly.

"Do you feel all right, Jenny?" Tabby asked.

Her sister sighed. "Just wanting this pregnancy over with."

Tabby looked Jenny over more closely, remembering their neighbor who'd gotten so sick when Tabby was a teenager. The ambulance had had to rush her to the hospital. Tabby narrowed her gaze on her sister's face, then moved to her hands and feet.

"I know you're a doctor and everything, but Jenny, you've changed in just a couple days. Your hands and feet are swollen. Your face looks puffy. You're complaining of a headache. We had a neighbor like that, and she was really sick. Like an ambulance came and picked her up sick."

Jenny stared at Tabby for such a long time she began to feel uncomfortable. At last her sister took a deep breath. "You ever heard the phrase 'physician, heal thyself?'"

"Yes," Tabby replied, drawing the word out warily, wondering if she had overstepped her bounds.

Jenny stood, putting a hand to the small of her back. "I think you should drive me to the hospital. I'll call Evan on the way."

She gave Tabby the keys. Tabby helped her into the SUV before running around to the driver's side. Just before she put the big vehicle in gear, Jenny touched her arm.

"Thanks."

An hour later, Tabby sat wide-eyed in the waiting room on the maternity floor. She had spent more time than she cared to remember as a child being shuffled around to one emergency room or another so that as an adult she went out of her way to avoid hospitals and doctors. Except now she had a sister who was a doctor and, right now at least, also a patient. Evan was in the labor and delivery room with Jenny where they had gone ahead and induced after confirming preeclampsia.

"Tabby?" She looked up at the sound of her name. Jake Allred stood there, looking big and comforting at the moment. "Holly said I should come sit with you. You okay?"

Tabby's chin trembled a touch, but she nodded. "How did Holly know?"

Jake shrugged. "I think Jenny or Evan called her, but sometimes Holly has feelings about things. You know?"

Tabby's eyes widened. "She does?"

Jake nodded. "Yeah. Like last Christmas. Noelle's biological father kidnapped her. Holly kept insisting everything was going to be fine. Sure enough, the woman who was engaged to him walked into the Christmas Eve service carrying Noelle. Isn't that the damnedest, 'scuse me, I mean the darnedest thing?"

Tabby wiped a finger below each eye. "Yeah. It is."

Jake sat next to her and took her hand. "A lot of folks wanted to talk about Holly when she first got here. Unmarried. Pregnant. But Holly has a way about her. Everybody loves her."

Tabby slipped her hand from Jake's. "I don't seem to have that same effect. In fact, pretty much the opposite."

Jake patted her knee. "You will. Sometimes it takes a while for Mountain Meadow to welcome you, but it will. Be patient."

* * * *

Joe had been coming up with reasons to see Tabby again all day long. He finally stopped by her house on his way to church to invite her over to watch a movie after the service was over. Her car was in the driveway, but there was no answer to his knock. He thought he'd heard voices earlier so he walked around to the front porch, but no one was there. Tabby's school bag sat there, though. Joe walked back to the kitchen and stuck his head in the door.

"Tabby?"

The cat dashed between his legs and into the house, but there was no sign of Tabby. Joe flicked back his cuff to check his watch. He might have time to call Jake once he got over to his office. In the end, though, he didn't need to. Sometimes, it seemed the ladies' worship committee grapevine worked in his favor.

"Did you hear, Pastor Joe?" Betty Gatewood was the first to greet him when he arrived. "Doc's gone into labor a month early. She's at the hospital right now. Came over to see the new school teacher, she did, and now she might lose the baby."

"Ladies," Joe said, trying to keep his voice calm when he was tempted to snap at them instead. "I'm sure there's no connection between Doc's visit to Miss MacVie and a slightly early labor. Just coincidence." He was beginning to feel as though he'd booked a front row seat at the Mountain Meadow witch hunt.

He had seen something similar last year when Holly came to town, but not like this. What was the difference? Was it him? Joe sighed. He'd been warned in seminary that a single pastor had a target on him. Everyone pictured ministers as married, so a single one just screamed "I need a wife."

Was all this animosity over Tabby just because he'd shown an interest in her, or was there more? Did it have something to do with her artwork?

Joe prided himself on taking time to talk to his parishioners after services, but on this night, he was doing his best to rush them out the door. When he saw there were still no lights on inside Tabby's house, he went straight to his Mustang and drove to the hospital.

Tabby stood near a window in the waiting room, staring out into the near darkness. She turned when he came into the room, as if she'd sensed him there. The loneliness and fear in her expression nearly undid him. They met in the middle of the room. Joe wrapped his arms around her and rocked her gently back and forth. He stroked her back and pressed his face into her hair. It overwhelmed him that she would let him get this close to her. As her shaking eased, he whispered, "Are you all right?"

"Yes. How did you know I was here?" Shadows lingered in her golden eyes.

Joe touched the tip of her nose and sighed. "The church lady grapevine. I managed to piece enough truth out of the gossip to put two and two together. You want to talk about it?"

She nodded, but before she could say anything, Evan strode into the room, hair disheveled, his eyes searching for her, and his expression betraying no surprise at all when he saw her in the arms of the Baptist minister.

"Excuse me, Pastor," Evan said and pulled Tabby into his arms before he gave her a kiss on each cheek and laughed. "I have a healthy baby boy and a wife who's already barking orders at nurses after one of the quickest labors on record. If you ever need me for anything, Tabby, I'm there for you. You are a part of our family. Remember that."

Joe arched a brow. "So Jenny's okay with that?"

"Damn man!" Evan laughed. "She'd be crazy not to be. Look at those eyes. They're the spitting image of Jenny's. God, Tabby! I told Jenny there was something about you, but she wouldn't believe me, and damn if you didn't already know what was going on before she did."

Tabby tugged urgently at Evan's sleeve. "Stop. Don't talk so loud. It was a lucky guess, and you're—stop swearing!"

Joe kept Tabby's hand firmly clasped in his own. "I guess God will forgive a man who's just become a father."

"Damn right," Evan agreed. "Come on in. Jenny wants to see you. You go, too, Pastor. I'm going to find a cup of coffee." He was already ushering them both down the hall.

Jenny cradled the baby in her arms. Joe wouldn't exactly say she was barking orders. She looked tired and a little overwhelmed, but when she saw Tabby, she held her hand out and smiled. Joe saw the resemblance and wondered why he hadn't noticed it sooner. Maybe it was the difference in the height and the hair color, but the eyes were amazingly similar. Tabby wouldn't turn loose of his hand, so he came right along with her, a sheepish grin on his face.

Jenny looked at their clasped hands, smiling faintly before she frowned and said, "Pastor, I feel it fair to warn you this baby's Presbyterian, so no birthing room conversions or baptisms."

"Now, Doc, you know we Baptists don't take to sprinkling babies. We like to dunk 'em once they're old enough to admit they've done wrong. The more they were wrong, the longer I hold 'em under. I almost drowned at my own baptism."

Jenny laughed before her eyes went back to Joe and Tabby's entwined hands. "I see you didn't waste any time."

"Evan already snapped up the prettiest girl in town, but fortunately for me," Joe said, his eyes going over Tabby's face, "her beautiful sister moved in next door."

Tabby blushed and looked at the nurses still tidying things up. They were taking in every word. As if she knew it would be all over town in no time, she shifted uneasily. Joe wanted to stake a claim, but he didn't want to make her uncomfortable.

Jenny held the baby out and said softly. "Hold him, Tabby. He might not be nearly as healthy if it weren't for you opening my eyes to what I should have already seen. I guess it's true that we often can't see what's right there in front of us."

Tabby glanced around in a panic, but the nurses had left and shut the door quietly behind them. With a sigh and a nervous swallow, she took the swaddled baby and held him close to her, nestled in the crook of her arm. She closed her eyes, and the expression on her face made his heart skip a beat. She needed family. She needed to feel close to people. Her stepfather had a lot to answer for.

Jenny's head tilted. "How does it feel to be an aunt?"

"You have no idea how relieved I am that you are both all right. He's beautiful, Jenny," Tabby whispered and looked at her sister before glancing at Joe. His gut twisted seeing her with the baby cradled so protectively in her arms. He composed his own personal mental painting—Tabby holding a baby they created together.

Their eyes met. As if she'd read his mind, her lips parted. If they'd been anywhere else, Joe would have hauled her in his arms so she could feel how much he wanted her in that moment. He blinked, unsure how he'd fallen so hard, so fast. But it was there, and they would eventually have to deal with it.

Jenny cleared her throat. "There will be none of that in here, you two." Tabby blushed, and Joe cleared his throat a little uneasily. "I think you both need to come to dinner at our house sooner, rather than later. Though I would never have guessed in this day and age, I suspect you could benefit from a little counseling."

Tabby shifted and Joe shifted his gaze to stare at the ceiling. Was their inexperience that obvious? If the church ladies had any idea how virtuous he truly was, Joe was sure their attempts to match make would have been that much more intense. Single, a minister, and a virgin. He was surprised there wasn't a neon wedding ring flashing over his head.

"Jenny?" Tabby questioned. "If you're tired, I can get a nurse."

Jenny shook her head and opened her eyes. "I want to ask you about this afternoon, Tabby." She glanced at Joe. "Is this something we should talk about in private?"

"No. Joseph knows about the letter."

"I have to tell you, that surprises me." Jenny's gaze raked over him. "It also shows me how high the level of trust already is between you."

While Tabby pulled a chair near the bed, Joe hovered next to the window to give them space and some measure of privacy. Jenny stretched her hand out, and Tabby took it. Joe's chest tightened. Tabby needed this sense of family—of normal family. If a sister was all she could have, then so be it. They needed that chance to bond.

"Did Mama ever talk about her life here?" Jenny asked.

Tabby shook her head. "Until she had me write the letter for you, she never said a word."

"Evan said he first saw you up at the top of the hill above the old home place."

"I went there to find you. That was the address Mama had given me."

"Instead you found the gravestone." Jenny captured Tabby's hand. "Neither one of us have had an easy life. Do you have any idea who your real father might be?"

Tabby shook her head. "Mama would never say a word about him."

Jenny squeezed her hand. "Well not only will my baby have a mama and daddy to love him, he'll have an aunt too. That is if you can forgive me for the way I acted to begin with."

"There's nothing to forgive. You're my sister."

"And we're overjoyed to have you in the family," Evan said as he walked in the door. His head swiveled to Joe. "Hey, Preacher."

As Evan's sharp gray stare became speculative, Joe felt his cheeks flush. Evan laughed. Joe stepped forward. "Maybe I should run you home, Tabby, so Evan and Jenny can have some time together."

Tabby smiled at him, and Joe's heart lifted. He had worried she might be overwhelmed by the sudden welcome into a family, but she seemed okay. He decided to ignore Evan's knowing look as they left.

Chapter 6

Joe wanted more time with Tabby, but it was too late to watch a movie. Tabby needed to get up early for school. He thought about ways to get what he wanted without depriving her the whole way back to their houses. In fact, he'd thought of little but Tabby since the kisses and caresses they'd shared the previous night. When he parked the car around the back of the house, he was still no closer to coming up with an excuse to spend time with her when Tabby unexpectedly helped him.

"Joseph? W-would you sing for me before I go home? You have a guitar, don't you?"

He could have kissed her in sheer relief that she handed him the means to keep her with him.

"Yeah. Come on in." He brought her to the living room, closed the drapes, and turned on a single lamp. "Sit on the couch. I'll get us some sweet tea and be right back."

After handing her the glass and setting his down, he took off his tie and loosened his collar before rolling back his sleeves. Tabby sipped her tea and closed her eyes. He could almost see the tension ease from her.

"Play for me, Joseph."

He would do anything for her. The sudden realization startled him but didn't disturb him. He set his glass aside, lifted his guitar, and sat cross-legged on the floor in front of her. He checked the tuning, then began to play. As his voice joined the music, he watched Tabby sigh with pleasure. Joe wasn't sure how long he played. When he stopped, she was asleep. He didn't take it as an insult. It was not a commentary on his music or his singing as much as it was a sign of her trust. She felt secure enough to fall asleep. He eased down next to her and cradled her head against his chest.

He loved her. The thought slipped into his brain quietly and peacefully. He had always figured it would be some sudden and overwhelming revelation. Instead, it simply was. He hadn't looked for it, and it didn't matter they had known each other for just days. He felt complete when he was with her.

Loving Tabby wouldn't be easy. Joe was enough of a realist to know that. She didn't fit other people's image of a preacher's wife. That was one factor, but the biggest obstacle might be Tabby herself. Marrying a minister, even dating one, wasn't on her list. Somehow, someway, he would convince her to trust him enough to marry him. In the meantime? Lord help him, he didn't know if he could wait. He ached to touch her and caress her, to hear her gasps and moans of pleasure for him, only for him.

As he studied her face with its long, sooty lashes, dark winging brows, and narrow, straight nose, he decided those must be features she'd inherited from her father. The eyes and the mouth she definitely had in common with Jenny. His thumb lightly brushed her full lower lip. Joe couldn't help it. That mouth of hers was incredibly sexy, making him ache in ways he'd never had trouble dealing with before, but this was different. All the reasons he'd given to other couples about waiting for intimacy suddenly jumped up and bit him in the butt. It was a whole lot easier to preach it than practice it. He knew his body wouldn't be satisfied until he could touch and kiss her everywhere. Even then, he suspected he would only crave more of her.

Suddenly, he found himself staring into her intense golden gaze.

"You took the bad feelings, the bad memories away," she murmured. "When I listen to you, I wish I could curl into your voice and wrap it around me like a blanket."

Joe was speechless, but what he was thinking and feeling must have been there in his expression, for suddenly her breathing altered, and she slid her hand inside his shirt. His name floated from her lips on a breathy sigh right before she pressed them against his throat. Joseph swallowed, and his hands tightened on her. He tilted her face so he could kiss her. How could he not when he craved her as he craved food or water or air? Surely there was nothing wrong in this? It was a natural expression of what he felt for her, a natural expression of his love.

He held nothing back as he kissed her. Their tongues tasted and explored. He nibbled at the lush fullness of her lower lip and feathered kisses along her jaw to the hollow beneath her ear. Their breathing grew ragged and uneven. Joe brought Tabby's hand back to his chest again and undid his buttons.

"Touch me," he whispered hoarsely, feeling his mind spin out of control as her fingers caressed his chest. "Yes, oh yes, darling."

He cupped her breasts through the thin silk of her blouse, feeling her nipples harden beneath his gently exploring hands. He wanted more, needed more. His mouth descended, brushed the silk aside, and suckled the coral tip of one breast. She moaned and arched against him.

Joseph began to understand what it was his fellow soldiers had gone on and on about in talking about the women they'd left behind. His heart pounded as he shifted so he lay beneath her. When her hips moved against him, he groaned at the intensity of his arousal. He was hard, so hard it was nearly painful. The weight of her pressing against him was amazing. She straddled him, the very heart of her resting against him. It was exquisite. She moved again, unconsciously rubbing him, caressing his erection, and clouding his mind. Even through their clothes, he felt the moist heat of her. They continued to move against each other, both of them panting for breath.

He ached. Heat suffused his face as he realized what was happening to him. "Tabby, I-I…" he ended on a groan as his head slammed back against the couch, and his eyes opened wide in surprise and embarrassment. Lord help him, he couldn't have been more mortified if he'd stood up in front of his congregation stark naked.

* * * *

Tabby felt him, pulsing and hard against her stomach, and it took her a moment to realize what had happened. "Joseph! I'm sorry. I-I didn't mean to…" She saw his embarrassment. "Oh, Joseph. Don't be embarrassed. Not with me."

He looked at her, and his beautiful warm blue eyes were shadowed with mortification. "Tabby, I've never…"

She paused, then hugged him tightly and laughed ruefully. "Oh, Joseph, neither have I. I've never even kissed anyone like I have you."

"You haven't?" When she shook her head, he laughed, too, and hugged her against him. "I kind of thought that, but I didn't know for sure. We're a pair of throwbacks. I'm almost thirty and you're what? Twenty-two… twenty-three?"

Tabby smiled at him. "Twenty-three. I—I guess we should slow down a little, huh?"

Joe grinned sheepishly. "That didn't work so well in my case."

She touched his face, stroked the tips of her artist's fingers along his lean cheek. "We need practice."

Joe's eyes widened in surprise. The idea of being free to touch him made Tabby's lips part. Joseph laughed softly. "Stop that, Tabby. My halo is slipping. Before it slides too far, I should walk you home."

Tabby sighed. "I know. Neither one of us can exactly flaunt our relationship."

He cupped her face in his hands. "That you even say we have a relationship means more than I can tell you. I guess we do need to be careful, but that doesn't mean ashamed."

He walked her to the door, pulled her close, and hugged her. "Are you ready to date a minister yet?" he murmured.

She touched his cheek. "I think the real question is whether you're ready to date the girl everyone's gossiping about."

He touched his lips to her forehead. "Definitely."

Tabby slept deeply and dreamlessly, so when she awoke the next morning, she felt more rested than she had in a while. Trying to keep in mind her problems from the beginning of the week, she dressed conservatively in black slacks, low-heeled pumps, and a long-sleeved white cotton blouse with a high collar. Normally she would have simply put her hair back in a braid, but she took time to twist it up and pin it. Finally satisfied she was as plain and conservative as she could make herself, Tabby headed to school. The faculty was still standoffish, though, some even cold. At least, she thought with relief, Mr. Underwood had unbent enough to nod and smile at her politely.

The real deep freeze was coming from Miss Harris, the new kindergarten teacher. Tabby toyed with the idea of taking a look at the town's Facebook page, but decided she was probably better off remaining in blissful ignorance.

She would have the little ones today—kindergarten, first, and second graders. The day proceeded more smoothly, and Tabby relaxed. When the kindergarten students filed in, she immediately started them on creating color wheels, so they could see how colors blended to form new colors. The second graders were next, and with them, she was again working on pre-testing line drawing skills. After lunch, her first graders came.

Tabby noticed one particular student right away—a quiet girl with beautiful blue eyes and long, dark curls. Her skin was like porcelain, and while Tabby took note of her exquisite beauty, it was her dress and her manners that were all too familiar. Even on this warm afternoon, Melodie Matthews wore a long-sleeved Tinker Bell shirt and a skirt that covered her almost to her ankles. What leg showed was covered in pale pink socks that disappeared into Cinderella sneakers.

A gut-wrenching familiarity made Tabby nearly sick. How often had she gone to school dressed this way, even though the weather was still far too warm to be in a long-sleeved shirt? Tabby took a deep breath. She didn't need to put her own emotions, her own background off on this child. It could be that Melodie's parents were extremely conservative.

The little girl sat by herself, the paper on the table in front of her, and the charcoal pencil untouched. As Tabby moved around the tables, she tried to figure out if the little girl was separating herself or being ostracized—maybe a bit of both—and her heart went out to her.

Tabby sat next to her, folding her long frame into one of the small chairs. "Do you need help getting started, Melodie?"

The little girl shook her head without meeting Tabby's eyes.

"I'll show you what to do, and you can try, okay?"

Melodie lifted her gaze to Tabby's. Without saying a word, she touched Tabby's hand to stop her from picking up the charcoal. For a moment, their eyes met, and there was such sadness in those big blues depths that Tabby nearly gasped. She couldn't tear her gaze away. It was truly like looking into a reflection of her childhood.

"My mommy says not to draw," Melodie whispered. "She says you're a bad woman, but you don't look bad."

Tabby blinked rapidly and shook her head. She glanced around the room, but none of the other children seemed to have heard Melodie's earnest whisper. Looking more intently at her than she had before, Tabby saw nothing, no obvious signs of what she suspected was happening to the little girl.

Tabby smiled, wondering how to communicate her suspicions to the child without alarming her. If Melodie's home was at all like Tabby's had been, the girl was probably well-coached in what to say and do.

"I'm not a bad woman, Melodie. In fact, I bet I'm a lot like you. If you'd like, I'll keep your drawings for my class in a file no one else needs to see." She handed the girl the charcoal and watched in amazement as the little girl began to fill the page with the most exquisite drawings of angels. They were childish and untutored, but showed incredible raw talent.

"Those are beautiful, Melodie." Excitement stirred within her at finding a kindred soul, a talent to be nurtured and developed.

Melodie smiled at her. "Angels are supposed to protect us. Do you think they really can?"

Tabby inhaled deeply, trying to tread carefully. "I think angels do the best they can with what they know. They're probably busy, though, as many people as there are for them to watch over, so sometimes we might have to help them."

Melodie stared at her intently. "Like you're here to help me." She slid the paper over to Tabby. "Here. I'm done with this."

Tabby looked at the clock. It was nearly time to go. She instructed the children on how to put away their supplies. Melodie's drawing she would keep in its own file, locked in the bottom drawer of her desk. After the kids left with their regular classroom teacher, Tabby sat staring at her desk.

She swallowed the excess saliva pooling in her mouth as memories and fears flooded through her. No one had helped her. Mama had tried, but Tommy just beat her too. Every once in a while someone at school got suspicious, but that never went anywhere. Tabby was too afraid to say anything, and Tommy was too smart to hit where it would show.

The law in Virginia required Tabby, as a teacher, to report suspected abuse, but what had she truly seen? What had Melodie actually told her? Nothing.

Their entire conversation could be interpreted as an imaginative little girl who liked to draw angels and decided that Miss MacVie was there to help her as a teacher. Nothing else. She saw no visible signs of abuse. Simply because she saw herself in the child wasn't enough. It would be easy enough to accuse her of transferring her experiences to a child and a situation that were completely different.

Tabby slipped the drawing into her bag, turned off the lights, and drove home. She wanted to talk to Joe, but when she got there, his Mustang was gone. Tabby did something she rarely did. After opening the cabinet, she took out a small bottle of bourbon, splashed some in a glass, and drank it down neat in one swallow. After coughing and wiping the tears from her eyes, she dragged heavy, unwilling limbs up to the third floor of her house. She had to get the images out of her head. The memories from her own past were simply too dark.

She switched from lethargy to frenzy when she reached her studio. Her movements were feverish as she moved the painting of Joseph to a safe spot before she slapped a fresh canvas on the easel. She glanced down at her clothing. She couldn't afford to get paint on her slacks and blouse. They were some of her best clothes. Tabby stripped them off until she stood only in her underwear in the middle of her studio. She folded her clothes neatly and set them outside the studio door. This shouldn't take long.

She pulled a long-sleeved smock from the hook where it rested and carefully buttoned it from its high neck down to mid-thigh where it ended. She picked up a pencil and sketched broad general sweeps on the canvas, allowing the pain to flow as she felt sure it flowed for Melodie, as it had flowed for her. Then she painted, losing herself and all track of time while she wrestled with her memories and worried about how to help her student.

* * * *

Memories of Tabby's exquisite body haunted Joe as he made his rounds, visiting people in the hospital as well as traveling around to older members who were shut-ins. At his last visit, he encountered Jeanie Underwood who also conveniently showed up with a large casserole. It would have been rude to refuse to stay, so he dutifully choked down baked spaghetti and a couple of glasses of too sweet, sweet tea while the two women made not so subtle inquiries into his love life.

For a moment, an errant flash of temper he forcefully suppressed, made him want to look at them and say, *Why ladies, my love life is pretty freaking good. Just last night I prematurely ejaculated while feeling up the delightfully sinful Miss MacVie. Had I not disgraced myself like a hormone-crazed adolescent, I might have been able to talk Miss MacVie out of her clothing, so I could actually see what I was climaxing all over.*

Instead, Joe smiled charmingly, admitted he'd met someone whom he was interested in but they were simply friends, then politely excused himself by saying he needed to work on his sermon for Sunday. When he pulled the Mustang in and covered it up, he saw Katie sat on his porch railing now, watching him intently with her faintly glowing golden eyes. A glance at Tabby's house showed him the light was on in the studio. She might get angry with him, but he decided after the day he'd had, he was going to intrude anyway.

He sprinted up to his room and changed into a pair of comfortably worn khakis and a lightweight cotton shirt. He slipped his feet into flip-flops and grabbed two cans of Coke before he dashed across the driveway and onto her porch. Katie, he noticed, had disappeared.

As he walked through the darkened kitchen, his sensitive nose picked up a smell all too familiar from his childhood. *Whisky?* Joe frowned as he noticed the bottle and the glass on the counter. His nose wrinkled when he picked it up, and now his expression grew taut as he looked down the hallway to the dimly lit stairway.

He remembered all too well finding Tabby collapsed from exhaustion amid the wreckage of her paintings, but he didn't hear any sounds. He hadn't smelled liquor on her then. No way he would have missed that. Some of his mother's best friends had been named Jack and Jim. The fact the bottle was still in the kitchen and still three-quarters full was a good sign, surely.

Nevertheless, he took the stairs two at a time until he once again halted in consternation outside her studio door. To one side was her partially finished painting of him, and to the other side were the clothes he'd seen her depart in that morning, neatly folded and stacked on top of her black leather flats. Taking a deep breath, almost afraid of what he might find this time, Joe slowly turned the knob and opened the door.

The first thing that struck him was the single-minded concentration with which she painted. She was much more intense than she had been while he sat for her. Something raw and elemental colored her movements now, as if she was in a battle with the canvas. Her brush was her sword, and the paints were the wounds of that battle. The next thing he noticed was the expanse of shapely white legs showing beneath a paint-covered smock that ended just below mid-thigh. While many women wore skirts that short every day, Joe had never seen Tabby expose anywhere close to this amount of skin. As his gaze traveled upward from trim ankles to shapely calves and further, he noticed something else, a thin crisscrossing of whiter skin. His breath caught as he realized what he was seeing, a fine network of old scars.

Now his eyes lifted, and he noticed for the first time what she painted. A cowering child, cringing away from a detached hand holding a wicked looking switch coated in blood. Ghostly figures crowded the edge of the painting, some gazing on in frozen horror while others looked away, refusing to see. Even as he watched, Tabby sobbed and dropped her palette and brushes.

"Tabby, darling…" he whispered softly, hoping not to startle or frighten her.

She whirled, her loose hair flowing around her head and her golden eyes overflowing with silent tears. She held her arms out to him.

"Joseph!" she choked, and her whole body began to shake. He caught her as her legs buckled beneath her and swung her into his arms. She was nearly as tall as him yet willow slender, and he had no trouble cradling her until he could sit with her in the window seat. She had her face turned into his neck and clutched him in desperation. He realized one of his hands rested on the bare skin of her thigh, and he quickly smoothed the material of her smock over her legs, covering as much as he could.

"What is it?" he asked. "Tell me what's wrong."

Tabby shook her head. "I can't. Not yet. Just hold me."

He rocked her, his eyes riveted on the images in the painting. Was it her? Was this a painting of something that had happened to her? "Who's the child in your painting, Tabby?"

Silence. Tabby took a couple of deep, shuddering breaths. "A memory, but triggered by one of my new students. Oh, Joseph. She reminds me so much of myself."

Joe's eyes swiveled to the painting again. "You think she's being abused?" he asked slowly, the horror bleeding through in his tone. "Tabby… Did you tell anyone?"

She pulled away, jumped up, and paced the studio, her movements now agitated. "Tell them what, Joseph? Tell them that my student dresses like I did at that age so that none of the bruises I had would show? The closest thing she said that even remotely sounded like she was telling me about the abuse was that she knew I was there to help her."

Joe's eyes wandered to the painting again. "You saw no bruises?"

Tabby looked at the painting too. "No. It was like watching myself, Joseph. Abusive adults are so clever, and Melodie is already well-coached." She turned to face him. "I told you the man I thought was my father invited the minister and the deacons over on a regular basis to try to cast the demons out of me. Well, in between those sessions, Tommy tried to beat them out. It started when I began school and didn't stop until I hit puberty. Six years, Joseph."

He swallowed thickly. "No one helped? No one discovered it?"

Tabby shrugged. "There were a couple of investigations, but my mother and I were too terrified of him to cooperate with anyone else. I wore long skirts and long-sleeved shirts to school. No one wanted to talk to me anyway. I was a social outcast not only because of the way I dressed, but also because I had nothing in common with my classmates.

"Once or twice, a teacher or administrator would call social services, but they never found anything." As she spoke, she unbuttoned the smock she wore. Joe stared in fascination, but not in a sexual way. There was absolutely nothing sexual about this situation. He already had a gut feeling of what he would see. Tabby turned her back to him, slowly pulled her hair off her back, and let the smock fall to the ground.

Joe gasped. "Tabby!" he whispered hoarsely. Long scars crossed her back from her shoulders to her buttocks, disappearing beneath the lace of her panties, only to reappear on her thighs.

Her shoulders slumped, and her head dropped forward. "Six years, Joseph. This is what he did to me while no one could prove anything. My mother and I were too scared of him to speak up, to volunteer any information. We enabled him. How do I help this little child when I couldn't even help myself?"

Joe retrieved the smock and put it back on her before he turned her into his arms and held her. Tears burned the back of his eyes. He wasn't sure if they were in sympathy to the pain she had endured or in fury at the man who had inflicted it. Both emotions warred inside him. He took her out of the studio, turned off the lights, and made her go with him downstairs where he settled her on the couch in the living room and brought her a can of Coke.

He sat next to Tabby and stroked her hair and shoulders as she poured out what had happened to her. Joe swallowed against the painful lump in his throat, praying God would take away the desire he felt to find Tommy MacVie and kill him. When at last Tabby lay curled against him, emotionally exhausted, Joe kissed her forehead.

"Think about Melodie for a few days, Tabby," he said quietly. "I won't advise you to pray about it. I'll do that for us both." Fingers that already held the cloth of his shirt in a death grip tightened even more. "Maybe the answer will come to both of us."

"She draws angels, Joseph," Tabby whispered, "the most beautiful angels, and someone beats her."

"Shh," he soothed. "We'll figure out how to help her."

Tabby looked into his face in the dim light. "Would you stay with me tonight? I-I don't want to be alone."

Joseph touched her cheek. Propriety said he should go home, desire told him to take what he knew was there for the asking, but what was truly right won.

"I'll stay with you, Tabby."

He would hold her. He would sleep with her, but he would do nothing more than kiss her, no matter how much that might cost him.

He found her nightgown, tucked her into her bed, then stretched out next to her on top of the covers, still fully clothed. For the first time since he had made the decision to become a minister, Joseph questioned the strictures that circumscribed his life. Tabby curled against him with a trust he wasn't sure he deserved. Her body was beautiful, and he wanted her, but not when she was so emotionally vulnerable. He wanted her when they could come together joyfully.

Joseph watched her sleep and gently stroked her dark hair, letting his fingers trail down to scars that extended onto her upper arms. Joseph looked at her narrow, beautiful face with its fine features and winging brows, and was touched once again by a sense of familiarity. She looked so serious when she slept, when those gorgeous golden eyes weren't sparkling with excitement and interest in what she found around her.

She sighed in her sleep, and her hand slipped down to lie across his hips. Joseph swallowed and closed his eyes with pleasure and pain as his body responded to her innocent caress. Lord, if this was a test, he was awfully close to flunking. He gritted his teeth while he silently prayed for strength.

At some point, he fell asleep, not waking until dawn began to touch the interior walls of Tabby's bedroom with its faint glow. Joseph slipped silently from her bed, grabbed his shoes, and tiptoed downstairs. Katie Scarlett brushed past him as he eased out the door and made sure it shut noiselessly behind him.

As he dashed down the porch steps and across the driveways between their two homes, a flash of silver caught his eye. Joseph's gaze switched to the street where a four-door sedan had slowed. Crap. It was Dennis Underwood. As their gazes met, Joe smiled and waved as if he had nothing at all to be concerned about. And he didn't. The night he'd spent with Tabby had been totally and completely G rated.

Chapter 7

Tabby felt almost weightless. Friday afternoon and she had survived her first weeks in a new town, she reflected, as she changed into her cycling clothes. They hadn't been entirely smooth. There were her concerns over Melodie and the continued cold shoulders from the elementary faculty. However, Tabby could do nothing with either of those situations other than keep her eyes open and be as professional as possible.

Joe's car was gone. He was probably working at the church or out on calls, so Tabby decided a long ride would be exactly the thing to help her clear her head. Katie sat on the porch railing with her gold eyes scrunched into inscrutable slits as she half dozed and half watched her mistress warm up. Tabby made sure to thoroughly stretch the muscles in her calves as well as the front and the backs of her thighs. There was nothing worse than a cramp while riding. She remembered one time at college when she had nearly run into the back of a truck trying to massage a cramp in her calf. Boy had that been scary. There was no room for distraction riding on any roads.

It took her a few minutes to get out of town. The afternoon was warm and a little breezy, but not enough to make riding difficult. The road she chose wound along a wide, shallow creek. Even though it was a state highway, it was nearly deserted and gave her plenty of time to think about her new job. While she was pleased overall with how things were going at the middle and high school levels, Tabby was still uneasy with the elementary classes. In addition to the cold shoulders from the faculty and the principal, Melodie Matthews worried her.

Tabby reviewed everything that might be a sign the child was a victim of abuse, but so far the only things she had seen were the long sleeves and long skirts, the little girl's withdrawal from the other children, and the rather cryptic comments from her mother. But simply telling a child she was not to draw, while odd, wasn't an indication of abuse.

In her heart, she knew Melodie was being abused. Somehow, she had to get the girl to admit it or show proof of it because, despite her certainty, she had nothing concrete. Melodie's attire and demeanor could simply be a shy child with strictly religious parents. From what she was able to gather, that description apparently fit the Matthews to a T.

The father was partner in a logging company. The mother was a stay at home mom. She attended a conservative non-denominational church. It brought such a sense of déjà vu to Tabby that it nearly made her sick to her stomach. Maybe she could talk to Dr. James, the middle and high school principal, on Monday. He might be able to give her guidance, where she didn't trust Mr. Underwood to do the same.

Tabby paused along the edge of the road to check her odometer. That was far enough. As she became better acquainted with the area, she could map out routes that would bring her in a circle, but for now, she simply turned around to head back to town. She heard a vehicle approach behind her, but it didn't pass. A glance over her shoulder showed a pickup hanging a few feet behind her back wheel. Lord how she hated that. It was either an overly cautious farmer or…the first wolf whistle made her cringe. Yep. That.

"Hey, baby! Nice ass!" a teenager leaned out the window to call. "Wish I was your bicycle seat."

Right. She had never heard that before. Tabby ignored them, until they pulled alongside; then she turned to look the three boys full in the face.

All three turned beet red, and the one on the passenger side said, "Oh shit! Get outta here, man! It's the art teacher."

The truck swerved as the driver stomped on the gas. Afraid they would accidentally hit her, Tabby veered onto the end of a long, paved driveway that wound up through manicured pastures to a large red brick home that looked like it had been there for centuries. The bike began to wobble. As she tried to free her shoes from the toe clips, her front wheel caught a rock and tossed her onto her butt. She lay there for a second, a little dazed, but mostly humiliated and angry. Tabby groaned as she sat up and looked at her skinned palms. That would make riding home miserable.

"Are you all right?" The question, voiced in a deep, pleasant baritone, came from somewhere far above her.

She started, a little afraid after her encounter with the teenagers. Her heart pounded as she looked up and up. The sun was behind the tall man who stood a few yards away, breathing as though he'd run. Tabby put a hand across her brow to shade her eyes, but she still couldn't see him well.

She took a deep, steadying breath. "Yes. I think so. That was clumsy. My hands are a little skinned up."

"I'm sorry I can't be a gentleman and help you to your feet, but I've reached the end of my leash."

"Huh?" Tabby examined the man again, confused by what he said. He didn't make sense. Was he crazy? That was all she needed. Horny teenagers stalking her in a pickup truck and now a crazy man rescuing her.

"Electronic tether," he clarified, lifting the cuff of his well-cut slacks to show a black nylon band with a small electronic tracking device on it. He stepped slightly to one side so she could see him more clearly. His mouth twisted with bitter amusement when he saw the way her eyes widened in alarm.

"I promise I'm not an ax murderer or even violent. My wife's up at the house. She saw what was happening and sent me down to make sure you were okay."

"Oh. Thanks." She didn't know what else to say. He didn't seem friendly, and he was a bit scary now she got a good look at him. Not in a wild, mountain man way. No, he was well dressed, and his steel gray hair had been carefully trimmed, even if it was a bit mussed right now. He was so cold and remote looking, as if he allowed nothing or no one to touch him.

"Your tire's flat."

Tabby sighed. "That's kind of how my life's gone lately."

"Would you like a glass of tea? I could help you with the tire too."

She was tempted to refuse, but she did have to repair the tire, and there was something else in his voice. A reluctant loneliness? She smiled as she stood and said, "Sure. My name's Tabitha MacVie."

He held out his hand, but when she showed him her skinned up palms, he smiled, and put his hands behind his back. "Stoner Richardson. If you'll hand me your bike, I'll take it up the drive for you. Your hands must hurt."

"A little." Tabby took off her bike helmet and the long ponytail she'd had tucked under it fell down her back. "Thanks for checking on me."

He looked down at her as they walked up the drive. She guessed he must be around six-four, a lean man with gray hair. His thick, black brows arched over penetrating gray eyes and an aquiline nose. "I have a daughter about your age, I guess. She's twenty-six. I don't get to see her much."

He said the last reluctantly, as though he were trying to find some common ground, but didn't wish to reveal anything about himself.

"I'm twenty-three."

He laughed self-deprecatingly. "I won't tell you how old I am. Suffice it to say that the twenty-six-year-old is the younger of my children." Tabby looked up at him again and smiled. Then she blinked and her smile faded. Stoner Richardson. She ducked her head, but not before he saw the change in her expression. "Ah. I see something has finally connected. Is it my prison sentence or who I am?"

Tabby stopped, and he did too. "You're Evan's father."

The man's wall of reserve was a mile thick. "I am," he responded stiffly. "How do you know my...him?"

"He's my brother-in-law." If it felt strange to say it, the reaction she got was even stranger. Stoner Richardson stumbled and uttered a crude expletive. Tabby's brows rose. In that at least, he and Evan did have something in common.

"Jenny Owens had no sister," Stoner challenged, his brows now drawn together in a suspicious glare.

"I'm her half sister," Tabby corrected.

"Mary Owens was your mother?" His voice suddenly lost some of its cultured veneer. There was a rawness to it that struck her instantly, but unlike so many other people, she couldn't read this man's thoughts and feelings.

"Did you know her?" Tabby asked. She wanted to talk to someone who might remember her mother from a time before Tommy MacVie had beaten her into a scared shadow of herself.

Stoner Richardson looked away and swallowed. "Yes, I knew her. It was years ago, though. I-I'm afraid I don't remember much about her."

"Oh." Tabby was disappointed. "That's okay."

Stoner cleared his throat. "What brings you here?"

"I'm the new art teacher for Mountain Meadow Schools."

"Really? Are you an artist too? Or do you only teach?"

Tabby blushed. "I paint. Mostly oils."

They reached the house with its imposing stone pillars, but he continued walking around the back to a small workshop. He propped her bike next to the door and disappeared inside. Tabby glimpsed a partially finished table with beautiful inlay work. He stepped back out with an air hose in hand to which he had attached a tire tip and a pressure gauge. As soon as he attempted to put air in, it was obvious the rock she hit had also sliced the inner tube and tire. Stoner frowned, but Tabby just released the tire kit hooked under the seat. After squatting next to him, she quickly and efficiently popped the tire from the rim. She stripped out the tube and yanked the tire off the wheel.

"What are you doing?"

Tabby turned. With him squatted next to her, they were almost on the same level. "Changing the tire, Mr. Richardson."

"Call me Stone or Stoner. You know how?"

Tabby sat back on her haunches and laughed. "Of course I do. When you ride a bike like this as much as I do, you learn how to take care of it. Trust me. It's no fun to push a bike with a flat tire for miles. I could even pump it up with my hand pump, but if you don't mind, sir, I mean Stoner, your air hose will work a whole lot faster."

She worked the new tire onto the rim, inserted the tube, and carefully snapped the tire's remaining edge inside the wheel. "There. All ready for air." She held out her hand for the hose. "If you don't mind, I'll do it. I had a guy at a service station start to fill it like he had all day when I told him it took a hundred pounds of pressure. Next thing I knew…pop! My inner tube was in shreds."

"I'll bet the guy at the service station was, too, when you got done with him."

Tabby tilted her head at Stoner's comment. "No. It was an accident. He didn't mean to do it. People shouldn't be punished for things beyond their knowledge or control." Her gaze skittered to the building behind them. "Hey, may I see your shop? Are you building furniture?"

Stoner flushed. "I-I'm not very good yet. It was a hobby of mine years ago, and since I have…well… I have a lot of time on my hands, I decided to take it up again."

He was obviously proud of his shop, but she sensed his uncertainty when it came to his work. Tabby ran her hands over the round occasional table with its Queen Anne legs. He was carefully working an intricate geometric inspired inlay pattern into the top of it. She touched the table, marveling at the workmanship. "It's beautiful. You must have incredible patience."

He chuckled. "Not a word most people would attribute to me, but thank you, Tabitha."

"Tabby," she corrected. She glanced at her watch. "I should go. I've got an hour ride back to town."

"What about the tea? And your hands?"

Tabby grimaced at her scraped palms. "I'll be okay. Maybe some other time."

"Sure." But it was obvious he didn't believe her. Impulsively, Tabby leaned forward and kissed him on the cheek. His brows drew together in a frown, but she saw him swallow. "Thanks," he said gruffly. "It was nice to have company for a little while."

"I'll be back." She told him earnestly. "This was a pleasant ride, well, except for falling." This time he nodded and smiled.

When she reached her house, Joe was pushing his mower back and forth across his lawn, and Tabby noticed her lawn was already mowed. He waved to her as he continued to push the mower, and Tabby nearly fell off her bike again as she gazed at his bare chest. She had never seen him without a shirt on. The man had muscles. And abs. Beautiful. The golden tan on his face and arms covered his upper body too.

She dashed into the house and washed the road rash on her palms, wincing at the sting before carefully examining her hands to make sure she'd gotten out any stray bits of grit. After taking down two glasses, she filled them with ice, then tea, and started to push the door back open with her hip, but Joe already leaned against the doorjamb. It finally struck her that she no longer heard the mower. He had a towel slung over his shoulder but still wore no shirt. Tabby swallowed as she stared at his broad chest with its covering of darker hair.

"I poured you some tea," she said breathlessly, looking away from his bare chest and moving back so he could open the door and step inside. "Here."

He smiled slowly. "Thanks. I stopped in to invite you out to dinner. There's a steak place over by the interstate. I checked and they have several vegetarian dishes as well. What do you say?"

Tabby looked from him down to the sweat staining her own shirt. "We'll need to shower first."

Dead silence greeted her. When she looked up, Joe gazed at her with such heat in his eyes she spilled some of her tea. He set his glass down on the counter as he advanced, took her glass, and set it down too. Tabby smelled newly mown grass mingled with clean, male sweat. A slow, heavy throbbing began inside her.

"Together?" he breathed.

Her startled gaze met his intent one. "Joseph? I haven't... I mean... you... me..."

He touched her cheek and leaned closer so that his lips were a whisper away from her. "I need to kiss you, Tabby." And he matched his actions to his words. She leaned into him, against him, feeling the heat of his skin from the sun and the work.

"I need to touch you," he groaned against her lips as his hands moved restlessly along her rib cage. "I need you to touch me."

She couldn't think. Her heart beat like mad, and his scent flooded her senses. He captured her hands and stared into her eyes.

"Feel me, Tabby," he whispered and drew her hips into his. "Feel how much I want to be with you."

She moaned as the intensity of it shot through her. Her legs went weak as she imagined what it would be like to have this man make love to her. Joseph cupped her bottom, holding and supporting her against him.

"It's too much, Joseph," Tabby gasped.

"Shower with me," he coaxed. "No more, no less. Only what you want."

"Yes."

They left a trail of clothing from the kitchen, up the stairs, and into her bathroom where the master bath had been remodeled at some point in recent years and included a walk-in shower big enough for both of them.

For an instant, Tabby simply stopped and stared at him. Joseph returned her look, his face flushed with a mixture of excitement and shyness. Did she look that same way? So hungry? Joe moved first, his fingertips trailing across Tabby's cheek, down the column of her neck to the pulse beating in the base of her throat. His eyes drifted lower.

"You're so beautiful."

Tabby's hands fluttered nervously, sudden shyness making her want to cover herself from his gaze. Joseph shook his head.

"Don't. You have no need to hide from me."

She looked at his chest, then lower, and sucked in a nervous breath as she saw his erection. Joe adjusted the spray in the shower. He pulled her in with him. His hands gently stroked along her upper arms as the water beat down, and he lowered his head to kiss her. It began tenderly and teasingly, but the passion that overwhelmed them soon had them gasping and groaning while their hands continued to touch and explore. Joe's tongue probed the inside of her mouth, and Tabby met him thrust for thrust.

When she caressed his flat nipples, he sucked in his breath on a startled moan. After grabbing the soap, he turned her and lathered her back, down the line of her spine, and over the smooth round globes of her buttocks.

"Don't look at them, Joseph," she choked, knowing his eyes were on the scars that crisscrossed her. His fingers brushed her as if touching the finest porcelain. Tabby trembled. She had never felt such tenderness or such passion. She ached with a need she only barely understood. "Joseph!"

He knelt and kissed one of the thin, pale lines. "I wish I could take away every bit of pain you felt."

He stood again, gently turning her and washing her front, his hands lingering on her breasts before his hand slipped lower. Tabby sucked in a breath, and he paused. "Is this all right?"

Her decision. He was leaving it up to her. Tabby knew that if she told him to stop, he would. But that was not what she wanted.

"Yes," she murmured, and he slid his fingers into the curls between her thighs.

* * * *

"You're so hot," he told her, his voice hoarse. His heart hammered, and he wondered if he was even still breathing. The silky feel of her jacked his already aroused body even higher. Joe continued to stroke and play her with his fingers. She whimpered and pressed against him. He leaned his face against hers. Lord help him, he wanted her so much, had waited so long to find a woman who accepted him as simply another human being with the same amazing feelings surging through him as she felt. He wanted her by his side and in his life.

"Yes, Tabby. That's it," he encouraged. His finger slipped inside her, and she clung to his shoulders, trembling from her kiss-swollen lips to the tips of her toes so that it nearly collapsed her legs. Okay, his were about to collapse too. Joe kissed her deeply as he continued to slide his finger in and out of her tight, wet heat. Encouraged by the small sounds she made, Joe slipped a second finger inside. Tabby sobbed against his mouth and twined her arms around his neck.

"Joseph!" she cried out, burying her face against his chest as she shook.

"Shh," he crooned. He was determined to hang onto his control, so what they were doing didn't end too soon. Just seeing her pleasure, though, made him burn even hotter, but he held her and stroked her until she calmed down. Then her belly rubbed against his erection, and her fingers found him, circled him, and it was his turn. He shook as she caressed the full length of him. Her hand was like a glove around the velvety skin of his shaft, and her stroking left him nearly mindless. "Oh, Tabby. It's incredible."

Joe groaned and leaned back against the wall of the shower, pulling her against him and trapping her caressing hand between them. His hips moved in rhythm with her stroking until he reached down and stopped her. He wasn't going to lose it like some horny teenager a second time.

"I can't take any more, Tabby. I don't want this to end too soon."

With the water still beating down on them both, he looked deeply into her golden eyes. "I want to love you, completely. I want to join myself to you, make love to you totally, but only if it's what you want too."

He was giving her the choice, and now he waited, not even daring to breathe, for her answer. Tabby's golden eyes were wide, filled with an expression of wonder. He had done that, put that look in her eyes. He would do it again and again if she would let him, especially if it made her glow like she now did.

Tabby stood on her tiptoes and touched her tongue to the shell of his ear before she whispered. "Yes, Joseph. It's what I want, more than anything."

Towels turned into seductive toys. They kissed, touched, and stumbled together to her bed. As the afternoon sunlight spilled over them, Joe aroused her to a fever pitch with his hands and his mouth. As he knelt between her thighs, their eyes met. Joe swallowed.

"I will do my best not to hurt you," he murmured. He trembled as he guided himself into the opening between her slick, wet folds. She was hot and so wonderfully tight around him he nearly lost control and plunged forward. He glanced up, seeing nothing but encouragement glowing in her golden eyes. "Tabby," he groaned and pushed all the way into her. He stilled at her gasp, afraid he'd hurt her, but then her hands stroked his cheek, reassuring him.

"It's all right, Joseph. I'm not in pain."

He moaned and began to move. It took them a moment or two to find a rhythm that stimulated them both, but soon he was driving into her, his hands bracketed on her slender hips. He felt her tense around him and stared down at her as she arched and cried out. It was the most wondrous sight he'd ever seen and sent him spinning over the edge too.

They lay next to each other, breathing heavily. Joseph stroked the tangled hair from Tabby's face and kissed her softly. "I love you, Tabby."

"I love you, too, Joseph."

It was that easy.

They smiled stupidly at each other and laughed as they tumbled out of bed. While she dressed, he pulled his shorts back on and dashed across to his house to change clothes.

* * * *

Joe grinned. He was staring out the window of his church office. Again. He had been trying all morning to tweak a few details in tomorrow's sermon. Instead, visions of Tabby flowed through his brain. He loved her. He'd told her so, and she'd said it back to him.

A knock sounded softly at Joe's door.

"Come on in," he called, the grin still firmly in place.

John Gatewood entered, his expression somber. "Got a minute, Joe?"

He stood and waved the older man to the chair in front of his desk. "Always. How can I help you, John?"

Gatewood sat, pursed his lips a moment, then blew out a heavy breath. "You know what a fine job we all think you're doing."

Joe sat back down and leaned back a bit in his chair. "But? Because I sense you're here for more than just handing me a compliment, wonderful though it is."

Gatewood rested his elbows on his knees as he clasped his hands together. "There's talk, Joe. About you and the new art teacher. Some of it doesn't reflect well on either you or her."

"So, are you here simply to let me know as a friend, or are you here as a representative of the church council?"

"A bit of both. I have to ask. Are you in a relationship with Miss MacVie?"

"It's still early, but yes."

"Serious?"

"Yes."

Gatewood leaned back, now resting his elbows on the arms of the chair. "It's a small town, Pastor. A small town in a conservative community. For your sake, and especially for her sake, you need to legitimize it and be very circumspect in your behavior."

Joe pinched the bridge of his nose, feeling a headache coming on. "Has there been a complaint?"

"Talk only, at least about you. But I'll tell you right up front, I don't think Miss MacVie has many friends among her colleagues."

"And I think that's a lot of unfounded jealousy," Joe responded, tamping down the resentment taking root. This was because of who he was, not because of who she was. "Tabby is a gentle, beautiful woman who had the misfortune of moving in next door to me. You know as well as me, John, that every time I turn around, someone's trying to hook me up with a wife."

"Human nature."

"It might be, but when I marry, it's going to be a woman of my choosing, not simply someone to run the ladies Bible study or the church bake sales."

John Gatewood stood, hitching up the khaki pants he wore, then smoothing a hand over his balding head. "I don't disagree with you. All I'm saying is be careful so this doesn't get out of hand."

Joe came around his desk. They shook hands. "I appreciate you coming by. I'll do what I can."

Chapter 8

Tabby felt the heat and intensity of Joe's gaze every time she moved around her kitchen Saturday night. She had decided to give him a sampling of how she normally ate, cooking Portobello mushrooms that she had grilled, then stuffed with a cheese and herb mixture, served with wild rice and grilled marinated veggies. He'd watched her the entire time, his eyes following her movements as they talked. Rather than making her paranoid, his attention made her feel wanted. Whenever she came within reach of him, he would snag her hand or her shoulder and pull her in for a quick, soft kiss.

Tabby smiled, overjoyed at being able to put her job from her mind while she basked in Joseph's attention.

"What did you think of the mushrooms?" she asked as they sat on the floor in the living room, their empty plates on the coffee table.

"Dinner was delicious, Tabby. I'm surprised. I didn't think I would end up feeling so full without the usual meat on the plate."

She grinned at him. "Dessert's a little more traditional. I made apple pie."

He rolled her underneath him and pinned her to the floor, the press of his hips against her belly not doing a thing to hide his desire for her.

"That's it," he growled with mock ferociousness. "I'm not releasing you until you agree to marry me."

She stilled and stared at him, his words like a dash of cold water, slapping her with bitter memories from her past. She didn't want that immediate feeling of being trapped. "Don't, Joseph. Don't tease about something like that."

His blue eyes searched her face. "I'm not teasing, Tabby. I want to marry you. I love you. You know that. I love you so much."

Panic squeezed her chest. She didn't want to feel that, not with Joseph, but it was there. "I haven't even agreed to date you. Marriage is a big leap."

He touched her cheek, his brow furrowed in confusion. "Tabby, we've already made love with each other. I think we've already taken a big step beyond just dating. I told you I love you. You said the same. Taking this to the next step is logical. Do you doubt my feelings…or not return them?"

Logical? She didn't feel logical. "I do love you."

He rolled away from her. "Then what is it?"

Tabby sat up and hugged her knees. "There's… There's more to marriage than love. You know that. Especially for you. You're a minister. You need someone who can be a helper."

His brows drew together in a frown. "I need a wife and lover, not an assistant pastor."

"It's not that simple," she protested. The last thing Tabby wanted was for him to make a commitment to her that would drag down his career. "And I haven't exactly had the best examples of what marriage is. Tommy beat my mother and me."

"You think I would do that to you?" Joe demanded. Now there was a hard edge to his voice she had never heard before. The patient, understanding man he'd always presented to her was suddenly stern, his blue eyes frosty.

"No." Tabby leaped to her feet and began pacing. "Never. You would never do that. I just… I lived under his thumb for so long, and I've had to fight so hard to be independent. I-I don't know that I can be a marriage partner. I don't know that I can be a wife."

Joe started to reach toward her, then dropped his hand and shook his head. He raked a hand through his tawny hair. The light was gone from his eyes.

"You're right. If you can't trust me not to crush your spirit, then we're not ready for marriage." He stood up, staring down at her in frustration. "Maybe we need to slow things down a bit. I would never expect you to take on a role in the church as my wife. It's true, people do have expectations of me, but those are their expectations, not mine. But you need to be able to believe that, and right now, you can't trust in that, can you?"

Automatically, she started to deny it, but closed her mouth and didn't say anything. Everything in her past experience told her there would be demands, and that ultimately, she would let him and everyone else down. That was one thing she couldn't bear.

"I should go home," Joseph finally said when she still didn't speak. "I'm not giving up on you or us, but maybe we need a little time and space to think."

With that said, he turned on his heel and left, the door shutting quietly behind him.

Tabby stared after him, tears welling but not falling. She'd glimpsed something with him that was so amazing, but how could it ever be? The pastor and the psycho painter? Joe might accept her. He might say he had no expectations of her, but other people would. Tabby shuddered.

* * * *

Joe tossed and turned all night, berating himself for rushing her, then walking out. They had known each other for less than a month. What had he been thinking to rush her and himself? He'd let his desire cloud his logic. Gatewood had pointed it out to him, and somehow he doubted he'd heard the last of that conversation.

He paced the floor in his room as he thought, but thinking was difficult when he knew Tabby was right next door. He was due a vacation. Maybe it was running away, but he was going to take that week now. He needed some space to clear his head. He'd drive to a friend's place in Tennessee and go trout fishing. Some quiet time away from everyone might give him a chance to think. It would give Tabby room as well.

Maybe it was circumstances, but they'd both rushed together without knowing much about each other. He'd known of her fears about organized religion, but he'd chosen to ignore them and the role his religion played in his life in his headlong desire for her. And he had shared virtually nothing of his own past with her. Nothing that would help her understand why what he did was so important to him.

Joe started to knock on her door the following morning before heading over to the church, but her bike was already gone. He needed her trust, and he knew that was something he didn't have right now. Joe rubbed his chest. Lord that hurt. For the first time in a long while, he had to use his notes to deliver his sermon.

He could almost swear when he told the worship committee that he wished to take a week's vacation there was relief on the faces of the men across the table from him. He narrowed his eyes and looked at each committee member.

"Was there something you wished to discuss?" he inquired.

"No," John Gatewood said, not quite able to hide the relief in his smile as he glanced down the table to Dennis Underwood, who also shook his head. "No. You're right, Pastor. This is a slow time in the church calendar, so now would be a great time for a vacation."

Joe smiled tightly at them and stood. "If you'll excuse me then, I'll put a call in to see if I can get a visiting minister to preach next Sunday. We'll cancel tonight's services. I'd like to get on the road."

"Excellent idea, Pastor," Underwood said heartily. Joe studied Underwood for a long moment, but then shook his head and left.

He wanted to say something to Tabby, let her know he was leaving town to give them both some space, but when he walked back to the house, her bicycle was still missing. He took the stairs two at a time, shoved a few changes of clothes into a duffel bag, slipped his feet into his running shoes, and tossed everything into the back of the Mustang.

He checked Tabby's house one more time, but saw only Katie dozing on the porch railing in the afternoon sun. Joe sat down on the steps, knowing she was sometimes gone for a couple of hours, but when another hour passed and she still hadn't returned, he stood up with a sigh. He scribbled a note but ripped it up. Handling this wasn't something that needed to be done in a note or a text. It needed the back and forth of a true conversation. They would find a way to work it out, but right now space was what they needed. His lips tightened briefly, and with a shake of his head, he got into the car and drove off.

* * * *

Tabby had heard Joseph singing as she pedaled past the red brick Baptist church that morning. She had left early, deliberately trying to avoid him, and had stopped in at Mercer's for some oatmeal before continuing. Now, as she rode out of town, the singing floated on the breeze. Even with the voices of the entire congregation joining in, she picked out his clear tenor as she passed the open doorway.

Her stomach knotted. She hadn't liked how things ended last night, but she didn't know how to approach him, how to make him understand. It wasn't him. It was her. And that sounded so cliché, yet it was the truth. He was wonderful, patient, and loving. Her own fears were what stood between them now.

Making love with Joseph had been incredibly beautiful. Just thinking about it now made her glad the morning breeze was cool on her heated skin as she pedaled. The wonder in Joseph's eyes made her feel, for the first time in her life, as if she were someone worthy of being loved. It might have been her first time, Joseph's, too, but it hadn't felt awkward. It had felt pre-ordained—right up until he'd mentioned marrying her.

Marriage was the next step for him, and probably should have been the first, but Tabby couldn't make that leap. She swallowed nervously, her breathing tight. Images of Tommy and how he'd controlled both her mother and her superimposed themselves. The logical part of her brain knew Joseph would never do that, but this wasn't logical. It was a gut level emotional response she couldn't control.

At first, she'd been concerned because he was a minister, and she still wasn't convinced it would be as simple as Joseph seemed to believe, but the real source of her concern was the issue of control. She could never allow another person to confine and command her the way her father had. Tabby had sworn never to give anyone that much power over her.

But she also knew living together wasn't an option. He was probably already in trouble, for all they knew.

With the need to get away for a while driving her, Tabby pedaled toward Stoner Richardson's place. Today she had brought her sketchpad and pencils in her backpack. She would sketch his house and take it to him as a gift for his help. It would be a nice thank you, and it would help keep her mind off Joe and the sudden snag their relationship had hit. When she thought of Stoner, his tall spare frame and his lean face, it filled her with an odd sense of comfort and security. Maybe that was foolish given the electronic tracker he wore, but Stoner had been nothing but helpful after she'd fallen off her bike. Today, she could use a little comfort.

Tabby found a spot across the road and settled on a large rock. She lightly created her perspective lines first, did a rough outline of her composition, and began drawing and shading her final sketch. After adding a few last finishing touches, she grinned, rolled up the completed drawing, and slid it into a protective tube before putting her sketchpad back into her pack.

The Richardson driveway was too steep to ride up, so she pushed the bike to the top. After leaning it against the hitching post next to the walkway, Tabby knocked on the heavy front door. Her eyes widened when an older gentleman answered.

"May I help you, miss?" he inquired in a distinctly British accent as his eyes raked her from head to foot dismissively.

Tabby blinked. A *butler*? "I-I'm looking for Mr. Richardson. Stoner…Richardson."

The butler gave an audible sniff as he eyed her attire, and Tabby hurriedly pulled her backpack in front of her.

"Who shall I tell the senator is calling?"

Senator? "Uh. Tabby. I mean Tabitha MacVie."

He waved her to a straight-backed wooden chair that sat in the front hallway. "Wait here, please, Miss MacVie."

He marched away. Tabby swallowed as she looked around the ornate front hallway with its crystal chandelier and wide, curving staircase. She felt like the hick cousin who'd wandered into a pasha's palace. Was the floor actually polished marble? What was she doing here?

Once she'd heard the word senator attached to Stoner Richardson's name, she recalled who he was. She had studied him in school, for heaven's sake. She didn't belong in a place like this. She bit her lip and stood, ready to flee.

"You're not leaving, are you?"

She spun around, guilty heat flooding her face. Stoner walked into the front hall. He wore khakis and a comfortably faded blue dress shirt, much like he had two days earlier. She fumbled inside her backpack and pulled out the tube with the sketch inside.

"I brought this to say thanks for your help the other day." Tabby eyed the ornate hallway. She didn't belong in a place like this and hated how nervous it made her. "I-I should go, sir. I-I don't belong here."

He caught her trembling hand and frowned. "Did Peterson pull the stuffy butler act with you, Tabby?" She eased her hand from his grasp and shook her head, not meeting his eyes. She didn't want the man to get in trouble. "Well, you must stay long enough this time to have a glass of tea with me and allow me to open my gift. It would be rude not to allow me to thank you in person."

"All right." Tabby realized she'd been manipulated, but she didn't mind. Stoner took her hand and drew it through his elbow.

"Come back to my study with me. I'm afraid you've missed Catherine. She's gone to church and, I suspect to visit my son and their new baby." He stopped and stared at Tabby. "I don't know why I didn't make the connection. You're the young woman Catherine mentioned, the one who recognized the changes in Jenny."

As they entered the room, Stoner paused and pressed an intercom on the wall. "Peterson, please have a tray with some iced tea and snacks brought to my study for my guest and me."

"Right away, Senator."

Stoner grimaced. "Have a seat, Tabby, while I look at what you've brought me."

She sat nervously, her eyes never leaving his tall, lean frame. With large, elegant hands, he tapped the rolled paper from the tube and flattened it on the table in front of him. He said nothing as he studied it, and Tabby's stomach twisted in knots. When he looked up, his cheeks were flushed and a curious sheen brightened his eyes.

"This is marvelous. If you do more than sketch, I would love to have you paint it."

She smiled. "Thank you. I do paint. Houses and landscapes aren't my usual subjects, but I could try."

"I would pay you, of course," he assured her.

Tabby dropped her gaze. Somehow, that didn't feel right, but she didn't want to make him angry. "We can talk about it," she finally commented.

Peterson arrived with the tray and poured them each a glass of tea before taking his leave. Stoner sat back in his chair. "What's wrong?" he asked quietly.

She smiled at him, but she was fairly sure he wasn't fooled. Still, she had to try. "Nothing. What could be wrong? It's a beautiful day...."

"And something has made you miserable. I still have some connections around here. Shall I have him driven out of the county? Tarred and feathered?

"No. It's not Joseph's fault."

Stoner sat back with a satisfied smile on his austere face. Tabby gaped at him, then had to laugh at how cleverly he had manipulated her into giving him a name. "That is unfair, Stoner."

"Hmm. Given your address—and yes, when all you have is time on your hands, I was able to ascertain where you live—you must be speaking of the young minister at the Baptist Church. Joseph Taylor."

Tabby nodded miserably. "He asked me to marry him last night."

His brows shot up. "Shouldn't that make you happy? Or don't you care for him in that way?"

"It did. I do care for him."

Stoner frowned. "Then what's the problem?"

Tabby stood and paced the room. She stopped at a picture of Evan and Jenny, obviously taken at their wedding, and looked at Stoner curiously. "I thought you and Evan weren't on speaking terms."

"We're not. Catherine procured it for me. And don't change the subject."

Tabby tilted her head and grinned. "It works with most people."

"I'm not most people."

"I'm beginning to see that," she mumbled and turned to study the portrait of him that hung over the mantel. It was a standard state-style portrait with him looking off at an angle and his hand propped on the back of a chair. She looked back at Stoner. "This artist didn't know you at all, did he? This is way too bland. He hasn't captured the ruthlessness that made you such an excellent politician, but such a...."

He studied her now with narrowed eyes. "Such a lousy father?"

Tabby's eyes widened. "No. That wasn't what I was going to say. Trust me. I know lousy fathers. Mmm. I'm changing the subject again."

"You do it well. You've still not answered my initial question about what the problem is between you and Joseph Taylor, you've also left me hanging with an incomplete comparison of how my ruthlessness has shaped me, and now you've teased me with how you know about lousy fathers."

Tabby grinned at him. There was something about this man she enjoyed more than she would ever have expected. He was like Evan in many ways, but harder…and sadder. She sat down in the chair next to him and stared at him before she sighed. "I'll answer your initial question first. The problem is me. I love Joseph, but I'm afraid to marry him because I'm afraid of marriage. I'm afraid I'll lose myself. I'm not easy to live with. I'm moody, and when I paint, I forget everything and everyone else. I lock myself away for hours, days sometimes. How could I make a marriage to a man like Joseph work?"

"Hmm. That does give you something to think about, but perhaps you're also underestimating him. Has he seen your moods? Your intensity about your work?"

"Yes," Tabby said slowly.

"Then he obviously already feels he can live with that."

She ducked her head. He was right. She wasn't giving Joseph enough credit. She wasn't trusting in him…exactly what Joseph had told her last night. Stoner pressed a handkerchief into her hands.

"Don't cry, Tabby," he admonished. "Take action."

She blinked her tears away and thrust the snowy square back into his large hands. Impulsively, she kissed his cheek. "How do you know exactly what to say?"

Stoner shrugged. "Old age. It's supposed to bring wisdom, but I'm still waiting."

Tabby laughed in pure enjoyment. "You're not old. You're experienced."

"You're changing subjects again," he reminded her and prompted, "My ruthlessness made me such an excellent politician, but such a…?"

Tabby regarded him intently as she whispered, "an unhappy man."

He frowned and turned his face away.

"I'm sorry," she whispered.

"Never apologize for being honest, Tabitha. It's a quality I should have prized a lot sooner in life." He looked back at her again and continued quietly. "Now for the last. How do you know about lousy fathers?"

Tabby stared at him and lifted her chin. If it was honesty he prized, then she would give it to him. "My father beat me. From the time I was six until I was twelve, he beat me bloody. He beat me until I passed out, and if my mama tried to stop him, he beat her too."

"Tabby…." His gray eyes clouded with pain.

She narrowed her gaze on him fiercely. "Don't feel sorry for me. I survived, and I'm free of him. He may have scarred my body, but I won. He didn't break me. And when Mama finally told me the truth, he lost any hold he ever had on me."

"Surely your mama left this man, didn't she?" he asked with a casualness that the tapping of his fingers on his chair belied.

Tabby wandered the room and studied the other paintings in it. They were all well done and very conventional. She had her back to him when she replied. "In a manner of speaking. She died last summer from cancer."

There was the sound of breaking glass behind her. She spun to see Stoner's tea glass shattered on the floor and blood welling from a cut on his hand. Tabby snatched up the handkerchief he'd laid on the table and wrapped it around his palm as she squatted next to him.

"Are you all right? What happened?"

"Yes, Stoner. Tell us…what happened?"

Side by side, they looked up at the same time to stare at the slender, blond woman outlined in the doorway. It had to be his wife. Catherine Richardson's face paled before she recovered herself and shut the door behind her.

"You must be the young woman I saw being harassed on the road Friday afternoon."

Tabby stood, but before she could say anything, Stoner spoke up. "Catherine, this is Tabby MacVie. Tabby, my wife Catherine. Tabby is *Jenny's* sister."

Tabby would have sworn there was a look of relief on the older woman's face. "Ah, that explains why you looked so familiar. I see it now. You share your mother's eyes." She turned her attention to her husband. "What have you managed to do, Stoner?"

He smiled, but it didn't seem nearly as free as earlier. "My glass slipped. When I attempted to save it, I crushed it and cut my hand. It's nothing serious."

Tabby looked uncomfortably between the two of them, sensing some underlying tension. She shifted from one foot to the other and picked up her backpack. "I—I should go. I still have lesson plans to review, and…." She blushed. "I need to talk to Joseph."

Stoner laughed. "That's my girl."

Tabby smiled faintly at Stoner and turned to Catherine politely. "It was nice to meet you, Mrs. Richardson. Bye, sir."

"Don't forget," he called after her. "I still want to talk to you about commissioning you to paint Richardson Homestead."

Tabby turned her head over her shoulder and grinned. "Okay."

It buoyed her spirits until she arrived back at the house. When she saw Joe's Mustang was gone, she frowned, but decided she would simply catch up with him later. When the house remained dark and the car was still missing by late that night, Tabby stared out her living room window with a stricken expression. Where had he gone?

She tossed and turned through the night.

When Joe was still not home Monday evening, Tabby did something she had sworn she would not. She plugged in her laptop and logged on to Facebook. Everyone in college had teased her about her aversion to social media. She had dealt with enough wagging tongues growing up. This was different. In one of her high school classes, she'd overheard one of the girls whispering to another about the picture of Tabby on the town's Facebook page.

Tabby had a gut feeling that there had been something behind Joseph's sudden proposal. Had he looked at that Facebook page? It took her a couple of minutes to locate Mountain Meadow's page. There was a picture of her arriving at school in her cycling pants. With it was the opening salvo, "Is this what our new art teacher considers appropriate attire?"

From there, the comments simply went downhill, all of them aimed at her and hinting she was doing her best to distract the town's beloved Pastor Joe from the righteous path. Tabby looked at some of the names. When there was what appeared to be someone's real name, they were people she didn't even know. One comment, from someone calling himself Hot Rod Redneck, stated, "Y'all are just jealous 'cause she's got one hell of an ass on her." Right after that was a post from a concerned parent calling for the board to dismiss Tabby.

Ignoring the heavy, painful thud of her heart, Tabby powered down her computer and closed the lid. It was starting all over again. The adult version of what she had experienced as a child. She needed to talk to Joseph, find out how much of this garbage he had seen. Even worse, had some of these people actually said something to him?

Tabby called Jake, thinking he might have an idea of where his pastor was. When she hung up the phone, she was stunned. Joseph was on *vacation?* He would be gone through Sunday? Tabby blinked back sudden tears. She knew they'd hit a rough patch, but he'd left town for a week without saying one word to her? Her throat tightened and the pressure built in her eyes and nose. Had she pushed him away that much? Had he let *gossip* get between them? She would not cry. She would not.

But it hurt. After being so careful not to open herself up to anyone, she had finally relaxed with Joseph. She'd let him inside her defenses, and he'd walked away. That hurt.

* * * *

Joe worried about Tabby. She was constantly on his mind, but he resisted calling her, wanting to give them time to think. And part of what he had to think about was his conversation with John Gatewood. Joseph had let the conversation push him into a marriage proposal that had been way too premature; he understood that now. Tabby had to be able to trust in him.

Now two days later, he sat in the cool evening quiet outside his friend's cabin. The conclusions he had reached while he thought made him cringe. He had not acted in her best interest, in his parishioners' best interest, or in his own best interest. He loved Tabby, but he'd allowed his desire for her to overshadow what he knew was right for him, for her, and for his faith.

The sex had been wonderful and beautiful. He would not regret what they'd shared. It was the ultimate expression of the love he felt for her, but he also knew he'd gotten things mixed up. Out of order. She deserved better. Their love deserved better than the way he'd handled everything.

Joe had never been a hellfire and brimstone preacher, nor like those televangelists who cried over their relationship with God at the drop of a hat, but he felt strongly that he must lead his congregation by example. In the past few days, he'd set a poor example indeed. He'd put the physical part of his relationship with Tabby above everything else in his life. He needed God's forgiveness, and he needed Tabby's as well, but he'd start with God. Joe slid off the chair and onto his knees, his hands over his face. His life had been far from perfect, but he'd tried hard to turn it around. He'd find the right way and turn this around too. He prayed he wouldn't lose Tabby in the process.

* * * *

Tabby didn't mean to eavesdrop. Of course, maybe she was meant to hear the remarks greeting her just as she was about to step into the teachers' lounge at the elementary school Tuesday morning.

"Have you seen the latest comments on the Facebook page? Busy Betty said Miss MacVie was chasing Pastor Joe so hard he had to leave town to get her claws out of him." Tabby recognized the voice of Miss Harris, the new kindergarten teacher.

"Hers or her cat's?" another teacher asked.

"One in the same, if you ask Mr. Underwood's wife. She thinks Miss MacVie's a witch." The comment was followed by snarky, disbelieving laughter.

Tabby closed her eyes. It was starting all over again, made even worse by the vicious comments on the town's Facebook page. The motivation this time around appeared to be jealousy, but that wasn't always the case. She thought about all the times God-fearing people had called her evil because she didn't create art that made them feel comfortable and safe. They tried to blame what they didn't understand on magic or possession, when the truth of the matter was she simply had an artistic talent that focused on subject matter most people found disquieting.

Her stepfather had tried to pray the demons out of her when he wasn't trying to beat them out. Hypocrites! As if they were completely without any vices or faults. She started to turn away, then saw Stoner's face in her mind, heard his voice telling her not to cry but to take action. With a flip of her braid, Tabby stalked into the lounge and smiled at both women.

Tabby had overheard her own share of gossip around the school, and up until now had tried to ignore it. Sometimes, though, standing up for herself meant giving someone else a good smackdown.

"Good morning, ladies." Tabby smiled at them. She looked the kindergarten teacher up and down. "The next time I see Joseph, Miss Harris, would you like me to tell him what you fantasize about during his sermons?"

Tabby spun on the other woman, who was snickering slightly, and swept her gaze over her. "Or perhaps I should tell *your* husband how you help Mr. Powers check out what's stored in the gym's equipment room? I had never realized badminton rackets could be used in quite that way."

She purchased her water from the drink machine and left them still open-mouthed inside the lounge. She had a half hour free between classes, so she walked into the office and asked if she could see Melodie Matthews's permanent file. After the secretary handed it to her, Tabby sat down at the desk reserved for reviewing student files and went through its contents. She was particularly interested in comments from her kindergarten year, any pattern to absences, and the medical information the parents had supplied.

Tabby's suspicions grew. A pattern of missed days before and after weekends clearly existed. Even documented changes in the child's behavior between the start of kindergarten last fall and the second grading period were there to see. Melodie went from being a happy well-adjusted child to being shy and withdrawn. She looked at the picture taken at the beginning of kindergarten, and that alone told Tabby a lot. Melodie was wearing a cap-sleeved Minnie Mouse shirt. The long sleeves were something new.

As she handed the file back to the secretary, Tabby asked, "Is Melodie here today?"

"No. She was out yesterday too. Her mother called to say she had a stomach virus."

Tabby smiled. "Thanks anyway."

She wanted to talk to someone, but Mr. Underwood made her nervous, plus he still treated her like she'd stepped in dog poop or something. Tabby stopped at her house after school and grabbed her camera, her sketchpad, and her colored pencils. She was going to visit Stoner. She thought about talking to Evan or Jenny, even Jake, but if she went to any of them, they would have to report it. The same was true with Dr. James, and Tabby just wasn't confident enough yet she had enough facts. They must believe her based on what *they* could see, not what *she* knew based on her own experience. She was sure Stoner could be a sounding board for her.

Tabby stopped along the road and took several pictures of Stoner's house from different angles. She would plug the camera into his computer, and he could pick the angle he liked before she did her preliminary sketches. This time when Peterson answered the door, Tabby smiled at him. She was dressed in a long silky skirt, a silk camisole, and a matching jacket. Her hair fell in its usual loose braid down the length of her back.

"Good afternoon, Miss MacVie. The senator is in his study if you wish to follow me. I'll announce you."

"Very proper of you, Peterson," Tabby muttered in a mock English accent.

He peered over his shoulder with an arched brow. "Quite so, miss."

Tabby laughed. "That's impressive. You've put me in my place."

Peterson paused before he rapped on the door. The barest hint of a smile played about his lips. "Apparently not, miss." At Stoner's muffled response, Peterson opened the door. "Miss MacVie to see you, Senator." He turned and stared at her. "He's been a bear today. Careful."

"I heard that, Peterson." Stoner was seated at his desk, but his chair was turned sideways, and he was gazing morosely out the window. Without greeting, he demanded, "Have you ever gone hunting, Tabby?"

She set her things down cautiously and eased into the smooth leather chair across from his desk. "I'm a vegetarian, Stoner. Since I don't eat meat, I choose not to hunt it either."

He turned and examined her as if she were some strange new species. "A vegetarian? Is it a religious thing or a fad?"

"I'd say neither. Call it having too many unique foods served to me that I could either eat or be beaten until I 'chose' to eat. I've had everything from bear to snapping turtle with some stuff in between that could well have been road kill for all I know. Now I simply choose to eat other things. I will eat cheese. I'm not that strict."

Stoner sighed. "It was never the kill that drew me to hunting. I enjoy going out with a pack of hounds—on foot, on horseback, it doesn't matter to me—watching them work and hearing their voices when they find. I miss it, and my sentence has hardly even begun."

"You can still enjoy walking around on your farm, can't you?"

His mouth twisted and he glared out the window. "Yes. Like a dog on a leash. I set foot off the property, and an alert gets sent to the sheriff's office."

He looked so petulant, so lost. Tabby searched her backpack for her camera. "I took some pictures of the house, so you can pick what angle you'd like it painted from. Wanna see?"

He glared at her. "Trying to cheer me up when I'm busy wallowing in self-pity?"

"Yes. Is it working?"

The stiff set of his shoulders relaxed, and his gray eyes suddenly twinkled. "Maybe."

He looked at the pictures, picked an angle, and they haggled over the price and the timeframe. Tabby glared at him. "You drive a hard bargain, Stoner. You must have been tough in negotiations in Washington."

"I was."

"Why did you quit?"

"My mistakes were about to catch up with me. It was easier to leave with my reputation still intact."

Tabby studied him a moment. He fascinated her in a totally different way than Joseph did. They were light and dark with personalities to match. "I want to sketch you."

He laughed. "You could hang it next to my senate portrait and entitle them 'Oh How the Mighty are Fallen.'"

"I want to sketch you doing your wood working."

"It won't reveal some nobler side to me, Tabby," he stated quietly and coolly. "I'm not a nice man."

"Neither are you a monster. I've seen those."

He arched a dark brow at her. "I suspect you have."

"Before you ran for office, you were an attorney, weren't you?"

"I studied law. I keep up with it, but I couldn't practice even if I wanted to now. The bar frowns on felonious attorneys. You need Evan if you want a legal opinion."

"Maybe later. I-I just need a sounding board right now. And someone with a legal background would definitely be a plus."

He leaned back in his chair. "I'm listening."

Tabby outlined what she had seen of Melodie that first day along with what she gathered from the little girl's file. He listened and shook his head. "It's not enough to bring charges, but it might be enough to have social services launch an investigation. Is this child Mike Matthews's daughter?"

Tabby slowly nodded her head.

Stoner grimaced. "He's a member of the school board, honey. Did you know that?"

She glared at him. "It doesn't matter. I know this is happening, Stoner."

Tabby stared at him helplessly, wariness warring with an overwhelming need. He was a practical man, a realist. She saw the steadiness in his eyes, the world-weary expression, then gave him her trust. She stepped around the desk and turned her back to him.

Shrugging out of her jacket, she said, "Lift up my shirt and look." She heard his soft hiss as he did. "I hid that my whole life," she spat as she spun around to glare at him, "from numerous investigations. No one ever saw because I hid it and wouldn't let them look. I did exactly what I'm sure Melodie is doing."

He stared at her intently, his eyes narrowed. "There is a vast difference between fact and belief."

Tabby paced restlessly to the window. "I am an artist, trained to look at things with a critical eye, trained to translate what I see onto paper or canvas. Because of that critical eye, I see details many people might miss."

"Just like you noticed the changes in Jenny that even she, as a physician, hadn't yet picked up on."

"Yes." She closed her eyes and swallowed. "I will have Melodie in class again Thursday."

Stoner leaned back in his chair, but when he spoke, his voice urged her on. "Then see if you can get her to go to the nurse with you and show you both. Be her advocate, Tabby, like no one was for you."

She sighed and nodded. "I will. Thanks. I needed someone to say it to me." She grinned at him. "You're good for me."

He picked her jacket up off the floor and handed it to her. "Damn it all. You have managed to shake me out of my dark mood when I was so thoroughly involved in feeling sorry for myself. I think I'm going to work in my shop. You ready to sketch now?"

Tabby smiled, thankful for the easy acceptance he gave her. "Sure."

They walked out the back of the house, Tabby still marveling at its size and rich appointments. Inside the workshop, she sat on a stool in the corner and sketched him working, the way his hair fell across his forehead, how his brows drew together in concentration over narrowed eyes and his hawkish nose. She drew his hands in various poses, fascinated by the contrast between their size and the elegance of their movements. He moved like an artist and concentrated as intensely at his work as she did at her own. When she had enough sketches, she closed her pad and simply watched him.

He straightened after a while and rubbed his back. With a grin he asked, "How's your love life?"

Tabby picked at the corner of her notebook with her index finger. "Wrong question."

"You didn't talk to him?"

Tabby looked away from his too sharp gaze. "That's a little hard to do when he's left town."

"Pardon me?"

"You heard me." Tabby looked back at Stoner, drawing her brows. "On vacation," she whispered, "and he didn't say anything to me." Her chin wobbled for a minute, so she bit her lip to stop it. Stoner came over and rubbed her shoulder.

"That's not all. Did you know the town has a Facebook page where people gossip?"

Stoner sighed. "Yes. I was one of its favorite whipping boys earlier this year."

"Well, I am now. There's even a post calling for me to be dismissed from my job."

"I'm sorry, honey."

Catherine poked her head inside. Stoner smiled at her. She seemed startled and came all the way inside. "Peterson said Tabby was sketching you."

"She finished. I was just asking her about her love life and offering some sympathy. Tabby's the latest target of the town's Facebook gossip. Plus, she and the preacher have hit a rough patch."

Catherine's brows arched. "Pastor Joe?"

Tabby blushed and nodded. "We had a fight. He asked me to marry him, and…"

"You didn't exactly say yes, but you didn't say no," Catherine finished for her.

Tabby blinked in surprise. "How—how did you know?"

Catherine looked at Stoner. "I did the same thing to this one. As I recall, we didn't speak for a couple of months."

Stoner laughed. "I had forgotten that. Just how did you make that up to me?"

When Catherine's face flushed, Tabby pushed at Stoner's arm. "Stop that. And quit thinking what you're thinking."

He jerked back and stared at her. "You can read my mind?"

Tabby gathered her sketchpad and pencils. "Anyone could read your mind. It's time for me to go home. Thanks, Stoner. Nice to see you again, Mrs. Richardson."

Chapter 9

Tabby nearly missed the ringing of her phone that night. She was in her studio working on Joe's painting, so it wasn't until the third ring that it sank in. She sprinted down the steps and snatched the phone off the nightstand in her bedroom.

"Hello?" She was slightly breathless.

"Tabby. It's Joe."

She cradled the phone close to her ear with both hands, trying to still their trembling and the tears that rushed to her eyes. "Wh-where are you?"

"A friend's cabin in Tennessee, not far from where I grew up. I'm sorry I left without telling you. It was wrong."

Tabby swallowed and blurted, "Oh Joseph! You hurt me… And I miss you so much."

He sighed. "I'll be back Sunday afternoon. We need to talk, but I don't want to do it over the phone. Some things need to be said face to face."

Tabby's hands shook. Was he going to break it off completely? He sounded so restrained and serious. "Joe?" she whispered. "Are we talking to work something out? Or are we talking to end things?"

There was a short silence on the other end of the line. "I guess that depends on you, Tabby. I promised myself I would quit rushing you, quit rushing us. You have to know you can trust me."

She sank onto the bed, so relieved she felt lightheaded. Tears trickled down her cheeks, and she raised one hand to scrub them away.

"I do know that. Deep down. I do know I can trust you. I'm so sorry for the way I acted," she choked out. She tried to keep the sob silent, but it ended in a soft hiccup.

"Shh, Tabby." Even through the phone connection, his voice soothed her. "We both acted with our hormones instead of our hearts and our heads. You're right about one thing, darling. You realized it even before me. My congregation does have certain expectations, and I have to lead them by my own example. So far, I haven't set a good one."

Tabby swallowed. "Does that mean you're sorry you made love to me?" She couldn't prevent the pain that stabbed through her.

There was a brief silence. "No. Never that, Tabby. It was beautiful. You're beautiful. But as much as I didn't want to accept it, I do have constraints on my behavior. I do have a higher standard I have to live up to. When I make love to you again, it must be within a committed relationship."

Marriage. Somehow the idea wasn't nearly as frightening as it had been a few days ago. "I'm willing to see if we can work out a compromise," she murmured.

"That's all I can ask. We'll talk Sunday when I get back."

"Okay. I'd like that. I truly would. Good night, Joseph." Tabby set the phone back in its stand and nibbled on her bottom lip. She realized she would compromise almost anything to have him in her life, and suddenly that scared her even more. Was that what her mother had done? But there was no comparing Joe to Tommy MacVie, so she had to quit doing it.

She returned to her studio and shook off her melancholy. She had only a few finishing touches to add to her painting of Joseph. He was dressed in a simple white dress shirt, his head thrown slightly back with eyes lifted heavenward as he sang, and his hands spread palm up at waist level. She had painted the light so that it seemed to come from him. His halo. She smiled as she finished the painting and left it on the easel to dry.

Tabby yawned, took her sketches of Stoner out, and examined them. As she studied his hands, she noticed how long his little fingers appeared in her drawings and wondered if it was just habit, kind of like an El Greco—not that she was comparing herself to the famous artist. She looked at her own pinkies and shook her head. Tabby yawned once more, setting the sketches and her sketchbook aside on the window seat. It was late, and she was exhausted. She wanted to be alert tomorrow to see if she could make any more headway with Melodie.

* * * *

Tabby knew at once when the little girl entered her room the next day that something else had happened. She wore a turtleneck even though the temperature was well into the seventies, and most other little girls still wore T-shirts. No pants again either. Once again, it was a long skirt. Tabby remembered how hard it was to wear pants when her legs were bruised. Skirts weren't nearly as painful. Most telling of all was the way the little girl appeared to have withdrawn from everyone around her.

Melodie wouldn't even look at Tabby when she sat down next to her. "We're working with crayons today, Melodie," Tabby prompted. "Free drawing for the first ten minutes. You may use whatever colors you like and draw whatever you wish."

Melodie picked up a black crayon and drew a witch. "My mama says you're a witch, but I don't think so. I know you're here to help me." It was a whisper of sound.

Tabby touched the little girl's hand, feeling the way she flinched ever so slightly.

"I want to help you, Melodie," Tabby said quietly, "but you must help too. I was like you, but I wouldn't tell anyone or show anyone who hurt me."

"I've told you," the little girl said simply and looked at her with trusting blue eyes.

Tabby stared at her speechlessly. Melodie didn't understand that simply mentioning her mother in conversation wasn't an indictment of her parent. Tabby couldn't bring herself to tell her otherwise because she feared if she pressed the girl anymore, she would deny everything. Tabby had been down that road too. She swallowed and nodded. "Yes, you have, honey. I'll do something. I promise."

She wasn't optimistic that approaching her principal would work, but what choice did she have? That was the chain of command. After the buses left that afternoon, Tabby returned to the office, requested Melodie Matthews's permanent file, and asked for a few minutes of Mr. Underwood's time. The principal regarded her with borderline hostility as she related what she suspected, and what she'd found in the little girl's file.

"Is that all, Miss MacVie?"

Tabby swallowed, smelling defeat. "She told me."

"What did she tell you?"

"She told me her mother is always telling her not to do things."

"And you see that as something out of the ordinary?"

"Not necessarily."

"Did she show you any evidence?" His tone grew colder.

"No. I asked her to let me take her to the nurse, but she refused." Defeat curled around her heart. She wasn't sure exactly what she had done wrong in this man's eyes, but it was clearly something. Surely arriving early that one day in her cycling pants didn't warrant his coldness? Perhaps he was reading and believing the trash posted on Facebook.

Dennis Underwood tapped the file with his pen. "I'll look into it. Your job is to report it to your administrator. You've done your job, Miss MacVie. I'll handle it from here."

She was dismissed, and she had no idea if he would even do anything. As she left school, she remembered Melodie's trusting blue eyes. *I've told you*. Then Stoner's words—*don't cry, take action*. Instead of going home, she drove to Jenny's house. It was time to bring her sister into this.

Tabby was in luck. Not only was Jenny at home, but so was Evan. They welcomed her with hugs and kisses. Evan eyed her curiously. "Mother says you've made a friend." He glanced at Jenny. "We can't say we approve of your choice."

Tabby plucked at her skirt. "If you're referring to Stoner, he kind of rescued me when I was being harassed on my bike."

"He was off the farm without his ankle bracelet?" Evan inquired sharply.

Tabby laughed. "No. He calls it his leash. And yes, Evan, he had it on. By the time he reached as far as he could go, the teenagers were long gone, but I'd dumped myself at the end of the driveway and flattened my tire. He helped me take my bike to the house to change it."

"But you've been back since then, according to Catherine. She was here this morning," Jenny explained. "She speaks highly of you and you're effect on Stoner."

Evan grimaced. "I certainly hope you haven't bonded. That would be a dark and twisted place to be."

Tabby frowned. "You shouldn't say that, Evan. He's kind to me, and he's funny. He makes me laugh."

Evan gaped. "Are we talking about the same man I know as my father?"

Tabby tilted her head. "Maybe not. The man I know is sad a lot of the time, except when he's working in his shop."

"Mother mentioned he was building furniture," Evan tossed off casually. "I suppose it passes the time."

Tabby's eyes glowed. "It's more than furniture, Evan. It's art. He's doing the most beautiful inlay work on an occasional table. You should see it."

Jenny glanced at her husband and back at Tabby. "I rather doubt that will happen any time soon."

Tabby thought of the lonely man who talked about missing the sound of his hounds hunting, the man whose large, elegant artist's hands were capable of manipulating complicated inlay. She looked at Peter, sleeping peacefully in Evan's arms, and shook her head. "He's different than the man you knew even a few months ago."

"Leopards don't change their spots, Tabby," Evan commented coolly, his thick brows drawing together over eyes as stormy a gray as his father's.

Tabby glared back, her brows furrowing over her tawny cat eyes. "Sometimes they do. I would give an arm and a leg to have someone like him for a father rather than the man who called himself my father."

Jenny looked at the way Evan and Tabby had squared off to glare at each other and shook her head. "Now, now. Tabby, sit down. You had a reason for stopping by. I could see it when you came in. Something has upset you."

Tabby took a deep breath, glancing at Evan sheepishly. "I'm sorry, Evan. Right now, my friendship with Stoner is one of the few things going right in my life."

"We heard you're having some problems with Joe," Jenny commiserated. "Is that it?"

"No, although I seem to be the popular one to beat up on Facebook at the moment, that's not my main concern. I think a little girl at school is being abused at home, but I don't think anyone will do anything about it."

Evan leaned forward. "Why don't you tell us what you know?"

When she finished, his brow was furrowed once more. "It is sketchy, but Tabby, legally you've done your job. Even if abuse is discovered later on, you've done your job and reported it to your administrator. Of course, telling us is a good backup too."

Tabby rubbed her face with a shaky hand. "Evan! You're not getting it. *She* thinks she's told me." Tabby jumped up, nervously pacing the kitchen. "It has to be her mother. It has to be. Melodie must be so frightened. She might be like…." She froze with her back to them and swallowed.

"Like you were?" Jenny interjected.

Tabby pivoted and stared at them both. "Tommy MacVie beat me. That's the story Mama felt was mine to tell. From the time I was six until I was twelve."

"Why did he quit then?" Jenny asked.

When Tabby actually smiled slightly, Jenny and Evan looked at each other.

"The last time he put his hands on me, it was different. Since he was still convinced I was possessed by demons, I told him Satan took care of his own and if he touched me in the way he was thinking, his penis would shrivel up and fall off."

Evan's gray eyes widened. Then he guffawed. "Oh my God! And he *believed* you?"

Tabby frowned at him. "Evan, you shouldn't take the Lord's name in vain, and yes, he believed me." Tabby laughed. "I prayed hard for the next week for God to forgive me for telling such a lie."

They talked her into staying for dinner, and as it turned out, Tabby made it, cooking eggplant Parmesan. She even allowed herself one glass of wine. It wasn't often she could eat with family. By the time she went home, she felt much better about the entire situation. After bending down to give Katie Scarlett a scratch behind the ear, Tabby unlocked her door, still wrapped in the warmth of having a sister and brother-in-law, a family she could call her own.

When she arrived at work the following morning, Dr. James was there at the door to greet her. One look at his face told Tabby something was wrong.

"I need to see you in my office," he stated. Tabby gulped, nodding her understanding. She stepped into his office and saw Mr. Underwood was there. Dr. James waved her to a seat across from him.

"Miss MacVie," Dr. James began. "As you're aware, your contract contains a morals clause. A complaint has been filed that you're in violation of that clause. A tenured teacher would have more recourse, but since you're still in your probationary year, the school system can choose to suspend you and not renew the contract."

Tabby folded her hands in her lap. "What is it that I am supposed to have done, Dr. James?"

He paused and shifted his eyes to Dennis Underwood who picked up the conversation. "I saw Pastor Joe Taylor leave your home early last Friday morning. It was obvious he had spent the night there. I thought seriously about trying to overlook it, but I discovered another incident occurred later that same day. I wanted you fired outright. We must maintain high standards for our young people."

Dr. James sighed. "I would prefer you be given a hearing before the school board at their next regularly scheduled meeting." He checked his calendar. "So that's scheduled for October sixth. You may have an attorney or your education association representative present with you. Until then, you are suspended without pay pending the results of the hearing. If the decision is made to reinstate you, Miss MacVie, then your pay will be reinstated as well."

Tabby gaped at them. "You're suspending me for having a romantic relationship with Joseph?"

Dr. James sighed. "The morals clause in contracts is an ambiguous one that is largely defined by the standards in individual communities. I'm not saying you have no grounds for an appeal. You should be ready to make that when you go before the board. For now, I will need your keys and your ID. Then I'll escort you from the building."

Tabby sat still and silent, momentarily in shock, but then she looked up at Dennis Underwood. "All I wanted was to teach, Mr. Underwood. I didn't ask to fall in love with Joseph Taylor. And quite frankly, I'm not exactly sure what it is you believe we've done wrong."

Underwood eyed her coldly. "That discussion can take place before the board."

Tabby shook her head in frustration. "What is the real problem here? Melodie? I didn't ask to teach a student I feel is being abused and in imminent danger at home. The law requires me to tell you about it, and I have. You may send me away, Mr. Underwood, because the child's father is a school board member, or because I don't fit the image you want for your minister, but I promise you this will not go away.

"I went straight from your office yesterday to speak with my sister, Dr. Jenny Richardson, and her husband, Evan, the commonwealth's attorney." She had the satisfaction of seeing Dennis Underwood flinch. Tabby stood up and stared at him. "That might be in violation of school policy, but I had to act according to my conscience. No one will do to that little girl what was done to me when I was her age. Even if it costs me everything I have, I will stand up for her because I know firsthand what she's suffered, and standing up for her—being her advocate—is the right thing to do."

Tabby slapped her keys and her ID on Dr. James's desk. "If you're ready, Dr. James, so am I."

She went straight to her studio when she returned. After staring at Joseph's portrait for several minutes, Tabby tossed a cloth over it, carried it downstairs, out the back door, and over to Joe's house. It would be safe all the way over here if one of her moods hit. She marched back across the driveway, up her steps, and let the kitchen door slam behind her as she raced up to her studio.

Tabby painted in a frenzy of disturbing images. This was no longer the wild, nearly subconscious painting of the past. Tabby was aware of everything she did. By early afternoon, she had finished a partial self-portrait. It was a nude of a woman seen from the back. Every scar she bore was starkly visible as she held the hand of a child who was being pulled by grasping, clawed fingers. She put her palette down, cleaned her brushes, and went down to her bedroom to change into shorts and a tank top.

No more would she hide her scars. If she was going to stand up for children like Melodie, then she could not afford to hide what had been done to her. She would ride out to see Stoner and tell him what had happened. He would put it in perspective for her, like he had so many other things. She swung her leg over the seat of the bike and pedaled strongly out of town.

Tabby played over and over in her mind the scene that had taken place in Dr. James's office. She still couldn't believe Mr. Underwood was using her relationship with Joseph to boot her out on a morals clause. She recalled the night in question. Joseph had held her while she slept. He'd stayed to comfort her, and that was it. They were discreet. They were in love.

What right did these holier than thou hypocrites have to judge them? But she knew it wasn't totally about her relationship with Joseph. She had simply rattled the wrong cages by dressing differently, by not fitting the mold they had already pre-made for her. Why was it so hard for people to accept her? It was more than the art. They hadn't seen it. So the only thing she could attribute their animosity to was that, different as she was, she had driven into town and snatched Pastor Joseph Taylor from beneath their noses. All Tabby had done was fall in love for the first time in her life.

Her fury made her ride fast and hard, stretching her muscles and pushing her body until sweat soaked her. She braked slightly coming down a hill and around a curve, noticing her rear caliper grabbed unevenly. She would adjust it when she reached Richardson Homestead. These bumpier country roads meant constantly tweaking and adjusting brakes and gears on the lightweight racing bike.

Tabby rounded the last curve and shifted, glancing down as the derailleur struggled with the gear change. When it finally completed its shift, she glanced back up, saw the large delivery truck directly in her path, and found she had time only to brake and swerve sharply to the right.

* * * *

Jenny snatched the phone up as soon as it rang. "Tabby?"

"Have you talked to her today?" It was Evan checking in from the office and already in a foul temper. "The town grapevine operates faster than 4G. News of Tabby's suspension is already everywhere, including plastered all over Facebook. It was pretty much the sole topic of conversation at Mercer's. I swear, if I find out Dennis Underwood has leaked any of this information, I will help Tabby hand him his ass on a platter."

Jenny couldn't dismiss a faint feeling of unease. Between what had been in her mother's letter and what she had learned from Tabby, her younger sister's life had been rough enough. How many more blows could one person be expected to handle before they simply caved in to the pressure?

"I tried Tabby's phone earlier," Jenny said, "but it was busy."

"Keep trying her. I'll check in at her house in a bit. First, I'm pulling a criminal record check on Mike and Missy Matthews. As accurate as Tabby was about your situation, I don't think we can afford to sit by and do nothing about her feeling about that little girl."

"Thank you for believing her, Evan. She needs a support network. It's something she's never really had, so we have an opportunity to help Tabby as well as the Matthews."

Jenny finished nursing Peter and put him down for his afternoon nap. This was the time when she normally grabbed some sleep as well. Her strength was nearly back, though certainly not as quickly as Holly after Noelle's birth, but then there was an eight-year difference in their ages. Jenny yearned to get back to work and wondered how to break the news to Evan.

Peter would be able to come to the clinic with her, or they could find a nanny, but as the town's primary physician, it was almost inconceivable for her to be out too much longer. Dr. Razawi was a talented, dedicated doctor, but he would need a break sooner rather than later, and he didn't have the surgical experience Jenny had.

* * * *

Stoner was livid. He had ordered extremely specific, highly specialized wood from the hobby store in Roanoke. It wasn't like he could make the trip to buy it in person. The delivery driver had come all that way, and the order was completely screwed up.

"How could you not double check something before you started a two-hour drive? I feel like I've stepped into the *Wizard of Oz*. You should be fired for not having a brain."

"Sorry, Mr. Richardson. I was told it had been checked. I assumed they knew what they were doing."

"Damn. I hoped to finish this table this weekend." He scowled. "Go. Take your sorry butt off my property." Stoner knew he was overreacting, but damn it all, life was a piss pot to begin with right now, and this kind of shit made it that much worse.

The truck driver muttered under his breath and gunned the engine unnecessarily as he careened down the driveway. Stoner saw Tabby on her bike as the delivery driver made a too wide turn back onto the state highway. Stoner bellowed and started racing down the hill from his house before he ever heard the squeal of brakes. He never even slowed down as he sprinted across the imaginary line that would trigger an alarm at the sheriff's office. The only thing on his mind was the disaster unfolding before his eyes.

Tabby tried to swerve, but it wasn't soon enough. As Stoner ran, her and her bike went airborne. Even from a distance, he heard the sickening crunch of metal and bone, and helplessly watched her body-jarring slam to the pavement.

He shouted at the driver who was already out of the cab, "Don't just stand there, asshole, call 911!"

Stoner tried to wipe the horror from his expression as he knelt on the road next to Tabby. Blood spurted from a gaping wound at the top of her thigh. Jesus. Her femoral artery must be torn.

Tabby's eyes fluttered open. "You're off your leash...." she whispered before her head lolled to the side.

Stoner tried to put pressure on the spurting bright red blood, but pressure alone wasn't going to stop it. "God! Help me!" he cried hoarsely, and for perhaps the first time in his adult life, he truly meant it as the prayer it should be. Stoner pulled out his pocketknife and ruthlessly cut Tabby's shorts out of the way. The snapped metal frame of her bike had left a gaping wound in her thigh and cut her femoral artery. It was too close to the groin to tourniquet. *Jesus!* He hadn't seen an injury like this since Vietnam. Fighting his own panic, he reached into the wound, found the artery, nearly as thick as a finger, and pinched it off.

Behind him, he heard the truck driver throw up. The man was useless as tits on a boar hog. Stoner felt a mixture of relief and horror when he heard Catherine.

"Stoner, the sheriff's office just called. What's... Oh my God! Is that *Tabby*?"

He glanced over his shoulder at Catherine's deathly pale face. "Katie!" he snapped, using the name he hadn't called her in years. "Pick up my phone. Call 911. I can't move. She's torn her femoral artery, and I'm pinching it shut. If I lose my grip, she'll bleed out in minutes."

As he listened to Catherine make the call, her cool voice sounding only slightly agitated, he calmed. Years of marriage to him combined with years as a politician's wife made her an absolute ice cube most of the time. And right now, that was a good thing. Stoner's eyes focused on Tabby, examining her for any other injuries. Her cheek was grazed, and it looked like she might have a dislocated shoulder. She still wore her helmet, though it was cracked. None of her other injuries appeared critical, but what did he know?

He knew he held her life in his hands.

"They're on their way, Stoner. They weren't too far away. Ten minutes at the most," Catherine said. "What can I do?"

He looked at his wife. "Be ready to hold her absolutely still if she comes to. If she moves, and I lose my grip, Katie, she's dead."

Chapter 10

Joe couldn't stand it any longer. All he was doing was spinning his wheels. While he'd stood in the river with his fly rod, he'd made his peace with God, not in catching fish, but in the simple rhythmic back and forth of casting. He'd managed to lose himself enough that he could figure a few things out.

Now he was anxious to get back. The drive from his friend's cabin was a tedious one, especially stuck behind a truck. As narrow and twisting as the back roads and state highways were, it was almost impossible to pass a car, let alone any larger vehicle. Joe tamped down his impatience until he turned off on Highway 8 and the truck he followed didn't. With a smile, Joe accelerated. Not much farther now.

It was time to make his peace with Tabby, so they could move forward in their relationship. His phone call had at least reassured him she was open to that idea. Thank heaven. He wasn't sure what he would have done if she'd been hostile. Well, maybe beg.

Joe had always been so busy brushing off overtures from within and without his congregation that his response to Tabby had turned the tables on him so completely it had knocked him off a foundation that hadn't been quite as secure as he had so arrogantly thought. He was back on track now, though. He had his priorities in order and was ready to spend serious time doing a little old-fashioned courting.

He wanted her to know more about him, who he was, where he came from. She'd opened up some to him, now it was time he did the same for her. He'd asked her to take him on trust without even giving her any background about himself whatsoever. That hadn't been fair. He knew that now. So if courting her was what it took, then he would do it. And he'd be patient.

Joe sent up a silent prayer he could actually do that.

He would ask her again to marry him, but this time he would do it right. His proposal wouldn't be while they were locked in an embrace on the floor. He would take her to dinner, at Mercer's where they had first gone. Then they could go for a drive. He'd do what Jake had suggested. He would take her out publicly. He would make their courtship so public there would be no need for the gossips to go to Facebook or their phones because it would all be right there for them to see.

The blare of an ambulance siren made him glance in his rearview mirror even as he slowed and eased the Mustang to the edge of the road. The crew shot by, and he pulled back onto the roadway. After rounding another curve along the neat fences of Richardson Homestead, he saw a panel truck in the road, along with the ambulance. Joseph pulled over and jumped out.

His National Guard unit had spent two years in Iraq. It was one of the reasons he was already near thirty and just preaching in his first church. Seminary had been delayed. He was lucky that his unit was a medical one, so he was able to serve his country without putting some of his personal beliefs about non-violence to the test. Now, jogging up the road to the accident, Joe wondered if he would need to help. There were few enough paramedics in Castle County, and he'd lent a hand before in some emergencies.

He saw Catherine Richardson first, standing slightly to one side. Her clothing was spattered with blood, and Joe's alarm grew. Was the senator involved in this in some way? He searched and found his gray-haired head next. Stoner was huddled side by side with the paramedics who already worked frantically over their patient. Even from this distance, he could tell from the body language the situation was not good. He heard fear in one paramedic's voice, urgency in the other.

"Keep hold of that artery, Senator. I'll clamp it off just above your fingers. What's her BP, Tony?"

Joseph saw Catherine hurry toward him. He slowed down to smile reassuringly and would have moved on, but she reached out and grabbed his arm. He noticed again the blood staining the knees of her slacks and the front of her shirt.

"Pastor. Wait!" The urgency in her voice surprised him. She was always cool and unruffled.

He stopped and touched her arm. "Are you hurt, Mrs. Richardson?" He glanced toward the accident scene. "What's happened?"

Her mouth opened and shut before she whispered, "Joseph, it's Tabby."

The shock of her words was as great as if someone had grabbed him by the throat. In fact, he wanted to shake his head and ask her to repeat it, but he'd heard her. His head swiveled in slow motion. Now he saw things he hadn't noticed before, or maybe hadn't wanted to notice. Tabby's bike helmet was discarded right behind the paramedic who was busy hooking up an IV. The twisted frame of her bicycle sprawled in the middle of the road. There was so much blood…too much blood.

He shook off Catherine's arm and started walking. Tabby. Walking turned to running. He swallowed thickly, squelching the panic that threatened. *Tabby.* He reached her side and saw exactly what Stoner clenched between his fingers.

"Tabby!" He gasped past the pain and tightness in his chest, fighting the knowledge that the woman he loved might already be beyond any help he could provide.

The older paramedic looked up in relief. "Pastor! We can use an extra hand here in a minute when we get ready to move her."

"We could use him right now," Stoner gritted and glanced over his broad shoulder. "Talk to her, son. Let her know you're here."

Joseph didn't even question how the senator seemed to know so much about him. He found a spot near her head, and while he watched with a practiced eye what the paramedics were doing, Joseph talked to her.

"It's Joseph, Tabby. I'm here, darling. I came back early so we could talk like I promised. You have to hang on for me, so we can have that talk. There are so many things I need to tell you, things I should have talked to you about before."

Tony looked at him. "It's true? You're seeing her?"

Joe never took his eyes off Tabby's still face. "I want to marry her as soon as I can convince her."

Stoner lifted his eyes to Joseph, who saw in the older man the same calm determination he felt. "If we can stop her bleeding to death, Joseph, I don't think convincing her will be much of a hurdle."

Joseph nodded. He touched Tabby's head and closed his eyes as he prayed. He opened his mind not only to God, but also to the woman he loved in the hope she could feel the strength he wanted to give. He would gladly take her pain as his own. He would do anything. "Feel me, Tabby," he whispered near her ear so softly no one else could hear him. "Feel what I feel. Take my strength."

Her lids fluttered open. "Joseph."

Their eyes met. Understanding lay in hers. Joe also saw how weak she was, and his heart missed a beat. "Don't move, darling," he told her. She blinked.

"Hurts." Her voice was weak and slurred.

"I know, but you're going to hang on. You're strong. You can do this. You're a survivor."

More sirens punctuated the noise around them followed by the sound of feet pounding the pavement. Sheriff Sam Barnes rounded the truck from the other direction with a trooper right behind him. As soon as the trooper saw the situation was under control, he set up flares and pulled the truck driver to one side to question him.

Sam studied Tabby, his mouth in a grim line as his gaze darted to the truck driver and back. "Damn," the sheriff whispered.

Joseph returned his gaze steadily. "I couldn't have said it better myself."

The older paramedic looked around. "Sorry y'all, but this is gonna have to wait." He looked at Stoner. "You ready, Senator?" At Stoner's nod, the paramedic continued. "Okay. I want to test this before you completely turn loose. Now, ease up on the pressure you've applied so I can see if these clamps hold."

Joe held his breath, knowing that this was critical. If they couldn't stop the loss of blood, Tabby had no chance of making it to the hospital because maintaining a manual hold on the artery while traveling would be impossible. "All right. Good, good. Now a little more. All right. Take your hand out."

God, if ever there was a time for some intervention, Joe prayed, *now was it.* He sucked in a deep breath, only now conscious that he'd been holding it. The older paramedic glanced at his partner. "Get the stretcher. You help him, Preacher."

"Let him stay," Stoner spoke, before the protest had even formed on Joe's lips. "She needs him right now. Just keep a hold of her, Preacher."

As if he could or would do anything else. The paramedic nodded. "Sam... You radio ER, tell them we've got the patient stabilized. She may need to be airlifted later, but they will have to do at least temporary repairs to this leg before she can be flown out. Have them call Doc."

Sam's eyes widened. "She just had the baby three weeks ago."

The paramedic stared at him. "She'll have to do it. Razawi is exhausted. Besides, Sheriff, where've you been? This is her sister. It's an emergency, so she sure isn't going to sit around and wait for another doctor to be called in from out of the county. Anyway, ain't no law says she can't treat her." The paramedic shook his head. "And to top everything else off, this girl's wearing a medical ID for a rare blood type." As soon as Sam left, the older paramedic looked at Stoner. "Get that trooper. I want everyone here to help move her so we can make sure these clamps stay put. The more people we have help, the less we'll jostle her."

Stoner nodded. "Bill? What is her blood type?"

Joe wanted to tell them to stop talking and get moving.

"O negative, so she can only receive O negative, and this girl needs a transfusion bad."

"Son," he interrupted, "I'm O negative."

The paramedic looked at him and slowly smiled. "Then get ready, sir. This time when you ride with the sheriff, you're going to the ER to get stuck like a pig."

Joe was getting antsy. They needed to get Tabby out of here and to the hospital.

Bill, the lead paramedic, looked around at all the faces crouched around Tabby. "Okay. On three. One, two, three, lift. Easy. That's it, Mrs. Richardson, slide the stretcher underneath her. Steady. Okay. Lower her. Let's load her and get her out of here." He looked at the sheriff. "I need the senator to come with us. Can you bring him?"

Joe watched Sam's gaze dart between the two men, but Sam didn't question them. Joe guessed he and Sam were in the same boat. They'd seen enough injuries where Tabby's was to know exactly which artery the paramedics had clamped. "Get in, Senator. This time you can ride in the front."

"Careful, Sam," Stoner growled. "You only have me on a leash for two years."

Sam glared at him. "Yeah, but I can make your leash a whole lot shorter."

"Stoner! Sam!" Catherine interrupted them. "This is not the time. You need to follow that ambulance."

Stoner looked at Catherine, and all Joe saw there was love and admiration. "Sorry, Katie."

"I'm going to follow you, Sheriff," Joseph stated quietly. "Mrs. Richardson. You're welcome to ride with me, though I'm afraid it will be with the top down."

She smiled graciously. "Hair, I can brush. Let's go."

* * * *

Evan wanted to share what he'd discovered with Tabby, so he stopped by her house. While neither one of Melodie's parents had a criminal record, he'd discovered a couple of interesting facts about the little girl's mother. She had lost a baby near full term just a year earlier. Shortly after that, she had been hospitalized for an attempted suicide and treated for postpartum depression. Past experience told him Melissa Matthews had real potential to be a time bomb waiting to explode. There were several notorious cases where young mothers, depressed in the wake of even a normal birth, had gone over the edge... And that could be dangerous for any children in their care, like Melodie.

When he parked the Tahoe, he noticed the church secretary outside Joe's door. When she saw him, she turned to hurry back over to the church. Evan knocked on Tabby's door but got no response. Her car was there, but he didn't see any sign of her bike. She must have gone for a ride to clear her head. Well, that was healthy. Running always helped him.

As he started back down the steps, he noticed the cloth-covered frame near Joe's back door. Must be what the church secretary brought, but damn it sure looked like a picture. Curiosity getting the better of him, he crossed the driveways, took the two steps in one stride, and lifted the cloth over the painting.

"Damnation," he muttered in amazement. Tabby must have painted it, and she'd caught the very essence of the man. He wondered idly if it was because she was in love with him, or if all her work was this dynamic. If so, what the hell was she doing teaching? Shaking his head, Evan replaced the cloth cover and sprinted back out to the car. He wanted to talk to Jenny and get her thoughts on launching his own investigation on Melodie Matthews.

His cell phone rang as he turned down Maple toward his big Victorian home. The caller ID read home. "Hi, honey."

"Oh, Evan! Thank God I reached you. Where are you?"

"About a hundred yards from the house. What's wrong?" Alarm coursed through him at the tone of her voice. "Are you okay? Is Peter all right?"

"He's fine. I'm walking out the door with him now. Pick us up. I'll explain as we go." And she hung up. *Go? Go where?*

Evan wheeled into the drive and jammed the car into park. Jenny was already waiting on him.

"Where are we going?"

"The hospital," she replied, handing him the baby's carrier. "I have to prep for surgery."

While Evan finished fastening Peter's infant carrier, Jenny climbed into the passenger seat and buckled her belt. As soon as Evan was back behind the wheel, he noted Jenny's pale, set face and asked quietly, "Why you?"

"Razawi's been up all night. They're bringing in an accident victim right now. Torn femoral artery, other leg trauma, and a possible dislocated shoulder." She paused and looked at Evan. "It's Tabby, Ev."

"You can't operate on your own sister. Damn it, Jenny!"

She stared straight ahead, her chin jutting stubbornly. "I have to. Razawi's only good to assist right now. Evan, if I don't get that artery fixed, at best she'll lose her leg, and at worst..."

"She'll die."

"Yes."

Evan pulled up to the emergency entrance, and Jenny hopped out. Razawi was already at the door. They fired medical terms back and forth that Evan didn't even try to comprehend. Only two phrases caught his attention. Medical Alert tag and rare blood type. God! That was all they needed.

After parking the Tahoe, he grabbed Peter and headed back to the emergency room just as the ambulance turned into the entrance, cut its sirens, and came to a halt. The sheriff's car was right behind it closely followed by Joe Taylor's Mustang...with his mother inside? He sprinted down the sidewalk, only to stop abruptly. His eyes widened as he watched his father get out of the sheriff's car, but this was a man he'd never seen before. His hair was disheveled, his face was pale and tense, and his clothes were covered in blood.

Fury welled up in Evan. He thrust the infant carrier with the sleeping Peter into his surprised mother's arms, dropped the diaper bag, and went toe-to-toe with his father. Evan grabbed his dad's shirt at the throat, mindless of the blood that now stained his dress shirt and tie.

"What the fuck did you do to her, you son of a bitch?" he snarled in his father's face. He shook off Joseph and Sam as he slammed his father up against the cruiser. "Wasn't Jenny enough for you? Did you have to hurt her sister too? The girl thinks you hung the moon!" His voice broke.

"Evan!" Sam Barnes growled. He was a big man. Nearly as tall as Evan and Stoner and a much heavier build, but he still struggled to pull Evan off his father. "He saved her life, man. He put his hand inside her leg and pinched her damn artery shut until the paramedics could clamp it. Now let him go! They need him in there."

"For what?" Evan snapped, but he relaxed his hold slightly. "Jenny has her now. She'll take care of her. Why the fuck do they need him?"

Stoner stared at Evan before his gaze dropped to the silver bracelet Evan wore on his wrist. "Blood," he whispered hoarsely. "They need my blood. They need your blood. Oh, Jesus, Evan. She's my daughter. Your sister."

And Stoner Richardson sobbed.

Evan released him and stepped back, blinking his eyes in disbelief. "She's *Jenny's* sister, old man. Jenny's!"

An orderly came out. "Mr. Richardson. We need you inside." When both men turned, the orderly said, "Both of you. Doc says both of you."

Evan glanced at his mother, who stood holding Peter's infant carrier while Joe Taylor wrapped his arm around her shoulders. She had heard his father. Why didn't she look at all shocked?

* * * *

As soon as Jenny walked through the doors, someone was shoving a chart in front of her. She stared at the blood typing information on the chart, looked at it again, and recited the information from memory. It was the same, exactly the same.

"Doc, the sheriff brought Stoner Richardson with them. He's the one who pinched her artery shut until the ambulance arrived." Razawi yawned. "Sorry. Glad you could get here."

Jenny looked at her colleague, but she already knew the answer to her question before she asked it. She needed to hear it so it would sink in. "Why are they bringing him in?"

"He's O negative, like the woman."

"He's her father," Jenny murmured.

"What!"

She laughed incredulously and with absolutely no humor whatsoever. More loudly, she stated, "He's her father."

"How do you know that? I mean O negative is relatively uncommon, but not like AB positive or B neg—"

"Raz, look at this!"

As he looked at the chart and saw everything that followed the O negative, Jenny rattled off from memory what was on it. Razawi looked up at her. "How did you remember all those other antigens?"

"I memorized it years ago in high school as a joke. It's Evan's blood type. It's his father's blood type. It's bad enough they're O neg, but add in the rest of this, and it further narrows what blood they can accept in transfusion."

"Jesus."

"As much blood as she's going to need, it's a miracle to have two such exact matches. We can transfuse and not worry about a reaction." She looked at an orderly. "Get the two Richardsons, probably already at each other's throats if I know Evan, and start pulling blood. Two pints from each of them. No more than that. Although if you wanted to let the older one bleed out…no never mind. You never heard me say that."

"Say what, Doc?" The man's expression was bland.

Jenny smiled at the orderly. She turned to Dr. Razawi. "Okay Raz, let's do this. Did you call Roanoke about flying in an orthopedic surgeon? I'd rather pay to fly one in than risk flying her out."

"Yeah. He's on his way. Dr. Jarrett Campbell. Private plane. I already have a deputy standing by at the air strip to get him here."

"Cool. Campbell's one of the best there is." Jenny wasn't at all as confident about what they would be facing in surgery as the front she put on for everyone else. Knowing Campbell would be the surgeon flying in to help with the orthopedic end of Tabby's injuries was an enormous relief. She brushed aside the fatigue of her recent childbirth and dug deep down inside. Saving lives was what she was trained to do. While she couldn't do the complicated surgery likely needed to make sure Tabby could lead a normal life, she could fix the artery that would save her sister's leg and keep her alive until a specialist could handle the orthopedics.

* * * *

Stoner lay side by side with Evan, their arms extended as two techs expertly located veins and hooked them up to draw blood. Only a life and death situation could have led to his son lying next to him, and Stoner didn't want to think about the life that was on the line right now.

Evan spoke to the tech hooking the bag to Stoner's arm. "He'd like to donate about ten pints all at once."

The tech gaped at Evan. "You want me to *drain* him?"

Stoner met Evan's glare as his son added, "It would save all of us a lot of misery."

Stoner glared. "You always were a self-righteous asshole."

"Tell me what it's like, *Dad*? How do you treat a woman so badly that she would run away and never tell you she bore your child? Then you turn around a few years later and try to destroy her other child? How does *that* work, *asshole*?"

Stoner's jaw tightened. He shut his eyes and shut his son out, but he couldn't shut out the pain.

Mary. She'd been Mary Sinclair when he'd first seen her. Sweet sixteen and as beautiful as a mountain sunrise—all golden from her hair to her shining eyes. He had felt like someone had punched him in the gut the minute he'd laid eyes on her. She had been working at Tarpley's. He'd teased her all that summer. Nothing more than that. He was already engaged to Catherine, but he had looked at Mary Sinclair, and she had looked right back.

He hadn't seen her again in years, not until he had caught that scum Owens with his still on Richardson property. He had threatened to turn him in. He was as self-righteous as Evan back then, as idealistic. God had Owens opened *his* eyes!

Stoner swallowed thickly. He didn't want to think about this now. He knew he would have to explain it all eventually, but not now. Tabby was who mattered. Tabitha...his daughter. There was a wonder in those three words that he wanted to see fulfilled. He had failed more often than not with both Evan and Erin, but now he realized how quickly he'd connected with Tabby right from the beginning. He wanted to be able to make it Tabitha Richardson before she and the preacher made it Tabitha Taylor. If she would let him. *If she lived.*

"Dad..." Evan's tone lacked heat now.

"Don't. Not now, Evan." Stoner's voice was choked.

* * * *

Evan's brow knitted as he stared at his father's profile. He still reeled in disbelief, but the transfusions were real enough. Perfect matches. Evan knew how rare their blood type was. It was all tied to some antigens that made transfusions tricky. That was why they wore the medical alert bracelets. They could only receive O negative blood, and not all of that was compatible.

Tabby. He thought of her this time from a different perspective, not from Jenny's tawny eyes, but from the other and far more numerous things they all should have seen. Her straight black hair. Her winging brows and distinctive nose. Her height. She had to be around five-ten. Jenny's sister. His sister. She was a tie that bound them all back to the man lying beside him. The man Mary Owens had confessed in her letter to loving. The man she had refused to identify even then in order to protect him.

Evan tried again. "Dad..."

Stoner shook his head, and his jaw muscles worked. He turned away, but not before Evan saw the tears. His father never cried. The senator had never been anything other than a cold, callous, hard-nosed son of a bitch. Evan always felt his father loved no one. Not his mother, not his children, and often not even himself. He had to strain now to hear his whisper.

"How did I fuck it all up so badly? Oh, God. Please, don't take her away when I've just found her." For a change, Evan realized it was a prayer rather than an imprecation on his father's lips. "Don't let me lose this last part of Mary. I should have looked harder. I shouldn't have given up. I should never have believed that scum Owens and what he said about her." His father sobbed harshly, his broad shoulders shaking and his breath catching in hoarse rasps. "Instead I let her go, let her end up with a man who beat her, beat my *daughter*...."

When Evan saw his father wipe his eyes and his nose with his free hand, he reached into his pants pocket and brought out his handkerchief.

"Here, take my handkerchief." He swallowed as Stoner took the folded linen and scrubbed his eyes. "She'll make it, Dad. She's one of us. Look what she's already faced. She's a survivor."

The techs unhooked the second bags from each of them, and while one tech headed toward the operating room with the last of the blood, the other removed needles, put pressure on arms, and cautioned both men to remain lying down. She looked at them severely. "Both of you listen up. I know how all you damn Richardsons are. You're stubborn, arrogant, and pig-headed. But you have both just donated double the amount of blood we normally allow. Your bodies have been reduced to about eighty percent capacity. If you try to move before I tell you, you'll faint, and we're all too busy and too tired to pick up stupid, hulking giants who won't listen to reason."

"You have such a charming bedside manner," Evan drawled. He glanced at her name tag. "You wouldn't by any chance be related to Sam Barnes, would you?"

"Second cousin."

Stoner smiled at her. "You're much nicer than him. He's a prick."

She narrowed eyes on him. "Flattery will get you a bedpan on your head." And the door snapped shut behind her.

Evan glanced at his father. "Now, that's the Stoner Richardson I know."

Stoner looked at him and sighed. "You don't know me at all, Son. That little girl on the operating table knows me better than you, your sister, or sometimes even your mother."

He turned his face away.

"You never *let* us know you," Evan protested. "You shut yourself away from us."

"I was there for your basketball games. I taught you how to hunt. What do you mean I shut myself away?"

"*Senator* Richardson was there because that was what he was supposed to do," Evan said, unable to keep some of the bitterness out of his voice. "But Stoner? The Stoner Richardson Tabby knows was never there."

* * * *

"Her blood pressure's dropping, Jen," Razawi interjected quietly.

"Check on the blood. We need to get those other two pints in her. I'm estimating she's lost about twenty-five to thirty percent. We're praying for a miracle here. Let's get the rest of it in her while I fix these smaller vessels. Five more minutes and I should have it. Once we get circulation going again through this leg, we can slow down, give her a chance to stabilize more before—"

She was interrupted by alarms blaring. Jenny looked up. Her blood ran cold. "She's crashing!"

Razawi barked orders. A nurse rolled the defibrillator over. Jenny kept working on the leg while he pulled the sheet off Tabby's chest and prepped her. He took the paddles from a nurse and glanced at Jenny. "Clear, Doc."

"Clear." Jenny held up blood-coated gloves and turned to a nurse. "Change these." She needed new gloves to keep working effectively, but she also couldn't bear to see Tabby's body jerk from the shock. There was silence for a moment. Jenny's mind, heart, and breathing had stopped along with everything and everyone else, tensed and waiting. Beep, beep—the regular beep of the heart monitor unfroze every man and woman in the operating room. Jenny sighed and turned back to work.

"Don't you die on me, Tabby!" she growled. "Between our mama and your son of a bitch of a daddy, you've gotta be way tougher than Evan or me put together."

Chapter 11

Joe paced nervously around the surgical waiting room. He had yet to hear anything about Tabby. He'd already sent so many petitions to God, he was afraid it might be construed as nagging or begging, but he was more than ready to do that too. He glanced at the clock again. Over an hour gone. The door from the hallway opened. Catherine and Joe immediately looked up. Evan entered the room, nodded to Joe, and crossed over to Catherine. He held out his arms for his sleeping son. Catherine looked from Evan to the door.

"Where's your father?"

"He'll be here in a minute. He was washing up while someone found him a shirt to wear."

"Evan…"

He looked at his mother coolly. "You weren't surprised to hear Dad say Tabby is his daughter. Why?"

Catherine shifted uncomfortably. "You just have to see them together, Evan. Their looks, their mannerisms. From the moment they first met, they communicated at a level I've never been able to achieve with your father."

Evan's gray eyes assessed her. "Okay. I'll accept that for now. But there's more you aren't telling, Mother."

No matter how much Joe might have liked to give them privacy, there was none to be had in the small waiting room. He rested his hand on Catherine's shoulder. The time to discuss Tabby's ever growing family was later. He couldn't wait any longer. Directing his question to Evan, he asked, "Have you heard anything?"

Evan shook his head. "They took a total of four pints of blood from Dad and me. I don't know, Joe. I'm sorry."

Four pints? Joe closed his eyes. From his own experience, he knew that was an enormous amount—especially if they needed all of it. Joe's gaze shifted again as Stoner entered the room. His khaki slacks were still covered in Tabby's blood, and the white polo shirt someone had found him with Castle County Regional Hospital emblazoned on the left breast only served to accentuate his pallor. He looked… God, he looked old and frightened. The man who had maintained an icy façade during his entire arrest and trial proceedings earlier in the year had now cracked wide open.

Evan cradled Peter in his arms and stared at his father. Stoner's hooded gaze gave away nothing. Evan sighed. He started to turn away. Joseph watched the byplay, allowing it to distract him for a moment from the worry that threatened to overwhelm him.

"Please," Stoner murmured, with a gesture toward his grandson. "May I hold him?"

Evan's eyes narrowed as he watched his father. A faint flush stained the older man's cheeks. Evan stepped closer and gently transferred the baby into Stoner's arms. As Joe looked on, Stoner touched Peter's dark curls with a trembling hand. "He's beautiful, Son."

Stoner's Adam's apple bobbed as he swayed back and forth with the baby cradled in the crook of his arm. "My grandson."

He blinked several times. Joe's throat ached as he watched the older man battle the emotions building to a crescendo until, with a flush on his cheeks, he held the baby back out to his son.

"Take him, Evan. Here."

As soon as the baby was safely back in Evan's arms, Stoner knelt down in front of Catherine. Evan and Joseph eased away from the older couple to give them some privacy, even if it was only an illusion in such a confined area.

Stoner took Catherine's hands in his. "I'm sorry, Catherine. It was a long time ago. I never knew. Mary just disappeared."

She studied her husband unblinkingly. Joe didn't know much of their history, but he knew enough from what had come out during Stoner's conspiracy trial to know the man couldn't have been easy to live with. And yet, Evan's presence was proof she'd managed it for more than three decades. She gently touched his cheek.

"We've both made some big mistakes, Stoner, things that go back almost to the start. But this isn't the time or the place to take them out and talk about them. Tabby is who matters right now. Everything else we can deal with later."

"You won't hold my weakness against her?"

Catherine smiled. "Never. She's made you happier than I've seen you in years. How could I object to someone who can do that?"

He pulled her hands to his face and bowed his head. Joe saw the moisture on his cheeks as Stoner groaned, "Oh God, Katie."

"Damn it, Dad!" Evan barked, snapping everyone back to the present. "You're turning into a fountain."

"Fuck you, Evan," Stoner snarled.

"That's more like it. What was it you always said…?"

Stoner jumped to his feet. "Don't cry. Take action. And right now, if you weren't holding my grandson, I'd flatten you."

Evan handed Peter to Catherine. "I'm ready. Go ahead, old man."

Both men glared at each other, standing toe-to-toe. Joe stepped between them. Someone had to. "Gentlemen. Aren't you forgetting why we're here?"

Joe had caught their attention. If he looked as frightened as he felt, no wonder they stared at him.

"Come on, Evan," Joe pleaded, not sure how much longer he could wait with no news. "Can't you find out something about Tabby? Please?"

* * * *

Jenny blew out an exhausted breath and looked at Razawi. "Okay, remove the clamps. Let's see if this will hold."

She had repaired both the femoral vein and the femoral artery. Around the operating table, everyone held their breath as blood moved through the repaired artery. Jenny noted some bleeding from the capillaries and actually smiled. "Looks like it's getting to the right spots. Okay. Go ahead and slowly raise the temperature in her leg to encourage circulation while we wait on our orthopedic surgeon."

An intercom buzzed in the operating room. "Yes?" Razawi responded.

"Call came in from the deputy. The plane's landing now. They should be here in twenty minutes."

Jenny looked at Razawi. "I'm going to step out, talk to my family and nurse the baby, then I'll be back to scrub in again. How you holding up?"

"I'll be fine to hold things down in here. If you can assist our orthopedist, then I can crash for a while."

Jenny nodded. Once she was in the scrub room, she stripped off her gloves, gown and booties, pulled the cap off her head, and shook out her hair. After closing her eyes for a moment, Jenny took a deep breath to steady herself and hurried to the waiting room. She peeked inside to see what awaited her before she stepped through the door. Stoner and Catherine sat together. Jenny's eyes widened when she noted their clasped hands. As much as she hated Stoner, Jenny admitted there was a vulnerable look to him she had never seen before.

Joe sat near the window, his mouth moving silently, probably in prayer. She admired him for a faith so steadfast he could look peaceful even now. Then she caught sight of Evan and felt some of her tension ease. He rocked and bounced Peter who had obviously decided he'd reached the point where only mommy would do. Jenny instantly felt her milk let down as she pushed the door open.

She went straight for her son and took him into her arms. "I don't have a lot of time, so let me nurse the baby while I bring you up to date."

Stoner and Evan looked like they wanted to protest, but Joseph smiled peacefully. As Jenny turned sideways and lifted her shirt, she heard Evan snap, "How can you look so damn peaceful, Preacher?"

"If we were going to hear bad news, do you think Jenny would nurse the baby first?"

Jenny turned to look at Joe. He wasn't her type, but she could see he would be perfect for Tabby. His steadiness would balance her volatility. He watched her from his angelic blue eyes and smiled. "You almost lost her, didn't you?"

Jenny's eyes widened. "Yes. How did you know?"

His eyes filled and overflowed. So the calm was just iron control that had finally broken.

"Sorry. I guess everything's finally hitting me." He scrubbed the heel of his hand across both eyes. "I felt her, almost as if she was here with us. I asked God to send her back."

Stoner cleared his throat. "Jenny? Is she…?"

It was difficult to meet the older man's eyes, even harder to be polite, so she looked at Evan and Joe instead. "She's through the repairs to the vein and the artery, and circulation in her leg looks good. Her vitals have stabilized. While we're waiting on the orthopedic surgeon, they'll take a couple of X-rays to check for any fractures to the femur, hip, and pelvic area. I'm sorry, Joe, but I have to ask—is there any chance she's pregnant?"

Joseph Taylor blushed scarlet, and Evan laughed. "I think you can take that as a no. Good thing, too, because now she's my little sister, I'd have to strangle you."

Joe coughed a couple times, and suddenly Jenny saw every eye in the room zero in on him with expressions that ranged from understanding to the desire to hang him by his toenails. "We—uhh…" Joe stopped awkwardly.

Jenny tapped her cell phone and called down the hall. "Pregnancy test my OR patient before you X-ray."

Joe swallowed, shoving his hands into his pockets.

"It's okay," Jenny tried to soothe him.

Simultaneous growls erupted from Stoner and Evan. Jenny smiled at them, and both men calmed down, though Stoner continued to frown at Joe.

Evan sat next to Jenny and stroked her hair off her face. "How are *you*?"

She bit her lip and leaned her head on his shoulder. "Better now. Better with you and Peter here."

Stoner walked away, out of the room. He returned a couple of minutes later with some orange juice and handed it to Jenny. Her initial instinct was to refuse it, but seeing the anguish and fatigue—the humanness—in his expression, made her pause.

"I thought you might need this," he explained stiffly. "Surgery takes a lot out of you. So does nursing a baby."

Jenny focused on the juice, removing it from his hand without meeting his gaze.

"Thanks, Dad," Evan said as Jenny drank it.

Sam Barnes stuck his head in the door, his eyes searching for Stoner. "I need to get you back, Senator. The state folks are giving me hell."

Before Stoner could say anything, Evan snapped. "I'll take responsibility."

Sam looked around at everyone, then back to Stoner before his enigmatic gaze eventually settled on Evan. "You call 'em then and let 'em know what you're doing. If you take responsibility, he has to be in your custody until he returns home."

Evan glared. "I know the law, Sam."

"Just sayin', buddy." Sam saluted him and disappeared back through the door.

"Prick," Evan and Stoner said together. Then they amazed Jenny by smiling ever so slightly. It served to cut at least some of the tension in the room.

* * * *

Tabby floated in and out of awareness. She'd heard Joseph while she still lay on the road and would swear she'd heard him again later, but that didn't make sense. She remembered Jenny's voice and a confusion of images. Joseph, people at a party. A big house. The operating room. Always the operating room and that horrible buzzing in her ears as she faded in and out of consciousness.

There was a different doctor in the surgery now with Jenny. He was tall and abrupt with quick, clever hands that found delicate muscles, ligaments, and tendons while he barked orders to the nurse assisting.

He straightened and looked at Jenny. "If you'll close her thigh, Doctor Richardson, I'll take care of the shoulder. Any other injuries?"

"No. She was lucky."

Tabitha fought the drugs trying to pull her back into that pain-free haven of sleep.

The tall surgeon looked at Jenny. "Damn lucky that Senator Richardson had the God given good sense to find that artery and pinch it. Otherwise, she would have bled out before the ambulance could get to her. She looks like him."

Tabby imagined herself with her artist's eye. She did look like Stoner. For the first time in her life, peace filled her, not borrowed peace, but peace of her own. She knew who she was. She had a place to belong. Time slipped away from her again....

"Tabby. Can you hear me? Come on, honey. Wake up for me."

It was Christmas, and Tabby wasn't sure which gift to open first. She had Joseph. She had a family. She had Jenny, and there were more people, but she couldn't remember all of them. They were family. Why couldn't she remember? It had all been so clear in her dream.

"Tabby! It's Jenny. We need you to wake up now."

She blinked in the dimly lit room. "Jenny." Her voice sounded funny, and her throat hurt. "Did Daddy beat me?"

"No, honey. How old are you, Tabby?"

How old was she? Tabby had to think. She remembered high school. College. "Twenty-three."

"Where are you?"

"In bed." Tabby coughed when she tried to laugh.

Jenny sighed in disgust. "God help us."

The red-haired surgeon scowled from beneath thick blond brows. "Is that supposed to mean something I'm missing, Doctor?"

Jenny looked over her shoulder. "Tabby, this is Dr. Jarrett Campbell, the orthopedic surgeon." To the other doctor, she said, "It means she's fine. She's being a typical Richardson—smart asses, all of them."

"Don't cuss."

Campbell's brows rose. "And giving orders. Just like a woman."

Jenny smirked. "Also just like a Richardson. Okay, sis. Dr. Campbell's finished and I have a whole line of people outside waiting to see you. Who do you want first?"

No hesitation. "Joseph."

"He's a good man, Tabby."

"I know." She wished her voice sounded stronger.

She closed her eyes until she felt Joseph's touch. Without opening them, she smiled. "Joseph," she whispered.

He leaned his forehead against her hand and murmured a prayer of thanks.

"You were right," Tabby said. "I didn't trust you enough."

She opened her eyes to find him searching her face.

"Do you now?" he asked.

"Yes." She wanted to apologize, but Joseph laid his finger against her lips.

"We can talk about it more later. You have others to see."

The surgeon touched her hand from the opposite side of the bed. "I'll be staying a few days. We'll talk. For now, take it easy."

After he left the room, Tabby drank her fill of Joseph's beautiful face.

"Are you sure you're up to seeing everyone?" he asked.

"Just Stoner."

"You scared me for a while there, Tabby. But it's not your time. You have important things still to do."

He motioned over his shoulder to someone beyond Tabby's sight. As he backed from the room, soft footsteps brought Stoner to her bedside. His gray eyes were dark with concern as he looked her over, and Tabby realized he was trembling.

"Daddy," she whispered and touched his hand with the fingers of her good right arm.

"You knew?" Her father's expression showed an uncertainty it was difficult to reconcile with his reputation. However, Tabby had always seen a different side of him.

She shook her head. "I heard."

"Oh, Tabby," he groaned, sitting in the chair next to her. "I didn't know, honey. Please believe me. I would never have given up trying to find her...you... I didn't know."

Tabby gazed at him steadily. "It doesn't matter. I loved you before I knew. I still do."

He stroked her hair and touched her face. His eyes were red-rimmed and his face pale. He had never looked dearer to her. "I was so afraid. When I saw the blood, and I couldn't get the pressure to stop it."

"But you did. Just because I was your friend," she whispered to him. It was slow and halting, but she had to get it said. "I used to dream I had a different daddy. After he beat me, I would dream I'd be Cinderella, but my fairy godmother would bring me a new daddy. Then I met you. I told Evan I would give an arm and a leg to have a father like you. I guess I nearly did."

He half laughed, half sobbed. "Oh Tabby. That's not even funny."

"It is. Admit it. Laugh."

He held her hand against his face as his laughter built from an awkward chuckle into a deep rumble that shook his powerful frame.

* * * *

What Joe really wanted was to be out of the hallway and inside the room where Tabby was. Instead, he was practicing the patience he had spent years cultivating as Jenny explained to Evan and him that Tabby's recovery could be a lengthy process. She would have to rehab both her shoulder and her leg. "It will be difficult for her to stay in her house. She will need someone who can give her almost constant care."

From behind the slightly cracked door of Tabby's room, Joe heard Stoner Richardson laugh. Tabby laughed, too, but it was followed by a groan.

Jenny pushed open the door so they could see inside. Stoner held Tabby's hand against his cheek as he murmured, "I love you."

Jenny pulled the door quietly shut again and looked first at Joe, then at her husband. "Have we entered the Twilight Zone or an alternate universe? That cannot be the same man who is serving a sentence for conspiracy in my gang rape and another for conspiracy to commit murder…again mine. Please tell me I am hallucinating."

Catherine Richardson stepped forward with the sleeping Peter in her arms and smiled. "No," she said softly. "You've entered Tabby's world."

Evan looked at his mother. "Does this mean we've found our solution to Tabby's living situation while she recovers?"

Catherine smiled. "Of course. I've already called the decorators to redo your room. It will make a splendid studio with its northern light and with the connecting bathroom into Erin's room."

Evan raised his brows. "Throwing both of us out?"

Catherine arched one brow. "You've both been gone for years. I'm not keeping shrines."

Jenny laughed.

The door opened, and Stoner looked at them all huddled outside, but his gaze rested on Joe before moving to Jenny. "Tabby wanted to know if it would be okay if the preacher sang to her?"

"Are you asking me?" Jenny put a hand on her heart. She closed her eyes briefly. "It is the Twilight Zone." She looked at Joe. "Are you up to it?"

"Sure."

Jenny glanced around the darkened hallway of the ICU. "This is so against regulations. Everybody go in. And Joseph? Don't sing too loudly."

Tabby smiled tiredly as she saw everyone, but her eyes were for Joe alone. He leaned over to kiss her gently on the forehead. He'd come so close to losing her, yet now he felt as though he'd been given an incredible gift.

"What do you want me to sing, Tabby?"

"'Thankful,'" she whispered. "Sing 'Thankful', Joseph."

He smiled. "It's perfect."

His eyes never left hers as he sang, but he still saw what was happening around him. Evan had his arm around Jenny as they cradled their son. Stoner stood behind Catherine and smiled down at her as she looked up at his face with a renewed tenderness. As the lyrics flowed from Joseph's throat with the added depth of his own immense gratitude that Tabby was still there, still loving him, Evan exchanged a long look with Stoner. While it wasn't exactly loving, there did seem to be an offering on both ends to open the door to communication.

Tabby smiled and closed her eyes. Joseph bent and kissed her forehead when he finished, thanking God with every breath he took that they had a second chance.

They left quietly. Stoner stared at Joe as if he'd never seen him before. "Son, that voice is truly a gift from God," he said quietly.

Joe smiled softly. "It's the first song I ever sang to her. The day she asked me to pose for her."

Evan chuckled, drawing everyone's attention. "The painting's done. It's on your porch, but you could very well be the last person to see it."

Joe laughed. "What makes you say that?"

"I talked to Jake a little while ago, and he said there's been a steady stream of church ladies sneaking a look at it all day long. Well, I did too."

Joe swallowed nervously. "Please tell me I'm decently clothed."

Evan and Stoner both looked at him expressionlessly, but it was Stoner who finally asked, "Is there some reason you would wonder, Preacher?"

"Uh…"

Jenny glared at father and son. "Stop it. There is none so pious as…"

"…a reformed whore," Catherine finished.

Evan grinned. "Don't worry, Pastor. You're fully clothed and angelic enough that no one would ever think you could be anything but fully clothed."

Jenny looked at her in-laws. "On to more important things for the moment." She paused for a heartbeat. "Stoner and Catherine, please stay with us until Tabby can go home with you. You'll be closer to her, and—and Evan and I both insist."

Stoner studied Evan's serious expression. "Can you swing that with the state?"

"Yes. You're in my custody."

Stoner nodded at Evan and Jenny. "Thank you."

Joe wondered exactly what it had cost Jenny to extend that invitation to Evan's father. As far as everyone knew, Stoner had masterminded a vendetta against Jenny that had kept her and Evan apart for more than a decade.

When Joe arrived at the parsonage a quarter hour later, the first thing he saw was the cloth-covered frame. She had set the frame here. His eyes drifted to her third floor window. Something had happened. Something besides her accident. She had needed to get her emotions out, deal with something that had upset her enough she felt she had to completely remove his portrait from the house. It must have been bad, but Tabby was a survivor. The scars on her back were proof of that.

Joe carried the painting inside. When he came back out for his duffel bag, Katie was on his porch, rubbing between his legs and crying pitifully. As soon as he opened the door again, she darted inside his house. He started to shoo her back out, but found a can of tuna for her instead. "Think of it as comfort food, but don't get too used to it."

The cat meowed, then purred while she sniffed the can.

Restless, he made himself a sandwich and poured a glass of tea before he sat down to listen to his messages. The sheer number of them was not a good sign.

"Pastor, this is John Gatewood. It's Thursday evening. Just got off the phone with Dennis Underwood. He's getting ready to fire Miss MacVie for violation of the morals clause in her contract. He saw you coming out of her house early last Friday morning. You and I have already talked about this, but Underwood isn't willing to let it go. I tried to talk him out of it but couldn't. We need to discuss possible ramifications for you and the church."

Heaven help them. This was going from bad to worse.

Beep.

"Pastor." Joe started at the obviously disguised woman's voice. "The Lord has seen fit to cast that harlot from our schools. Now you must cast her from your bed!"

Oh for heaven's sake. *Beep.*

"Joe—It's Jake. If you get this message before you get home, you need to head this way. Dennis Underwood's gotten Tabby suspended for a violation of her morals clause. She's going to need our support. Maybe you should talk to Evan too."

Beep.

"Pastor—It's John Gatewood again. The church council called an emergency meeting for Sunday evening. We'll need you there."

Joe hit the pause button. This was worse and worse. What had happened to the peace and unity he and Reverend Calloway from the Presbyterian Church had helped foster at Christmas? Was it all evaporating simply because he had fallen in love with Tabitha MacVie? He'd marry her tomorrow to make it all go away, but there were other considerations.

Like finding her father...and brother, giving her a chance to get to know her family before they formed their own.

He had a feeling both Stoner and Tabby would want to change her name to Richardson before he asked her to change it to Taylor. Joe wouldn't deny them that opportunity no matter how long he had to delay their marriage for it to happen. She deserved a chance to have a real daddy and a last name that didn't belong to someone who'd abused her, and Stoner deserved a chance to enjoy a daughter who was so obviously a kindred spirit.

Joe hit the play button again to hear the same disguised voice. "God has seen fit to punish that jezebel. Beware his wrath before it turns on you!"

This time anger stirred. Joe was tempted to erase her messages, but decided to leave them. They were disturbing, but he was still vaguely hopeful they were simply a childish prank. If not, someone sick was out there.

"Pastor." It was his final message, and he was relieved to hear Holly Allred's voice. "Jake told Tyler and me about Tabby's accident. Ty is beside himself. If you can...that is if you're up to it...if you could call and reassure him, I know he'd appreciate it."

Joe looked at his watch. It was nine, not all that late for a Friday evening, and the walk might clear his head. He'd visit instead of call. His eyes went to Tabby's portrait of him. Now he understood why she'd left it on his porch. She had to have done it this morning after she was put on leave. He remembered the last time she had been upset and moved the painting to keep it safe. He glanced at her house again. He would look later. For now, he'd check on Tyler.

While he knew she would never deliberately try to hurt herself—and never involve anyone else—he wondered if everything she'd had to face on her own today had distracted her. Joe's mouth thinned. If only he'd been here... But he couldn't live his life on if onlys. No one could.

* * * *

Surely the sky had fallen, Evan thought. He could scarcely believe Jenny had extended an invitation to his father. Her discomfort in leading

Stoner and Catherine into their home was more than obvious. As they stood awkwardly in the front hall, her smile was just a bit off as she said, "I'm sure you would both like to freshen up. The guest room is upstairs on the right. There's a bathroom attached to it. Fresh towels are there and a robe on the back of the door." She looked at Catherine. "I'm afraid that's all I have to offer in the way of clothing because of our height difference. Stoner, Evan should be able to loan you whatever you need, and Catherine, we can launder yours."

His mother waved her hand. "Not to worry. I called Peterson while you were settling Peter into his car seat. He should be here shortly with bags for Stoner and me as well as sandwiches and potato salad."

Evan wondered if Jenny would feel affronted at Catherine taking charge, but from the tension leaving her expression, all she apparently felt was relief and gratitude. She had to be dog-tired. "Thank you. That's marvelous."

"It's the least we can do," Stoner mumbled. "You saved Tabby's life, and you've opened your home to us...to me."

Jenny held up her hand. "I—I'm too tired for this. Can we... Can we keep it impersonal? I'm not ready for anything else."

Catherine smiled. "We'll go up."

Evan moved forward. "I'll get you some pants, Dad."

Jenny carried Peter into the living room and stretched out on the couch to nurse. When Evan came down a few minutes later dressed in jeans and a lightweight cotton sweater, she had fallen asleep with the baby at her breast. He saw Peter was dozing, so he picked the infant up and burped him. He knelt next to Jenny and gently shifted her. "You need to switch sides, honey."

"Mm. You do it, Ev..." she mumbled. He smiled at her tenderly and deftly rearranged things before helping the baby latch onto the opposite side. When he was sure they were both secure, he turned to pour himself a bourbon. Stoner stood in the doorway.

"You're a good man, Evan. A good husband and a good father."

"Thanks. Jenny makes it easy. Would you like a drink?"

"Hell, yes. At this point, you could just hand me the decanter."

Evan splashed the whisky into a heavy glass and handed it to his father, eyeing the older man with the feeling he'd never seen him before. "You know, I don't know that I could have done what you did today. How did you know?"

Stoner shrugged his broad shoulders. "A short tour of duty in Vietnam. I saw a lot worse, but none that hit me as hard as what I saw today." He closed his eyes at the memory. "That damn truck tossed her like a rag doll, and I couldn't get the pressure in the right spot. Blood spurted like a damn hose. When I reached for the artery, all that idiot truck driver could do was stand behind me puking up his guts." He paused to clear his throat, carried the whisky to his lips with a shaky hand, and swallowed. "Thank God your mother arrived. Katie was cool as a cucumber. She called 911, then knelt right there with me, holding Tabby when she came to for a moment and tried to move. I couldn't have saved Tabby without her."

Catherine, dressed in a terry cloth robe, slipped her arm through her husband's, smiled at Evan, then Stoner. "Some people are worth the fight."

The doorknocker rapped at that moment. Stoner smiled. "That will be Peterson. No one else would rap exactly two times with such precision. I'll get it, Evan. You keep an eye on that wife and baby of yours."

* * * *

A few minutes later, just next door, Joe rubbed the back of his neck before ringing the bell on Jake and Holly's house. She opened the door, her face bursting into a big smile when she saw him standing there.

"Oh, Pastor Joe, come in. You must be tired. You could have called. How is Tabby? How are you? Someone phoned Jake and told him Jenny had performed surgery. Is it true Senator Richardson saved Tabby's life?"

Joe held up his hands. "Whoa!"

Holly laughed as she shut the door. "Sorry. You know how I get. Jake says he could use me in interrogations because I could make a wall talk. Come to the kitchen. We have some leftover pot roast I could heat up. Would you like some?"

Joe nodded, thinking of the small sandwich he'd eaten. "You have no idea how wonderful that sounds."

She grinned before calling up the steps, "Tyler! Pastor Joe is here. Tell Jake." She turned back to Joe. "Jake's giving Noelle her bath. She already has him wrapped around her little finger."

While she fixed a plate to heat for him, Holly asked about his vacation, shared an amusing story about trying to fish with Jake over the summer—they had both fallen in the lake—and managed to weasel out of him the fact that the church council was apparently ready to jump down his throat about Tabby. Joe looked at her in admiration. He once heard Evan describe her as a tornado of happiness, but she was the perfect foil for Jake.

"Hey, Pastor." Tyler skidded into the room and slid into the chair next to him. "How's Miss MacVie? Alex said his cousin told him blood was spurting out, and it was everywhere! Oh, sorry. You're eating. Is she going to be okay?"

Joe decided that between Holly and Tyler he was caught in a hurricane. Jake walked in at that moment with a sleepy Noelle nestled against his big chest. Though he and Jake were of a similar height, Jake was built more like a bear than a mountain lion. "Slow down, Ty. The man's had a tryin' day."

Just his presence seemed to settle the other two. Holly set coffee down in front of Jake and him before pouring a glass of tea for Tyler. He swallowed a bite of the melt-in-your-mouth pot roast and grinned. "If you would invite me to dinner once a week, I would sing your praises. I have the feeling I'm about to become a vegetarian when I finally convince Tabby to marry me. She eats cheese, but nothing else." Joe set the knife and fork down.

"Now, to answer some of your questions. We left Tabby sleeping at the hospital about an hour ago. She lost a lot of blood, even as quickly as the senator was there to help her."

Jake nodded. "I lost a buddy from just such an injury. It doesn't take long with an artery that big. That he would know what to do—and do it—now that surprises me."

Joe smiled. "Then you're in for a lot more surprises in the next few minutes. Tabby struck up a friendship with him after she fell off her bike at the end of his driveway a few weeks ago. He was outside and saw the whole thing happen today. The delivery truck was leaving Richardson Homestead, the guy made the turn too wide, and never even saw her. Stoner ran all the way down there. When he couldn't stop the bleeding with pressure, he cut her shorts off, reached in, and grabbed the artery."

Horrified, Holly put a hand to her face, and Tyler interrupted, "It's big enough to do that?"

"Second largest artery in the body, Tyler," Jake said. "Lucky the wound was big enough. Guess it must have been too high for a tourniquet."

Joe nodded. "I got there right after the ambulance by sheer coincidence, and ran up to see if I could help, not knowing it was Tabby." Joe closed his eyes for a minute. Holly covered his trembling hand with hers. "There was blood everywhere. Stoner was covered with it, and Catherine had a fair amount on her as well, just from holding Tabby still." Joe shook his head. "Bill Brewster was the paramedic. Tony was assisting."

Jake nodded. "Lucky. Bill's the best."

"Anyway, as we prepared to move her, he mentioned she had a rare blood type, which it turned out was the same as Stoner's." Joe could see Jake, at least, already understood the significance. Joe looked at Holly. "It's also Evan's blood type."

"Oh," she said with dawning comprehension. "So did they give blood?"

Joe nodded. "Jenny had them take two pints from each of them."

Jake shifted. "They had to transfuse four pints? That's...Jesus, Joe! Oops, sorry. That's a lot," he finished, his gaze darting to Tyler, as though Jake knew exactly how touchy saving Tabby had been.

"They nearly lost her once on the operating table," Joe said. "I've never prayed so hard in my life, and I do a lot of praying." Holly patted his hand. "But she made it. Jenny fixed the arterial damage and restored circulation. They flew an orthopedic surgeon in rather than move Tabby, and he fixed everything else. No broken bones, but between the leg and the dislocated shoulder, she'll take a while to heal."

Joe looked at Tyler. "She will be all right, Tyler, but you should get ready for a few changes. I suspect within the next week, she and the Richardsons will be asking the court to change Tabby's last name from MacVie to Richardson."

"Why?" Tyler asked.

Joe smiled. "As it turns out, Tabby is Senator Richardson's daughter."

Tyler frowned. "But I thought she was Jenny's sister."

Joe laughed now. "Think of Tabby as a bridge between Evan and Jenny. Stoner is Evan and Tabby's dad, but Tabby's mom was also Jenny's mom."

"So, she's like a half sister to both of them?" Tyler asked.

"That's exactly right." Joe smiled.

Jake sipped his coffee, then leaned back in his chair, his hazel eyes thoughtful. "I suspect she may be a bridge in more ways than that."

Joe smiled. He admired Jake immensely. The man was quiet, but he saw and understood more than people thought. Then, in his quiet way, he set about fixing things. It was one of the things that had him shaping up into an excellent police chief.

"She already is. Evan was at Stoner's throat when they both arrived at the hospital. Literally. Both Sam Barnes and I couldn't get him off. Now Catherine and Stoner are guests next door."

"What!" Jake leaned forward. "Jenny and Evan have his parents staying under their roof? What about Stoner's house arrest?"

Joe shrugged. "Evan told Sam he'd be responsible for his custody until Tabby can go home with Stoner and Catherine."

"Tyler," Jake said in a deadpan voice, "look out the back and see if any pigs are flying."

Holly and Joe laughed. Tyler said, "Huh? Is this some weird adult thing again?"

"Tabby's going to stay at the Homestead?" Holly asked.

Joe nodded, feeling a little glum. "Yes. She's going to need a lot of help. I—I can't do it until we're married. It seems some folks in town are already prepared to stone her as a harlot and run me out of town. Stoner and Catherine have the room, and as Stoner points out, it's not like he has anywhere else to go. But more than that, he wants some time with her. He knows I want to marry her. I think he's all right with that, though I plan to talk to him about it, but I think he needs to be there for her to try to make up for the past."

Jake frowned, shaking his head. "What you describe doesn't fit the Stoner Richardson I know."

"We all saw a man today who doesn't fit anyone's picture of Stoner Richardson. I think Evan kept picking fights with him because he was so uncomfortable with his father crying."

"Crying?" Jake arched his brows in disbelief. "Stoner?"

Joe shook his head. "I'm telling you. Tabby got to him in a way no one else has, and it happened even before he knew she was his daughter. Even Catherine admits that. It's made such a difference she was more than happy to take Tabby into their home."

Holly smiled and looked at Jake. "Loving parents don't always have to be related by blood. Jake's loved Noelle from the moment he delivered her, even though she isn't his biological daughter."

"She's mine in every way that matters," Jake finished. "I'm relieved to hear Tabby will recover. It will be interesting to see how Jenny and Evan's relationship with Stoner changes." Jake cleared his throat. "On a different topic, Joe, did you get my message?"

"Yes. I also had a message from John Gatewood. The church council has called a meeting Sunday evening, and they want me there." Joe sighed. "I don't want to lose my job. It's more than a paycheck. You both know that."

"Yes," Jake said, "but I also know there're a lot of rumblings out there about Tabby and you. I'm sure half is fiction like it was with Holly and me. We just need some strategy."

"Like a political campaign." Holly waggled her brows. "Hmm. I wonder where we know any people who might have experience in that area."

Chapter 12

Tabby now knew the real meaning of feeling like she'd been hit by a truck. On top of that, every time she fell asleep, a nurse was there to check her blood pressure, adjust her IV, and make sure she knew who she was and where she was. For the first few days, she was in and out of it so much the only visitors she could recall for certain were Joseph and Stoner. Having them with her gave her the strength to get better.

Most of the hospital staff was helpful, but Tabby had been on the receiving end of treatment that bordered on rude from a couple nurses. No doubt it went back to the Facebook page, or maybe a nurse who, like the kindergarten teacher, had harbored her own fantasies about a future with Joseph.

The final blow, though, was when her breakfast tray was set in front of her the first morning she was allowed to eat solid food. She smelled it even before she lifted the lid. Eggs and bacon. Tabby pushed the tray and table away in revulsion, spilling coffee on herself in the process, so she cried out.

"Tabby? Are you all right?" Joseph asked. Stoner filled the doorway right behind him.

She saw them and burst into tears. She hated being weak, hated feeling helpless, but most of all she hated being in the hospital. It made her feel trapped.

"J-Joseph…Daddy… I want to go home. I can't breathe here."

She held Joe's gaze, could see he recognized her mood. He'd seen it the night he found her in her studio with the torn up canvases. Without saying a word, he crossed the room, took her uninjured hand in both of his, and pressed it against his face. "Shh, Tabby. It's okay. Look at me, darling. It's okay."

Stoner lifted the lid on the breakfast tray, saw the eggs and bacon, and his mouth thinned. Grabbing the call button, he rang the nurse. Stoner's gray eyes narrowed furiously. His voice dripped icicles as he pushed the tray into the woman's hands.

"I know my daughter-in-law would have noted her sister is a vegetarian, so take this shit back to the kitchen and bring a new tray."

The woman made the mistake of trying some feeble defiance. "I'll be happy to have an orderly take care of it."

Stoner drew himself up even taller than his already immense six-five frame. Years of power and leadership oozed from his very pores. "Unless you wish to wear this tray and its contents, do it yourself. Now."

"Is there a problem?" Jenny asked from just beyond the nurse's shoulder, looking as if she was ready to rip Stoner's head from his shoulders if he was harassing anyone. Then her brows lowered over her golden eyes as she smelled what was on the tray, and her attention turned to the unfortunate nurse. "You okayed bacon and eggs for her breakfast? Didn't you read her chart?"

Jenny stepped around the woman, with her back to Stoner, and put her face close to the nurse's. "You might not like my sister, and you might not like me, but you will be a professional. Blink wrong around this patient again, and I'll have you tossed out. Now, take the tray and bring one that complies with a vegetarian diet."

The nurse backed out of the room with the tray in her hands. Jenny began flipping through Tabby's chart as nonchalantly as if nothing at all had occurred. Stoner chuckled. Jenny arched one brow and eyed him coolly. "What's so funny?"

"Damn," Stoner said in amazement. "I thought I was a son of a bitch, but I can't even hold a candle to you. You must really give Evan a run for his money."

Tabby watched the byplay between the two cautiously. She wondered if Joseph knew their history, but who didn't after such a public trial? Jenny glared at Stoner for another instant before poking him in the chest. "That's right, and don't you forget it." Then she spoiled the whole effect by laughing.

"Joseph?" Tabby whispered softly. "I think you should pray for all the staff until I get out of here. Between my sister, my father, and probably my brother, too, I think they're going to need all the help they can get."

He laughed and touched her cheek with his lips as he whispered into her ear. "You'll be all right in here with two watchdogs like them. Three counting me. I love you, Tabby Richardson."

That sounded wonderful. Almost as good as Tabby Taylor might sound. Her feelings must have shown. Joseph grinned and kissed her on the forehead. "It's who you are, who you should be as soon as you and Stoner can make the name change legal. You might wear the scars Tommy MacVie inflicted, darling, but there is no reason now to bear his name, not if you don't want to."

Stoner, who'd heard the last part, rounded the other side of the bed. "I would erase it all if I could, Tabby, so at least let me give you this much. Catherine and I would like you to come home with us while you're recovering. We can even fix you up with a studio so you can paint."

Tabby looked from Stoner to Joe. "What about my cat?"

Joe coughed. "Uh… I can take care of her. She's sort of moved in with me already."

Jenny pointed to the door. "Out. Right now she is still here and, unless I can get a look at her, likely to stay. I need to examine my patient, and neither one of you need to be here for that."

After the door closed behind them, Jenny came around and leaned down to kiss Tabby's cheek. "Hi, sis. I didn't get a chance to tell you I'm glad you're still here. It was a little touch and go there for a bit."

Tabby plucked the sheet covering her. "I have the strangest dreams from then."

"It's not unusual. Do you recall them?"

"I saw Mama. Other people, too, like I was at a big garden party."

"You miss her, don't you?" Jenny asked softly.

Tabby sighed. "Yes. I wish you could have known her like I did, Jenny. She wasn't what your daddy said. You look so much like her; it's why Stoner was afraid of you."

Jenny's head swiveled up from where she was checking the bandage at Tabby's hip. "*Afraid* of me? Tabby… He nearly destroyed me. You have no idea. Look, I'm glad you're my sister. I'm glad Evan is your brother. We love you. I'm even glad you seem to have such a great relationship with Stoner, but don't expect me to, and don't expect it from Evan either."

Tabby didn't say anything for a moment. She wouldn't push. She had come to know Stoner pretty well, and his reactions whenever Jenny came up in a discussion were revealing. If only they would all sit down and talk. "Jenny, could you at least work with him to help Joseph? There are people in his church who think he should be fired. Mr. Underwood is one."

"Yeah. I can do that. Evan too. Jake already called us. We're meeting this afternoon to talk about it. We'll let you know what goes on, but right now, let's look at some of those other abrasions on you. The sooner we can get you out of here, the better for you."

* * * *

Joe studied the group assembled around Jake's kitchen table, surprised by how just seeing them together made his chest tighten with gratitude. His and Tabby's friends and allies. Jake's house was neutral territory. Joe watched them gather as though they were already all family, even if a few of them didn't want to acknowledge it. Jake and Holly, Jenny and Evan, Catherine and Stoner...all there to help Tabby and him.

Another knock sounded at the door. Jake stood up with a small smile.

"I asked Sam to join us. Figured we might have to call in some favors, and he could help us...."

"Twist arms?" Evan inquired. "Or play poker?"

"Provide gentle reminders," Holly said with a smile. "It sounds much nicer, don't you think?"

Evan and Stoner looked at Holly's innocently smiling face, and Stoner inquired, "Are you Evan's press agent? If not, you should be."

"I'm an accountant."

"Damned missed calling, if you ask me," Stoner muttered.

Sam walked into the room, nodded to the women, then shook hands with Joe and Evan. He nodded coolly to Stoner and sat as far from him as possible. Stoner, it seemed, had few fans. Joe stood up and looked around at everyone gathered around the table in support. He felt humbled.

"I'd like to start us off with a prayer, if you don't mind. A little divine help couldn't hurt." Joe kept it straightforward and simple, asking for guidance and patience. When he finished, everyone said amen. "Thank you all for your support. I can't tell you how much it means."

Stoner stood and took charge. Joseph saw the look of surprise on Sam's face before he turned his penetrating look on Evan and Jenny. Joe smiled. Things were changing. Joe hoped the price of the miracles happening wouldn't be his career.

"Holly," Stoner began, "If you're like most accountants, you're organized. Can you take notes?" At her nod, he continued. "I think we should begin by outlining the problems we face, then formulate a plan of attack to assist Joseph and Tabitha."

"As I see it," Jenny said, "Tabby's biggest problem is having come into the community as a stranger and immediately claiming the town's most sought after bachelor, a little like Holly last year with Jake."

"There's another problem," Jake offered. "Tabby didn't fit the image everyone had of an art teacher. Remember the last one was the motherly-teacher type not a gorgeous college grad."

"Nor does she fit what everyone believes my wife should be." Joe smiled grimly. "While they're looking for someone to organize the church bazaar and host sewing circles, I simply want a woman to love and support me, not be an adjunct church employee."

"Okay," Stoner said. "We have at least one concrete issue that must be handled and that's the school board meeting to consider the question of a morals clause violation. I'm guessing your meeting, Preacher, will center on the same issue. So." Stoner looked hard at Joe. "What were you doing coming out of my daughter's house before dawn?"

Every eye was on him, and Joe blushed.

Evan snorted in exasperation. "The first thing you and Tabby must do is control the blushing, for God's sake. It instantly makes you appear like you've done something wrong."

"Evan," Holly said. "You will not use the Lord's name in vain in my house."

"Yes, ma'am," he said meekly. If Joe hadn't been feeling so much like he was on the hot seat, he might actually have laughed.

"I had gone to Tabby's house the night before with two soft drinks. The light was on in her studio, and I wanted some company. When I got up there, she was upset and painting in an absolute frenzy. I'm sure it's still in her studio. It's one of her students. The one she believes is being abused."

Jake and Sam both went on alert. "Did she report it to her administrators?" Sam snapped.

"The day before she was put on a leave of absence," Evan snarled, "but we'll come back to that. I've already set wheels in motion on my own investigation."

"Anyway," Joe went on, "The whole situation reminded her too much of her own childhood. She showed me the scars." He swallowed. "I calmed her down and helped her to bed. She asked me to stay with her. I did, but not in any sexual way. She was under the covers. I slept on top of them, fully clothed."

Stoner grimaced. "I appreciate the fact you did the honorable thing, but it still looks bad."

Joe saw how somber everyone's expressions were. This was not going well. The silence hung heavily as they realized it would indeed come down to perceptions.

"I vote on the gentle art of arm twisting," Holly said, breaking the silence.

Stoner arched a brow. "I like you. You're like a Santa's elf who's gone to the dark side. Okay. Who's owed favors or has any dirt on a school board member?"

And so the lists began. One for the school board and one for the church council. "We should start with the church council, since that meeting's tomorrow evening," Holly reminded them.

"Jim Tarpley won't vote to fire me," Joe said. "I don't believe John Gatewood will either."

"Underwood is a yes we won't be able to change. He's the one behind it," Stoner said. "Who's he most likely to influence? We'll have to get to them first."

As they made up the list, among Evan, Stoner, Sam, and Jake, they covered all but one council member. Surprisingly, Jenny was the one who spoke. "That one's mine. I can't say why."

Stoner arched a brow. "Arm twisting with patient confidentiality? Isn't that unethical?"

"Isn't that the pot calling the kettle black?" Jenny shot right back. "These folks are messing with my family. Besides, I won't have to say anything as soon as he realizes Tabby's my sister."

Joe gaped at all of them as he listened to the private sins of his church elders being discussed as if they were common knowledge. Of course, in Mountain Meadow, they likely were.

"Okay, then. Who's going with Joe to make the speech?" Evan looked around the table.

"What speech?" Stoner asked.

"The 'let he who is without sin' speech," Holly clarified.

"I will," Jake volunteered. "No one expects a speech from me."

Holly smiled. "Combined with the phone calls this evening, that should be enough to save Joe's job. Then we can work on improving his and Tabby's image."

Stoner nodded. "Okay. Let's move on to Tabby. Making it public that she's Evan's sister will help. She's already agreed to the name change, so we can begin working on the legalities Monday. Catherine can also work on some of her friends in the community. That will help build the idea that she's not a stranger, that she belongs here and always has."

"I don't hear how you're helping," Sam commented.

Stoner's jaw clenched. "I think we can all agree I'm not much of an asset. Besides, as soon as it gets out she's my daughter, a lot of disapproval will shift to me." He shrugged. "I'm used to it."

"I believe we should host a showing of Tabby's work at the Country Club," Catherine said into a silence that had become strained.

"Her painting of Joe is brilliant," Evan offered.

"A lot of her work is disturbing," Joe told them. "In fact, Tabby believes that's what spurred a lot of the abuse she lived through. It will make a few people uncomfortable. But I have to agree—everything I've seen her do is brilliant."

Jenny patted his hand. "You're in love with her, so you're biased. Stoner's an art connoisseur. Maybe you should show him what's in her studio so he can decide if we should move forward with plans for a showing."

"Yeah, but he's also her dad," Holly said. "We need someone to offer a second opinion who doesn't know anything about art and has no vested interest."

Jake laughed. "Why didn't you just say Sam and be done with it."

Holly pouted at him. "I was trying to be nice."

"That's okay," Sam grumbled. "Y'all go ahead. You think just because I split my time between the sheriff's office and my farm that I don't get any culture. I'll have you know I picked up one of those beach scenes that matched the colors in my orange-flowered couch over at the flea market last weekend."

When Jenny, Stoner, and Catherine gaped at him, Sam laughed. It was a rare sound that made everyone's jaw drop. "Just kiddin'. My couch is brown leather."

Jake and Holly shook their heads.

"Now the final order of business," Stoner said and looked right at Joe. "When can we announce your engagement?"

The room went silent, but all eyes turned to Joe. "As soon as I can get her to say yes."

Jenny tapped her fingers on the table. "While you gentlemen check out the paintings, why don't Holly, Catherine, and I head over for a womanly visit with Tabby. I think we can help her see the light."

* * * *

Walk? Tabby was beginning to think the surgeon Jenny had brought in was a sadist, but Jarrett Campbell's lean cheeks creased in a smile as he patiently said, "Yes, Tabby. You heard me correctly. I want you up moving around. I won't ask you to run a marathon, climb Mount Rogers, or even walk unassisted. It will be a little awkward for you because of the shoulder issue, so that's going to preclude crutches. Your best bet for now is to have someone walk with you to provide support, since even a walker is not possible. In a couple of weeks, you might be able to use a cane."

Tabby was staring at him, horrified by what she was hearing. A couple of weeks before she could use a *cane*?

"As for the shoulder, I'll want that immobilized for three weeks, then we'll begin physical therapy. Three months from now, you'll probably not even realize it was injured."

"Three months?" Tabby whispered blankly. She swallowed thickly. "Dr. Campbell?"

He was looking at the incision critically. "Hmm? Your sister did an outstanding job with this. She's wasted as a GP. She should have specialized as a surgeon at a larger hospital."

"Jenny's not wasted," Tabby said stiffly. "She's needed. She listens, and she heals people inside and out."

Jarrett Campbell's gaze snapped to hers, a strange expression crossing his normally intense face. "Is there a criticism in there, Tabby? I'm one of the top orthopedists in the country. I heal." He covered her incision and sat down in the chair next to her.

"You had a question, Tabby?" When she blushed, he chuckled. "Do women even do that anymore? Blush? Now what was your question?"

"Joseph and I want to get married. Can we…I mean…how long will it be before we can…you know," she stumbled in acute embarrassment.

He raised his sandy brows in cynical amusement. "Have sex?"

Tabby nodded, her mortification now complete.

He frowned. "Is he a vigorous lover?"

Tabby's mouth dropped open. "I—I don't think…"

"None of my business, huh?" Now he was smiling.

Tabby looked away and blinked away the angry tears in her eyes. "Never mind. I'll ask Jenny," she mumbled.

He laid his hand on top of hers where she plucked nervously at the cover on her bed. "I'm sorry." He sighed. "I get so used to dealing with jaded, cynical people. I can honestly say I've never encountered a couple as modest as you two. It's refreshing." He removed his hand.

"I can't give you a timeframe. There's certainly no reason why you couldn't go ahead with the ceremony, but you may want to wait on truly consummating it until you're more comfortable moving around. Certainly, you'll have to wait for the incision to close."

This time it was Jarrett Campbell who paused and looked uncomfortable. "Look, maybe you *should* talk to your sister about this. There are ways to show your love for each other without," he paused and cleared his throat, "without engaging in active intercourse."

Tabby nodded. "I'm sorry if I embarrassed you."

Campbell smiled. "You must love this guy a lot."

"You have no idea."

He stood and patted her hand. "I'll have the physical therapist come up here to begin working with you. Push—but not to the point of pain. Are you taking your medication?"

"As little as possible," Tabby said. "I don't like how groggy it makes me."

He inclined his head. "I'll see if we can't find something else to minimize that."

With a smile, he was gone. Dr. Campbell wasted no time. The physical therapist appeared in a few minutes to help her walk down the hallway and back again. After that, she manipulated the muscles in both legs.

Tabby was encouraged by the therapist's pronouncement that she expected someone as physically fit as Tabby to make a speedy recovery. Tabby wanted that. She wanted to be whole for her wedding. She swallowed. That could mean months. Plus, he hadn't even asked her yet. Her mouth drooped.

The door eased open to admit Jenny, followed by Holly and Catherine Richardson. Tabby smiled wanly.

"You've left Evan and Stoner alone together?" Tabby asked. "I don't think Jenny will let me donate blood to them yet if it gets messy."

"No way. Besides, they're not together. Evan and Jake are discussing how to proceed with your student," Jenny supplied, "and Stoner went with Joe and the sheriff. They're working on getting your studio moved."

Tabby's eyebrows rose. "Y'all don't waste any time."

"Well," Catherine explained. "There is an ulterior motive. We want you to think about doing a showing of your work. Stoner is a connoisseur, so he went to take a look at what you have."

Tabby thought about that for a moment. "I don't paint Norman Rockwell type art."

"Joseph mentioned that," Catherine murmured, "but honey, no one's asking you to paint only happy people or pretty flowers. Good art should make us think."

Tabby nodded. "Okay. Is this to help Joseph?"

Holly smiled. "And you. We've launched a campaign, Tabby, but we need to know where your feelings stand."

"My feelings for Joseph?"

"How soon can we plan the wedding?" Jenny asked. When Tabby suddenly burst into tears, Jenny's glance swiveled to the other two women who tactfully withdrew, closing the door behind them. Jenny sat down next to Tabby and stroked her face. "What's wrong, honey?"

"I asked Dr. Campbell about…you know…making l-love. He said he couldn't give me a timeframe, but he did say it would be about three months before I was completely back to normal a-and at least two weeks before I could even use a cane. I-I want to be able to walk down an aisle to meet Joseph…not be wheeled there. And what kind of a marriage can we have if we can't be intimate?"

Jenny stroked Tabby's hair. "Do you love Joe?"

"So much I ache when I'm not with him."

"Do you want to marry him?"

"Yes. I look at him, Jenny, and can't think of anyone else with whom I'd want to grow old. He makes me laugh. He gives me peace. He sings to me. He's my best friend."

Jenny smiled. "You're ready. Honey, let me call the other two in so we can all talk about this. There are times in every marriage where a couple has to express their love in different ways. Intercourse is just a piece of that. When Holly and Jake first moved in together, Holly had just given birth. Sex wasn't possible. But you can touch each other, learn each other's likes and dislikes. If you go ahead with your marriage, you can go ahead with that as well. As for walking down the aisle? Your physical therapist already said you walked down the hall and back. Stoner will support you, and Joe will be there at the altar to support you."

"Here." Jenny handed her a tissue. "Wipe your face. You need some serious girl talk."

"What's that?"

"We give you advice, and you ignore most of it."

Holly and Catherine came back in. As all three shared stories with her, Tabby realized they were right. She could do this. She would do this. Finally, she looked at Catherine. "If Joseph is okay with it… Could we both stay with you until my doctors say I don't need constant supervision? I need him close to me."

Catherine touched Tabby's cheek. "Of course."

* * * *

Joe slipped the key from above Tabby's kitchen doorjamb and unlocked the door.

Sam snorted. "Like that is not the first place a thief is going to look."

"Sheriff," Stoner said softly, "are you comparing my future son-in-law to a thief?"

"Oh get off it, Senator. You know that's not what I meant. You always twist things…."

"Gentlemen," Joe interrupted quietly. "Can we stay focused on why we're here?"

"Sorry," they both said in unison.

Stoner glanced around the house as Joe led the way upstairs. "This doesn't reflect what I know of Tabby at all. In fact, she doesn't seem to belong here."

"She bought the house furnished, sight unseen through an Internet auction," Joe said. "You won't see Tabby's influence until we get to her studio."

Stoner stepped inside the studio. "She's prolific. What a great space."

Joe hung back as Stoner and Sam wandered around the room. Stoner picked up her sketchbook and flipped through it.

"Who's the kid who looks like Holly?"

"Her brother, Tyler," Joe said.

"I see there are dozens of sketches of you, Preacher." Joe smiled as Stoner continued to turn pages. "And me," the older man added, his voice a little soft with surprise.

Stoner had reached the easel. With hands that shook slightly, he undraped the painting. "Oh, God."

Joe and Sam came to stand next to him.

"I guess this must be what you termed disturbing?" Sam said.

"It's a self-portrait." Joe touched the canvas, as if in doing so he could somehow erase the scars Tabby had so realistically painted. "It's very realistic, Sam."

"Yes, it is," Stoner agreed.

"Who did that to her?" Sam's voice was hoarse.

"The man she thought was her father," Stoner growled. When Joe laid his hand on his shoulder, Stoner blew out a ragged breath. "That's why she's so concerned about Melodie Matthews."

"If the guy's still alive and kicking," Sam commented, "she might still want to worry about herself."

Stoner shifted from examining the painting to staring at Sam. "You think he might try to find her? I got the impression he was probably glad she'd left."

Joe shook his head. "She told me one of the reasons her mother wanted her to find Jenny was to have some protection. He apparently threatened to kill Tabby if he ever found her again."

"Maybe you should back off putting her in the public eye," Sam began.

"Sometimes being in the public eye is the safest place to be," Joe said. "People know who you are, and that might scare someone like Tommy MacVie away. From Tabby's descriptions, he sounds like a coward."

Sam nodded. "I see your point. Still, I'd like a picture of the guy so my deputies know what he looks like. This art goes public, and it won't reflect well on him at all."

They sorted the paintings into two stacks, those that could be put into a showing at the country club and those that might be too disturbing for their intended audience.

"I think she has some brilliant work here," Stoner commented, "but as I was told, I'm biased. So what is your artistically plebian opinion, Sheriff?"

The tension between the two men was palpable. Whatever had sparked their animosity obviously ran deep. Sam looked as if it would give him great pleasure to flatten the older man. Joe handed Sam another painting, holding it long enough so the sheriff had to meet his gaze.

Sam's face was like stone. He slowly exhaled before he spoke. "I think your country club showing stack is right on. I also think your other stack could be set up as a show that should travel nationwide to illustrate the horrors of child abuse and help raise money for its victims."

Stoner stared at the big, burly man next to him as if he had never seen him before. "You have depths to you that surprise me, Barnes."

Sam looked at Stoner. "And you have a heart inside you that surprises me." He scratched his head. "You know, if Erin's turned out anything like Evan and Tabby, you're a lucky man."

Stoner's expression turned remote. "Thank you. Let's get these out to Evan's Tahoe. I'll see to packing up her paints and brushes if you all will take care of the canvases."

It was evening before Joseph cleaned up and drove to the hospital. He was nervous. He clutched a honey colored teddy bear, and in a small silk bag around its neck was the diamond ring Stoner Richardson had handed him in the study of his big house. "It belonged to my grandmother. If you want it for Tabby, son, it's yours." It was perfect, and Joseph liked the idea that it was a gift from Stoner as well. His blessing on their marriage, and her own link to her new family.

Joe pushed the door to her room open and gazed tenderly at her. She slept, her head turned slightly toward him. As quietly as he could, he crossed to her bedside and tucked the teddy bear into the crook of her arm before he sat down to wait, content just to be with her. The past few days had been so traumatic, he felt like he'd barely had time to breathe, and there were still so many hurdles facing them.

He leaned his forehead against the side of her bed. God never promised life would be easy. There would be obstacles, but part of him wished the first ones they had encountered were a little smaller. He drew a shaky breath, then stilled when he felt Tabby's hand stroke his hair.

"Joseph," she whispered. "I've missed you today."

He brought her hand to his lips. "I know. I've missed you too."

She smiled. "I'm glad you're here. I'm sorry you're in trouble because of me."

He stroked her fingers. "If it hadn't been us, Tabby, something else would have come up. The issue, with some members of the church, isn't really about you and me. It's about understanding and tolerating differences. Maybe it's best this way. We can get through this together." He looked deeply into her eyes. "You have a whole army of people who love you, Tabby. People are pulling together who I thought would never find a way back to each other's hearts. That's because of you."

"Oh, Joseph…"

He dropped his gaze to the teddy bear. "I brought you a present. He has something to give you too. Shall I help you?" Tabby looked at the small silk bag around the stuffed animal's neck and nodded. As Joseph tipped the ring from the bag into her palm, he whispered, "This wasn't exactly how I pictured doing this, but in the end, the setting isn't nearly as important as the words. Will you marry me, Tabby? I want to marry you, not to salvage your job or my job, not because of any gossip, but because I love you. There's no other woman I want beside me, no other woman who brings out the best of me. I promise I'll stand by you and do the same."

Tabby's gaze held worry. "Joseph, I'm afraid I'll hurt your work."

He stroked her hair and smiled at her. "Never. Tabby, you may have an aversion to the church itself, but you live by example every day. Anyone who looks at you, who spends time with you, can see that. You've already changed so many lives since you arrived." He leaned down to kiss her cheek. "You know, there's a question you've never asked me."

"What's that?"

"How I ended up in the ministry to begin with. Or did you think I was born that way?" When she looked uncomfortable, he touched her cheek. "Don't worry about it. A lot of people are hesitant to ask how and why I made the decision. But I want you to know.

"Some of my childhood probably wasn't a whole lot different than yours. My family was poor. My father…like your stepfather…was abusive, and my mother was an alcoholic. Her escape, I guess."

She squeezed his hand. He stroked his thumb over hers.

"I got into a lot of trouble, even committing some petty crimes. It got worse as I became a teenager. Then one night, my best friend, Ash, and I got into a fight with some kids from the next county over. One of them pulled a knife." He paused, swallowed at the memory. "I watched Ash bleed to death. Everyone ran. I couldn't leave him to get help, and I couldn't save him by staying."

Tabby's eyes filled. "It's why you work so hard with the kids, isn't it?"

He sighed. "Yeah. I changed that night, and I made a promise to Ash that his life would mean something."

Tabby bit her lip and stared at the ring. "I want to say yes, Joseph. But how can I begin to live up to you?

"I'm not perfect, Tabby. Not even close. I need you. You make me human, see me as a man. I need that. Please take me, flawed as I am." Joe had trouble choking out the last part. He kissed her fingers and hid his face.

"There's one more thing that you should know. I...I can't be a...wife to you...not physically right now."

He took the ring from her and slipped it on her uninjured right hand. "Tabby, I love all of you. I would marry you tomorrow if you could never be a wife to me in that way." He touched her head and her heart. "This is what matters. I look forward to the time when you're healed enough for us to be lovers, but until then..." He shrugged. "We'll find our own ways to be intimate."

Tabby smiled. "Holly and Jenny, and even Catherine told me that, but I wanted it out in the open."

He smiled. "What else did they tell you?"

Tabby blushed. "This and that."

Joseph laughed. "Marry me. As soon as we get over this hurdle with the church council, I know just the man to perform the ceremony. You could call him a cohort in crime, I guess. Will you marry me soon? Even if Stoner and I have to hold you up?"

"You already lift me up, Joseph, every day. So yes, I'll marry you, and maybe I can return the favor."

Chapter 13

As soon as Joe walked into the church council meeting with Jake, he saw that their efforts had already borne fruit. He couldn't help thinking that the meeting had turned into a farce. Dennis Underwood stood isolated from the group, and many members greeted Joseph with a hearty handshake, Jim Tarpley at the front of the line.

"Joe, sorry your vacation was cut a little short, but I guess it turned out to be a lucky thing for Tabby."

Joe smiled. "It was. It was a fortunate thing for both of us, but I'll explain that later."

John Gatewood opened the meeting with a prayer. When he finished, he looked at Joe. "Pastor, as you know, your covenant with us includes a pledge that you will lead your flock through the example of your own life. That is a promise to us that your behavior inside and outside this church will be moral and above reproach. Is that also your understanding?"

"Yes."

"A charge was placed before this council that you left Tabitha MacVie's home before dawn a week ago Friday. Is this true?"

"Yes." Joe would give them the truth no matter the cost. While he loved his job, his main concern right now was Tabby.

Several of the men shifted uncomfortably. Jake looked around at all of the council members and said quietly, "Perhaps you should listen to Pastor's explanation. You know our faith tells us we've all sinned and fall short of the glory of God."

Jim Tarpley spoke up. "I know that for a fact. I certainly haven't lived a life so blameless that I would dare cast stones."

Joe stood, the stress of the past few days making him feel tired beyond his years. This wasn't going to be easy, but he needed everything out in the open. If he withheld information, then Joe knew the council and the congregation's trust in him would be gone, and he could no longer be an effective minister to any of them. "I appreciate what you're trying to do gentlemen, but if the sin of lust occurs just from the thought, then I'm guilty. I went to Tabby's house the evening before Mr. Underwood saw me leave looking for comfort, not only in her friendship, but I hoped physical as well. I've been attracted to Tabby since I first saw her.

"When I arrived, she was in her studio distraught over a student for reasons of which Mr. Underwood is fully aware. It was Tabby who needed the comfort, not sexual or even romantic. She simply needed a friend. She asked me to stay with her because she feared she would be unable to sleep. And that's exactly what we did—sleep. When Mr. Underwood saw me, I was leaving Tabby's home after sleeping with her, but not after having sexual relations with her. I had indeed gone to her house with the intent of kissing her at the very least. So if that's a violation of the moral conduct you expect, then I'm guilty. If I showed poor judgment in staying with her, then I'm guilty."

Joe glanced down at the table, recalling how things had gone so wrong, before he continued. "I asked Tabby the following evening to marry me, and she turned me down because she feared her aversion to organized religion would hamper my ability to minister to my flock. She has reason to be wary of churches. The man she thought was her father beat her as a child and misguidedly sought help from his own church to change who she was. Despite that, Tabby doesn't suffer from a lack of faith in God, simply a lack of trust in the humans who say they represent him. I had to overcome that hurdle before we could be friends."

He met the eyes of each and every council member, many of whom shifted uneasily. He wasn't going into any more details about his relationship with Tabby. That was their private business.

"I'm happy to say I asked Tabby again yesterday evening to be my wife, and she's agreed. So, let me get this out on the table right now since you have brought me here based on the covenant you made with me, and I want no misunderstandings or misconceptions. Your agreement is with me. Tabby is not a part of that. If that's not acceptable to this council, then we should deal with it, and you may accept my resignation. My calling is mine. Tabby has her own gifts and uses them in her own way. I hope each of you will see that as you know her better." Joe looked around at all of the council members. "Thank you. Jake and I will step outside so you may discuss the matter and make your decision."

When the door closed behind them, Joe's shoulders slumped, and he rubbed the back of his neck tiredly. "All I want is to be at Tabby's side right now, to support her while she recovers." He turned to Jake. "I love this church and this community, but, Jake, if I have to make a choice, I'll choose Tabby. Maybe God is telling me preaching is not the gift I should be using."

"Bullshit." Jake blushed furiously at Joe's raised brows. "Sorry. You have an amazing gift, Joe, not just as a preacher but also as a pastor. We need you. In the community and the church. They'll realize that, and they would have done so without any of us making phone calls to help it happen. You'll see."

Jake grimaced. Joe wondered if it was the strain of stringing so many words together.

Just a few minutes later, John Gatewood and Jim Tarpley opened the door to invite them back in. The chill in the room had thawed perceptibly. The mood was relaxed and accepting. The only person who still seemed ill at ease was Dennis Underwood, but he'd begun to look uncomfortable from the moment Joe mentioned the thought was as much the sin as the deed. Joe's jaw tightened as he wondered whether Underwood had entertained his own lustful thoughts about Tabby. After all, the man did seem to have his own personal vendetta going.

* * * *

Tabby heard the slight movement of her hospital room door the next morning and turned her head eagerly toward the sound. Joseph entered, casually attired in khakis and a faded blue polo shirt that only made the blue of his eyes that much brighter. She searched his expression, which gave nothing away, hoping for some indication about how his meeting with the church council had gone.

"Well?" she finally asked as he approached her bed.

His expression was all blank innocence. "Well what?"

"Joseph! How did it go last night?"

He sat in the chair next to her bed and took her hand. Tabby's heart began to thud. What if they had fired him? Finally, he looked up and smiled, his straight, white teeth gleaming.

"Everything's okay, Tabby. I still have my job. They've given me an official reprimand, and yes, that will go in my personnel file, but the council followed it with a vote of confidence."

"Oh, thank heaven."

"I'm relieved they decided to follow the idea that we are all sinners deserving of forgiveness. Jake and Jim Tarpley were a tremendous help."

"I'm so happy for you."

He brought her hand to his lips and kissed her fingers. "Happy for us. I have to tell you, the meeting wasn't one of Dennis Underwood's shining moments. You still have that hurdle to face."

"It's something I will have to think about."

He touched her cheek, stroking gently. "Get well first."

A short time later, Tabby looked up from where she and Joseph still quietly talked. Jarrett Campbell walked into the room, dwarfing Jenny who was right behind him. "Good morning, Tabby," he greeted her cheerfully. "I'm flying home today. Do you know what that means?"

Tabby smiled. "I can go home too?" She looked at Joseph and beamed. Evan and Stoner had already stopped by to get her signature on the petition to change her name. She noticed the relationship between the two continued to thaw. Stoner also confided he was phoning in the announcement of Tabby and Joseph's engagement. Three weeks. They would wait that long so Tabby could at least have her shoulder out of the immobilizer. Joseph would have done it tomorrow, but Tabby drew the line. She was girly enough to want to be able to look decent in a wedding dress.

As she waded through the paperwork and instructions for her release, Stoner returned with Evan. Tabby felt a surge of love. This man was her father, but he was also her friend. She knew he wasn't perfect. She also knew he wasn't nearly as evil as he had been painted.

"If you don't think you'd be too tired, Tabby," he said, his voice rough, "Catherine and I would like to have a family dinner this evening. We want you there, Joseph, and"—he turned to Evan—"we would love to have you, Jenny, and Peter as well."

Evan's expression was remote. "I won't speak for Jenny, Dad, but I will discuss it with her and let you know."

Stoner sighed and nodded. "I understand. Catherine should be here with Peterson in a moment. You will be sure to let the state folks know I am back on my leash?"

Evan's mouth twisted. "Yes, sir."

"I'll find a wheelchair while you check to see if Mrs. Richardson is here yet, sir," Joseph offered in an attempt to leave Tabby and Evan alone for a minute.

After the door closed behind them, Tabby invited him to sit down. "I haven't had a chance to tell you how happy I am to know you're my big brother."

Evan smiled crookedly. "You were a little out of commission when I discovered you were my baby sister. I'm glad I could be there for you."

She touched his lean, elegant hand, so like their father's and so like hers with the long, sensitive fingers and, she smiled, the extra long pinkie. "You're conflicted about Daddy, aren't you?"

"Does it show that much?"

Tabby grinned. "Yeah."

"So much has happened…."

"Please, Evan, please come tonight," she begged. "He needs to talk about it. And I think we all need to hear what he…and your mother have to say."

Evan arched a brow. "She knows something she's not telling."

"I think so too."

Evan stood up, paced over to the window, and spun around to stare at her from across the room. "He never gave any kind of an explanation to us last year when the shit hit the fan. He pleaded guilty to the conspiracy charges without batting an eye. I wanted a trial at the time. I wanted the fight in court. I needed to see him humiliated, but he pleaded guilty, shut himself up in that damn house, and wouldn't talk to anyone. But you know what it's all about, don't you?"

"Some of it. He's said some things."

Evan raked his hands through his hair. "I'll talk to her. I won't promise she'll be there, but I'll come."

Tabby smiled in relief. "Help me up. I hear Stoner and Joe."

* * * *

Stoner paced the family room like a caged tiger. In the background, Joseph picked out a tune on the piano while Tabby rested on the sofa nearby. Catherine was in the kitchen, conferring with Peterson and the cook over some last minute adjustment to dinner. Meanwhile, Stoner was going quietly crazy. He was so afraid Evan and Jenny wouldn't show that his upper lip was slightly damp with perspiration. When he heard the doorbell, he nearly dropped his bourbon. A moment later, the door to the room opened and Jenny walked in carrying Peter, Evan a step behind her.

Stoner sighed and relaxed. They would eat dinner first so everyone would have a chance to be more comfortable. He set his glass down and crossed the room. Ignoring Jenny's slight flinch, he kissed her cheek and shook his son's hand. Evan's brows rose, and Stoner knew his son felt the tremor in his hand. He swallowed. Hell, he hadn't been this nervous the first time he ran for political office.

"I'm so glad you could come. Catherine will be thrilled…and I am too. Would you like a drink?"

Jenny shook her head, but Evan smiled and nodded. "Bourbon…neat."

While Jenny took Peter over to Tabby and Joe, Evan followed Stoner to the wet bar. "You're more on edge than I think I've ever seen you, Dad. Is there anything wrong that we should know about?"

Stoner handed his son the glass but didn't quite meet his eye. "No. I just…damn it, Evan," he whispered hoarsely, "I want my family back. Even before I knew who Tabby was, I saw how I had isolated myself. Nearly losing her… Well, I realized I couldn't live with the lies anymore. I had to get the truth out in the open."

As Evan sipped his bourbon, Stoner felt his son studying him. "Sometimes the truth is better left alone," Evan finally said.

"That's what I thought. But I've had months to realize I was wrong. I should have told the truth years ago before any of this happened. I could have saved everyone so much pain." He shook his head and tried to smile. "Sorry. Let's enjoy dinner. We can talk later."

Joe helped Tabby into the dining room. She was seated to Stoner's right with Joe to her right. Catherine was wise enough to seat Jenny next to her, leaving Evan on Stoner's left. Years of acting as a politician's wife served Catherine well. She managed to keep the conversation flowing and safely off the eight hundred pound gorilla that hovered over them.

Stoner was grateful. He had nerves enough for everyone. Her first sign of tension was when she asked Peterson to bring coffee and after dinner drinks to Stoner's study. Only the faintest tension was palpable in her voice. Tabby settled on the couch with her foot propped up and her back resting comfortably against Joseph's side.

* * * *

Evan helped Jenny get into a comfortable position to nurse Peter, then stood near the window with his hands jammed into the pockets of his slacks. It gave him a chance to observe. His mother, he noticed, hovered around the coffee tray, and there was a faint tremor in her hands. Stoner stood near the empty fireplace, a brandy snifter dangling from his elegant hand. Evan would have sworn his father's eyes rested on Jenny with as much love as they did when he watched Tabby, but that was ridiculous. It must simply be a trick of the light, or wishful thinking.

"Dad?" Evan prompted somewhat sharply. He wanted this over with so that no matter what came out, they could deal with it and move on. Chances were it would make little difference. If that was cynical, then so be it. He'd had an excellent teacher.

His father swallowed and slowly gazed at everyone in the room. His mouth twisted. "This is a long story. I don't offer it as a justification or an excuse. I simply want to tell it. Maybe… Maybe if I had told your mother years ago, Evan, all of this could have been avoided." Stoner pressed one hand against his forehead for a moment as if he were trying to decide where to start.

"I did a short stint in Vietnam. I could have gotten a student deferment, but I was filled with all sorts of ideals about serving my country, so I went. It was an eye-opening experience. I came back and tried to settle into my old life. Daddy and Mama wanted me to get married and start a family, so they began introducing me to suitable girls. Katie was one of them." He paused and smiled softly at Evan's mother. "We fought like cats and dogs, though. The summer I turned twenty-one, right before the end of the semester, she agreed to marry me. I came back home for the summer to help on the farm as high as a kite that Katie had said yes."

Evan turned away from the window, intrigued despite himself at hearing his father reveal so much about the past.

"That was the summer I first saw Mary. She worked in Tarpley's store, and I had come in to get cigarettes. She was sixteen years old and as pretty as you Jenny, all golden hair and big golden eyes. I felt like I'd been punched in the gut. I had a huge crush on her, but I was already engaged to Katie, and Mary was too young. It didn't stop me from flirting, but by the end of the summer, flirting was all I had done. I went back to school, back to being engaged to Katie, and put Mary out of my mind.

"Catherine and I married the next year. I finished law school just a short time before you were born, Evan, then joined a firm in Charlottesville. I was never coming back here if I could help it."

Evan met Jenny's gaze. His father had always given the impression that Richardson Homestead was the most important thing in his life.

"Hard to believe, isn't it? Daddy burned me out working the farm and shoving family history down my throat. I wanted no part of it. I was young and idealistic. I had a beautiful bride and a son who was the pride and joy of my life. Then three years later, your grandpa died. It was ruled a massive heart attack. Only one other man and I knew what actually happened. Daddy made some risky investments and lost almost all his personal fortune. There was still the land, my trust fund, and Mama's money, but Daddy was too proud to touch it or ask for it. He committed suicide."

Evan's mouth tightened. This was a version of the family history he had never before heard.

"I didn't tell anyone. Not Catherine, not your aunts, and definitely not your grandmother. Instead, I came back here and tied myself to the farm I hated. I felt like someone had hung an albatross around my neck." Stoner paused, his jaw working. "I used my influence to get the man who knew my secret elected sheriff, a reward for his silence. I poured my own money back into the land, made some sound business decisions, and managed to restore much of the money that was lost without anyone ever knowing.

"It was about that time that the sheriff, Sam's uncle, began his crackdown on the moonshiners. He'd heard rumors that the Owens family wasn't only making shine, they were growing another cash crop as well. I discovered a marijuana crop, along with a still, down in our river bottom while I was out with my beagle pack."

Stoner paused as though to gather his thoughts. "Catherine and I were having problems, mostly my doing. I was unhappy and foisted that on her. She had a difficult pregnancy with Erin. Both she and the baby were sick a lot. I felt frustrated and trapped. We argued constantly until I suggested she should visit her parents for a while and leave me the hell alone." When Stoner paused to shake his head, Evan glanced at his mom, but he couldn't read anything there. All the years as a politician's wife had given her a poker face even stronger than his dad's.

"I was shocked as hell when she did." Stoner smiled sheepishly. "She up and took you and your sister off to her folks for an extended visit. Neither one of our families would countenance divorce.

"Anyway, I wanted—needed—someone to take my frustrations out on, so I kept an eye out to see who was growing pot on my land. Eventually, I caught Billy. He offered me a percent of his crop and some of the take on his shine, but I wanted none of it. The crop disappeared—harvested I now realize—and he moved the still. A few months passed, and I found it back on my land again, along with a newly planted marijuana crop.

"I was livid and already sore as a bear anyway because Catherine had once again refused to come home, so I rode over to Billy's place. That's when I saw Mary again." Stoner stared into the empty fireplace grate and absently rubbed his hand over his cheeks.

"I saw you first, Jenny," he admitted. "You sat outside on the porch playing doctor, of all things. You had all your dolls lined up as patients. It's funny now remembering. I had forgotten that until just now. I asked after your daddy, and you looked at me with that golden hair and those golden eyes. It was like getting punched in the gut all over again. Before you could say a word, your mama came out. I wanted to grab you both and run."

"Stop it!" Jenny hissed. "Don't you make out like you gave a damn about my mama."

Catherine murmured, "He did, Jenny. He came to Richmond and asked me for a divorce. He said he was in love with someone else and wanted to marry her. He didn't tell me her name, but I found out later. I wouldn't release him."

Evan stared at his father as if he'd never seen him before. Trying to absorb all this new information about his dad was mindboggling. Stoner looked to Tabby, who smiled encouragingly. When Evan darted a glance at his newfound sister, all he saw was serenity. He wished he could be that calm.

"Anyway, I saw Mary and fell for her all over again. She looked tired, as if Billy's lifestyle had taken its toll. I harassed Billy to get his pot and his still off my property, but it was an excuse to see Mary. More and more when I came over, I found that Billy had taken Jenny off somewhere so that when I arrived, only Mary was there.

"We struck up a friendship. She could always make me laugh. It didn't seem to matter what kind of mood I was in. I fell for her hard, and I saw the same emotions in her eyes, but we were both married." Stoner paused again. His jaw tightened. "Then Billy showed up at my house one night, drunk as a skunk, said he was leaving Mary because she was a no good slut. I hit him. Told him again if he didn't get his shit off my land I'd go to the sheriff.

"He said he needed that crop because his girl was sick. Fool that I was, I didn't realize he was talking about his mistress. I thought he meant you, Jenny. He said he'd make me a deal. If I would let him harvest this one last crop, he'd turn a blind eye while I visited Mary."

Stoner stopped abruptly and returned to the bar to pour himself another brandy. Evan saw his dad's hand shake so much the decanter clinked against the glass and some of the liquid slopped onto the bar. He tossed back the liquor and poured another. Evan took the two steps needed to bring him to his father's side and took the decanter away.

"That's enough, Dad," he said quietly. "Are you okay?"

Stoner nodded. He turned back to all of them with eyes that were over bright. His mouth twisted into a parody of a smile. "I was so naïve. I thought I could have it all. I would get Mary, and Jenny would get the help she needed.

"I moved Mary into a cabin near Sam's property line. We were together almost constantly, and I realized I had to find some way to get her away from Billy for good. I wanted it to be a surprise so I didn't tell her my thoughts. Besides, I had to end it with Catherine before I could say anything to Mary, so I went to Richmond. When I got back with Catherine's refusal still fresh in my ears, Mary had disappeared.

"I searched for Billy and nearly beat him to death trying to force him to tell me where she went. Then I saw you standing there, Jenny, as healthy a little girl as you could be. Billy laughed at me, said he'd gotten great photos of the crops I was growing, and he'd turn them over to the DEA if I so much as opened my mouth. He told me Mary got tired of both of us and took off with another man. I looked for her for months, even hired a detective, but I couldn't find her anywhere. It was as if she simply disappeared."

Stoner stopped again. He looked hurt and alone in a way that Evan had never noticed. It was what Tabby had tried to tell them. He glanced at Jenny and saw her gaze waver, as if what she heard simply had too much of a ring of truth for her to continue to deny it.

"I gave up eventually," Stoner whispered, "and I sat back and started taking a hard look at my life and what I wanted out of it. Mary was gone, but I thought I might still be able to salvage what I had with Catherine. After all, I had two beautiful children with her, and I was missing their childhoods. So… We patched things up, but it was never quite the same. That was my fault too. I didn't have that part of me to give anymore… until I met Tabby. In my heart, I knew from the first who you were." He smiled tenderly at her. "But I'm getting ahead of myself and everything else that happened."

He took a deep breath. "I set my sights on a political career as single-mindedly as I had approached everything else in my life. The only other thing I allowed room for was hating Billy Owens. Because you were a constant reminder of what I had lost, Jenny, God help me, I started to hate you too. I told myself you were a child, Mary's child, and you looked just like her, but I couldn't get past the fact you were also Billy's daughter. He made sure I knew that every time I saw you together.

"So I hated him, and I hated you for being a reminder of what I could never have. I came back from my first year in the senate to find Evan infatuated with you. I figured it would go away, but every year when I returned home from Washington, you and Evan had simply grown closer."

Evan rolled his shoulders to ease some of his tension. This was harder to listen to than he'd expected, and it must be torture for Jenny.

"I hated your father so much. The last thing I wanted was to be tied to him or his family in any way. Well in that, I wasn't alone. Billy didn't want it either. He pretended it was because he wanted bigger things for you, but the bottom line was we both hated each other and would have done," he paused and corrected himself, "did do anything we could to keep the two of you apart."

Two steps brought Evan to the back of the couch where Jenny sat. He dropped a hand to her shoulder, feeling her tension.

"Billy sold a lot more than shine and pot by that time. He told me if I could pay off a few high school kids to make it look good, he'd see Evan would be left in no doubt that you were the same as the rest of his family. He traded someone a few ounces of pot for some roofies. I remember asking him what the devil that was supposed to be, and he told me it was just a little something to loosen you up."

Stoner stopped and turned his back to them, staring out the window. "I didn't know," he choked. "Didn't know you were pregnant. Not until years later. I used to sneak onto Billy's farm up to the trees behind the house. It was where Mary and I first made love. After your daddy died, I was able to go there more often. Then one afternoon, after you'd come back to town, I went up there and saw." His voice was filled with horror. "My grandchild. I—I'm sorry. Damn."

Stoner strode out of the room.

Evan's heart pounded. Anger and empathy nearly brought him to his knees. He knew exactly the pain and grief his dad was feeling because he'd felt it himself. The anger he felt told him his dad didn't get to just walk away from this. Evan started to go after him, but paused in mid-step as Jenny handed Peter off to Joe.

"I'm going with you. I want him to finish. I want him to tell me. He owes me."

They found Stoner standing on the terrace out back, not staring down at the pool as one might expect, but with his eyes looking over toward Sam Barnes's farm and the small cabin near there. Jenny stopped just a few feet away, and Evan wrapped his arms around her from behind, wanting her to know she had his support.

"You have a real flare for the dramatic, Stoner," she spat. "But I won't let you off the hook that easily. You owe me."

His dad sat on the low stone wall. "You're right. I do. I know from the court documents what your daddy told you. I also knew that it was simply my word against a dead man's."

"Exactly." Jenny rubbed her temples as if they ached. She was as tight as a bowstring. "Now you want me to believe you over my own father."

Stoner sighed tiredly. "There was never any deal beyond my finding the teenagers for what was supposed to be a setup, and that was all. Mike Saunders stepped way over the line. I saw that tape and recognized it for several things. Ultimately it landed me here, but it also ended my political career. Mike threatened to make it public seven years ago. I've always suspected he was paid off by competition in my own party. That's when I said I wouldn't run for another term."

Jenny trembled in Evan's arms. She was a strong woman, but this was so beyond what anyone should have to hear. Any illusions about her father that she might still have clung to were being ripped away.

"Let's say I believe this. Why did you pay for my education? Why did you show me that damn tape? Why did you continue to threaten me to keep me away from Evan, and why the *hell* did you hire Mike Saunders to *kill* me?" She raked a hand through her hair. "Stoner, how can I believe you with all of that stacked against you?"

He stared at the cabin again. Evan wanted the same answers from him that Jenny did. Between Stoner and her father, they had ripped more than a decade from him and Jenny.

"I paid for your education because I felt guilty about what had happened to you. Oh, make no mistake," Stoner continued in a weary voice, "I was overjoyed when you and Evan split. After all, I still hated your father with a passion. I made it possible for you to get the education I thought would keep you away from my son. When you refused the money, I was desperate. All I could think of was you coming back, and Evan and you getting back together. I wanted him to have the political career I had to give up. Your career would keep him here, so I threatened and tried it again when you showed signs of forgiving him.

"I was so used to thinking of you as Billy's daughter, that I hated you as much as Billy. I was sure you would eventually turn out like him. I called Mike because he was a slimy bastard who would do anything for a little money and power, but I didn't hire him to kill you. He was supposed to scare you, God forgive me, maybe even rough you up some, but never kill you! He took that on himself."

Jenny stepped out of the Evan's embrace and right into Stoner's face. "If all of this is the truth, why did you plead guilty to everything?"

That was what Evan had wanted to know too. If all this was true, his father's actions at the trial made no sense.

Stoner's concentration rested completely on Jenny. He reached up with a shaking hand to touch her cheek. When she flinched, he dropped it without making contact. He stared once more at the cabin. "Hadn't there been enough pain? You lost your mother to your father's lies and manipulations. You already hated me, almost as much as I hated myself. So it was easy to plead guilty. It saved you and Evan the trauma of my trial, and it left you at least some illusions about your father."

Jenny waved her hand in dismissal. "I no longer have any illusions about my father. Those were destroyed the day he left me with no way to get help. But you? Why come clean now if that's how you feel?"

"Finding and almost losing Tabby made me realize the past needed to die. If the truth didn't come out, your father would still be dead, but the rest of us—you, Peter, Evan, Tabby, and Catherine—would lose the chance to become a family. I want us to have a chance to be a family. You don't have to forgive me. I've done unforgivable things, but if you could open the door a crack, that's all I ask."

For the first time Evan saw not arrogance, but self-defense when he looked at his dad. Stoner was afraid of rejection. He had felt rejected by Catherine, then by Mary. Only Tabby had walked into his life with an open heart and mind. He was too hemmed in by his own isolation now to let down all his defenses, though he had certainly thawed like a snow cap in springtime compared to what he had been. Evan and Jenny had to be the ones to reach out, to make the first move.

Jenny stood almost perfectly still. Almost. Her fingertips tapped her leg, betraying the emotions she must be holding rigidly under control. Evan watched them, his own emotions in turmoil, but knowing he couldn't react until he saw which way Jenny's reaction would go. First and foremost, his loyalty was to his wife.

"I've hated you for so long, Stoner, I don't know how to start." Her words were barely louder than a whisper.

For a second, the man who had been such a remote, cold version of the father Evan had really wanted appeared uncertain. His Adam's apple bobbed before he opened his arms to Jenny. When she stepped into his embrace, Evan's throat closed with emotion.

Stoner hugged her and whispered, "If I'd gone with my gut all those years ago, if I'd taken you and your mama and run, I could have had you all."

Jenny shook her head. "No. There's a reason for everything. Holly taught me that. We just haven't been shown yet what it is." Jenny stepped back and glanced at Evan before she turned to take Stoner's hand.

"Come back inside," Evan told them both. "I have a feeling that the earth hasn't quit shifting beneath our feet."

* * * *

Tabby studied them when they returned. Jenny's arm was tucked in Stoner's elbow. Evan was just a step behind, and all of them were smiling. She blinked against the sudden tears in her eyes. Her dream of a family was becoming reality.

"I guess it's my turn to confess now."

Everyone in the room stared at Catherine. Tabby had known she was hiding something. Now it seemed tied to this mess.

"Katie?" Stoner inquired. "What on earth could you possibly have to confess?"

She looked at her husband and sighed. "You're not an easy man to live with, Stoner. You're an even harder man to love. I've alternately loved and hated you for thirty-five years."

She tugged at her earring, an unusual gesture from the normally poised woman Tabby had come to know. "Five years ago, I answered your private line when you were out hunting one morning. A woman asked for you. She sounded much older than the political groupies who flocked to you in Washington, so I drew her out. She had called from a pay phone in Asheville, North Carolina."

"Katie, what did you do?" Stoner whispered.

Catherine's eyes went to Tabby. "It was your mother, honey. It was Mary. She told me who she was, said she didn't want you to know— didn't want Stoner to know—but she was desperate to get you away from there so you could go to college." Catherine reached into her pocket and drew out a sketch that bore the creases of being folded and unfolded time and time again. "She said you had incredible artistic talent, so she sent me this as proof."

Catherine handed the sketch to Stoner who gasped. It was a sketch of him sitting on the porch of the cabin, looking as he had around Evan's age. When he passed it to Joe, he held it for Tabby to look at. She touched it, smiling in nostalgia.

"I called it 'Mama's Memory' because she talked about it so often from the time I was a little girl until I left for college. She never told me who the man sitting in front of the cabin was. I always wondered what happened to it."

Catherine smiled. "I flew to Asheville, and we met for lunch. I think your mama was ill even then, honey, but even if she wasn't, I could see how life had worn her down. She showed me your picture. I saw so much of Stoner in you. She described your talent and the trouble with your stepfather. I set up an account for you, jointly in your name and hers, to help you with college. When I heard she passed, I made sure you found out about the teaching position here."

When Joseph twined his fingers through hers, Tabby realized she had tears welling in her eyes. The letter would have brought her here to visit, but it was Catherine who had opened the door for her to move here, to get to know her family. Joseph tucked a handkerchief in Tabby's hand so she could wipe her eyes.

"That explains why you weren't shocked to hear Dad was her father the day of the accident," Evan mused. "You already knew."

"Forgive me," Catherine said, staring at Tabby contritely. "Despite having helped you, Tabby, I was still prepared to dislike you. After all, you were my husband's love child, conceived and born after I had already given him children, after I had been married to him for ten years. But then I saw how you two meshed, how you changed him. Suddenly, I was looking again at the Stoner I fell in love with decades ago. He laughed without that awful cold edge to it. He used to lock himself in his study or his wood shop and stare morosely into space, and suddenly he was creating, talking, smiling, even making jokes about his house arrest.

"I will never forget his face that afternoon he knelt next to you, keeping you alive until the ambulance came. I knew if we lost you, we would lose him before anyone else had a chance to see the real Stoner."

Catherine rose from her chair, crossed the room, and cupped Tabby's cheek in her palm. "Tabby, I couldn't love you more if you were my own child. You've given me back my husband. I don't think he's called me Katie since before Erin was born."

She bent and kissed Tabby's cheek before resuming her seat. Tabby looked at Stoner, Evan, Jenny, and Catherine. Her family. Almost. She finally asked the question that had bothered her through this whole story. "Where is Erin?"

Evan twirled Jenny's hair around his fingertips. Stoner frowned thunderously. Catherine sighed.

"The last time I heard from Erin, she was the cook on one of those sailing boats somewhere in the Caribbean. What do they call them?"

"Windjammers," Joe supplied.

"Not hostessing at the topless bar in St. Thomas anymore?" Evan inquired mildly.

Stoner made a choking noise. "What?" He glared at Catherine. "You didn't tell me about that."

"It was only for a few weeks between life guarding for the hotel and being a nanny for the owner and his third wife." She looked at Tabby and Joseph apologetically. "Erin left for school at eighteen, and when she was able to access her trust fund at twenty-one, she disappeared. We haven't seen her in five years."

"We should invite her to the art showing." Tabby said it quietly, but she refused to let it drop until Stoner nodded.

Chapter 14

Tabby was awfully tired. Joe helped her to her room. Evan and Jenny had left with Peter a short time earlier. Stoner invited Joe to spend the night and gave him the guest room across the hallway from Tabby.

"Is he deliberately tempting us?" Tabby yawned.

Joe laughed. "That didn't sound convincing, darling. You're not supposed to yawn if you're being tempted. Besides, you did ask if I might stay here while you're recovering."

"Can we kiss?"

"I can if you can." He smiled and helped her into a chair. He sat at her feet and took her shoes off for her. His hands gently massaged her arches, then her calves, easing the tension she felt from walking so cautiously. Light gleamed off the golden hair of his bent head, and his massage was doing much more than relaxing her.

"Joe?"

"Hmm?" he responded absently. He had shifted behind her, unbraiding her hair and brushing it out.

"Will you mind living here for a while until I get back to where I was before the accident?"

"Not at all. You and your dad are good for each other. As much as I love you, I can't ignore my parishioners or my work. There will be times when I can't be with you because I have to visit people, lead Bible studies, work on my sermon. This way, I can do those things knowing someone is watching over you, someone who loves you as much as I do. Best of all, when I can grab some spare time, you'll be right here."

Tabby turned her head to smile up at him. "I do love you, Joseph. I hope you don't get tired of me saying it."

"Never." He set the brush down and settled her carefully on his lap. His kiss was soft, his hands cupping her face. Tabby ached to be able to touch and caress him. He was so beautiful. Her lips parted, and Joseph groaned as he slipped his tongue inside to explore. Their breathing grew ragged. Heat flowed through her, settling in an empty feeling deep in her belly.

There was a discreet knock at the door. Stoner stuck his head in. "Look, I gave you time to help her get ready for bed. After all, you are her fiancé, but you don't have permission to be in here all night. So get busy, get her tucked in, and say good night before I get my shotgun."

Joe laughed. "Yes, sir."

Stoner stared hard at both of them. "Look. Don't touch."

"Yes, Daddy."

As soon as the door shut, they resumed their kiss.

* * * *

Stoner watched the news outlets and the Internet like a hawk. By the weekend, Tabitha *Richardson*'s engagement had made news not only in Virginia, but neighboring states as well. It wasn't every day that a disgraced former U.S. senator announced the engagement of a daughter no one even knew he had. Castle County's weekly paper, *The Messenger,* had juggled numerous calls for photos of both Tabby and Joe. Eventually, the wire services picked up Amanda Brown's story of Tabby's accident and near death, and how the senator literally held her artery closed with his bare hands. Suddenly, the phone rang off the hook at Richardson Homestead.

If Peterson answered, he simply said that the senator and his family were not available. If by chance Stoner got one of the calls, he usually hung up with a terse "go to hell" until he caught Tabby frowning at him and decided he should simply let Peterson continue to screen calls. Stoner knew from experience that the interest would die down pretty quickly. That suited the hell out of him. He wanted Tabby left alone so she could recover.

He had discussions with both Joe and Sam about the publicity. Sam had located a driver's license photo of Tabby's stepfather and distributed copies to his deputies. Joe and Stoner had taken a good look at it too. As plans moved ahead for the art showing, both men decided some caution was warranted.

In addition to Tabby's story making it to traditional media, Stoner found it plastered on the Internet. He read the article and saw the mention of his other children. Erin's name jumped out at him. Stoner rubbed the ache in his chest. When Catherine couldn't reach Erin by phone, she had sent her e-mail about Tabby and the upcoming art exhibition, but she'd heard nothing in return. The last thing any of them wanted was for Erin to find out about Tabby by reading it in a news story. Stoner hated the disappointment that rose in him when he thought of Erin.

If she showed up at all, it would surprise him. Erin and surprise usually weren't two words anyone wanted in the same sentence.

* * * *

Evan's cell phone chimed just as he returned to his office in the courthouse after grabbing a sandwich at Mercer's on Tuesday. As soon as he saw the caller's identity, he swiped his thumb across the screen.

"Hey, Jake! What's up, man?"

"Took a call about an hour ago from Dennis Underwood. Any chance you can come out to Mike and Missy Matthews's house?'

Evan's heart sank. Shit, if anything had happened to that little girl Tabby was so worried about, she would be crushed. He was already turning away from his office door with its gold stenciled "Commonwealth's Attorney" lettering.

"What's going on, Jake?"

"They're dead. Melodie's MIA."

"I'm on my way."

He made it in record time. Now, Evan stood beside Jake outside The Matthews's house. Jake was tapping his cap against his thigh, always a sign something was bothering him. Well, something was bothering Evan too—the knowledge that Tabby had not overreacted and everyone else had underreacted.

Jake cleared his throat. "Mike and Missy Matthews are both in there. You might want to take a look, see if you need to gather additional evidence, but it seems pretty clear cut, Ev, as a murder-suicide. There are signs a pretty violent struggle took place. Mike's dead in the kitchen from multiple stab wounds. Kitchen shears appear to be the weapon. They're lying nearby. Plenty of blood. Missy's in the master bath downstairs with slit wrists, knife on the floor next to her. So far, we haven't found Melodie."

Evan stared at the big home and shook his head. "You think she's dead?"

Jake grimaced. "I don't know. We found traces of blood behind the couch in the den that don't fit any of the spatter patterns for Mike or Missy, and there's blood upstairs in the little girl's room, but not enough to be consistent with a fatal injury. There were also hair samples—more than normal hair loss, like it was pulled." Jake blew out a breath and resumed tapping his cap against his thigh. "My men have searched the house, and we can't find her anywhere. We've tried calling her name. I even brought her teacher over."

"*Yes.*" Evan slapped Jake on the back. "That's it. You just brought the *wrong* teacher, Jake." He pulled his cell phone out and called Jenny.

"Hey, honey. What are the chances I could bring Tabby over here to the Matthews's house?"

"She's not up to a whole lot of moving around yet, Evan. How much of an emergency is this?"

Evan hesitated telling her. Jenny had known Missy. They'd gone to high school together. In the end, though, there wasn't much choice. He needed her permission to bring Tabby over.

"Mike and Missy are both dead. Melodie's missing."

"Oh no! Tabby was right about everything. But, Evan, she's still so fragile."

"I'll help Tabby, and I'll only keep her here five minutes, I promise. Jen, you know she's got a connection to this little girl. It looks like a murder-suicide, but we can't find the little girl anywhere. If Tabby—"

"You think Melodie will come out of hiding if she knows Tabby's looking for her?" Jenny sighed heavily. "Five minutes, Evan. You have to promise."

"I swear to you, five minutes only, then I'll personally take her back to Dad's. I love you." He shoved his phone back into his pocket.

"Call Sam. Have him bring Tabby here. We'll have five minutes. I'll call Joe. I want him here with Tabby." When they finished their calls, Evan looked at Jake. "Let me take a look. It might not need additional investigation for Mike and Missy, but until we find the girl, we have to keep looking for evidence."

Evan had seen some grisly sights, but this was one of the worst. Added to it was the fact the coroner put the time of death more than forty-eight hours ago. He braced for what they'd find inside, his stomach tight. Before they entered, Jake handed Evan a mask, gloves, and booties. Evan put on the booties and the gloves, but shoved the mask into his pocket. The things always made him feel smothered. He took his handkerchief out instead and held it over his nose. They looked at Mike's body first.

"From the way items were broken," Jake explained, "it looks to me like he dragged Missy through the house in here, maybe to use the phone. His cell phone's still in the car in the garage."

"Are you sure he wasn't dragging the girl?"

"Possible but not logical. He could have carried her. Anyway, it looks like once they got in here, Missy somehow got hold of the kitchen scissors and went to work on him. We've already lifted prints from the shears consistent with the size of her hand and bagged the scissors for evidence. They'll print Mike and Missy at the morgue so we can match it up. From the blood on both sides of the back doorknob and on the deck railing, I believe Missy came outside after she killed Mike."

They stepped out onto the deck, into the fresh air, and Evan took the handkerchief away from his face to breathe deeply.

"You think she was looking for the girl?"

"I want to believe that," Jake said. "There are bloody prints throughout the house. If it's Mike's blood, that would fit a scenario of Melodie still being alive after Mike's death."

Evan pinched the bridge of his nose. "Jesus, Jake. How could a woman do that to her husband?"

"I think the theory you were looking into is probably correct. It goes back to the baby she lost last year. I—I keep thinking what it would have been like, you know? What if when Holly went into labor we had delivered Noelle, and she had been dead? Can you even imagine?"

Evan shuddered. "No way. It would be tough enough as a father, but to be the one to carry the baby for nine months, feel it alive and moving inside of you, then...nothing?" Evan shook his head. "It ripped me up finding out what Jenny had to go through with that miscarriage. I was scared shitless when she delivered Peter."

One of the sheriff's detectives, who had come to assist in the investigation, poked his head around the corner. "I've got what looks like the girl's church clothes from Sunday, and sir, your sister just pulled up with Sam."

* * * *

Tabby sat in the cruiser. She wasn't ready for this. She was still trying to absorb the news that Melodie's parents were dead. Fear churned heavily in her stomach that Melodie couldn't possibly have survived.

Evan opened the door and squatted next to her.

"Don't get your hopes up, Evan. I know she trusted me to help her, but if she's alive, she must be so traumatized."

"Just try, honey, that's all we ask. She needs our help. Her mama and daddy are dead. They've spotted blood in Melodie's room we think belongs to her, but we can't find her, Tabby."

Tabby closed her eyes, clutching Evan's hand for a minute. *Please God,* she thought, *help me find this little girl. Let me help her like she trusted I would.*

"Help me up."

"Tabby," he warned. "You have to take it easy."

Her gaze lifted beyond him to where Joseph stood, outlined against the trees and the afternoon sunlight that filtered through them. He looked tall and golden. Even from this distance, his innate peacefulness flowed over her, soothed her. "Joseph," she called. "Help me. Take me inside. I want to go to her room."

"Tabby," Jake said. "You need to be prepared. Mike and Missy Matthews have been in there dead for two days. Melodie's room is upstairs…."

Tabby looked at all three men. "One of you can either carry me or I'll crawl, but I will get there. That's what you brought me here to do, and I promised her I'd help her."

Her voice rose, and two of the investigators looked around. Joseph stepped forward and held out his hand. "I'll help."

It was slow going. By the time they stood at the base of the staircase, Tabby stared at Joe, feeling a little light-headed. "I can't do it, Joseph. I can't get up those stairs, but I feel sure it's where she would try to hide. Some place where she felt safe, and some place far away from what happened down here."

He smiled. "If you can't do it on your own, then I'll carry you. Put your good arm around my neck. I'll try not to jostle your other shoulder. We'll do this together, Tabby. You'll help Melodie. You'll find her."

Tabby gazed into his warm blue eyes and knew he was right. His confidence bolstered hers. Jake led the way into Melodie's room with Evan bringing up the rear. As Joseph set Tabby on her feet, he kept his arm around her waist to support her. She saw the blood-spattered paper, and her heart missed a beat.

Tabby closed her eyes and leaned heavily against Joe. "I know it's a lot to ask, but could the rest of you go downstairs for a few minutes."

Joe squeezed her hand. Evan nodded to the other men standing in the doorway. Tabby waited until she heard the last one finish going down the steps.

Tabby sat on the edge of Melodie's bed, looking around the room. The walls were painted a pale pink, the windows trimmed in white with lacy curtains that gave everything outside a kind of fairytale quality. A lot of pain could be hidden in even the best of surroundings. Tabby struggled to her feet, limping to the table and the paper lying there. Angels. Melodie loved to draw them, and in this picture they seemed to be hovering over someone… Tabby's eyes filled. It looked like her. Melodie had been drawing her.

Tabby sucked in a shaky breath.

"Where are you, baby?" Tabby said softly. She stared around the room again, thinking back to her own childhood. Melodie's room had a ceiling like Tabby's childhood bedroom in the attic they had converted. Tabby chewed her lip. Her room had contained a crawlspace at the back of her closet. What were the odds....?

After limping slowly to the double doors, Tabby opened them and flipped the switch that turned on the light.

"Melodie," she said in a louder voice. "It's Miss MacVie. Everyone's worried about you. I'm worried about you."

Nothing stirred.

"Oh, sweetie, I know you're scared. I know your mama hurt you, but she can't hurt you anymore." Tabby paused, clearing her throat to ease the tightness of the tears clogging it. "I'm here to help you, but I can't stay long. I can see from your drawing that you know about my accident. I'm still hurt, and I bet you are too."

"Please come out now, honey. It's safe. It's just me. No one else is here until you tell me it's okay, but I need you to come out for me."

Tabby leaned against the door, supporting some of her weight as she waited. She thought she heard a slight noise, but wasn't sure. The seconds ticked by with incredible slowness.

After an eternity, what appeared to be simply a stack of storage boxes moved. One box at the base pushed outward to reveal a hole only large enough for a child. Slowly, a little girl with tangled black hair and blood still on her face crawled out. She crept cautiously forward, clutching her teddy bear and a blanket in one hand. Her other arm she tucked close to her. It was bruised and discolored between the elbow and shoulder. Blood stained her shirt and her face was bruised as well. She didn't say a word, but as she looked at Tabby absolute trust shone from her eyes.

"Oh, honey," Tabby said, and her voice broke. "I'm too hurt to come to you."

Melodie stumbled over to her and carefully leaned her bruised head against Tabby's uninjured side. "I knew you would come," she whispered. "You said you would help, and you came."

Tears choked Tabby stroked Melodie's tangled hair. "Everything will be all right, but we need to get you out of here. I can't pick you up, honey, because I'm hurt, too. Is it okay if I ask Joseph, Mr. Evan, and Chief Jake to come up here?"

Melodie trembled but slowly nodded. Tabby gently caressed the little girl's tangled hair as she called down the stairs. Melodie examined the three men who soon surrounded them, but her eyes came back to Joseph. She held her hand with the teddy bear and blanket out to him.

"You can carry me," she said. Joseph blinked and swallowed, then bent down to lift her carefully in his arms. She leaned her head against him trustingly. Her blue eyes gazed steadily into his. "You're the man who sings. Will you sing to me too?"

"Anytime, sweetheart," he murmured, his voice a husky rumble. "Anytime."

Tabby bit her lip as the tears flowed. When she started to sway, Evan caught her and lifted her into his arms. "I've got you. Let's get you two back downstairs. Jen will have my head."

Jake put his arm on Evan's shoulder as they left the house and said quietly, "The girl has to be examined, Evan, but I'm afraid the hospital will traumatize her even more. Can you get Jenny to look at her at your house? I'll contact social services and see what we can do about placing her somewhere temporarily."

"Could she come home with me to Daddy's?" Tabby asked.

Jake seemed surprised. "I don't know. Evan?"

"I'll talk to the judge, Tabby, while Jenny's making sure Melodie doesn't have any serious injuries. Right now, we need to get her away from here so we can move the bodies."

As soon as Jenny had looked at Melodie, Tabby and Joseph were cleared to take her to back to Richardson Homestead. From the moment Stoner stared into Melodie's solemn blue eyes, Tabby could see he was a goner. Melodie had taken one look at him and lifted her arms in complete trust. He picked her up, cuddled her close, and asked if she liked dogs.

"I do, but Mama said we couldn't have one 'cuz they stink."

Stoner grinned conspiratorially. "We have lots of dogs here. And if you go to sleep like a good girl tonight, I'll take you out tomorrow morning to show you the puppies we have."

Melodie's mouth formed an O of surprise. Some of the sadness left her face. "Oh, Mr. Stoner, that's awesome. Even Jamie Gardner doesn't have puppies."

Joseph wrapped an arm around Tabby's waist. She leaned into him gratefully as they watched Stoner climb the stairs with Melodie in his arms.

"Has it struck you just how much his life has changed?" Joseph whispered into her ear. "How much he has changed? In befriending you, he found a daughter. Now he's opened his home and his heart to a lost little girl. Let's pray he can soon claim her as a new grandchild."

Tabby sighed, a mixture of weariness, sorrow, and relief. "I wonder how often he missed these same opportunities with his own children? Probably too many times to count."

"I suspect you're right."

"I think that's the past, though. I have the feeling he'll be making up for lost time."

Catherine joined them, her gaze moving from the staircase to Tabby. "I should have let you meet him five years ago. I should have told him then instead of trying to exact my own revenge. You have made such a difference in him, Tabby. I..." she paused to gather her composure before she finished. "Thank you."

Tabby touched her arm. "She doesn't have any other family, Catherine. Joe and I have already talked. We—we want to see if the court will give us custody once we're married, and I'm back on my feet."

"That's a big burden for a young couple, but if any two people can handle it, you can." She looked up the steps again. "You'd also get an instant grandpa."

"We were just saying that. We'd also get a grandma." Tabby smiled.

Catherine nodded. "I love Peter, but it would be nice to have a little granddaughter to spoil."

Melodie settled in quickly. Tabby thought it was possible she didn't fully comprehend that her parents were gone for good, but for now, she appeared to be adjusting. Evan stopped by the following afternoon to tell them the judge had given temporary custody of Melodie to Stoner and Catherine, who let out a small sigh of relief. Tabby had worried they might not get custody because of Stoner's criminal record.

While Melodie sat at Stoner's desk drawing pictures, Evan said quietly, "Jake and I will need to take a statement from Melodie. We'll bring a social worker and a child psychologist with us. You all may sit in as well, if it makes her more comfortable."

"Isn't there any way to spare her that?" Tabby asked.

Evan shook his head. "Although we've pretty much pieced everything together, she is the only surviving witness to what happened. If her statement verifies what we have already gathered, then that will be it. The case will be closed."

Tabby nodded. "It might be for the best. It might help her put some closure on it."

"There are two other things you should know. Dennis Underwood put in a request for early retirement effective immediately."

Tabby felt relieved at that news, but certainly no sense of triumph. There were no winners and losers in this whole situation—only losers. Melodie had last her parents. Tabby had lost her job, and so had Dennis Underwood.

Stoner arched his thick brow. "Was that his idea?"

"Jake and I stopped by his office this morning. When I pointed out that some people might construe his failure to immediately report Tabby's suspicions to social services as negligence that resulted in not only injury to the child in question but also the deaths of both her parents, Dennis decided it was time to retire and pursue other interests."

"What was the second thing?" Stoner prompted.

Evan's lips thinned. "Missy Matthews's minister and his wife have contacted an attorney to begin proceedings seeking custody of Melodie in the absence of any other blood relatives."

"No," Tabby stated fiercely, her heart thudding heavily. "No, Evan. You can't let that happen. You'd be putting her right back into the atmosphere she came from."

"We can fight it," Evan said and looked at Stoner, "especially if you and Mom will agree to temporary guardianship. You still have a fair amount of clout around here."

"You don't even need to ask, Son," Stoner said. He lifted his gaze to meet Catherine's. Tabby smiled. She couldn't help it. Amid all the tragedy, this new closeness between her father and Catherine filled Tabby with hope for the future.

* * * *

Joe returned after Wednesday service still feeling somewhat weighed down by a tragedy that touched his own congregation. He would have to set aside his own personal feelings to minister to the Underwoods, but right now, he wasn't sure how to do that. As he entered Richardson Homestead, Melodie ran to the front door and held up her arms for him to pick her up. He swung her up so she could wrap her legs around his waist. Her exuberance wiped away his bad mood. Faced with her smile, all he could do was give her a kiss and a grin. He glanced up the steps and caught Tabby's golden gaze. He was the luckiest man alive, and he'd thank God every day for the blessings that had come to him in the form of Tabby and this sweet little girl.

"Hi, sweetie." Joe kissed the little girl's cheek. "Already had your bath?"

"Mama Catherine helped me 'cuz Tabby can't yet. I needed one too 'cuz Tabby let me help her paint!"

"She did? She's never let me help. I only got to pose for her."

"I got to hold her pal-palette, and she showed me how to mix some colors."

"Wow. What's she painting?"

"Mr. Stoner making furniture."

Stoner approached them, held his arms out for Melodie, and she went into them happily. "Give Joseph a chance to say hi to Tabby, honey."

"Okay." Melodie turned her face to Joe again. "Will you sing for us later? Sing about angels before I go to bed?"

Joe laughed. "For my favorite littlest angel? Of course I will. You want me to sing for everyone?"

"Yes. Peterson too. Sing in here. It'll sound way cool."

Joe glanced around the big front hall and realized that she was right. Singing in the hallway would sound great. "All right. Why don't you round everybody up while I say hello to Tabby?"

When it was just the two of them, he took her into his arms, careful to protect her shoulder, and kissed her deeply. "I've missed you. I think about you all day long. Do you have any idea how awkward that is sitting in the middle of the countywide ministers' council meeting?" His lips parted over hers, and he teased her mouth with his tongue. Their breath mingled and Tabby relaxed against him. Joe let his right hand slip down until he could cup her bottom. "Mmm. You feel so good here like this. I never want to let you go," he whispered against her ear. "I've found a minister for us. The church council has given its okay for Reverend Calloway to perform the ceremony."

Tabby giggled at hearing the Presbyterian minister's name. "A truly ecumenical wedding service."

He touched her cheek and looked at her tenderly. "I think what happened with Melodie and her parents has shocked everyone out of their sanctimonious attitudes and brought the community back together again. They saw how allowing pettiness, spite, and gossip to become too important clouded their minds so they didn't see some other truths."

"Like a little girl being abused by a mother who was in desperate need of help?"

Joe stroked his fingers across Tabby's cheek. "Yeah. Once we're married, Evan says he'll help us work on adopting her." He kissed Tabby on the nose and grinned at her. His finger traced the neckline of her blouse. "Mm. I have to stop before Stoner goes for the shotgun."

"Damn straight," a deep voice muttered behind them.

"You shouldn't cuss, Mr. Stoner!" Melodie whispered wide-eyed with just a hint of a shadow in her expression. Stoner looked down at the little girl tugging on his sleeve and scooped her up.

"You're right, Melodie. I'm sorry."

Peterson, who had just walked in with the maid, stopped dead, his jaw dropping open in an undignified way as he gaped at his employer, no doubt because he had apologized for swearing. After Peterson had collected himself, he brought chairs for Catherine and Tabby. Stoner sat on the stairs with Melodie while Peterson, the maid, and the cook hovered near the entrance to the narrow hallway that led to the kitchen area and the servants' wing.

Joseph smiled at all of them, and then his eyes settled on Melodie. "This song's for you, sweetie. It's called 'I'm Your Angel.'" He closed his eyes for a moment, and in a gesture Tabby had become achingly familiar with, he began to sing, looking right at Melodie. "No mountain's too high, for you to climb all you have to do is have some climbing faith...."

Tabby never ceased to be amazed at his clear, melodic voice. She glanced around the hall and observed the stunned expressions on everyone else's faces. Only Stoner and Catherine had heard him sing, but that had been in the hospital room when he had needed to sing softly. Now his bell-like tenor rose powerfully in the huge front hall. When the last note faded away, Melodie stared at Joe with shining eyes. "Oh, Joe!" She laughed. "You don't just look like an angel. You sing like one too."

He laughed, half embarrassed. "Come on, sweetie. I'll put you to bed. Kiss everyone good night." He looked at Tabby. "I'll be back in a few minutes, darling."

* * * *

Tabby watched Joe disappear up the stairs with Melodie. She was still watching the second floor landing when Stoner said, "Good God, Tabby. Joe shouldn't be in a pulpit. He should be in a recording studio."

Tabby smiled. "He's needed here, Daddy. Maybe once he's not, he can explore using his gifts in other ways."

"And what about you?" Stoner asked. "Will you go back to teaching?"

Tabby felt as if everything inside her shut down. "I don't know."

It was a question she'd been asking herself. She thought about it repeatedly over the next several days. She'd enjoyed teaching, but there were other priorities she needed to consider. One of them was Melodie.

She watched how hard it was for her to talk about what happened in her home, but she did and didn't leave out a single detail. They kept the little girl at home for the rest of the week to give her a chance to recover. She alternated between helping Tabby in her studio, and then, when Tabby rested, she could be seen outside with Stoner, romping with the puppies and walking with him, or sitting quietly drawing in the corner of his wood shop while he worked, nearly finished with the occasional table.

Catherine shared with Tabby the plans she continued to make for a showing at the Country Club. It would take place Saturday night. In light of what happened to Melodie, Tabby and Catherine agreed to set up two rooms at the club. One for the main party that would contain Joe's painting and some of her other lighter work, but another room would be set aside to raise donations for a national organization to prevent child abuse.

Tabby had to smile. Catherine, in her own element in planning any kind of fundraiser, ruthlessly played upon Tabby and Stoner's story. She twisted arms and called in favors until suddenly not only was the entire community invited, but everybody who was anybody in political circles and Virginia society was trying to wrangle an invitation. However, the coup that had overjoyed Tabby and widened Evan's eyes was that Sam had agreed to accompany Stoner, and on her own, Catherine had secured permission from the state for Stoner to be there.

When they gathered for an early dinner before the showing, Catherine looked around at all of them before settling her gaze on Tabby. "You should be prepared. Several media outlets contacted me. Stoner agreed to talk to them in a short press conference just prior to the opening, and we have granted them limited access to shoot video and photographs."

Tabby's eyes widened in alarm and her heart raced. "I don't wish to talk to them Catherine. It was hard enough to see my picture in the newspaper. I would rather avoid as much publicity as possible." Tommy MacVie's face flashed through her head. Some part of her expected him to make contact. Unless he'd moved into a cave, he must now know where she was. Tabby's stomach turned. It was simply too much to hope he wouldn't come sniffing for money or something.

Stoner patted her arm. "Catherine's already told them you will not talk to them, and I will reiterate it." He looked around at the other men gathered in the dining room—Evan, Joseph, Jake, and Sam. "I hope you will help Catherine and me keep them at bay. We wouldn't have done this, but Sam actually planted the idea for the exhibit to raise money for child abuse victims. This seemed like the perfect time to launch it. Catherine has already received inquiries from several museums and galleries."

"That's marvelous, Mother," Evan said.

Catherine shook her head. "It's not my doing, Evan. Tabby's work speaks for itself, and very eloquently." She looked at Joseph. "I turned down a six figure offer for Tabby's painting of Joseph just this morning."

Surprised chuckles rippled around the room, then grew louder as Joseph blushed. Tabby squeezed his hand. "There is no price for that painting. It will hang in our home, wherever that might be, for as long as I live."

They arrived at the club, and two white-jacketed attendants hustled out to park the cars. Joseph stuck to Tabby's side like glue. All of the glitter had completely overwhelmed her, and her stomach twisted in knots. She watched Stoner with amazed curiosity, seeing a side of him completely new to her, though it must be the norm for everyone else. In his tux, he appeared urbane and sophisticated. He radiated power and confidence, and Evan was no different. Catherine and Jenny both looked poised and sophisticated.

Tabby blinked, and that flash of being the poor, hick relation suddenly choked her. "Joseph," she whispered in a panic. "I don't belong here."

He touched her cheek with his fingers and kissed her lightly on the lips. "You have no idea how right you look. It's the perfect backdrop for you, and I am so proud to stand at your side."

He squeezed her hand. Tabby relaxed a bit, but the feeling that something was out of place persisted.

They stood inside the doorway to the club in a large front hallway that was plushly carpeted, walls lined with wood paneling and boasting a large stone fireplace at one end. Already some members of the press gathered, toting equipment in through a back entrance so they could set up around the lectern positioned in front of the fireplace. At an angle to one side was Tabby's self-portrait entitled "Scars."

Stoner stepped up behind her and touched her shoulder. "I'm sorry, Tabby. We'll keep you out of the limelight as much as possible, though you have such an incredible talent it will be harder and harder to do as you become better known."

Tabby glanced at Joseph, who nodded. She turned to Stoner and said, "You're the first to know, other than Joseph. As I watched the preparations for tonight, and saw how my work might benefit others, I made my decision about teaching, Daddy. I won't go back. There are many reasons, but I believe I'm meant to use my gift to paint more than to teach."

"I'm proud of you, honey." Stoner kissed her cheek, scowling after a flash went off.

"Good evening, Senator." A lean photographer with one earring dangling from his ear grinned as he stuck his head out from behind his camera.

"God, I should have known." But Stoner grinned back even as his words dripped sarcasm. "I guess I should be happy you decided to wear a tux, Mac." He stuck his hand out, and the shorter man grasped it in a firm handshake.

"Blending, Senator, like a chameleon. You should try it some time. Did you bring a watchdog with you?"

Stoner nodded to Sam. "The big guy, looks like a pit bull only not as friendly. I heard he came out of the womb that way."

"Daddy!" Tabitha whispered. "Sam is so nice. Remember, he was the one who came up with the fundraiser idea."

Now she had the photographer's attention. "Really? You must be Tabitha, the long lost daughter."

Joseph's arm tightened, and for the first time that she could remember, Tabby saw his expression harden. Stoner apparently wore the same look.

"Whoa!" Mac held his hands up. "I know. I know. She's not talking to the press. I'm on my way. I'll go talk to the Rottweiler with the marshmallow filling. "

Stoner frowned thoughtfully. "Perhaps you should go into the main room. It's only going to get more crowded with journalists here. Just imagine sharks around chum, and you'll get the general idea."

Joseph nodded, keeping his arm securely around Tabby's waist. "Let's find you a spot to sit down, Tabby. It's going to be a long evening."

"Joseph, I'm overwhelmed. Stoner, Catherine, and Evan... They're all used to this, but I'm not. I feel like I'll do or say something wrong, not to the press, but to their friends."

Joseph's blue eyes twinkled. "Tabby, does the Stoner you've known for the past two weeks care what anyone thinks?"

"No."

"Exactly. And how many of these friends have kept in touch with him since he was sentenced?"

"None that I know of except maybe Sam, which seems funny because they always act like they hate each other."

"Darling, you can do nothing wrong in your father's eyes. Nothing would ever cause him to turn his back on you. I think you'll find plenty of people here just like you and me." Joseph paused and smiled at her. "Besides, in the eyes of the Lord, we're all equal."

Tabby smiled. "The Lord might feel differently if he had to wear a tux. Help me into the main room. I want to show you my surprise."

She held his arm securely and pointed him to a painting that was still draped. It stood right behind a table that was also draped. Tabby's smile was mischievous as she sat in a chair next to them. "Go ahead, take a look under the cover while everyone's occupied with the press conference."

Joe looked, smiling as he glanced back over his shoulder. "You finished it. Does he know?"

Tabby shook her head. "Check out the table." After he peeked under the cloth, Tabby grinned. "Peterson sneaked them out late this afternoon and set them up for me."

"You think he'll be okay with everyone seeing his woodwork?"

She smiled. "He will once he hears the reactions. I'm telling you, Joseph, his work is as brilliant in wood as you all seem to think mine is in paint. It's incredibly complex, and he's only enhanced it with his finish. It's a beautiful table."

The press conference ended as the brunt of the guests began to arrive. Catherine and Stoner stood in the ballroom area. Tabby sat in a nearby chair with Joseph perched casually on the arm. Evan and Jenny hovered, talking to Jake and Holly. To anyone who didn't know them, it would have appeared to be a casual arrangement, but as soon as anyone from the media came anywhere in the vicinity, the circle tightened and shut Tabby off from curious eyes.

Outside that protective circle, Tabby watched Sam casually sipping a ginger ale. He was frowning, not unusual for him, but this evening she sensed his anger was directed at them. As she wondered about that, Sam's focus suddenly shifted toward the room's side entrance.

A young woman had come through the doorway there. In a room of tuxes and silks, this woman stood out. Her black, lace-up platform boots ended just below the knee, but there was still a long expanse of bare, slender thighs visible before her black leather skirt began. It was belted tightly around her hips, well below her navel. Her arms were bare except for a dozen bangle bracelets glittering silver in the muted light. Around her neck, she wore a black leather collar. Her makeup was dark, throwing her pale skin into relief.

Tabby's eyes widened. She tugged on her father's sleeve.

"Who is that?"

As soon as Stoner and Evan saw the woman, they abruptly set their drinks aside and moved to intercept her. Sam had done the same. Tabby frowned.

"Sammy!" The woman slurred a bit as she spoke. "I came all the way from St. Thomas to meet my new sister. Where is the new golden child?"

It was Erin. Tabby's heart clenched. No one appeared happy to see her.

"Daddy and Evan," Erin slurred and giggled again as they closed in on her. "I wanna see my new baby sister."

Stoner's broad shoulders were stiff. "How dare you, Erin," he growled in an undertone that Tabby still managed to hear. "God almighty, even if you hate me, don't you have some respect for your mother? Or yourself? You're shit-faced...hell, make that stoned."

Sam stood next to her while Evan shielded her from the rest of the room.

"I'm glad to see you too, Daddy. What's it been now? Five years? No big open-armed welcome? No big party like the new kid?" She stared at Evan, weaving slightly on the high heels that still left the top of her head below his shoulder. "Hey, Evvie! Remember me? Oh, probably not—especially now that you have the new Richardson clone. Can I meet her?"

"No!" Stoner snapped. "Not here. Not now. Not when you're in this condition."

Sam stepped up and took her arm. "I'll take her home, Senator, and come back."

Tabby rose to her feet. It was time to meet her sister.

"Come with me Joseph." She needed his support, physically and emotionally.

"Put her in the guesthouse. I don't want her around Melodie in this condition," Stoner said as Tabby and Joseph reached them. Catherine and Jenny were close behind.

Erin's bloodshot blue-gray eyes narrowed. "Afraid I might contaminate something?"

Stoner's barely controlled temper was evident in his clenching jaw.

"Is this Erin?" Tabby asked. As Tabby reached tentatively with her uninjured arm to touch her sister's hand, her gaze met Erin's and she finally noticed Erin's bloodshot eyes.

Erin stared at her; then her gaze shifted from Evan to Jenny and back to Tabby.

"Oh my God, Daddy! You screwed Jenny's *mother*?"

Stoner raised his hand. It shocked Tabby because it sure looked as if he'd been about to slap her before he dropped his hand to his side. Sam covered Erin's mouth with one hand and effectively blocked Stoner with his own big frame, which was also odd. Sam scooped Erin's struggling figure up in his other arm and began removing her from the clubhouse.

Chapter 15

Tabby looked from Evan's expressionless face to Stoner's angry one. "Evan...Daddy?" Anger, frustration, and grief twisted their expressions. "What's wrong with her?"

Jenny put her arm around Tabby's waist. "She was stoned, honey. High."

Evan cleared his throat. "Sam will get her settled in the guesthouse. We can all talk tomorrow. Tonight is for you Tabby."

Stoner blinked. His strong face was pale and a little haunted looking. Tabby saw the sadness and touched his arm. She would help him now, and they could deal with Erin later. Evan was right. "Help me into the other room, Daddy. I have something to show you." He smiled, and if his fine gray eyes were just a little too bright and a touch sad, Tabby chose to ignore it, softly returning his smile.

"What do you have to show me, honey?" he rumbled.

"It's a surprise."

As they entered the main room, Catherine signaled for everyone's attention as Tabby made her way painstakingly to the covered portrait and the cloaked table. When they stopped next to the draped painting, Catherine joined them and looked up at the gathered guests. "Tabby has decided to unveil a portrait here tonight that she just finished. She calls it 'The Artist.'"

Tabby smiled nervously, then removed the cloth. It was the painting of Stoner working intently on the occasional table. The painting focused on both his intense expression and the elegance of his hands as he worked with such tiny detail. Applause vibrated around the room, but it was Stoner who Tabby watched. He swallowed a couple of times, pressed his lips together, and hugged her as tightly as he could without hurting her shoulder.

"It's beautiful," he murmured for her ears alone.

She kissed him on the cheek and leaned back. "It's you. The Stoner I know."

Catherine had Evan call for quiet again, and she smiled at her husband. "Tabby also had me sneak out the table pictured in the painting. Stoner just finished it, and she felt like everyone should see what she called the true artistry. Evan, if you would be so kind."

When the table was unveiled, those nearest gasped. The wood glowed rich and warm, a backdrop that made the geometric pattern of the inlay leap off the smooth surface.

"Good God, Dad." Evan was among those clearly astounded. "It's gorgeous!"

Echoes of that same sentiment spread throughout the room, in addition to amazement that Stoner Richardson was its creator. Tabby smiled at him. She was so proud of him, but it was difficult not to laugh because he was so stunned by the praise he received.

* * * *

Joe noticed Sam seemed particularly silent when he came back, but on all other counts, the evening was a success. While Evan drove home, Tabby leaned against Joseph tiredly. He stroked her hair and kissed her forehead.

"Easy, Preacher," Stoner said from the front seat, as if he had eyes in the back of his head. "You still have two weeks before you put a wedding ring on her finger, but I think between your engagement, your meeting with the church council, and tonight's showing, we've managed to allay everyone's desire to tar and feather Tabby and defrock you."

Tabby smiled at Joe, who enjoyed the way she seemed to fit so comfortably into his side. "It was a wonderful evening."

"There's one more thing for you to deal with," Sam growled from the seat behind Tabby and Joe.

Erin.

Joe knew Tabby wanted to know more about her, wanted to find out why she seemed so lost, and why everyone else seemed not to know what to do around her. However, they soon realized Erin had disappeared.

Stoner read the note Erin had left and crumpled it in his fist. "Damn her!" he muttered. "God! She's self-destructing, and I don't even know where she is to try to stop her."

"We can start at the truck stop," Sam said. "Your car needs to be picked up anyway."

Stoner looked at his watch. "It's been two hours since you dropped her here." He shook his head. "She's long gone by now."

Sam looked at Stoner levelly. "Your car still needs to be picked up. I'll go."

Joe spoke up. "I'll run you out there. I need to head into town anyway to get ready for services tomorrow."

Sam nodded. "Thanks, Joe. I'll bring your car back, Stoner, and try to find out something."

Stoner nodded, his face somber. "Thanks, Sam."

Sam's tension was almost a living thing as they drove toward the interstate. Other than their poker games, Sam Barnes kept to himself, even when he showed up in church. So it had surprised Joe tonight when Sam was the first one to recognize Erin, the first one to intervene, and he had noticed, even if no one else had, the way the big man had put himself between father and daughter.

"Erin seems troubled," Joe said quietly.

Sam snorted. "You're being way too kind, Preacher. Completely screwed up might be more accurate." Sam's hand clenched on his knee. "Erin's issues could fill a book. I don't think we have time to get into them."

"You've known her for a while then?"

"I saw her for the first time when she was nine. She broke her arm sliding down a waterfall on my farm. She's been nothing but trouble since."

They reached the truck stop. The Cadillac was in the parking lot. Joe waited for Sam until he returned with the keys. Leaning down into the window, Sam said, "The keys were right where she said they'd be. I also spoke to a trucker who said he saw her hop a ride with a southbound driver."

"She's long gone by now, then."

Sam's eyes turned toward the interstate, his mouth a thin line. "Yeah. I'll let the Richardsons know. Thanks for the ride, Preacher."

* * * *

Tabby wished it was different, but Erin's shadow hung over them. Catherine sent her e-mail, wanting to know that she had made it back to the Virgin Islands okay and inviting her to the wedding. Erin replied she was fine but wouldn't make the wedding because they would be in the middle of a two-week island-hopping trip. Tabby wasn't sure that was the truth, but it was a convenient way out of having to come home again.

Stoner shut himself in his wood shop for a few days. When he finally emerged, it was as if he had simply shaken off a bad mood and decided to move on.

Tabby observed it all, her concern deepening. They had put Erin in a neat little compartment, locked the door, and shut her out of their lives. If Tabby had discovered nothing else from her own experience and Melodie's, it was that family secrets refused to stay hidden. She seriously doubted they had seen or heard the last of Erin. And why should they? She was family.

A shiver snaked down her spine. Tabby still had her own family out there somewhere. Tommy MacVie might not be blood kin, but he was still a threat. She needed to talk to Joseph about it.

The showing and the long lost daughter angle of her story made national headlines. Stoner, the handsome former senator gone bad, was always good grist for the journalistic mill. There was even a story the following weekend on a nationally syndicated magazine show. But what concerned Tabby most of all was the discussion of child abuse. There was no way to avoid it. Even though she had never named Tommy MacVie, those who'd known them in Asheville would know. Her name was a matter of public record. There'd been no way to keep that private. The one thing Tabby remembered all too well about Tommy MacVie—he always exacted his revenge.

Tabby continued to work on the painting of Richardson Homestead. She had lost her helper, though. Melodie had returned to school, and Tabby was feeling a little bit lonely during the day. Catherine and Stoner finished preparations for the wedding and reception Saturday. Joe was busy with calls. Even though they had decided to postpone a real honeymoon until Tabby was completely healed, he was trying to get things cleared off his calendar so he could take a few days off after the wedding.

Tabby paused with the brush in hand and smiled. She had worked hard with the physical therapist, who was extremely pleased with her progress. She could now walk on her own, though she used a cane some of the time to keep from overdoing it, and they were going to take her out of the shoulder immobilizer the following day so she could begin therapy. Jarrett Campbell had flown in over the weekend and had grinned at her.

"You're a remarkable young woman, Tabby, and your recovery is nothing short of amazing." He paused. "You're getting married next weekend, aren't you?"

"Yes."

He winked. "Other than watching what you do with that arm, I think you're good to go for whatever else you have in mind." When she blushed scarlet, he laughed. "Seeing you blush is about worth the plane ride down here and back."

Tabby's reflections were interrupted as Katie wrapped herself around her legs, and Tabby looked down to smile at the cat. Stoner had reluctantly given the okay for her to bring Katie to the Homestead. Joseph was staying in the guesthouse for the time being because Catherine had insisted on redecorating the parsonage for them. Tabby grinned. That was one upside of the week that remained until she and Joe would be together. The guesthouse gave them a chance to sneak a few minutes alone, though it seemed to her that Stoner spent more time than necessary hovering.

Thursday evening, Evan arranged a guys' night, which taciturn Sam had somehow been talked into hosting. Jenny had turned Tabby bright red when she told her that Evan and Jake were determined to give Joe a few tips before his wedding night. So when she saw Joseph Friday morning, Tabby blushed. He had chuckled and pulled her into his arms.

"How... How was your evening?" she asked breathlessly.

He leaned in and kissed the side of her neck. "Very informative," he growled against her ear.

"Joseph!"

He laughed. "We played cards, darling. While Sam and Evan smoked cigars and Evan drank bourbon, Jake and I proceeded to take their money. We play poker just about every month." He looked around. "Where are Catherine and Stoner?"

"Catherine had something she was taking care of for the dinner at the club tonight, and Stoner is working in his shop. Melodie is at school, Peterson and the cook have gone shopping, and I just saw the maid go out to clean the guesthouse for us."

He pressed her against his lean body. "So we have the house to ourselves?" At her nod, he wrapped his arms around her and began kissing her. "Mmm. One more day. Should we practice a bit?"

Tabby laughed softly. "Absolutely."

They settled on the couch in the family room off the kitchen. Joseph pulled her onto his lap and gently stroked her cheek as he kissed her. As their mouths opened to each other, his hands moved over her, caressing her rib cage down to her hips and along her thigh. Tabby trembled, heat and desire building inside her. She slipped her hand between his shirt buttons to touch his chest and felt his instant response to her questing fingers. His hips shifted, his erection pressing against her bottom.

"I am so ready for this marriage," he groaned against her. "It has been pure torture to keep my hands off you."

She chuckled gently and wiggled a little on his lap. "I can tell. How much practicing can we do?"

Joe groaned as he leaned his forehead against hers. "Not too much more, or Stoner will shoot me."

They heard a knock on the kitchen door. Tabby laughed. "That's probably the florist. Catherine said she was expecting him this morning. I'll get it since you're a little indecent at the moment." She blushed as her gaze dropped to the bulge in his slacks. Joe laughed as he tucked his shirt back in and smoothed his hair. "I'll come help as soon as I calm down a bit."

Tabby was still laughing as she opened the kitchen door.

"Well, Tabitha! Here you are getting ready for the wedding, and you didn't even invite your papa?"

Her smile evaporated, and her heart thumped like a caged bird. Tommy MacVie filled the doorway, a faded John Deere cap pushed slightly back on his head. Old habits die slowly. Even as she cringed from him, she automatically stepped back, giving him room to walk in before she had time to think and shut the door.

"Papa," she whispered faintly, automatically.

His eyes narrowed. "At least you remember who I am," he hissed. "But I don't hear enough respect in your voice, and you haven't invited me in. Maybe what you need is a reminder." He grabbed hold of her hair and jerked it as he examined her face. "Your lips are swollen. Have you been fornicating with your preacher before your wedding? Is that what you've been doing? Just like your mama, spreading your legs out of wedlock."

"Don't talk about Mama!" Tabby cried, but as weak as she still was, she didn't dare do anything.

MacVie sneered. "You know your pitiful little story cost me my job?"

Her eyes widened in surprise, and he continued. "Didn't realize you'd made national news, did you? Well, your daddy made sure to drag me through the mud, and they fired me at the plant. Looks to me like he's well-to-do enough he should recompense me for everything you cost me."

From behind them, Joseph spoke in a voice Tabby had never heard before. It was flat and cold. "Take your hands off her."

MacVie spun Tabby around, making her cry out from pain as his hand yanked her hair again.

"You must be the preacher boy." He eyed Joseph contemptuously. "Pretty thing, ain't you? But pretty don't mean shit. What are you going to do? *Pray* I release her?"

Joe walked slowly forward, his eyes never leaving MacVie. "Perhaps you didn't hear me, Mr. MacVie, I said take your hands off Tabby. Do it now. If you want to hit someone, hit me. Stop putting your hands on women and children. That's a coward and a bully's way. *Hit me!* Or can't you do that because I'm a grown man, so you run the risk I might hit back."

Tabby's eyes widened at the cold, measured fury in Joseph's face. MacVie released her and shoved her aside. She staggered and caught herself against the kitchen table. Joseph stepped instantly between them, protecting her.

"I ain't letting some pussy preacher from some heathen church tell me what to do. You'll take your whippin' like the boy you are!" He swung at Joseph, his eyes widening in surprise as Joseph expertly blocked the blow. He tried again, and again Joseph blocked him. Time after time, as MacVie pushed his attack, Joseph simply stopped him with his arm or a dodge of his body. "Why don't you stand and fight like a man?" MacVie shouted in frustration. "Fight!"

How often over the years had she heard her stepfather's voice raised in rage against her and her mother? Her instinct was to run, but she wouldn't leave Joseph, whose calmness helped her with her own fears.

Joseph smiled. "That goes against my personal beliefs, Mr. MacVie. What kind of an example would I set for my congregation if I allowed myself to give in to the urge to pound you senseless for all the years that you took your temper out on a child?" Joseph stepped in close to MacVie and stared him down. "No matter how much of a scumbag you may be, *I* won't hit you."

Stoner Richardson's big frame filled the doorway, and he snarled, "Fortunately for me, I don't feel any such compunction!" He spun MacVie around and slammed his fist into the man's face. The John Deere cap finally went flying. MacVie had just a moment for a surprised expression to cross his face before he dropped like a rock to the kitchen floor. Stoner stared down at him, then looked at Joseph and Tabby. "Y'all all right?"

When they both nodded, Stoner suddenly started shaking his hand back and forth in front of him. "Son of a bitch! That hurt! Damn! I guess I must not be as young as I once was. Call the sheriff, Joseph. I'll take this trash outside until someone can come pick it up."

Joseph grinned. "It would be my pleasure."

He turned to Tabby who leaned, wide-eyed against the kitchen counter, and took her in his arms. "Are you all right? Did he hurt you anywhere?"

She shook her head. "Just scared me mostly." She buried her face against his chest and shuddered. "I kept trying to convince myself he'd forget about me. But I think I always knew he'd be back."

Joseph stroked her back. "Don't worry, Tabby. We'll take care of it. We'll make sure he can't come back to harm you again. Why don't you go on into Stoner's study while we take care of this? Do you need any help?"

Tabby looked down at MacVie. "No."

* * * *

Laura Browning

After Tabby left the room, Stoner sighed. "You know, Joseph, in the old days, I'd have been tempted to see Mr. MacVie met with an unfortunate hunting accident. You must be a good influence on me."

"What makes you say that?" Joe asked.

"Now I'm only tempted to break both his kneecaps so he can't ever walk again."

Joe raised his brows. "I would be mighty tempted to agree with that plan, but I'll call Sam. I'd prefer you be able to get off your electronic leash before too much longer."

Stoner looked down at the unconscious man. "Me too. Call Sam. What a shame. It would have been one time I truly felt justified in being unscrupulous."

Stoner grabbed MacVie by the collar, dragged him none too gently out the door, and down the back steps. He had just finished work in his shop when he'd heard the truck drive up. As he walked to the house, he had heard Tabby's cry. It made him smile secretly to see the way Joe stood up for Tabby without ever compromising his own beliefs. That boy was going to do more good for this family than he even knew.

They were in luck. Sam had run by his farm to pick up something and came on over when he got the call. With an economy of movement, he snapped cuffs on MacVie and stuffed him into the backseat of the cruiser before he radioed in for a tow truck to come impound MacVie's truck. He looked around at Sam and Joseph. "Tabby all right?"

Joe nodded. "Just shaken up a bit. She'll be fine."

Sam nodded and slipped behind the wheel of his cruiser. "I'll see to this. I'll send a deputy by in an hour. I'll need statements."

* * * *

By the following afternoon, Tabby had put MacVie out of her mind and sat in front of the mirror in the dressing room of the Baptist Church. Her eyes were wide and her smile shaky as she stared at Jenny and Holly while they attached the veil to her hair. Melodie sat in a chair nearby, swinging her legs and watching the way the puffy skirt on her dress bounced up and down with each movement.

"It's almost time," Jenny reminded softly. "Are you ready?"

Tabby nodded. A knock sounded on the door.

"Everybody dressed?" Stoner called through the wood panel.

"Come in, Daddy," Tabby told him, her voice sounding a little shaky to her own ears. Stoner looked impressive in his morning suit with its gray vest and black and gray striped tie. His eyes glowed with pride as he looked at her.

"Ready, honey?" he asked gently. "Your groom already looks nervous even with Jake and Evan standing next to him."

"I'm ready." Tabby stood and hugged him carefully. "I love you so much," she murmured. "I never thought when I came here that I would find so much. Not only did I gain a sister, I found an entire family and a better father than I could ever imagine."

Stoner's eyes met Jenny's, and he held out his hand to her. The smaller woman stepped forward and linked her fingers with his. "Tabby, you helped us all find each other."

"Time to go," Stoner said. He took Tabby's hand and tucked it through his arm. Jenny and Holly straightened her skirts, then their own. The church was filled with people. Many of Joseph's congregation, friends of Stoner and Catherine, but Tabby noticed none of them. As she followed Melodie down the aisle, her eyes were only on Joseph. He did indeed look like an angel.

As their eyes met and held, Tabby realized she had experienced many miracles since she arrived in Mountain Meadow. She had found a sister, a brother, a father, and even a daughter. The family she had always longed to have. But the biggest miracle of all was the man standing at the altar. He loved her without hesitation or reserve.

When Stoner placed her hand in Joseph's, she heard the tremble in her father's voice and saw the sheen of tears in Joseph's eyes. Tabby had never felt so sure of anything in her life as she was of this day, this moment, this man. There was no shyness or hesitation from either of them as they pledged their love.

When Reverend Calloway told Joseph he could kiss his bride, not a sound could be heard inside the Mountain Meadow Baptist Church. Joseph touched his lips to her forehead, her nose, and finally her lips. She couldn't wait to start her marriage to this man—her lover, her angel, her friend. Their fingers twined together, and their eyes closed. When they parted, everyone clapped, and Tabby and Joseph blushed.

Meet the Author

After a long career in journalism, **Laura Browning** changed gears and began teaching English. The change in pace allowed her to ramp up her love of writing fiction. After a push from her hubby, her hobby morphed into a book contract. When not teaching or writing, you can find her on her farm or in the woods with camera in hand. Visit her website at: www.laurabrowingbooks.com.

Enjoy this preview of book 3 in Laura Browning's
Mountain Meadow Homecomings series!

ERIN'S WAY

Available August 2016.

Chapter 1

Erin Richardson handed over some of her precious stash of cash and signed by the X for her rental car. Leaving a paper trail made her nervous, but reaching her destination quickly took precedence. Home sweet home. The black sheep of the family was returning to the fold.

Hating the heavy jacket she'd donned to keep out the last blast of winter cold, she tossed it in the back seat of the little sedan. The car would warm up soon enough. The bulky coat was a further reminder that she'd been forced to leave behind the warmth and her friends for the cold and uncertainty of the Blue Ridge…also known as home. Right. The place where she was headed had rarely felt like home, at least not as she had wanted it to be.

An image of a frowning face with snapping, dark eyes flashed in front of her. Sam. He was older now, but so was she. Not that it would make a difference. He was one more face lined up in judgment of her.

She slid behind the wheel and checked her reflection in the rearview mirror. A little different look than last fall when she'd dropped in on the 'rents so unexpectedly. Erin had kept the extra body jewelry but ditched the Goth-looking makeup and dyed her hair back to its natural color. This time when she returned home she wasn't aiming to shock as she had been at Tabitha's art showing. Erin was trying hard to fit the image of the senator's daughter. That would be a first. But now totally necessary.

After what had happened right before she left the Virgin Islands, it was important to lay low and fit in. Maybe she should get rid of the ring in her eyebrow. No. She'd keep it for now. That was one too many changes for her to cope with at the moment. If she suddenly turned up in plaid and pearls, she'd make her family more suspicious than they would be simply by her turning up at all.

One thing hadn't changed. Erin carried a bag of some high-grade pot, a few hits of ecstasy, and even a couple of Quaaludes she'd traded for with a guy from South Africa. She laughed humorlessly as she pulled out of Dulles and headed southwest in the rental. There was only so much goodness she could stand, and she certainly wasn't ready to give up her escapes from reality. It might at least brighten the dullness of where she'd grown up. Mountain Meadow. She shivered. Her last memories of her hometown were some of the most humiliating of her life. She was far from happy to be back, but life had a way of throwing curve balls. She wished it wouldn't throw so many.

With a long drive still ahead of her, she stopped at a Starbucks and wired up on a triple shot of espresso. As the miles slid by, her nerves tightened. She would so much rather still be on board the *Sprite*, but Andre Delacroix had certainly screwed that. Staying there after what she'd overheard? No way. She might be stupid, but she wasn't suicidal.

Just thinking of Andre made her stomach tighten. She was afraid Rick, the *Sprite's* captain, and the rest of his crew were underestimating how dangerous Andre could be. Rick was forever writing Andre off as nothing more than a spoiled rich kid, much as he'd originally thought her. While his opinion of her had certainly undergone a radical change, his opinion of Andre hadn't, and Erin was afraid they were all making a big mistake.

Her hands clenched on the steering wheel, her left leg adding a rapid tattoo. She still had part of a joint already rolled. Maybe a few tokes would calm her nerves, take her stress level down a notch. After all, if Stoner and Catherine were as uptight as ever, she'd need all the help she could get once she arrived in the middle of nowhere. A little brain fog might help blunt how underwhelmed her parents would be to see her. Maybe she could even pretend they would welcome her home. Erin laughed. Like that would happen.

Suddenly, surprising them didn't seem like such a great idea. In the back of her mind fear niggled that her parents would have asked her not to come if they had known of her plans ahead of time. How mortifying was that? She snorted. No more humiliating than being carried out of a party last fall tucked under Sam Barnes's arm like a little kid in the midst of a temper tantrum. That had accomplished essentially the same thing that evening. Erin had taken the hint and cleared out before they could actually kick her out.

She had never been able to do anything right in her parents' eyes. So now she was going *back*? Really. She needed her head examined. What was the definition of insanity? Oh right. Doing the same thing over and over again and expecting a different result.

Erin yawned. God, she had forgotten how truly boring this area was. No people, almost no traffic and certainly no lights. Nothing, as a matter of fact, to help her stay awake. Even worse, she'd already hit several icy spots where she felt the car's traction turn loose for an instant. After years of rarely driving at all and only in warm, sunny climates, the ice had certainly jolted her back awake. Erin shook her head and blinked her gritty eyes several times.

Shit, she was so tired she'd started to see things. Was that a deer in the road? Was it a pot-induced hallucination? That most recent bag had been a doozy. At the last minute, she stared into a white face and wide, startled brown eyes and yanked the wheel hard to the left. The car plunged off the shoulder of the road and through a dark board fence. The air bag exploded back at her, smacking her forehead and making it burn. Finally, the car landed at an odd angle, one wheel hanging over the bank of a creek. The only thing breaking the silence were the moos of panicked cows roaming in the darkness. *Wow, this was some fucking trip.* She slumped forward.

She wasn't sure how much time had passed when she groaned and touched her head. It was wet and sticky. She shivered. Her heavy coat was somewhere in the backseat. Why did it have to be so god-awful cold? She yearned for blue skies, even bluer water and hot, steamy nights. She could use a drink. Something alcoholic and on the rocks would be perfect. She hurt. Where the hell was she anyway?

It was dark, but this didn't look or feel like St. Thomas. She fumbled with her seatbelt, and it finally popped open. Her legs refused to obey as she opened the door, so she stumbled and half fell out onto the frozen ground. God, it was slippery out here and so freaking cold! She rubbed her arms, her coat forgotten. Her teeth chattered and that only made her head hurt even worse.

Erin turned around and looked at the car. *Holy shit!* She was in the middle of a cow pasture, and her rental car was a mess. God, how stupid. As she surveyed the damage to the vehicle, she decided it would be a whole lot easier to handle with a little buzz going. Life in general was a lot easier to face when she was a little bit high. She'd discovered that early in high school. She went back to the car, pulled out her purse, fumbled around until she found another joint, and lit it. Breathe deep, hold, exhale. It was a routine. A couple of tokes and she felt her calm return.

She turned to look at the fence behind her. *Wow!* It looked even worse than the car, though God knew it was hard enough to see anything out here. Had she taken that much of it out? Erin giggled as she imagined a cartoon vision of fence pieces flying through the air like matchsticks. The image was like one of those old Road Runner cartoons where Wile E. Coyote keeps screwing everything up. Yep! That was her all right. Wile E. Coyote, the original screw up. Maybe she should check to see if the car she'd leased came from Acme rentals.

It all struck her as so amazingly funny. She sat on a rock, puffed on her joint, and giggled. Welcome back, Erin! Nothing like arriving in style in Mountain Meadow. *Daddy, I'm home!* A few more feet, and she'd have made a splash right into the bottom of a shallow creek. Wouldn't everyone be so proud of her?

Some things never changed.

As she toked the joint in her hand, she looked around blearily. Where was she? She couldn't be far from home. But God, it had been so long since she'd been here. Last fall didn't count. She hadn't even spent the night. So, yeah, where was she? A couple of blinks and she momentarily cleared her vision enough to see the dark silhouette of a cabin. As she looked at the hills and trees surrounding her, memories came back. Her cheeks flushed with humiliation. She was on Sam's land. Why did every mortifying moment of her life involve Sam? He was the only man who had ever made her breath catch and her heart pound, and he was the only man who had never shown any sign of wanting her. Life was so unfair.

* * * *

With his long, sock clad feet propped over the end of the couch, Sam had nearly dozed off when his phone rang. It had been a crazy day what with deputies on vacation or sick. Sighing impatiently, he snatched the cordless phone from its resting place on the table next to him. "Barnes."

"Sam? It's Stoner. Carter called me. There are cows out on the highway. He's not sure whose they are. He's already out there trying to round them up. I'd be happy to help, but that whole electronic tether thing…"

"Dang it, Stoner," Sam snarled. "I'll call the department and tell them to ignore the alarm and why. The neighbor kid who helps me is sick with pneumonia, but I'll be out there as soon as I get my boots on to see what's up." Sam slammed the phone down with a bang.

At that moment, he would gladly have strangled the judge who sentenced former Senator Stoner Richardson to two years house arrest for pleading guilty to conspiracy charges. It was nothing but a major pain in the butt, when it wasn't a downright joke. In the last six months, Stoner had probably spent as much time away from home as at it. Now he was going off the property again. If someone didn't suspend his sentence soon, Sam might go beg the judge himself so he wouldn't have to play watchdog for the wandering senator. He would have to talk to Evan about it. The guy had served half his sentence already and been a model prisoner.

Sam's already taciturn mood grew even more thunderous as he yanked on his coveralls, slipped his big white-stockinged feet back into thick-soled work boots and pulled a cowboy hat on. Sweet Mary. He'd be glad when spring got here. Better yet, summer so he could work in either a T-shirt or shirtless.

Most of all, he wished he wasn't going out in the dark to round up cows in the freezing cold. Just in case, he threw a roll of barbwire, some temporary posts, and his wire cutters into the back of the truck before he bumped down the drive.

Please let them be Stoner's Angus and not his Hereford crosses. It would please him to no end to have something to hang over the senator, but as he reached the road, he saw broad white faces reflecting back at him in the moonlight. It was his baldies. Stoner would never let him hear the end of it.

Crap!

Even in the dark, the tall, angular form of the former senator leaning against his pickup was plain to see. He spoke as soon as Sam got within earshot. "Carter's herded most of them through the gate, but we haven't located the break in the fence yet. You know, Sam, if you'd hire another hand or two…"

Sam spun on his neighbor, fists clenched, but only glared at him. "Not all of us drip money, Senator."

Stoner's two-way radio crackled. "I've found the problem, Mr. Richardson. An accident. Fence is busted pretty good here in the corner by the creek. Car's hanging with one wheel over the bank."

Sam instantly converted from farmer to sheriff. "Any injuries you can see? Do I need to radio for an ambulance?"

"Don't think so. There's a woman here. She seems okay, I guess. She's laughing."

"Laughing?" Stoner's mouth twisted.

Sam growled with anger. Probably some teenager out joyriding. Just what he needed, something else to drag him back into town tonight when all he wanted to do was crash. "Hop in, Senator. I'll give you a ride. You and Carter mind helping me put up a temporary fence?"

"Not at all."

"I know we haven't exactly been on the best of terms…."

Stoner cut Sam off. "That was years ago, Sam. Besides, looking back, I don't think you were the one at fault. Erin was out of control."

Sam nodded, deciding it was better not to respond. Erin always seemed to be at the middle of any discord. He might not be at fault for his actions, but his thoughts about the senator's daughter had been anything but pure. It was twelve years ago, so maybe it was time to let things lie. After all, Erin was gone and it didn't look like she would be back. Last fall hardly counted. He rubbed the back of his neck and frowned at the thought.

As they drove down the road, Sam used the radio in his truck to call in the accident and said he would handle it until they could get someone out in the morning. As he and Stoner climbed out of the truck in the darkness, Sam saw how much of his fence was smashed.

"Holy freaking cow! Could the stupid idiot have done any more damage?"

"Damn," Stoner added. "It almost looks like the driver did it on purpose."

"Or fell asleep at the wheel," Sam grumbled. Fools. Nobody needed to be out on a night like this one, especially just joyriding. Icy patches from the last storm were still refreezing at night, making driving risky.

In the pasture, on the other side of the car, they heard Carter's deep rumbles and a higher pitched voice.

"I'm fine, man. Hey, jerk, get your hands off me. Ooh! Was that *cow shit* I stepped in? Oh, God. Oh *gross*. That is so freaking disgusting. Man, I hate this place! I *always* hated this place."

Stoner looked at Sam, who saw the same shock of recognition reflected in the senator's features before both of them slipped and slid down the embankment in a sudden hurry, running across the pasture to the car. Sam skidded to a stop, all of his thoughts jumbling together, but what lingered in his mind was, *not like this, Erin, not like this.*

Erin looked up as she heard them and grinned. The grin started Sam's heart pounding until he saw her bloodshot eyes in the glow of the flashlight. "Hi, Daddy! Hi, Sammy! I had a little accident." Then she leaned over and vomited right at a very surprised Carter's feet. Sam doubted it was the puke that floored Carter. Hearing Erin call Stoner Daddy probably accounted for the look on the foreman's face.

As Stoner slowed, so did Sam. They approached cautiously, as if they had encountered a wounded grizzly and weren't quite sure how it would react. But then confronting Erin had always been that way. He never knew exactly which Erin would show up. Would she snap his head off or twine herself around his heart? Sam had been struggling with that since he'd first met her when she was nine. No matter how much he'd tried to forget her over the years, it hadn't happened. His feelings had just changed.

"Erin?" Stoner ventured quietly. "What are you doing here?"

Sam sniffed the air, inhaling an all too familiar odor. Any nostalgia he might have been experiencing evaporated. "Darn it, Erin. Have you been smoking pot right here on my land?"

She straightened, her eyes wary as she looked between the two men. "Don't worry, Daddy...Sam. I'm fine, just a little head injury. So nice of you to ask, and nice to see things haven't changed. Oh wait, I guess they have, because the last time you two were this close together, Daddy, you were trying to choke Sam at the same time you were calling me... Let's see. What was it? Oh yes, a 'white trash tramp and no daughter of yours.' Fourteen was such a good year."

She glanced at Carter's gaping jaw and smiled coolly. "Another fond memory of childhood in the Richardson household." Erin tilted her head back and laughed. "Hi, Daddy. I'm home!"